Look Always Forward

DIANE GREENWOOD MUIR

D1713180

Cover Design Photography: Maxim M. Muir

ISBN-13: 978-1517514266
ISBN-10: 1517514266

CONTENTS

CONTENTS   iv
ACKNOWLEDGMENTS   i
CHAPTER ONE   1
CHAPTER TWO   11
CHAPTER THREE   21
CHAPTER FOUR   32
CHAPTER FIVE   41
CHAPTER SIX   50
CHAPTER SEVEN   60
CHAPTER EIGHT   70
CHAPTER NINE   80
CHAPTER TEN   90
CHAPTER ELEVEN   102
CHAPTER TWELVE   112
CHAPTER THIRTEEN   122
CHAPTER FOURTEEN   131
CHAPTER FIFTEEN   143
CHAPTER SIXTEEN   153
CHAPTER SEVENTEEN   163
CHAPTER EIGHTEEN   173
CHAPTER NINETEEN   184
CHAPTER TWENTY   194
CHAPTER TWENTY-ONE   204
CHAPTER TWENTY-TWO   214
CHAPTER TWENTY-THREE   223
CHAPTER TWENTY-FOUR   235
CHAPTER TWENTY-FIVE   244
CHAPTER TWENTY-SIX   256
CHAPTER TWENTY-SEVEN   267
THANK YOU FOR READING!   279

ACKNOWLEDGMENTS

Writing these books is such a joy. I've met incredible people who are only in my life because of Bellingwood. What more could a girl ask for.

A special thank you to those people who answer questions for me when I ask. You'll meet a new character in this book who shows up courtesy of a few well-placed questions from Brad Hickson. He and his wife, Kate have become great friends and without him, Alistair Greyson wouldn't exist.

Jancie Ter Louw, another reader, has become an invaluable resource for Sylvie's new bakery. Her passion for recipes, food and its history will be peppered throughout the books as Sylvie expands her business.

Thank you to Rebecca Bauman, Linda Watson, Carol Greenwood, Alice Stewart, Fran Neff, Max Muir, Edna Fleming, Dave Muir, Linda Baker, and Nancy Quist for all they do to make these books happen.

These people will never know how much they mean to me. It isn't easy to trust people with the raw, barely edited version of my soul's work. They encourage me, while making corrections and asking good questions about the story. They each uncover unique issues and my book gets better and better. I appreciate their gift of time and attention.

CHAPTER ONE

"That girl is never here," Henry said, dropping onto the sofa beside Polly. "Where is she tonight?"

"Rebecca and Kayla are watching Molly. Jessie has to write a paper for her online class," Polly said.

He chuckled. "How does Jessie afford two baby sitters?"

"She doesn't, but since we're both nervous about either girl babysitting by themselves this summer, I'm supplementing."

"Of course you are." Henry put his arm around Polly's shoulders and she relaxed onto him. "Does Rebecca know?"

Polly shook her head, and then, recognizing she was tickling his chin with her hair, continued moving it back and forth.

"Stop that." He clamped his hand down on top of her head, trying to restrict her movement.

She ducked out from under his hand and said, "What do you want to do for supper?"

"Why aren't you up at Pizzazz with the girls?"

"Everyone was busy. It's no big deal. So what should we do?"

"You're the worst wife ever." He flinched backward before she could swat him. "I work my poor fingers to the bone all week long. Every once in a while I expect dinner to be on the table, but instead, not only do I have to make a decision about dinner, you probably expect me to pay for it."

"Either that or you can hire a cook." Polly stood up and waggled her eyebrows at him. "Tell you what. Take a nap and rest your weary overworked bones. I'll go to Pizzazz by myself."

"And bring supper back for me?" He grinned at her.

"Not on your life. If you want to live in that strange little world where wifey prepares your meals and meets your every need, I'm going to let you live there all by yourself."

Henry grabbed her hand and pulled her back down to his lap. "Nope. I'd rather live with you in whatever world it is you've concocted. So really, no plans for dinner?"

She gave him a quick kiss on the lips and pulled away. "Since it's such a beautiful evening, we can grill out. Chicken is marinating, veggies are wrapped in tin foil, and potatoes are already cooking. It's all downstairs in the kitchen, so whenever you're ready.

"You're a rotten woman, you know that?" Henry poked her side and kissed her cheek.

"Come on Obiwan, let's go outside and play while Mr. Fuddy Duddy gets into his comfortable clothes." She sashayed into his office. "I'll be the one relaxing with a glass of wine. Doug, Billy, and Rachel are joining us."

They finally put a patio in the back yard this summer. Henry had built eight Adirondack chairs and installed a fire pit. She'd given him a nice grill the week before Independence Day and they used it every chance they got. Whenever they sat down for dinner, someone joined them. Whether it was Doug, Billy and Rachel, or Sylvie and her boys, or Jeff or even Stephanie and Kayla, Polly prepared more than necessary, because it would always be eaten.

She was going to miss this when winter came. It was so much easier to put a meal on the grill than cook dinner in her kitchen. As soon as it turned too cold, they'd go back to pizza and takeout.

Polly filled the rolling cooler with food from the refrigerator downstairs and pulled it outside. She opened a bottle of wine and set glasses out on a table, then arranged the food so Henry could put it on the grill.

Obiwan and Han wandered through the back yard. The younger dog was doing much better. Obiwan was good for him and Polly worried less and less that he would run off. They stayed pretty close to wherever she and Henry were.

She sat down in an Adirondack and closed her eyes. The summer had been wonderful. It was hard to believe school was starting in a couple of weeks. She enjoyed having the kids here. Andrew had grown, adding at least three inches to his height. He was still lean, so much different than his older brother, but Sylvie had uncles who were tall. His additional height had given him more confidence with the horses and Rebecca finally convinced him that he should learn to ride. The three kids were finally spending more time with Eliseo in the barn.

Andrew and Rebecca hadn't changed all that much, though. Eliseo had put together a table they could drag outside and they were often found there, Andrew with his head in a book or his fingers on a laptop and Rebecca with a sketchpad.

The big horses had grown used to all of the dogs that ended up in the pasture with them. Eliseo brought his two, Khan and Kirk, nearly every day, and this summer, their sister Padme accompanied Jason and Andrew to Sycamore House. She was well-behaved after spending time training with Eliseo. Andrew and Rebecca were also in charge of taking care of Billy's dog and Doug's very playful puppy.

Jason was less thrilled to have his brother around, but he had a couple of friends who helped with the animals. Polly wondered if she shouldn't pay Eliseo hazard pay with all of the kids that were in his space.

Polly heard the back door open and turned her head to make sure it was Henry. "Do you need anything else?" she asked.

"It looks like you have everything here. Are you ready for wine?"

"Nah. Not yet. I'm just enjoying the quiet. I can't believe no one's here yet."

The sound of the cooler opening accompanied soft laughter. "You always have plenty of food for everyone, though."

"It can go back in the fridge." Polly stood and met him at the grill "How are things coming at the coffee shop?" she asked.

"Fine - same as yesterday. I spent today down the road at Mikkels' new place. We're laying the foundation next week."

"But we're still on schedule?"

"Labor Day weekend it is." He poked at her with his elbow. "I keep telling you that if you want to manage the guys, you'll know we're moving forward."

"They won't listen to me."

"Bet me. They know better than to mess with Polly Giller. Not only are you the scariest woman in town, you're the boss's wife."

"I'm not scary. Stop that."

"Yes, honey, you are." He leaned forward to kiss her and she backed away. "Okay," he said. "You're not scary. Gimme a kiss?"

"Whatever. But you're sure we'll be ready."

"You know better than that. You're up there enough."

Polly snickered and swatted his behind. "You're awfully good to me."

She *was* up there nearly every day. The front was finished and they were placing chairs and tables that she and Sal ... and Beryl and Andy and Lydia and Joss and everyone who had anything to do with the place picked up across the state. A few pieces had gone back to Henry's shop for additional repair, but for the most part, the furniture just needed to be cleaned.

The fire last May had made the upstairs apartments unusable. Henry's crew ripped those out and opened up the ceiling, giving the space an immense feel. The floor and wooden coffee bar that Henry's dad and Len Specek made had been scorched in the fire, but when Sal saw it, she fell in love with the beautiful patterns the fire created in the wood. It would be a great conversation piece. After ripping out the walls and replacing them, everything was finally coming together.

They'd begun installing appliances in the bakery two weeks ago and even though they were fully functional when the original owner closed his bakery in Strawberry Point, cleaning and small repairs were necessary. Sylvie was still testing and tweaking - something she'd be doing until long after the bakery was open for business. Jeff was interviewing baristas and servers while Sylvie came to grips with the fact that she needed more help now that she had two kitchens to manage. Rachel would stay at Sycamore House and Hannah's work hours were fairly limited, so additional employees were imperative.

They still had a big hole in their team at Sycamore Inn. Polly didn't mind working out there, but they needed someone there more regularly. Jeff had been right when he insisted that Stephanie and Kayla shouldn't live there. So far, everyone that she'd dealt with was polite, but some rough characters came through. Stephanie was too nice to take their harassment, but she had become adept as Jeff's assistant.

Polly poured a glass of wine and put it on the table beside Henry, then poured another and took it with her. Just as she was bending to sit down, tires squealed and the horrendous sound of two cars trying to occupy the same space rang out. She put her wine on the patio floor and turned to see Henry take off at a run.

"Call 9-1-1" he yelled as he ran past her. "This was a bad one."

Her eyes followed his path to the highway in front of them. She dialed and gave as many details as possible, while jogging toward the crash.

A man in his mid-forties had gotten out of an old Chevy pickup truck and was headed for the sedan in front of him, its passenger side crushed in the accident. He looked inside and then stood back up, his head thrown back. Polly waited for a wail; it seemed to be what he wanted to do.

Henry was on the other side of the car, speaking to the driver. Polly stepped onto the highway and saw blood pouring out of the young man's scalp, stepped back up onto the grass and bent over at the waist. Blood wasn't something she dealt with well.

"Do you need me?" she called out to Henry.

"Check him out," he said, pointing to the man now standing in the middle of the highway.

Polly did her best to keep her eyes averted and approached the man cautiously. "Are you hurt anywhere?" she asked.

"Don't bother with me. Help him," he said.

"I've called 9-1-1 and my husband is with him. I want to know if you've been hurt."

"I don't know. I don't know. He came out of nowhere. I didn't mean to hit him. All of a sudden, he was right there in front of me and I couldn't stop in time."

"What's your name, sir?" Polly asked.

He looked at her in confusion. "Why do you need my name?"

"Because I want to have a conversation with you. I'm Polly Giller and that's my husband, Henry. And you are?"

"Alistair Greyson."

With a name like that, Polly expected at least a British accent, but no such luck. He was quite ordinary looking, his thick dark hair smattered with silver. His scruffy face had a beard growth of at least three days that only accentuated his pallor. He kept darting glances toward the kid in the car and relief flowed across his face when they finally heard the howl of the emergency siren coming toward Bellingwood.

Two Bellingwood police cars arrived and Chief Ken Wallers got out and strode over to Henry. He looked inside the car, shook his head slowly, and then approached Polly and Alistair Greyson.

"What happened here?" Ken asked.

Greyson looked at the crumpled car and then back at his own truck, its front end ripped and torn apart. "I was just coming through town when all of a sudden, he was in front of me. I couldn't get stopped. He was right there."

"I need to see your driver's license and automobile registration," Ken said, steering Greyson away from Polly. She heard him ask, "Have you been drinking this evening?"

"No, thank goodness," the man said.

Ken cocked his head. "What does that mean?"

Polly stepped back onto her grass as an ambulance and firetruck came down the highway, but she continued watching. Greyson appeared confused and she wondered if he'd hit his head in the accident. Surely Ken was aware of how dangerous his condition could be.

Doug, Billy, and Rachel had come down from their upstairs apartment and were standing further down the street. As she looked around, quite a few people had come out of their houses to watch the action.

The EMTs spoke to Henry, he stepped away from the car and walked over to Polly.

"What's happening?" she asked. "Do you know who that was?"

Henry nodded and said under his breath. "It's Leslie Sutworth's kid, Denis. I don't know if he's going to make it. He wasn't wearing a seatbelt and bounced all over the inside of that car. Something in the passenger seat impaled his right side."

"Oh no. Was he talking to you?"

"He was for a while. I did my best to keep him alert. I knew I couldn't move him. I just wanted someone to be there with him."

"Did he say anything?"

Henry slowly turned to her and tears filled his eyes. "I need to talk to Ken."

"What?" Polly asked.

He took her hand. "Just stay with me, will you?"

"Of course I will. But what's going on?"

The two dogs had stayed on the property and were now standing beside Polly and Henry. Obiwan nuzzled at Henry's other hand and whined.

"He knows something's wrong," Polly said. "Are you going to tell me?"

Henry absentmindedly put his hand on the dog's head. "I can't say it more than once. Let me just get Ken's attention."

They stood in silence as the crew worked to extricate Denis Sutworth from the car. Ken finally looked up and over at Polly and Henry as he escorted Alistair Greyson to a squad car. He spoke quickly to the EMTs and crossed the highway to them.

"Thanks for staying with him, Henry," Ken said. "Did you two see anything?"

Henry nodded. "I did. The guy in the truck did nothing wrong.

Maybe he could have stopped faster, but it wasn't his fault." He took a deep breath and said, "And I talked to the kid."

"Is that one of the Sutworth kids? It looks like their car," Ken said.

"Yes. It's Denis."

Ken pursed his lips and gave Henry a grim look. "What did he say?"

"He said he did it on purpose. He waited for a pickup that he didn't recognize and then shot out in front of it. And Ken, he's been drinking... a lot."

"Damn it," Ken said. "Anything else?"

"If he dies, I'm supposed to give this to his mother." Henry handed Ken a folded up piece of paper. "I haven't looked at it, but it was in the pocket of his shirt. He made me take it out. I didn't want to touch anything, but he wouldn't stop begging me to pull it out and keep it."

"You're fine, Henry," Ken said, unfolding the piece of paper. "This poor kid has been trying to kill himself for a long time. No matter how much they do for him, he just can't hold on to anything that's good. He walked out of another facility last week and hitched a ride home. His mom called to ask if we would keep an eye out for him until they could get him in to see another set of doctors. He won't take his meds and insists on drinking himself into a stupor, even though he knows it spins him out of control. I can't believe he chose to involve someone else, though."

He gave a quick shake of the head. "I shouldn't be talking to you about this. I'm sorry. But thanks for staying with him until we got here." Ken started to walk away and then turned back to Polly. "I know it's late, but I suspect Mr. Greyson doesn't have any place to stay tonight and that truck of his isn't going anywhere. Do you have any rooms available at the Inn?"

"Sure we do," she replied. "Let me know when you're ready for me to meet you there and we'll take care of him for the night."

"He's going to the hospital in Boone first," Ken said. "How about I call you when we're coming back into town. If they keep him, I'll let you know that too."

"The chicken!" Henry exclaimed.

Polly watched Henry run back across the driveway to the patio. "Whenever you need me, just let me know. Life is nice, quiet and boring right now, so I don't have anything else going on."

Ken put his index finger to his lips. "Shh," he said. "Don't say that out loud. You never know who's listening." He walked back to the emergency workers and Polly wandered to the patio with the dogs. She looked up at the sound of feet beside her and gave Doug a weak smile.

"Is that Denis Sutworth?" he asked. "He was a year older than us in school. He's messed up."

"Just tonight or before?" Polly asked.

"Before. Is he going to live?"

She stopped when she hit the patio. "I hope."

Billy had run up to walk on her other side. "We heard the crash, but didn't see anything. That's a terrible sound. Who was the other guy?"

"Just someone driving through Bellingwood," Polly said.

"His timing sucked," Rachel said. "A few minutes earlier or later and he would have missed that car."

"It's a good thing you made extra," Henry said. "This isn't even fit for the dogs. Are you three joining us?"

Polly didn't feel like eating. She scooped up her glass of wine, surprised that it was still standing upright. The dogs weren't usually interested in anything alcoholic, but Han had a terrible habit of checking anything out that was at his level and these days, nearly everything was at his level.

"Rachel made cupcakes," Doug said. "We were just coming down with them." He headed for the door into the garage and the stairs leading to their apartment. "I'll be back."

"Put more chicken on," Polly said to Henry, opening the cooler. "There's no reason to go upstairs and worry. It's still a beautiful evening."

Billy and Rachel took their usual spots in the circle of chairs. Polly chuckled. Humanity just couldn't help itself, it created a pattern and then stuck with it. She looked up when the back door opened and Doug came out, preceded by two more dogs. Billy's dog, Big Jack, ran over to Obiwan and started their normal sniffing and greeting ritual. Doug's dog was still on a leash. Still learning boundaries, the pup had enough beagle in him to require that leash for a long time. He wanted nothing more than to run and play. She put her hand out for the leash when Doug walked past her and he smiled gratefully and handed it over.

"How are you this evening?" Polly asked, crouching down. Doug had wanted to name the dog Thor, but decided everyone was doing that. There was a dark brown eyebrow over one eye and he'd settled on Hawkeye, another character from the Avengers. Polly didn't spend time explaining other uses of that name, but gave Doug a copy of "The Last of the Mohicans" from her library. Sometimes it killed her that pop culture often overwhelmed literary references.

Hawkeye barked and then licked her chin, his tail wagging. He was a happy, social dog and loved being outside with everyone. She picked the pup up and snuggled his face, then walked over to the circle and sat down. Doug joined Henry at the grill and she watched them laugh together as they talked. She was glad of that. The wreck had been a shock. She looked out at the street as the deputies worked, measuring and taking photographs. The ambulance was gone and two flatbeds drove up to manage the vehicles. Polly turned away. She didn't want to watch the cleanup.

Han nosed her arm and Hawkeye yapped at him. She grinned and put the young dog down on the ground beside her, hooking the leash over the arm of the chair.

"Weird night," Billy said. "I hope Denis is okay."

"Me too," Polly responded. "I wonder what's next."

CHAPTER TWO

One night of observation in the hospital was the recommendation for Alistair Greyson. Ken had called Polly and told her one of his deputies would pick the man up the next afternoon and bring him back to Bellingwood. No one was sure what he would do without a vehicle, a problem that Polly fully understood. They still hadn't replaced her pickup truck. Polly had sworn to never drive the thing again after Joey Delancy and his serial killer partner used it.

For now, it was in the impound lot until the trial was over. She told Aaron that if any of his people wanted it, they could make an offer and she'd accept it, no matter what. She'd never gotten attached to the truck, carrying nothing in it that was important - except her dad's work gloves. Aaron had already returned those.

Polly wasn't sure why she was dragging her feet on buying another vehicle. She was going to need it once school began. Henry's T-bird was fine for her and Rebecca, but there wasn't room for anyone else. Henry had too much going on to let her drive his truck very often, so she borrowed Sylvie's car if she wanted to take the kids to Boone.

Whenever they drove past a car lot, Henry pointed at the shiny new vehicles. Polly couldn't work up enough reason to make the leap. For the most part, she walked. It was only a few blocks to the grocery store or anywhere else downtown. One of these days, necessity would outweigh her procrastination.

The next morning, Polly was at Sweet Beans with Sal and Sylvie when Ken called.

"Good morning," she said brightly, standing up and stretching. She'd been stacking freshly washed mugs and glasses into cabinets on the back side of the coffee bar.

"They're releasing Alistair Greyson this morning," Ken said. "Do you still have a room available at the Inn for him?"

"Sure we do. When do you think he'll be in town?"

"Bert's heading down. They'll be back in an hour or so."

Polly looked around the room at the piles of boxes to unpack. If she left now, Sal would be in a blithering puddle on the floor. "I'm calling Jeff. He'll meet Bert out there and take care of it."

"Thanks."

"How's the Sutworth kid?" Polly asked.

"Better than expected. Last night they weren't sure, but things improved overnight. They'll move him out of ICU today. He's got a long road ahead, though."

She sagged against the counter in relief. "Thank goodness."

"It's a pretty bad deal," Ken said. "I'm worried about Greyson, though. When I spoke with him last night, he was worried about Denis. He managed to make his way to ICU and spent time with Leslie while they waited. He's taking this pretty hard. And with his truck totaled, he's staying in Bellingwood."

"There are worse places," Polly said.

"Leslie took me aside last night and told me that they'd pay for his stay at Sycamore Inn for a week."

"You know that isn't necessary," she argued.

"I told her that. She feels terrible about the whole thing, though."

"If you see her again, tell her that's the last thing she needs to think about. We'll work something out. And if Mr. Greyson wants a short-term job, either Henry or I could put him to work." She looked around the room again. "I could put him to work here at the coffee shop for the next two weeks helping us get ready."

"Thanks, Polly. I'll let you go. Tell Jeff that Bert will buzz him when they're back in town."

They hung up and Polly smiled. She supposed this type of thing had happened in Story City when she was growing up, but she never saw it. Now that she was a business owner, it was fun to help take care of people when they needed extra help.

"What's up?" Sal asked.

"The guy who was in that accident in front of Sycamore House is staying at the Inn for a while. His truck was totaled and he doesn't have any way to leave town."

"You're putting him to work at the coffee shop?"

Polly shrugged. "I don't know. I'll talk to Henry. He probably needs a day or so to get his feet under him. Between the accident and the possibility of that poor kid dying, he's got to be a mess."

A bell rang and the front door opened. Two college aged kids came in. The first, a young girl, spoke. "Hello?"

Polly stepped forward with her hand out. "Hi there, how can I help you?"

"We heard that you were looking for help and want to apply for a job." The girl bit her lip. "Do you have applications? Are you really opening soon?"

"We do and we are," Polly said. "But we aren't taking applications here. You can either do it online or head to Sycamore House and talk to Jeff Lyndsay. He's managing all of that."

The young man laughed. "I told her we should do it online, but she insisted that we needed to meet you face to face. I'm Sky and this is Rena." He put out his hand and Polly shook it.

"Do you know where Sycamore House is?" she asked.

"We passed it on the way in, right?" Rena said. "That old schoolhouse with the trees and the horses?"

"That's it. Go in the front door and you'll see the office on your left. Stephanie is at the front desk. I'll call and tell her that you're coming to see Jeff."

Sky rubbed his foot on a scorch mark. "This is pretty cool," he said. "What a great use of this old building." He wandered over to the large bookcase on the east wall and stroked the wood. "Awesome work. Someone doesn't see the knots and pits in the wood as defects."

Polly wasn't sure if he was complimenting the place to get the job or what, but she liked the kid. He had an easy smile. His pony tail and skinny jeans would be perfect in most coffee shops, but she was pretty sure Bellingwood would have plenty to say about him. That would have encouraged her to hire him on the spot, but she'd promised Jeff to keep her hands off. Rena was dark-skinned and spoke with a smooth accent, probably Central American. Her long black hair was also pulled back into a ponytail, but it was so thick that wisps pulled away as she moved, framing her round face.

"We'll get out of your way," Rena said. "Come on, Skylar."

"Nice to meet you." He waved as they left by the front door.

Sal stepped up beside Polly. "He was kinda cute. Can we keep him?"

"We told Jeff we'd let him handle it. Now be good." Polly gave Sal a push. "Get back to work. We have to make a dent in these boxes."

Before Polly knelt down to her task, she called Jeff. He was going to throttle her. Two applications and a run to the Inn. She chuckled to herself and dialed his phone.

"Good morning. Are you working hard?" he asked.

"I am, but I'm about to disrupt your morning. Are you ready for me?"

"I'm still employed here, so I guess I'm always ready for you. What's up?"

"Two things. A couple of kids just stopped in to apply for jobs. I sent them to you. They should be there any minute."

"Okay, that's no big deal. What's the disruption?"

"Well, I need you to go out to the Inn when Bert calls."

"Bert? As in Bert Bradford? Why would he be calling me?" Jeff asked. "You haven't done anything stupid, have you?"

14

"Stop it, you," she said with a laugh. "You know that accident that happened in front of Sycamore House last night? Alistair Greyson is the man who hit the Sutworth kid. He was in the hospital overnight and needs a place to stay for a few days - just until he figures out what he's going to do next. His truck was totaled and..."

Jeff interrupted. "And you said that he could stay there while this was all worked out."

"Bert is going to call you when he gets into town." She lowered her voice to a whisper. "And Sal will kill me if I take off on her. We're never going to get this place put together."

"Got it. I'll take care of the applicants and this Greystoke guy."

"Greyson." Polly hesitated. "Greystoke is from Tarzan."

He gave her a wicked chuckle. "Just making sure you were paying attention."

~~~

The ringing bell on the door at the coffee shop jerked Polly awake. She sat up straight and jumped to her feet, not believing she'd fallen asleep in that position. A quick check of the time and she realized that she'd only been out for about a minute. She wasn't over-tired. Her nights were the regular amount of up and down with animals in the bed and too much heat or too cold, whether she covered up with the sheet or threw it all off.

"Polly!" Sal called. "Your kids are here, wondering what to do."

She made her way past the piles of boxes and smiled at the three musketeers: Kayla, Rebecca and Andrew. "What are you doing up here this afternoon?" she asked.

"Mom said we were driving her crazy, so we're supposed to come up and see if you need any help," Andrew said.

Kayla said, "We took the dogs out before we left."

"And now we're here," Rebecca said. "Can we help?"

Polly looked at Sal, who shrugged and pointed at the bookcases.

"Sure," Polly said. "See these boxes? They're all books. We need an interesting way to organize them on the shelves. Alphabetical by author is important, but we aren't sure how to sort them."

Andrew unflapped the first box and pulled out a stack of paperbacks. "Look at all of these books," he said. "Where did you get them?"

"I've been to every thrift store in five counties," Sal said with a dramatic sigh. "I couldn't leave it to Polly or she'd still be trying to decide what books to take and which to leave. I just bought books."

Rebecca and Kayla emptied boxes as fast as Andrew could open them and soon piles of books were scattered around the three kids.

"I don't know where to begin," Rebecca said.

Polly came back out from behind the bar and laughed at the mess they'd made. "You'd better start making decisions." She gestured to the bookshelves along the walls. "Those are empty. Help them find their new homes."

"You're really going to let people take these?" Kayla asked Sal.

"Most cost practically nothing," Sal responded. "At one place, the woman was so glad they were leaving, she gave me the whole box for a dollar. If someone needs a book badly enough to walk out of here with it, I don't care. I hope people will bring a book back if they take one. We'll see what happens, though."

Andrew was sitting beside a stack of books reading. He leaned back on his elbow and rested his head on a shorter stack.

"Andrew Donovan," Rebecca snapped.

He lazily looked up at her. "What?"

"You aren't here to read. You're here to help. Put that book down."

Polly chuckled at the two of them. "What do you have there, Andrew?"

"I don't know. It's some old book from before I was born."

She bent over and took it out of his hand. "Not much before you were born," she said. "But this is a good one. 'On Basilisk Station' by David Weber." Polly showed it to Sal. "Honor Harrington. Did you read those?"

Sal shook her head and then rolled her eyes. "No," she said. "I was never into sci-fi like you."

"Can I take it home tonight?" Andrew asked, standing up and holding his hand out to Polly.

Polly glanced at Rebecca, who had planted her hands on her hips and was glaring at the boy. Polly bit her lips together to hold back laughter. "You might want to take that up with Rebecca." Polly tossed the book to the girl. "Maybe if you hold it hostage, you can get some work out of him."

"Hey! Don't be throwing books," he cried. "You might rip it."

Rebecca held the book behind her back and said, "Give me an hour and then you can read. We have to figure out how to sort out all of these books first. No more getting distracted."

Andrew looked down at the piles of books and Rebecca swatted his arm. "Stop looking at them like they're chocolate. I said you could read later."

Polly and Sal glanced at each other and quickly looked away.

"We're separating these out. Non-fiction over here," Rebecca said, pointing to a table. "Science fiction goes on this table and we can put mysteries here and children's books over there."

Polly slipped behind the bar and found a stack of paper and markers. "Here you go, Rebecca. This should help. Maybe instead of piling things on tables, you could put signs in the shelves where you want them to go."

"Does it matter?" Rebecca asked, looking first at Polly and then at Sal.

Sal shrugged. "I don't care. Once you decide, I have decorations for space you have left over." She dragged another box out to the middle of the floor.

"Maybe we save that until they're done with this part of the project," Polly said. She grinned at Andrew, "He doesn't need any more distractions."

"Whatever," he said. He picked up a stack of books and walked across the room. "This is science fiction," he announced and stacked the books on the first shelf. "I don't care where anything else goes, but I'm choosing this one."

Rebecca shook her head and sat down at a table with the paper and markers. She made signs and handed them to Kayla. They whispered and pointed, and then Kayla took a sign and propped it inside a set of shelves. Polly found a box cutter and broke down the empty boxes. For the first time in days, brown cardboard gave way to open space. Even if Sylvie wasn't ready in the bakery, they could open the coffee shop as soon as Jeff hired baristas.

Polly had no doubt there would be customers when they turned on the open sign. Jeff wanted to do a soft open, just to work the kinks out. Once the bakery was going and everyone was comfortable with their positions, they'd set a date for the grand opening. That had made both her and Sal feel much better. Neither had any experience with any type of retail, so the thought of hundreds of customers a day was terrifying.

The doorbell rang again and Polly looked up to see Henry. She smiled at him and gave a little wave.

"This is more like it," he said. "Fill those shelves and this place will start looking like home." He strode across the floor and kissed her lips. Polly couldn't help herself. Whether it was his lips, the kiss or just his scent, she relaxed into him whenever they kissed.

"What are you doing?" she asked. "Checking up on us?"

"Come outside with me." Henry took her hand and gave her tug.

Polly stepped over a stack of books and followed him. "What's up?"

"Just come with me. You'll see."

He opened the front door and waited for her to go through, then taking her hand again, took her around the west side of the building.

"What am I looking for?" she asked.

"That."

Polly didn't see anything new. "What?"

Henry patted the hood of a red pickup truck. "This." He looked very pleased with himself.

"Is this what I think it is? For me? I thought we were going to look for a vehicle together."

"You don't like it?"

She raised a shoulder. "I guess. I guess I'm..." She walked to the driver's side "I'm surprised is all."

"You don't like it." His shoulders sagged and his voice dropped.

"No!" she exclaimed. "It's great. I'm just surprised."

"That was the point. I wanted to surprise you." He held out a set of keys. "I shouldn't have done this without you, right?"

Polly walked back up on the sidewalk and hugged him. "No. I'm just surprised. This is great. Where did you get it?"

"It's not new. It's used."

She took his arm. "You're so smart. You know I think new trucks are ridiculous. Used is better."

"Nate and I checked everything out. It runs like a dream and has all of the bells and whistles you had in your last truck. There is plenty of room in the back seat for all of your kids and animals." He was desperately trying to make this okay. "And it's red. Like your dad's truck."

"Henry, it's awesome. I can't believe I have a truck again." She giggled. "Are you going to tell me where it came from?"

He took a deep breath. "I made a deal with the guy who does my concrete work. He was planning to trade it in for a new truck. Since I know how he treats his vehicles, I knew it would be in good shape. The deal was just too good to pass up. Are you mad?"

"I'm not mad at all," Polly said. She kissed his cheek. "I just can't believe I finally have a truck again. Can we go for a ride?"

"Sure. You have the keys. Let's go."

Polly climbed in. The tan leather seat felt like butter and she ran her hands back and forth on the steering wheel while peering at the dash. "There's a lot more here than my last truck," she said.

Henry reached into the glove compartment, took out the manual and held it up. "Bed time reading?"

"I'd guess so." She popped the console open between them and looked into it. "This is clean. Everything is so clean."

"I told you, he takes good care of his trucks. Are you sure it's okay?"

Polly put the console lid back down and put her hand out, palm up. Henry took it in his. She smiled at him. "This was so unexpected. I'm sorry I didn't react well. I really was just surprised. All of my procrastinating and you took care of it. Thank you for fixing me."

He opened the glove compartment again and took out her dad's work gloves. "I hoped you would like it. I already made the transfer."

Her eyes filled with tears. "I don't know what I did to deserve you, but I'm always grateful."

Henry handed her the gloves and she held them to her nose, inhaling their scent. "I'm such a dope, aren't I."

"You're my dope. Now where shall we go?" he asked.

She passed the gloves back to him and he returned them to the glove compartment, tucking them under the manual. Then she looked at the key ring. There was no key and for that matter, no place to put one - anywhere. "I'm confused?" she said.

"Just push the button. As long as you have the fob, it will turn on."

"Wow. Big time," she said with a laugh and pressed the ignition button. The truck came to life and she breathed deeply. "I'm free again," she said. "Thank you."

CHAPTER THREE

Reaching down absentmindedly, Polly scratched Obiwan's neck when he placed his head on her leg. They were in her office the next morning before anyone else arrived. Han spent more and more time with Henry during the weekdays. He'd turned into a great companion and loved spending time at job sites or the shop. Jessie's little girl was in love with the big, goofy dog who spent time keeping her corralled. Once she started crawling, Molly was unstoppable. Marie Sturtz was more than happy to watch the child during the day. She'd turned most of the business work over to Jessie, stepping in to help only when needed. Bill and Len Specek had put together a covered play area in the back yard where Marie could watch Molly and somehow, Marie and Bill's living room had turned into a child's playroom.

Marie insisted that it took a village to raise a child and Jessie was helpless to stop the additional assistance she was receiving. It worked out wonderfully for her, but she confided in Polly that she felt guilty for accepting it all. Polly confided in Jessie that she was grateful Marie had a baby to play with because she wasn't planning to have one any time soon.

Jessie had named her daughter after Marie and Polly, combining the names to honor the two women who changed her life. Jessie's own parents still had yet to see their grandchild, which didn't surprise Polly. Kelly Locke didn't have a relationship with any of her children other than her son, Ethan, who still lived at home. It broke Polly's heart, but at least Jessie had a safe place to work and was establishing a life for herself and her daughter.

"Good morning," Jeff said. He came in to Polly's office and flopped down in a seat, dropping his messenger bag on the floor beside him.

Obiwan wandered over to sniff the bag and then nudged Jeff's hand for attention.

"I'm sorry for landing all of those people on you yesterday afternoon," Polly said. "How did the rest of your day go?"

He nodded. "It was good. The two kids should work out fine for the coffee shop. In fact, I'm meeting them up there later this morning. They'll help with setup."

"And Alistair Greyson?" Polly asked.

Jeff pursed his lips and grinned at her. "He's a character. He'll tell you to call him Grey."

"Grey Greyson?"

"Yep. I like him." Jeff rested his hand on Obiwan's head, which was resting on his knee.

"Cool," she said. "I told Ken we might hire him for a couple of weeks up at the coffee shop to help us get ready to open."

He shrugged. "Sure. That would work. He's not in a hurry to leave Bellingwood. We might want to think about helping him find something more permanent."

"What do you mean?" Polly creased her brow.

"I don't know," Jeff said. "He just seems like someone I want to keep around."

"How do you know he isn't leaving Bellingwood?"

"Some things he said. If Denis Sutworth lives through this, it sounds like Grey wants to spend time with him. He says he's had experience with messed up kids."

"Interesting," Polly said.

"Why do you say that?"

"Because from what Ken tells me, the Sutworth kid is going to need a lot of help. He's been in and out of psychiatric situations, refuses to take his meds, and is basically a mess. Do you think this guy can help?"

"I don't know," Jeff said. "Just wait until you meet him." He reached down and picked up his bag, then stood and stepped toward her office door. "He said he felt like he was here for a reason and that reason wrecked his truck the other day."

"That's odd," Polly responded with a smile.

"Yeah. You're right. It probably is." Jeff's shoulders dropped lower as he walked out of her office and turned into his own.

Obiwan came back over and sat down beside Polly.

"What do you think?" she asked the dog. He made a noise in his throat and lay down. Polly watched Stephanie and Kayla come in, Kayla heading for the stairs to go up to the apartment and Stephanie turning to come into the office. Right behind them were Sylvie and Andrew. He ran to catch up to Kayla and she heard Sylvie speaking to Stephanie before tapping on her door.

Polly looked up and smiled. "Come on in. How are you this morning?"

Sylvie shook her head. "Long morning already. Isn't it about time for the kids to go back to school?"

"Just a couple of weeks. Which one today?" Polly asked.

"No big deal. It was both of them. I had to pry Andrew off a stupid video game and Jason was grumpy for no good reason."

"There's probably a reason," Polly said.

Sylvie scowled at her. "I know. You're right. But I don't have time right now to get past his tight-lipped adolescent self. I have too much to do right now to put up with either of them and their bad behavior."

"So you're grumpy, too," Polly said with a grin.

"Don't start on me," Sylvie said, looking over the glasses she'd started wearing this summer. She still wasn't used to having them on her head, and more often than not, they were nowhere to be found when she tried to read small print. Her worries of getting old had almost turned into a crisis. A night of laughter and good food with Lydia, Beryl and Andy had reminded her that age didn't have to define her.

Polly put her hands up defensively. "I'm not starting. I promise."

"Did I hear you got a new vehicle?"

"Henry found the perfect truck for me. And I'm free again," Polly said. "Now if I can just keep this one out of the hands of serial killers and away from insane kids who want to run me off the road, I'll be happy. It's red and has everything a girl could want."

"I'm glad for you. I suspect Henry is glad, too."

Polly laughed. "I think he might have been worried about his poor T-bird. I drive faster than he does."

Sylvie stood up. "I have two events that I'm catering out at the winery. I'd better get busy."

She stopped in front of Stephanie's desk to let her know people would be coming in for interviews. Good, she was finally taking this expansion thing seriously.

~~~

Jeff tapped on Polly's door. "I'm going to the coffee shop. Can you hold down the fort?"

"Sure?" Polly was perplexed. "Are you expecting something to happen while you're gone?"

He laughed. "No. It's fine. I just wanted you to know where I was."

"I'll be up later with the kids. They're shelving books. Surely Stephanie can keep an eye on things here."

"Of course she can." Jeff glanced at her desk. "I'll see you later."

Polly looked back down at the paperwork in front of her. From bills to contracts, it never ended. She was ready for the coffee shop to open and things to settle down again. That familiar itch was starting to happen in the back of her mind. She hadn't yet identified what was on her radar, but it was time to be creative again. One thing that hadn't taken off in Sycamore House was artisan crafts. She'd originally had a vision of a place where artists and crafters could have classes and sell their wares. There were a few classes happening in the space across the hall, but she was located too far off the beaten path. Whatever her dream was would have to take place downtown where people could drop in without making an appointment.

Only in small town Iowa could four blocks be considered off the beaten path. There were open spaces downtown that would work. Bellingwood wouldn't know what to do with some of the bohemian artists she'd known in Boston. The only person she could imagine who would know what she was looking for was Beryl and that woman did her level best to stay under the radar.

Polly's eyes snapped open from her daydreams. Bellingwood needed an art gallery. Here they had a well-known artist living right in their midst and no one was showing her work. That was insane. How many other people like that lived in Iowa, hiding from the world that knew who they were? Henry had a friend who designed toys for a large firm in Chicago. He lived in Iowa so he could raise his family on a farm. She'd met a young couple earlier this summer at a wedding who were part of a wave of programmers and web designers that didn't want to live in Silicon Valley and were making an impact from the Heartland. So much was starting to happen here.

She wondered what Beryl would say to hanging her work in a Bellingwood gallery. Would the woman be able to say no to Polly? She chuckled. Beryl wouldn't have a problem saying no.

"Ms. Giller?" a man's voice roused her from her daydreams. She looked up to see Alistair Greyson standing in her doorway. His face had been banged up. One eye was black and blue and a bandage covered his chin.

"Mr. Greyson," she said, standing up. "Come in and have a seat. How are you doing today?"

He limped in, favoring his right leg, shook her hand, and sat down across from her. Obiwan ran right to him and after sniffing his hand, nuzzled his face under it for attention.

"I'm better than I expected," he said. "This is a beautiful dog."

"That's Obiwan. It looks as if he likes you."

Greyson bent over and rubbed the top of Obiwan's head with his cheek, a move that surprised Polly. "I'm quite fond of animals. This one has a heart that is true."

Polly had thought when she first saw him, that Greyson was ordinary looking. But in the time since the accident, he'd cleaned up, trimming his hair and his beard. The beard had much more gray in it than the hair on top of his head and it gave him a distinguished look. He had laugh lines around his eyes and an easy smile.

"Obiwan is a wonderful dog," Polly said. "He always knows what I need."

He nodded, taking her office and all of its contents in.

"Is there anything I can help you with this morning?" she asked. "Is your room okay? Do you need anything?"

"If it wouldn't be too much trouble, I was wondering if you could help me find my truck. I'd like to retrieve a few items before it is sent to its final resting place."

"Of course," she said. "Let me call the police station and ask where they've taken it. I guess I'm surprised they didn't get your luggage out of it."

"They most certainly did. But there are often treasures that don't appear to be so to those who are unaware of their nature."

"I see." Polly swiped her phone open and dialed a familiar number. Even after three years, it still surprised her that she had a close relationship with not one, but two local law enforcement agencies.

"Bellingwood Police," a voice said.

"Hi. This is Polly Giller and I have Alistair Greyson here asking about his truck. There are a few items he would like to retrieve."

"Hi there, Polly. Sure. The truck is over at the city yard. If you want to take him over there, I'll call down and they'll let you in. No problem. Ken wasn't sure if he'd gotten everything out of it."

"Thank you," Polly said. "We'll head over in a few minutes."

"No problem. I'll tell Ken you called."

Polly laughed when she hung up. "This is what's wonderful about small towns," she said to Mr. Greyson. "A quick call and we can get to your truck. Would you like to go now? They'll be ready any time for us."

He nodded. "Thank you very much. I didn't expect such an immediate response."

She asked. "How did you get here this morning?"

"I walked. My knee was giving me trouble earlier. I'm afraid the accident aggravated an old injury. But it isn't far and the exercise is good for me."

"We do have you out on the edge of town. I'm sorry about that." She glanced at the time. "Maybe after we pick up your things, I could take you to lunch."

He stood and stepped back, gesturing for Polly to precede him, "If you will allow me," he said with a bow, "I would like to take you to lunch."

Obiwan followed Polly out of the office and stopped beside her when she turned to Stephanie. "We're going to run a couple of errands. I'll be back later."

"No problem," Stephanie said. "I might not be here, but I'll have the phone. I need to run out to the hotel and help some people check in."

"Thanks," Polly said. Finding a manager for the hotel frustrated her. No one was right for the job. They had hired housekeepers - a woman and her daughter, Barb and Cindy Evering. But those who applied for the reception job stayed for a week or less and moved on. Polly's employees always became part of the family and sometimes people just weren't cut out to be responsible to a large number of odd family members.

"This is quite a facility you have here," Alistair said as they passed through the main foyer.

"It's ..." Polly wasn't quite sure what to say. Most words seemed trite in comparison to the depth of feeling she had for Sycamore House. "It's a wonderful place."

"If you are in charge, it must be," he said. Stopping in front of the door to the auditorium, he asked, "May I?"

She nodded and opened the door. He stepped in to the empty room, his eyes resting on the stage. He caught sight of the display cases.

"A fascinating collection of pop culture," he said.

"We discovered crates in the basement the first few months we were here - things that students had lost while the school was open. A custodian kept everything together year after year."

"A person could get lost in memories," he said, reaching up to touch the glass in front of a pair of black and white saddle shoes.

"We've offered to let people come in and take back any of their personal items, but not many have claimed them," Polly said. "I think they like knowing this piece of history is here."

He shook himself from his reverie. "Perhaps it is time to move on." He pointed to the back of the building and said, "To your trusty steed?"

Polly chuckled. "Let's go through the kitchen so I can introduce you to a couple of my friends."

"You are a woman who has many friends, aren't you, Ms. Giller," he said.

"I suppose I am." She led him through the auditorium and opened the door in front of the kitchen. They stopped at the counter and Sylvie glanced up from an oven.

"Hello there," Sylvie said. Her hair was pulled back and yet a few tendrils fell in front of her face. Her cheeks were red from exertion and the front of her apron looked as if something had exploded.

"You are a vision of perfection," Alistair gasped.

Sylvie looked down at herself, glanced at Polly and then at Rachel and said, "Who, me?"

"Your natural beauty shines through the work that you do." He turned to Polly. "Have you ever seen anyone so lovely?"

Polly shrugged. "He's right, you know. You are quite lovely in that getup. Sylvie Donovan, this is Alistair Greyson. He's staying at the Inn."

Sylvie stepped forward and put her hand out. Polly wasn't at all surprised when he turned it to kiss the back of her hand.

"Oh," Sylvie said. It shouldn't have been possible, but her cheeks turned an even deeper shade of red.

"Might I inquire as to whether you are free this evening?" Alistair asked. "I know it's short notice, but I don't feel that I can go another day without learning more about you. You are exquisite."

"I. Don't. Think. So," Sylvie said evenly.

"I apologize," he said. "I've pressed too quickly. But I've never..." He stopped and said again, "I apologize. Ms. Giller, shall we leave now?" His confidence was gone and he stammered out, "It was nice to meet you."

Rather than taking him through the kitchen, Polly pointed to the auditorium door. He went through it without waiting for her. She shrugged at Sylvie and followed.

"I do apologize," he said. "I've never met anyone so lovely. Please express to her that I did not mean to frighten or startle her." He quietly spoke to himself. "Sylvie Donovan. 'Tis a beautiful name."

"I'll let her know," Polly responded. "My truck is right through here." She led him into the storage room and out into the garage. It felt wonderful to be able to have her own vehicle.

Greyson walked into the garage and stopped in front of Henry's Thunderbird. "It seems that I am to be exposed to great beauty today," he said. "My mother told the story that my father married her for her T-Bird. This is very nice."

"It's my husband's. I've been driving it for the last few months, but we got my new truck just yesterday."

He trailed his fingers across the hood of the T-Bird as he walked around it and then turned his attention to the truck, climbing up into the passenger seat.

Polly opened her door and let Obiwan jump up and in. He leapt to the back seat before she had her seatbelt buckled.

"It's just a short drive to the city yard," Polly said.

"Then I probably could have walked."

"That's not what I meant." She was flustered. "I guess I was just making conversation."

"I'm grateful for the ride."

They rode in silence the few blocks to the yard. His battered truck was inside the fence. A gate opened when Polly pulled in front of it and she drove in and over to the truck.

"Hello!" a man said, coming out from a small building. "Are you Ms. Giller and Mr. Greyson?"

Polly jumped down and said, "Yes, that's us. He wants to get the last of his things."

"For what it's worth, it's all locked up. Here are your keys."

Alistair took the key ring from the man and pocketed a few after removing them. Opening the back of the truck, he drew out a long stick and leaned it against the side. He climbed into the bed and pulled out two white five gallon buckets. One was empty, the other heavy with a lid tightly clamped down.

"I just need to get a few things from the front. It will be only a moment." After two attempts, the passenger door finally opened. He dug underneath the seats and in the glove compartment, dropping things into the empty bucket.

"That should do it," he said. "There is nothing more in that faithful vehicle of any importance to me. It has earned its rest." He patted the back of the truck before picking up the second bucket. "I appreciate you saving my life. It isn't every vehicle that can be said of."

Alistair Greyson glanced at the long stick, as if trying to discern whether he would be able to take it up in his hands while carrying the two buckets. Polly smiled at him and put her hands on it.

"Let me open the back of the truck," she said. "You can put your things in there."

After putting the buckets in, he took the stick, stroked the wood, then laid it in the bed and waited for her to shut the tailgate.

"Thank you, kind sir," he said to the man who opened the lot for them. "I will speak with your Chief about the paperwork. I appreciate your care of my vehicle."

The man nodded, a slow smile stealing across his face. "Nice to meet you." He tilted his head at Polly. "Ms. Giller."

"Thanks," she said and got back in her truck, then turned to her passenger. "Would you like lunch?"

He nodded to the back seat where Obiwan was seated quietly. "You won't be able to take him into the diner."

"It's a beautiful day. He won't jump out of the truck if I leave the windows open. We can eat."

"Then I would feel quite privileged to share a meal with you. And please, allow me to express my thanks by bearing the cost."

"We'll see," she said.

CHAPTER FOUR

Unless she got an emergency call, Polly had nothing to do late that afternoon. She'd just returned from dropping the kids off at the coffee shop. Jeff promised to bring them back when he closed for the day. He and four new employees were finishing setup. Sylvie had introduced him to a woman she knew who could train them all in the basics of coffee and tea. Polly overheard some of it and chose to ignore it. She didn't need to understand the magic, it was enough to know that it worked and she got coffee to drink. Beyond that, they could learn how to froth, mix, bubble, or even swim in the coffee for all she cared.

Before moving the kids around, she'd dropped Alistair Greyson off in front of his hotel room. He'd gathered his two five gallon buckets and his stick and watched as she drove away.

He was such an odd duck. She didn't know what to make of him. His speech patterns were just a little off. It was right for him, but no one else spoke the way he did. Trusty steed? Faithful vehicle? And what was up with his sudden infatuation with Sylvie?

If Sylvie and Rachel weren't so busy in the kitchen, Polly would love to hear what they thought about it, but there was too much going on. When she'd picked Kayla, Andrew and Rebecca up, they were ready to get out of Sycamore House. Sylvie had fed them lunch, but apparently she'd been short-tempered with them. No one said anything, but they were glad to be gone.

"What do you think about it all, Obiwan?" Polly asked her dog. "Is there something I should be doing? Jeff told me I didn't need to stay at the coffee house, we have a strange new man in town, Sylvie doesn't want anyone in her kitchen and I don't want to sit in the office and twiddle my thumbs."

He rolled over on his back on the sofa and nuzzled her elbow. Polly obeyed and rubbed his belly. "You aren't helping. And by the way, what was up with all of that attention you gave Alistair Greyson? You're my barometer. Is he really a good guy?"

Obiwan's eyes closed and his body relaxed beside her. "Fine," Polly said quietly. "Sleep. You're useless."

When her phone rang, Obiwan's paws twitched, but he didn't move until she twisted to retrieve the phone from her back pocket.

"Hey there, what's up?" she asked Henry.

"I just drove past the inn and that guy we're putting up is outside pulling weeds," Henry said.

Polly chuckled. "He's what?"

"He's pulling weeds underneath the sign and it looks like he's been working his way down the front of the building. Do you know what's up?"

"Uhh, no. I took him over to the city yard to get the rest of his belongings from his truck this morning and then we had lunch, but I have no idea why he's doing yard work." She wondered if he and Jeff had talked about this. "Let me call Jeff. Maybe he knows."

"It's no big deal. He's doing a great job. I just thought I'd ask."

"What are you doing out and about?" she asked.

"Dad sent me to Ames to pick up supplies. I'll be at the shop for a while. Do we have plans for tonight?"

"No, it's quiet and since it's warm out, I thought we could spend it outside again."

"Sounds good. I'll see you later."

"I love you. Thanks for checking up on the inn," she said.

"I love you, too."

They hung up and she dialed Jeff's number. It went straight to voice mail, so she figured he must be busy.

Polly jumped up from the couch and Obiwan startled awake, his feet hitting the floor right behind her. He gave a bark and she looked down. "Sorry, bud. Didn't mean to freak you out. I can't sit still. I have that brand new truck in the garage and I want to put some miles on it. Do you want to go for a ride?"

There were a few phrases that the dogs recognized immediately and 'go for a ride' was one of them. He wagged his tail and trotted through the house to the back stairs. Polly poked her head in the main kitchen and left when she saw Sylvie run her hand across her forehead. Rachel was kneeling in front of the open oven and both were frazzled. Polly had tried to help in the past and had learned a quick lesson: Sylvie would ask for help when she needed it. Otherwise, Polly needed to stay out of the way when they were under stress.

Polly and Obiwan got in the truck and she backed out and drove toward the inn. She had to see this for herself.

She pulled into the parking lot and didn't see Greyson anywhere, but there were small piles of weeds in the parking lot. Polly drove around the building, pulled up under the canopy and rolled her windows down, telling Obiwan to stay. She opened the front door of the hotel, startling everyone as Grey was coming out, carrying a broom and a small trash can.

"What are you doing?" she asked.

"I'm gathering the weeds," he responded, as if it were quite normal for a guest to work on the property.

"But..." she started.

"Ms. Giller, I intend to stay for a goodly length of time. Remaining in that room, beautiful as it may be, with nothing to keep me occupied, would serve none of us. Please excuse me?"

She backed up and held the door for him. "You could find many other things to do in town, though. There's a library and several restaurants."

"You are correct, Ms. Giller, but this needed to be done and so I set my hands to it. In just a few minutes, it will be swept up and then won't it look beautiful?" He nodded back toward the inside of the building. "I assisted two of your guests with questions regarding their stay. You will find notations for all that I did."

"On the computer? You were able to access the computer."

He stopped and bowed his head. "I apologize profusely if I overstepped my bounds. It was quite simple and I was able to serve them without concerning any of you. You are all quite busy."

"Not that busy," she protested. "Wasn't Stephanie here?"

"Aye, that she was. But she had a multitude of calls come in demanding her attention. Once the admissions were complete, I assured her that all would be well."

Polly shook her head. "I guess all I can do is say thank you."

He bowed. "I am grateful for the opportunity. Now if you will excuse me, I would finish this project."

She watched him sweep up the parking lot, astounded at what was happening. But he wasn't about to let her stop him, so she got back in her truck and tried to decide what to do next.

"Come on, Obiwan. We have another stop to make."

Polly drove up town and parked in front of the coffee shop. She didn't know whether to be furious or grateful. Did the man assume too much or was he just being helpful? She snapped a leash on Obiwan's collar and they went inside.

Rebecca gave her a little wave when the bell on the door announced their entrance. Polly's heart surged with love. They'd talked a few times about Sarah's death, but Polly knew that she still cried herself to sleep some nights. As much as the girl missed her mother, it still overwhelmed Polly when Rebecca publicly acknowledged her. She knew it was silly, but that didn't stop her feelings.

"Where's Jeff?" she asked as she walked over to the kids. Seventy-five percent of the books had been shelved and while Polly could changes their arrangement, making room for knick knacks and signs, they'd done a nice job.

"He's in the back room with everybody," Andrew said.

"Everybody?"

Rebecca glanced at the back room. "There's like six people with him. They got everything organized and ready and he started training them on the register and stuff. I heard him say that a delivery was coming in tomorrow and if enough of them learn how to make the drinks they could maybe open this weekend. Wouldn't that be awesome? We could come here after school."

Polly slowly nodded. She hadn't thought about that. Sal wouldn't be thrilled that this place filled up with elementary aged kids in the afternoons. It made her chuckle. Hopefully the kids weren't drinking coffee yet, but hot cocoa would be a popular item when the weather got cold. The coffee shop was only a few blocks from the school and on a direct path to the library. Maybe Sal could work here during the early part of the day and spend her afternoons somewhere else. It made Polly chuckle. This could get interesting. Then again, she doubted that many parents would pay for coffee shop drinks. Maybe they'd be fine.

"What you three have done looks good," Polly said. She'd worry about kids and the coffee shop another day.

"You can put a lot more books in here," Andrew said, gesturing around the room. He was right. There were plenty of empty shelves. But all of that would come in time.

"Maybe you should donate some of yours," she responded with a smile.

His eyes grew big as he looked at her in shock. "Mine? I'm keeping my books."

She shrugged. "It was just a thought."

"It was a terrible thought. Don't have that one again, okay? Especially in front of Mom."

Jeff came out of the kitchen with six people in tow. She recognized the two kids who had stopped in the other day. There were two other young people, a woman about Polly's age, and then an older woman she'd seen in town.

"Polly!" he exclaimed and strode across the room. "Everyone, I'd like you to meet one of the owners of the shop. This is Polly

Giller. She owns Sycamore House and you might have seen Sycamore Inn out on the highway. Polly, do you remember Rena Acosta and Skylar Morris?"

She nodded and smiled at them, then put her hand out to shake theirs.

Jeff continued. "This is Benny Wilson and Julie Smith." He gestured to the other pair of young people and then put his hand on the woman who was Polly's age. "This is Camille Specht, who will be managing the coffee shop and then this," he got the attention of the older woman who had wandered over to see what the kids were doing, "is Helena Black."

Helena Black rushed back over and thrust her hand in front of Polly. "It is so nice to finally meet you," she said effusively. "We hear all about the famous Polly Giller and I've seen you around town, but I just haven't had the chance to introduce myself to you. My husband is Donnie. He farms out north of town, just down from your husband's aunt and uncle. They're awfully busy and we don't see them as often as we'd like. I heard all about your escapade a few months ago. How awful. To be kidnapped and held like that. You'd think they would have better security in those psychiatric places. You know, I had a great uncle who worked in Clarinda, back when it was for the criminally insane. He had a lot of stories, he said, but then he told us that he'd keep them to himself because he didn't want to give us nightmares."

She took a breath and Jeff stepped in. "What brings you up here, Polly?"

"I didn't realize you were so busy," she said and turned back to Helena Black. "It was very nice to meet you. In fact, it was nice to meet you all. I hope you enjoy working here."

Helena took a breath and opened her mouth, but Jeff said, "Excuse me," and took Polly's arm, guiding her and Obiwan away from the group.

They walked back outside and Polly giggled. "You're going to let her loose on customers?"

"She's a nice person," he said sheepishly. "But Camille assures me she can handle it. I like her. She'll be a great manager."

Polly shook her head. "I'm so glad you are handling all of this. You're so much better at looking past first impressions. Camille and Benny aren't from here?"

He chuckled. "What gave you that idea?"

"Because I didn't know we had any African Americans living in Bellingwood." Polly grinned. "It's our job to just stir these folks up, isn't it."

"I didn't hire them because of that, but if it's a side effect, all the better. They got used to Eliseo and they got used to me. This should be easy. And Camille is good. She's run a coffee shop before, but for the last three years, she managed a college food service. She wanted to move back to central Iowa and thinks this could be fun. I think she'll be a great help to Sylvie, too."

"They've met?"

"Sylvie introduced us. I think they met at a food conference. Now, did you need me?"

Polly creased her brows together. "I forgot. No. Wait. I remember."

"Helena has that effect on us." He laughed at his own joke. "No, that's not nice. Okay, enough. What's up?"

"Alistair Greyson was pulling weeds at Sycamore Inn." Polly put her hands in her pockets.

Jeff wrinkled his forehead, "Oh no! Were they special weeds?"

"That's not what I mean. He didn't do anything wrong, but why is he working? He was just in an accident and it seems wrong. And then, he took care of a couple of the guests, too."

"The horrors," Jeff said dramatically. "Should we send Ken to arrest him?"

Polly took a deep breath and scowled at him. Then she pursed her lips.

"Well?" Jeff asked. "I don't know what you want me to do. I could tell him that he's to sit in his room all day, but that seems like a rotten thing to say to the man."

"No." Polly swatted at him. "You're awful. I left thinking that maybe you should talk to him about a job. He seemed to fit right in out there, but now I'm back to thinking that he is just too weird.

He talks funny, he does strange things. Jeff, he carries his belongings in plastic, five-gallon pails and he has a long walking stick."

He laughed at her again. "I don't know what he has in the pails, but when I met him at the inn yesterday, he had his things in two duffel bags and a large suitcase. At least that's what Bert hauled out of his car and into the room. And five-gallon pails aren't that odd. Everybody has them."

"Whatever." Polly dropped her voice. "He hacked into the computer and left notes about what he helped the guests with."

"He probably watched me do it when I checked him in." Jeff shook his head at her. "You worry about the weirdest things. But were you serious about me talking to him about a job? Do you think he'd be a good manager?

"I don't know," she said. "When I say it out loud, it sounds odd. He just showed up in town and I know nothing about him."

"Except he has a walking stick."

"Yeah. That." She grimaced. "Forget I said anything. We should know someone better if we're going to hire them."

"It wouldn't be that hard to teach him how to use the system. If he stays, we could move him into the apartment. If it works out, great. If he up and leaves, we wouldn't be any worse off than we are now," Jeff said. "And it's not like we haven't set a precedent."

"Eliseo isn't a precedent. He's special," Polly said. "All of the animals said so." Then she remembered Obiwan's reaction to the man. "Crap," she said.

"What?"

"Obiwan liked Grey. In fact, it was kind of odd how much Obiwan liked him."

The dog looked up when she said his name.

"You're too nice to people," Polly said to the dog.

"He's really not, you know," Jeff said. "But he does know the difference between a good person and a bad person. He's proven that over and over. What do you want me to do?"

"I don't know," she said as she shrugged. "I just don't know. It felt kind of right. And I still think the man is as odd as they come."

"But you trust him, don't you."

Polly looked up at Jeff. "He's infatuated with Sylvie. He tried to ask her out the first time he met her."

He laughed out loud. "What did she say?"

"She said no. Definitively. And he felt terrible. But still, he asked."

"That could certainly mess with the status quo." Jeff bent over and stroked Obiwan's head. "I like the idea. I'll finish up with these folks and then head over and talk to Mr. Greyson. Maybe we'll have all of our employee issues dealt with in one day."

"It would take a lot of pressure off. So you feel good about this?"

"Camille will hire more part timers down the road, but she can start with this group." He turned to head back inside. "Any more bombs you want to drop on me today?"

He held the door as she and Obiwan walked back inside. "No, but the day isn't over yet. Thanks for listening and not thinking I'm insane."

Camille Specht had her employees washing down tables and chairs while she polished the top of the counter. She looked up and smiled at Polly, put down her cloth, and crossed the room.

"I'd like to get to know you better," she said. "I'm staying at the inn until I find a place to live. Would you have time for lunch in the next couple of days?"

Polly grabbed Jeff's arm and said, "Why isn't she staying at Sycamore House? She could be closer to Sylvie and much closer to this place."

"I don't know. It was just my go-to."

Polly said, "I'd love to have lunch with you. And let's do it whenever you have time. My schedule isn't as tight as yours. And please, you should stay at Sycamore House. We have four wonderful rooms available until you find a place to settle."

Camille glanced at Jeff, the question in her eyes.

"It sounds good to me," he said. "It looks like you just became part of the family."

CHAPTER FIVE

"Now be honest," Sal said. "What did you think of her?" They were at the Sycamore House kitchen table, drinking coffee.

"Think of who?"

"Camille. The manager we hired."

"She seems nice," Polly said. "Jeff moved her into Sycamore House this morning."

"Thank you!" Sal exclaimed. "Mark's house isn't big enough for a long-term guest and I didn't want her to have to stay at the hotel." She stopped and gave a sheepish grin to Polly. "Not that it isn't fabulous."

Polly laughed. "I get it. The rooms aren't big enough."

"Well, the rooms here are a lot bigger and so much..." Sal stopped again. "I'll just shut up now. Thank you for doing that. Can you believe we're about ready to open?"

"I certainly can't," Sylvie interrupted, dropping into a chair next to Polly. She flicked powdered sugar dust off her apron. "I haven't decided what I want to put in there for the opening yet."

Polly and Sal watched Sylvie work. They had offered to help, but Sylvie just rolled her eyes and pointed to the table.

"You need to quit worrying about it. People will like whatever you offer. And it isn't like there's going to be a big rush anyway," Sal said. "We aren't really telling anyone that it's even open."

"They'll find out soon enough," Sylvie retorted. "And you don't think they're not going to want to test me, to see what I've done?"

Sal laughed. "I kind of hoped it was going to be about coffee and tea. People in Bellingwood already know how good you are. Aren't you selling bread at the General Store already?"

"You're right. I know. I worry too much," Sylvie said.

"It's what makes you good at what you do," Polly offered.

She looked out the window to the back yard. Andrew and Rebecca were chasing the dogs in and out of the tree line and tossing Frisbees for them to catch. Exhausting all of them was a great idea, but she knew it wouldn't last long. Kayla had Hawkeye's leash and was trying to keep up with him as he chased the older dogs. When he got exhausted, he would flop down in the grass and she'd drop beside him. The rest period never lasted as long as Kayla wanted. Something would catch the puppy's attention and he'd give a tug on the leash and she'd be up and running again.

Polly and Rebecca had gone to a garage sale one Saturday before Rebecca's art lesson and found an old croquet set. Rebecca had never heard of the game and it had been years since Polly had played. They found instructions online, set the wickets up and it had become quite an attraction for the kids. Several of Jason's friends had also been over to play. Who would have thought that old game would draw kids together again?

Eliseo talked about putting a volleyball net up in the yard, but until the garden came out, Polly wouldn't let him. She could only imagine the destruction feet and wild volleyballs would inflict on his vegetables.

"Hey Jeff," Sal said. "How're things? Should I be up at the coffee shop?"

Polly turned. He had a silly grin on his face. "What's that look?" she asked.

"It's the look of a man who is content," he said.

Sylvie jumped out of her chair and ran to the oven just before the timer's bell rang. "A new hot date?" she asked.

He scowled at her. "No. I think I'm destined to be alone for the rest of my life." He sat down in Sylvie's seat. "No, I hired a manager for the inn."

"You hired him?" Polly asked.

"For a month. That worked out so well with Eliseo, I thought we'd try it again. One month and we all agree that he's a good fit, he stays. Otherwise, he'll move on and we'll start looking again."

Sylvie put two trays of pastries into a rolling rack. "Hired who?" she asked.

"Go ahead. Tell them," Jeff said to Polly. "It was your idea."

"That guy you met yesterday," Polly said. "The one who had been in the wreck out front."

"Victorian guy?" Sylvie asked.

Polly laughed. "I suppose he does act a little like that. But yes. Alistair Greyson." Polly looked over at Sylvie. "Are you going to be okay with him working for us?"

"Why do you ask?" Sylvie just rolled her eyes.

"He was smitten with you and made no bones about it."

"As long as he isn't a stalker, we'll be fine," Sylvie said. She blushed again. "It *was* flattering, but he threw me. I know what I looked like and there he was telling me how beautiful I was."

Sal looked back and forth between the two of them. "He told you that you were beautiful?" She realized what she had sounded like and quickly said, "No. I mean. You are beautiful, but this was the first time he met you and he said that?"

Sylvie laughed. "I know what you mean. I was a complete mess. It was embarrassing. But we'll be fine. I hope it works out."

"You just hired a guy who showed up in town?" Sal asked. "Just like that?"

"Maybe." Polly felt herself blushing. "But when I went out there yesterday, he was pulling weeds and cleaning up the parking lot. And he even figured out how to get into the system to help some of the guests." She looked up and around the room. "It seemed like a good idea at the time. How bad could things get?"

Sal wasn't having it. "He could be a thief or a murderer or anything. What if you've set your guests up to be killed or have their rooms broken into?"

"We'll run a standard background check, right Jeff?"

He nodded. "Of course. Stephanie's working on it right now. Just like we do for anyone that gets hired..." He glanced at Polly. "Anyone that gets hired now that I'm in charge. Polly would just trust people."

She swatted his arm. "I'd rather trust them than not. But that's why I have you. And hey, I trusted you."

"Yes you did," he agreed. "Smartest move you've ever made."

Polly patted his arm where she'd swatted him. "It really was. And I appreciate you every day. Especially when you hire people to do work I don't want to do. Is he moving into the apartment?"

"As we speak," Jeff said.

They had furnished the apartment at Sycamore Inn with furniture and appliances from Polly's father's house. It was still pretty sparse, but someone could easily move in on a moment's notice. She was also thankful that it emptied out much of the garage. There were still stacks of boxes left, but maybe when it got cold this winter, she'd make time to sort through them.

"When are you training him on the system?" she asked.

"He's coming over this afternoon to work with Stephanie, but he's pretty smart. He had it figured out before I even asked him. He's not afraid of computers or hard work."

"He said that limp is from an old injury," Polly said. "Did he tell you what that was from? Will it affect his work? It would be nice if Eliseo didn't have to ride the mower over there every week."

Jeff shook his head. "We didn't get that far, but he assured me that he was quite capable of doing whatever needed to be done."

Polly sat back in her chair. "It would be great if we finally found someone who would stay for a while."

Stephanie came into the kitchen with her coffee mug. "Here you are. I thought I'd lost everybody."

"Come over and join us," Polly said. "You can watch the kids playing." She chuckled. "Just look at those little red faces. They're having a blast. Maybe they'll head over to the pool this afternoon. Do you mind, Stephanie?"

The young girl nodded. "I have Kayla's swimsuit in my bag. She never knows when Andrew and Rebecca will want to go."

"I'm terrible at setting up schedules and making plans during the summer," Polly said. "I'm sorry."

"No, it's okay." Stephanie sat down on the other side of Polly and hesitantly touched her arm. "Speaking of schedules, I need to ask a question."

Polly turned to face her. "Sure, what's up?"

"Kayla and Rebecca want to go clothes shopping this Saturday. Since we've been going to Goodwill so much, Kayla has seen clothes there that she wants. It's such a good deal. Would you mind if I took Rebecca Saturday morning? Or would you rather take her to one of the bigger stores?"

"That would be great," Polly said. "If the girls can find fun things to wear for school, I'd much rather she spent her money that way." She leaned in to speak quietly. "I know they've been saving money from babysitting and working this summer. Is that what Kayla is using?"

"No. I won't let her. This one's on me."

"Well, you tell me how much you plan to spend on Kayla and I'll send the same amount with Rebecca. Will that work?"

Stephanie gave her a grateful smile. "Thank you for letting me do this. We might run to Target after we're done with the thrift stores. I want to get Kayla new underthings too."

"Rebecca would probably love to do that with you two. Just let me know how much I should send, okay?"

The girl took a deep breath and let it out. "I was worried it wouldn't be good enough, but Rebecca said she used to shop at Goodwill with her mom. And I know you can afford..." She paused, looked at Sal, and blushed. "Nothing. Just thank you."

Polly smiled at her. "No problem. The world's an interesting place, isn't it? You never know who you're going to be hanging out with. But I appreciate you taking the girls shopping. They'll have a great time."

She stood up. "I'm going to round up some young-uns before they get too overheated. The dogs have flopped onto the grass a couple of times. I suspect everybody is ready for something cool to drink.

"Anybody who is up town this afternoon should stop by the coffee shop," Jeff said. "Either that or give me an order." He looked at Stephanie and she smiled back at him. "We'll be making free drinks while the kids learn the ropes."

"Helena Black will appreciate being called a kid," Polly said.

Sylvie's head snapped up. "Helena Black? She's working at the coffee shop?" Then she dramatically clutched her chest and said, "Shoot me now."

"What's wrong?" Polly asked. She glanced at Jeff, who was watching with wide eyes.

"Nothing's wrong," Sylvie said, rolling her eyes. "She's just ... busy. And chatty. And interested in everything you're doing, but she never pays any attention, so her interest is always new." She pursed her lips and looked up at Jeff. "But don't worry, she won't last long."

"That's mean. Don't say things like that to me," he replied. Then he said conspiratorially, "But what do you mean by that?"

"She comes on strong for about a month or two and then gets bored. By the time she finally quits, everyone is praying for her to be gone."

"But her references said she was a great worker."

"She is. She'll work hard and she'll do a great job. But she's worked nearly everywhere in town as well as Boone, Stratford, and Webster City. She worked with me at the grocery store... for a couple of months." Sylvie realized that everyone else was in shock. "Don't worry," she said. "Helena is great with customers. They all like her. It's the rest of the employees that will want her to be gone."

Polly poked Jeff, "Maybe this one is your first mistake."

"Hey!" he said.

"Look. Mine was the guy who was high whenever he deigned to show up. You get to have at least one."

He gave her a little push. "Yours was a doozie."

"You're right there." Polly opened the door to the back yard and stepped out, then yelled. "Hey, who wants lemonade? Come in and head upstairs."

"I want lemonade," Sal said when Polly came back inside.

"Then come upstairs," Polly retorted.

"No, that's okay," Sal replied. "I've wasted enough time this morning. I'm going up to the coffee shop and order a crazy drink off the coffee menu and see if I can trip Camille up. She's amazing."

~~~

Jason and one of his friends, Kent Ivers, had agreed to go to the pool with the three kids that afternoon. Polly knew that Rebecca and Andrew could swim. Rebecca had taken lessons this summer and Andrew had been swimming since he was a kid, but Kayla was still a question mark. Rebecca promised to teach Kayla how to float and hold her breath, but Polly was much more comfortable knowing the two older boys would be there.

Polly had gone the first couple of times, but discovered that it embarrassed Rebecca, so after hovering in the background once or twice, she gave up and let them have fun on their own. They were just across the highway, the pool employed lifeguards, and Jason was in charge. After he'd dropped Joey Delancy a few months ago, his self-confidence had grown. He hadn't become arrogant, but that encounter had served to make him realize that he had important contributions to make in protecting others.

She walked out the front door and wandered through the garden on the corner, stopping to listen to the burbling of the water in the pond. There were no people there today, but it was a popular spot for people on their evening walks. She crossed the highway to head up town and realized that Alistair Greyson was in front of her. He was dressed in jeans, a white linen shirt, had a straw hat on his head, and was using his walking stick.

"Mr. Greyson," she called out.

He stopped and turned, bursting into a huge smile. "Why, Miss Polly Giller. What are you doing out today?"

She walked faster to catch up to him. "I'm going to the coffee shop to put their new employees to the test. They aren't open yet, but the kids need practice. Would you like to join me?"

"That would be lovely." He bent his arm for her to take it and said, "And call me Grey. Everyone does. Mr. Greyson is much too formal, don't you think?"

"Grey it is," she responded. "Jeff tells me that you are moving into the apartment at the inn and will be managing the place for us. Thank you for doing that."

He touched the edge of his hat and tipped his head to a woman they passed and said, "I understand that it was upon your recommendation he extended the offer. What a splendid idea you had. Just when I was beginning to wonder what this great, big wonderful world had for me to do next, all of a sudden there you are. Has anyone ever told you that you have a special connection with the movements of the universe?"

She looked at him sideways and realized he was sincere. "I've heard something similar to that in the past, but not put into those words."

"Hey old man," a high school age kid said. "Hasn't anyone ever told you that this look is out?" Two of his friends joined him and cut Polly and Grey off before they could cross the street.

"Young men," Grey said. "You are obstructing our passage. Please move aside."

"Move aside? Who do you think you are? We were here first," the first kid said.

"Are you kidding me?" Polly asked. "This is ridiculous." She started to step forward and one of the other boys blocked her. She stepped in and got up in his face. "Back away and let us through. I may not know who you are, but once I find out, I can make your lives miserable. Now grow up and back off."

"You might think you're a big shot, but everybody knows you're nothing." The first kid spat on the ground in front of her and crowded the other out of her way. He stepped in front of her, trying to intimidate her. He wasn't much bigger than Jason, but it was enough.

Polly refused to give way. She stared at the kid, holding eye contact with him until he broke it. But then he tried to move in even closer. In a flash, though, he was on the ground. She looked around in surprise. Grey had used the walking stick to sweep the boy's legs out from under him. The other two stared in stunned silence, while Grey remained cool and calm. The only thing that betrayed his anger was the flash in his eyes.

He tipped his hat at them and said, "Your deportment is severely lacking, young men. You never treat a lady in that manner." Grey took Polly's arm and guided her around the three boys and across the street.

"That was a smooth move," Polly said, her voice cracking as she worked to regain her composure.

He chuckled. "That, my dear, was from a former life. In fact, the life in which I damaged my poor, blighted knee. I'm afraid those young gentlemen thought I was easy prey, but mayhap they learned a lesson this afternoon."

"I don't know what made them think they could get pushy like that," she replied, opening the door to the coffee shop. She stopped to take a breath. The baristas had been practicing, the wonderful scent of brewed coffee filled her senses.

"The product of too much time on their hands, fears of returning to school soon, and confidence that they had safety in numbers. I'm a stranger in town..." He gestured down at himself. "And might I say I'm like none they've ever met before."

"That's just not right, though," she said "It isn't as if Bellingwood is a bastion of white middle-class..." Then Polly chuckled. "Actually, I guess it is. I do my best to bring color and interest and some people want nothing to do with that."

He propped his stick inside a tall umbrella stand just inside the front door and swept his arm toward the counter. "After you, milady. I believe they're awaiting our orders."

CHAPTER SIX

"We hardly ever see that girl," Henry said to Polly. This was a recurring theme. "Where is she tonight?"

"Jessie invited her to spend the night before school started. They're having girl talk," Polly said.

"It's really just you and me all alone - all night?" he asked, a wicked glint in his eye. He leaned over the sofa and groped her breast.

"Henry!" she exclaimed, laughing. "Stop that!"

He stood back up and with a proud smile, said, " No one's here. And don't tell me you hate it. You didn't say that last night."

Polly's face flush and she giggled. "Sometimes I don't know what to say to you."

"I know," he said. "I'm hilarious. Are we grilling out tonight?"

She wrinkled her nose. "I don't want to. Let's go out to eat."

"It's because I groped you, isn't it. You want to be out in public where I'll be good. You're afraid of me," he taunted her.

"That's me. Afraid of you."

Henry bent back over and kissed her cheek. "I love you anyway. Where do you want to eat?"

"I could do Mexican."

He scowled. "We did takeout from there for lunch."

"We need more restaurants in this town," Polly said. "I don't feel like driving all the way down to Boone."

"It's fifteen miles. You drove farther than that for a meal when you lived in Boston."

"Yeah, but..."

"Don't yeahbut me," he said. "Come on, let's go."

"I don't want to leave town when Rebecca is staying somewhere else." Polly chuckled as she said it.

But Henry bit. "You're kidding me, right?"

"Ahh, a little bit," she said and jumped up off the sofa. "Can we just go to Davey's? I feel like steak or pasta or a big salad."

He rolled his eyes. "You are too easy."

She followed him through the house and down the back steps, glancing back to see two very forlorn dogs at the top.

"We'll be back soon. I promise," she said to them. "Now go lie down and keep each other company."

"You think they understand you?" Henry asked.

"I feel better if I talk to them, so don't give me any trouble."

He held the truck door open for her and waited until she was settled before going to the driver's side.

"Are you always going to do that?" Polly asked.

"Do what?"

"Hold the door for me?"

He spoke in an exaggerated drawl. "Absolutely, ma'am. We boys are brought up to take care of our women. Because y'all are precious flowers, deserving of our undying attention."

"You're a weird, weird man."

Henry touched the front of his non-existent Stetson and nodded to her. "Yes, ma'am."

"I didn't tell you about the bullies today," she said. "Three boys got pushy with me and Alistair Greyson when we were walking to the coffee shop."

"In Bellingwood?" Henry sounded shocked.

"I know!" she said. "I forgot to ask Jason if he knew who they were. I'm half tempted to find out who they are and call their mothers. It was rude. And honestly, Henry, I didn't know whether they were going to get physical or not."

He had stopped at the end of their driveway waiting for traffic to pass. "In Bellingwood?" he asked again.

"Almost downtown. I've seen one or two before. I have no idea what they thought they were doing. It was a little scary."

"In Bellingwood," he repeated, shaking his head. "I just don't believe it. And no one came out to stop them?"

"We weren't near any shops. But, to be honest, it was kind of entertaining to watch Grey sweep their feet out from under them and put them on the ground."

"Tell me you didn't..." Henry glanced at her.

"Kick them in the balls?" she asked, laughing. "No, but I probably should have. Taught those little jerks a lesson. And then one of them made a point of telling me that even though I thought I was a big deal, in reality I was nothing."

"That's not true," Henry said. "You are a pretty big deal in this little town."

"I've heard nasty stuff before, though," she said. "Sometimes it bothers me that people think that. I'm just doing my thing."

"People get jealous of others and their success. You're doing a lot for Bellingwood. There are always people who are so negative, they can only imagine you have sinister motives behind everything you do."

"Me?" she asked, laughing. "Sinister? I don't even know what that looks like."

"They do. They'll always hope you fail or look for a way to trip you up. They want to drag you down into the gutter with them. It's just their way."

"That's ridiculous. Have I done something to hurt these people?" She paused. "I don't even know who they are. Are they just phantom complainers?"

"They're real and there are more than a few in town."

"You've heard them?"

He grew quiet.

"You've heard people saying bad things about me, haven't you?"

He nodded.

"I'm sorry," she said. "You shouldn't have to listen to that. Have you ever confronted them?"

Henry shook his head. "It's stupid to get into an argument with people like that. There's nothing you can say to change their mind, so why fight with them?"

"I know you're right, but it makes me even angrier that they think they can get away with bad-mouthing me in front of you. And other people who don't even know me."

"Everyone who is anyone knows they're wrong. They're just sad, sad people who have nothing better to do than to complain about good things. They're afraid of change and think that by making noise they can stop new things from happening."

Polly crossed her arms over her chest. "So the best thing for everyone else to do is just let them say terrible things. That makes a ton of sense," she said, marking every word with as much sarcasm as possible. "You know that kind of talk is insidious. Others hear it and then begin questioning whether or not it's true and before you know it, they're looking closely and making every little thing fit in with their negative belief about me."

"Now Polly, you know that isn't real." Henry drove past the entrance to Davey's.

"Don't try to placate me. This is how World War II started. Hitler's beliefs were insidious and people who should have stood up and stopped him, didn't."

He burbled out a laugh. "Bellingwood is World War II Germany now?"

"No!" she snapped. "But you know what I mean."

Henry drove into the parking lot of Sycamore Inn and parked. "You're right. I should be better about standing up for you, but seriously, Polly. Most of the garbage that comes out of their mouths is hooey and everyone knows it. These people are just looking for a fight and I don't particularly want to be the one to give it to them."

"Who are *these* people, by the way?" she asked.

He tried to wave her off. "I don't know. It's been a while since I've been anywhere to hear them. It's no big deal."

"It was a big enough deal today that three young punks thought they could get all up in my face and try to bully me."

Henry reached over and took her hand. "Find out who those little jack-asses are and I *will* stand up and protect you. Trust me on that."

Polly reached out and patted his arm, smiled, affected her own drawl and batted her eyes at him. "You're mah hero," she said. "Mah big, strong hero."

"Yes, ma'am, I am."

He back out and drove to Davey's.

Polly reached for the door handle after he parked the truck. "I feel kind of guilty."

"For what?" he asked.

"I should have invited someone to come to dinner with us. I get so busy that I don't think about it until it's too late."

"You're a nut and I love you," he said. "I think the world will be just fine tonight if you aren't taking care of it."

"Brat." Polly opened the door and hopped down. She waited for Henry to catch up and they went inside. The hostess seated them and Polly checked out the room. She could always count on someone interesting being here. Henry often told her that she had more fun watching people than actually spending time with him. That was true.

She'd never been able to find anyone since college who would play the story-telling game with her and she missed it. They would choose a few people and weave elaborate lives for them, based on nothing more than what they were wearing and doing at the time. There were international spies or housewives whose other job was much more interesting. They had created serial killers and bounty hunters, aliens bent on taking over the world and even little old ladies who lived with 87 cats. Maybe she should teach Rebecca and Andrew how to play the game. Their imaginations were still growing.

"What are you thinking about over there?" Henry asked. "You're a million miles away."

"Oh nothing. Just thinking about how interesting people are."

He glanced around the room. "You're doing it again, aren't you?"

"Watching? Yeah. I guess so." Then she saw him. "That's him," she whispered loudly.

Henry looked up. "Who?"

"The little brat who got all up in my face today. He's here with his parents."

"Who?" he asked again.

"He's behind you." She stopped him before he turned around. "No, don't look. I don't want him to know he got to me."

"Who cares what he knows?" Henry asked. "If he was bullying you on the streets of Bellingwood, I'd like him to know that I've got your back and he can't get away with it." He turned around in his chair and stared at the table with the young man.

The boy glanced up and caught his eye, then ducked his head.

Henry turned back to her. "Now it makes sense. Those aren't his parents. They're his dad's brother and wife. His parents were killed the winter before you got here. That's Heath Harvey. The poor kid has been in a lot of trouble. He just can't move on."

"Was he in the accident with them?" Polly asked.

Henry shook his head. "No, they were on their way to a basketball game in Ames. They shouldn't have gone out in the storm. His older brother was playing. Hayden, I think his name is. Anyway, Heath was home with a babysitter and it busted him up pretty bad. His uncle is a tough man. He farms out east of town. So, in one fell swoop, he lost his parents and had to move out of town, away from everything he was used to."

"You're almost making me feel bad for the kid," Polly said.

"Well, he shouldn't be acting like that, but those two no control of him. I hope he figures it out, but who knows."

"Is he Jason's age?"

Henry looked up from the menu. "Stop it. Don't make Jason get involved with that. He doesn't need to rescue the world with you.

That poor kid is finally done with a year where he had to figure out his own life."

"But..."

He put his hand over the top of hers. "I love you..."

"You already said that," she replied, interrupting him.

"But you don't need to get involved in every problem that rears its head in Bellingwood."

Polly picked up her menu and then said, "If I don't, who will?" She glanced back at the boy sitting sullenly at the table with his aunt and uncle. "Don't they say that kids' brains aren't fully developed at this age - that decision making and empathy and all of that is still being learned?" she mused out loud. "Is he just expected to figure it out on his own? Those people aren't going to help him. I mean, look at them. They aren't talking. And why didn't they have children of their own? Was it because they couldn't or because they didn't want to? Then they were stuck with a messed up kid they barely knew."

"Honey," he said. "Don't do this to yourself. You can't fix him."

"But I could show him something different. What if I offered him a job at the coffee shop or out at Sycamore Inn. It wouldn't be many hours, but he'd be with people I trust to be good to him."

"You have a brand-new manager at the coffee shop. Are you just going to throw employees at her and expect her to deal with them?"

"No." Polly stuck her lower lip out.

"And I don't know what you think you'd do with him at the inn. You don't even have a manager."

"Whoops," she said.

Henry put his menu back down again. "What's whoops?"

Their waitress stopped, took their order, and Henry looked at Polly again. "You said 'whoops.' What does that mean?"

"We hired Alistair Greyson to manage the inn."

Henry had started to take a drink of water and instead, put the glass back down on the table. "Who is the *we* in that equation?"

"We. You know. Me and Jeff. I had a crazy idea and he ran with it. It's the same deal we made with Eliseo. We'll try this for a month. If it goes well, great, we move forward. If it goes horribly bad, then everyone moves on and we start over. But I like him, Henry. He's a good man."

"I thought you said he was odd."

"Well," she chuckled. "That doesn't change whether or not he's a good man. He just happens to have a few odd affectations."

"Does he have any experience?"

"Did I?"

"Well no, but you were building a business, not running someone else's."

"And I had no business background, no idea what I was going to do once I started. I didn't know anyone in town. I had no connections."

He put his hand up to stop her. "Okay, okay. I get it. It just seems strange to hire someone like that right off the street."

"You mean like Eliseo? Or even Jeff for that matter. He walked in for an interview and hired himself."

"But Jeff had the education. And Eliseo is just ... Eliseo."

"And Grey is Grey," she retorted. "It's going to be okay. I have a good feeling about this. And besides, Obiwan liked him."

"If the dog likes him, I guess he's acceptable, then," Henry said.

"That's right," Polly said. "It's going to be fine. You'll see."

Henry smiled at her. "Your super power is finding dead bodies, not reading people or having good feelings."

"Don't start with me. There are going to be no more dead bodies." Polly glanced up and said, "Well, oh my. I wonder who the pretty boy is with her."

"That's mean. With who? I hate it when you look at things behind me and make cryptic comments."

"With her," Polly said, grinning and standing up. "Hello Beryl, how are you? You look wonderful this evening." She gave her friend a hug and waited while Henry stood.

Both Henry and Polly waited an uncomfortable moment for Beryl to introduce the man who was standing beside her.

He shifted on his feet and Beryl finally broke the silence. "It's nice to see you two this evening. I hope you enjoy your meal."

She tugged a beautifully knitted black shrug around her shoulders and turned to follow the hostess.

"Oh no you don't," Polly said, grabbing her arm. "You wouldn't dare."

"Oh honey, there are so many things that I would dare. Maybe you ought to clarify." Beryl lifted Polly's fingers one by one and then squeezed her hand gently before dropping it.

Polly put her hand out to the man and said, "I'm Polly Giller and this is my husband Henry Sturtz."

He shook her hand and then Henry's and finally looked at Beryl, laughter in his eyes.

Henry couldn't stand it. "Would you two like to join us this evening? We've only just placed our order with the waitress. I'm sure they can put our food on hold until you've ordered."

"We couldn't," Beryl said. "We have too much to discuss and it would be rude." She took the man's arm and led him away from the table, looking back over her shoulder at Polly with an immense smile on her face.

Polly and Henry sat back down and Polly just looked at him. "I don't know what to think about that," she said.

"What just happened?"

"Is she on a date?"

"Surely you would have heard about a hot date. Wouldn't you?"

Polly craned her neck to see where they'd been seated. "You'd think. Was she just being rotten by not introducing him to us? And how did he avoid the introduction so gracefully? I gave him a perfect lead-in and he ignored it. And I think he enjoyed ignoring it!" She pursed her lips. "I'm calling Lydia."

The waitress came with their salads and after she left, Henry picked up his fork. "Let's enjoy our supper and you can talk to Lydia tomorrow. Maybe Beryl is just messing with you and soon she won't be able to stand it. Then she'll tell you what's going on."

"I suppose you're right," Polly said. She glanced back at their table again. Beryl was laughing and touching the man's forearm. "But she's flirting with him."

"Eat your food," he said.

"If she was trying to hide him from us, she wouldn't have brought him to Davey's. They could have gone anywhere else and been more discreet than this."

"Exactly. It's probably nothing. Eat."

Polly looked down at her salad and then up at him. "This has been a weird meal so far. We should probably have played the story-telling game. It would have been easier."

Henry raised an eyebrow.

"Making up fictional stories about the people we see here. This real stuff is enough to make me insane."

CHAPTER SEVEN

Huffing out an exasperated sigh, Polly called Lydia as soon as they were back in the truck.

"Hello dear, how are you?" Lydia asked.

"Confused."

Lydia chuckled and asked, "Well, that's a new response. What's going on?"

"You tell me," Polly replied. "I just sat through dinner at Davey's watching Beryl and some strange man together. She was all dressed up and it looked like she was flirting with him. Who is it?"

"Don't tell me you didn't introduce yourself," Lydia said.

"Of course I did. I even caused an awkward silence hoping that one or the other one of them would cave in and introduce him to me. Beryl just ignored it and he wasn't helpful either. Who is it?"

"Hmmm," Lydia said. "I don't know of any special man in Beryl's life. Is she hiding a new beau?"

"They're hardly hiding if they're eating together at Davey's," Polly retorted. "Now do you know something about this or not?"

"I'll tell you mine if you tell me yours," Lydia said.

"Mine? I don't have anything interesting going on."

"That's not the rumor I've heard. You and Jeff have gotten awfully busy over there at Sycamore House. You hired a manager for the coffee shop and it appears you've rescued another poor soul and hired him to manage the inn."

Polly sighed. Nothing got past this woman. "You already know everything. Yes and yes. What more is there to tell you?"

"I want to hear all about these people. What do you think of them? Why did you hire them? Was it your decision or Jeff's? What does Henry think about all of this?" Lydia took a breath and before Polly could respond, she rushed ahead. "Not because Henry has any say in it, I'm just interested in his opinion. I know that he doesn't tell you what to do."

Polly laughed. "I knew that. Maybe we should have coffee or lunch in the next couple of days and hash out all of the gossip in town."

"We should get together," Lydia said firmly. "Another dinner with the five of us. What do you think?"

"I'm game. The only person we need to worry about is Sylvie. She's going out of her mind. I can't force her to hire someone, but until she does, she's stretched pretty thin."

"Let me work on her and we'll find a time. We can do it at my house again. It's been too long and I miss having you all come over."

"That sounds great."

"It's a plan, then. I'll make the calls tomorrow and work on a plan. I love you sweetie, have a good night."

With that, Lydia was gone.

Polly looked at the phone in her hand and then at Henry. "She hung up," Polly said.

"Did you find out what you were looking for?"

"No. She hung up. I don't know whether she deliberately ignored the reason for my call or if she was distracted by party. And I don't know what to do now."

He laughed. "That'll teach ya. You're too nice. You won't call her back either, will you?"

"I can't. If she's deliberately avoiding my question, she'll just keep doing it. If she was been ditzy, I hate pointing that out. I don't know anything more now than I did before I called. Well, except that we're going to have another party."

Henry pulled into the driveway and pressed an overhead button to raise the garage door. "Another drunken night of revelry?"

"Oh please no." Polly shuddered. "That was a once-in-a-decade kind of thing. None of us ever want to go through that again." She opened the truck door and turned back to look at him. "But it was fun. As much as we don't want to repeat it, all of us had a blast. Even Lydia and she was the one going through hell at the time." Polly leaned back on the seat. "Can you believe that was just six months ago? So much has happened. Everything keeps changing."

"It does," he agreed.

"Henry, we have a daughter who is going to be a seventh grader. She's only going to be with us for six more years and then she'll be making decisions about her future. How am I supposed to prepare for that?"

He put his hand on the console, palm up and she placed hers on top of it. Henry squeezed it lightly. "You know you're getting ahead of yourself, right?"

"I try not to think about it too often," Polly said. "It scares me to death. I don't want to miss anything, but I want to be ready for all of the big things that are ahead for her."

"You'll always be ready. Just slow down and enjoy the moments. Right?"

She nodded. "It's a nice evening. Do you have time for a long walk with the dogs?"

"I have all the time in the world for you." He jumped out of the truck and ran around the front so that he was beside her by the time she got to the door. He kissed her cheek and she took his hand and leaned into to kiss his lips.

"Sometimes I'm overwhelmed by my life," Polly said. "You're my only constant. When everything else is in chaos, you're steady and solid."

He broke from the embrace and opened the door. "Well, that sounds boring."

"Not boring. Never boring."

"Good. Because if you think I'm boring, I'm going to start making waves." He opened the door at the bottom of their steps and flipped a light on. The dogs were on the landing, waiting to be called. "Come on down, boys. Your mama has been much too philosophical tonight. She needs to get outside where grass is green, skies are blue and life is real."

Polly snagged two leashes and bent to kiss the top of Obiwan's head. Han bumped the older dog out of the way and she rubbed his neck, and waited for him to send his tongue across her cheek.

"He's a sloppy kisser," she said. "You need to teach him to be neater about that."

"I don't think so," Henry said. "That little boy has learned so much from Eliseo. I don't feel like I have much of a say in what he does after that. He's a goofy, goofy dog."

"We have the strangest little family, don't we?" she asked.

Henry snapped the leash onto Han's collar and they walked back outside. "Our family might look different than others, but we're happy. Now which way shall we go?"

"We aren't in a hurry. Let's go north and wander through town," she responded.

He nodded and clicked his teeth much like Eliseo did and Han stopped pulling and dropped in beside him.

"It always amazes me," Polly said.

Henry chuckled. "To be honest, it amazes me, too. It's like it's an on-off button. Eliseo should teach classes. We'd have a town filled with obedient dogs and even better, smart pet owners. You were lucky with Obiwan, but I'm pretty sure this one left his brains in New Mexico."

"Come on," she said as they crossed the highway. "He's a great dog."

"Yes," he agreed. "He's a great dog. But intuitive he isn't." They got to the other side and Henry bent down and slipped a treat out of his pocket. "I love you though. You're a good boy."

Han wagged his tail, his tongue hanging out of his mouth. Henry handed another one to Obiwan. "You're just a good dog all around."

"Wow," Polly said. "They even have you trained."

It was still early enough that there was plenty of activity in and around the restaurants and bars. People waved from their cars or smiled and said hello. She enjoyed being out on summer evenings. Next week the stores would stay open in the evenings as people prepared for the start of school. Then she had one more community band concert over Labor Day weekend. It was hard to believe they were coming up on three years in Sycamore House. So much had happened and she'd gotten to know more people than she could have ever imagined.

This was her home now. Story City was her dad's home and Boston was just a place where she used to live. Bellingwood was home. She no longer relied on Henry to tell her who people were in town. There were a few that she didn't immediately recognize. For the most part, though, even if she didn't know people well, she was familiar with who they were.

"What's that about?" Henry asked, startling Polly out of her thoughts.

"What's what?"

"Is tomorrow a big day at the coffee shop?"

"I don't think so. Why?" Polly asked.

"Lights are on. Do you have your keys?"

Polly patted her pockets. "No. You don't?"

"I dumped all the keys in the tray before we left for dinner."

She gave a one shoulder shrug. "Maybe it's Camille."

They crossed the street and stopped in front of the door to the coffee shop. Henry tugged on it and both of them were surprised when it opened.

"What in the heck?" he asked.

Polly put her hand on his arm. "I don't want to go in."

"How bad do you not want to go in?"

She looked down at the dogs. "Bad enough that I want Obiwan with me."

"Fine." Henry took her elbow. "Let's see what's going on."

He pulled the door open and Polly stepped in first, calling out "Camille? Are you here?"

The light coming from the bakery showed a mess in the main room. Books had been pulled off the shelves, tables and chairs were overturned and mugs that had been neatly stacked on the counter were broken on the floor.

"Damn it," she said. "What happened?"

"I'll call Ken," Henry responded.

"Let's see what the rest of the place looks like first," she said. "I don't want to tell Sal about this. She's going to freak out."

Henry flipped the main lights on. The damage wasn't awful, but it was apparent that someone had gone through the place.

"I can't believe no one saw this," Polly said. She strode across the floor and looked behind the bar. Everything was still in place.

Henry used his phone to capture pictures of the damage and she went down the back hallway to the kitchen, terrified of what she might find. Obiwan followed along quietly and stopped beside her in the doorway. She breathed a sigh of relief. Nothing there. It still looked as fresh and new as it had when she'd been here earlier. At least didn't have to give bad news to Sylvie. One friend in distress at a time was plenty.

The back door was open and Polly crossed the room to pull it shut. Who left things like this? They'd have to find out who had been the last person in and out of this place. Yes, Bellingwood was a small town, but obviously there needed to be some security.

When she got to the back door, Obiwan tugged on the leash. He pulled her outside to the back dock, filled with empty cardboard boxes and pallets.

"You aren't giving me a lot of confidence, Obiwan," she whispered as she let him pull her. She went down the steps to the alley and the dog walked to the end of their building. He sniffed at a stack of pallets and looked up at her.

"What's there?" she asked.

"Polly, are you out here?" Henry called from the back door.

"Just a second," she said and walked in front of Obiwan. It was pretty dark in this corner, so she took out her phone and turned the flashlight on. "Crap," she said, then bent down to rub Obiwan's neck. "*You* are the good dog. Thanks for finding her."

Polly called back to Henry. "Don't bother with Ken. I'm calling Aaron."

"Wh..." he started, then walked along the dock to where she was standing. "I shouldn't even ask, should I? What did you find?"

She pointed at the body of Julie Smith, one of the new employees, lying behind the stack of pallets.

Han tried to leap off the dock, but Henry held tightly to his leash. Polly and Obiwan walked back over to the stairs, she sat down and swiped a call open.

"Don't you have someone else to call when this happens?" Aaron said upon answering the phone.

"Maybe I'll buy you a cape and bright red oversized underwear you can wear over your uniform," Polly said. "You're my hero."

"You're about to mess up my perfectly calm evening, aren't you?"

"I can call Ken," she replied.

"Okay, why don't you do that?"

"Hey! I call you when I find a body. I call him when other things happen. I like to spread the joy."

She heard Lydia's voice in the background and Aaron said, "Yes, Polly found someone." He hesitated and said, "No, you can't come with me. You can talk to her tomorrow."

He came back to Polly. "Are you okay? Is it someone you know?"

"I know who she is. We just hired her at the coffee shop. But no, I don't know her very well and I'm fine."

He relayed the information to his wife and then said. "I'll call in the team. Why are you there anyway?"

"Lights were on inside and the place was messed up. There are broken mugs and books were pulled off the shelves. Tables and chairs were tossed around too. The place was all unlocked."

"Okay. We'll be there in a few minutes. Stay out of things, will you?"

"You're training me," Polly said. "You know I'll be good."

She put her phone back into her pocket and looked up at Henry. "There's a good walk ruined."

"Does Aaron want us to stay?"

Polly nodded. "Yeah. And I don't want to call Sal."

"You should wait to do that. Let them get in and started before she shows up all worried."

"You're right." She patted the step beside her. "Wanna join me?"

"I'll take the dogs home and come back. That shouldn't make a difference, should it?"

Polly stood up. "Would you? That would reduce the amount of chaos. I'll stay here with Julie." Her shoulders drooped. "I don't know anything about her. I don't know where she's from."

"It will be okay." Henry put his hand on her shoulder. "Don't take all of that on right now. Get through tonight and take care of the rest as it comes."

"I need to call Jeff. And Camille. Maybe I'll let him tell Camille. The rest of the kids are going to be upset. I don't want to tell Andrew, Rebecca and Kayla. They had fun with those older kids the last couple of days." She paused and handed Obiwan's leash to Henry. "Sometimes I think I have too much death in my life."

"We've been over this before. The death was already there. This isn't about you."

"You're right." She kissed him. "Thanks for dealing with the dogs. I'll just be sitting here in this creepy alley waiting for the Sheriff to show up."

He chuckled. "I'm not too worried about you. You're a scary woman. You'll take care of 'em." He walked with the dogs down the alley to the sidewalk and turned south to go home.

Polly took her phone back out and hovered over the keypad. Jeff first. He'd have more information. She swiped the call to him.

"Hey Polly." She understood the concern in his voice. She never called him in the evening. "What's going on?"

"Jeff," she started. "You aren't going to believe it."

"Believe what? If it were a dead body, you'd be calling the Sheriff. So what is it?"

"Well, actually."

She heard him take a deep breath and then say, "Excuse me. I need to take this in private."

"I'm so sorry," she said. "I didn't mean to interrupt you."

"It's okay. Now, what's going on?"

Polly explained to him what had happened in the last half hour and he quietly took it in. Then she said, "Jeff?"

"What?"

"You're not talking."

"I don't know what to say. Do you need me to come back to Bellingwood?"

"No," she responded. "I don't think so. There's nothing you can do. I'll call Sal and tell her about this. Aaron will probably want Julie's employment records so he can reach out to her family."

"You know where those are in the computer. And we should talk to Camille."

"Maybe we should let Aaron tell us what to do next and who to talk to," she said.

"Yeah. You're right. I'm really flustered."

Polly heard a car door open and then she heard the sound of the car starting in the background. "Jeff, what are you doing?"

"I don't know. I guess I'm coming up to Bellingwood."

"Did you just leave someone in a restaurant?" she asked with a small chuckle.

"Holy cow, I did!" he said. "What am I thinking? I need to go back in and apologize and then I'll be right there."

Polly smiled. She wasn't going to let him forget this anytime soon. "Stop talking and stop doing anything. If Aaron wants to speak with you tonight, he'll call. Otherwise, let them do their job and take care of Julie. I'm here. I can get into the system and give them any information they want. Camille is at Sycamore House if they want to talk to her. Handle your date and I'll let you know if there's anything else."

She heard the car turn back off. "I'm sorry I was such a dope," he said. "I'll be fine. He's never going to believe this."

"Who's that?" Polly asked.

"Uh huh. Whatever. I'll talk to you later. Have you called Sal yet?"

"No. You were my first call. I expected you to be the least crazy. If Sal ends up being the calm one about this, my world is upside down. You know that, right?"

"Good luck with it. Call me later."

"You won't still be on your date?"

"Uhh. No. If it wasn't dead before now, this effectively killed it. Call me. Okay?"

"I will."

Lights came down the alley and Polly grinned at her phone. She was rescued from calling her friend. Stu Decker got out of his SUV and walked over to her.

"I always look forward to spending time with you, Ms. Giller."

"Yeah, yeah, yeah. You're a brat."

He smiled at her, then turned serious. "Where is she?"

Polly stood up and walked with him over to where the girl's body was, then backed away, knowing that he would want to get right to work. He knelt down on his haunches and took in the scene, then stood back up.

"Did you see this stick?" he asked. "Do you know what it is?"

She walked back over to him and looked to where he was pointing. A long walking stick, covered in blood, was tucked up against the girl's body.

"I do," she said flatly. "It belongs to the man we just hired to run Sycamore Inn."

CHAPTER EIGHT

Even though she had tried, Polly's respite from the conversation with Sal didn't last long. Just after Henry came back, her phone rang.

"What in the hell is going on?" Sal demanded.

"There's been a murder," Polly said, as matter of factly as possible.

"In my shop?"

Technically, this wasn't inside the shop. "Well, not really," Polly said.

"What exactly do you mean by 'not really'? Denis just called and said the place was crawling with Sheriff's vehicles. And he said that he saw you and Henry go inside. Are you still there?"

She didn't want to point out the obvious. And maybe Sal wasn't quite as alert to Polly's superhero status as everyone else was, but she said, "There's been a murder. That means there was a dead body. So ... that means I'm here."

"Was it inside the shop or not?"

"Sal, honey. I think the first question you should probably ask is if we know the person. And yes, we do. It was Julie Smith."

"Oh for god's sake, it's going to be known as the jinxed coffee shop. I can't believe this has happened again. I can't catch a break."

"Salliane Judith Kahane, you stop talking right now and think about what you have just said to me," Polly said. "I can't believe you are being this self-centered when a young girl has been murdered. Get over yourself and start asking the right questions."

The phone went dead and when Polly looked at it, she realized Sal had just hung up on her. Sometimes being that girl's friend was full-time work. They had known each other for over fifteen years and there were times it was more difficult than others.

Aaron had walked over to stand beside her and asked, "We need to speak with Jeff Lyndsay, the woman you've hired to manage the shop, and Mr. Greyson. I understand he's been hired at the inn?"

Polly nodded. "Camille is staying at Sycamore House. Jeff will come back tonight if necessary and Grey should be in the apartment at the inn. He moved in today. Was his walking stick the murder weapon?"

He gave her a weak smile. "You know I'm not making any assumptions until we have more information."

"You need to see what happened inside, too," Polly said. "I can't tell if there was a fight or if someone deliberately tossed the place."

"We'll check it out." Aaron creased his brow. "Were you opening tomorrow?"

"Jeff was planning to. He doesn't want to make a big deal out of it until we get the kinks out. Just let people find us when they do. He's going to have a big grand opening later this fall. The employees need time to get their feet under them."

"And this girl was one of your new employees?"

"Yeah. I don't know her, but I can get into the employee records back at Sycamore House and find information. Do you want Jeff to come up tonight?"

"He'll be here in the morning. That's soon enough. Have you spoken with him?"

"Yes, while I was waiting for you."

"Sheriff?" One of the deputies called and Aaron walked away.

"How are you doing?" Henry asked, coming up to stand beside her.

"Sal's mad at me. I yelled at her."

"You knew it wasn't going to be easy."

Polly bit her lips together. "She drives me crazy. Always worried about the silliest things. She believes this place has a jinx on it now. It didn't matter that one of her employees had been killed. The only thing she worried about was whether it had happened inside or not and if it was going to mess up the building."

"Do we need to discuss finding money so you can buy the rest of this from her?" Henry asked.

"It crossed my mind. But I'm not ready to do that yet. She's poured so much of herself into this." Polly stopped. "And yes, I understand that's why she's so upset. But still ... property versus people. Will she ever learn the difference?"

"She's never had to be responsible for people before."

"The thing is," Polly said. "This is exactly what makes her so angry with her mother. This same behavior. She sees it in her mom, but has no concept that she's doing the same thing."

"If you yell at her a couple more times, she'll figure it out," he said. "Do we need to stick around?"

"I'll ask Aaron. You didn't happen to bring keys, did you?"

Henry pulled out two sets. "I brought the extra set. Figured maybe he'd lock it down when he was finished."

They found Aaron and gave him the keys, which he promptly turned over to Stu Decker.

While they were walking home, Polly heard her name being called. Turning toward the sound, they saw Jessie and Rebecca pushing a stroller.

"What are you two doing out?" Polly asked when they got close to each other.

"There was all of this excitement down here and we had to find out what was happening," Jessie said. She had moved into the apartment building that Sylvie and the boys used to live in. It was only a couple of blacks from the main downtown area.

Polly had hoped a relationship might happen between Jessie and Stephanie. Sharing expenses would have helped both girls, but neither was interested in an adult roommate. They had their own girls to raise. It made sense. It was hard enough having a husband in the same house some days. At least he knew better than to judge her when she didn't clean the place right away.

The truth was, even though having a roommate through college was one thing, she was glad when she moved into her own apartment. It had been a struggle at first. There were times when going to the grocery store was the only shopping she could afford. And other times when a surprise gift from her father was what put toilet paper in her bathroom.

If she thought about it, though, those were some of the strongest memories she had of her days in Boston and she was proud of herself for having made it through them.

Rebecca stopped in front of Polly and asked with a little condescension, "Did you find another dead body? Is that why you're here?"

Polly nodded, the seriousness of the evening falling on her. "I did. The Sheriff is taking care of her now."

The girl's mouth dropped open and her eyes grew wide. "Was it at the coffee shop?"

"It was out back," Polly said, nodding. "And once the Sheriff is done, you will have to come back up and re-shelve those books. Someone pulled them all down. The coffee shop is a mess."

"Who died?" Jessie asked.

Polly started to speak, but stopped when Henry took her hand. He gave a slight shake of his head and she smiled back at him. "Let's not talk about that tonight. I want the sheriff to do his job and then we'll talk after he contacts the family. Is that okay?"

"Okay," Jessie said. "I hope it's not someone we know." Then she screwed up her face. "It's bad that it is anyone, but if it's a friend, that makes it worse."

"It isn't anyone you know well. I promise," Polly looked into the stroller. Molly had a toy in her hands and was making small noises. "How are things with her?"

"She should be in bed now," Rebecca said. "But we wanted to see what was happening. We're going to make popcorn and watch a movie after she goes to sleep."

"Then you two should get back and start your evening," Henry said. "We'll see you tomorrow, okay?"

He took Polly's hand as they watched the two girls walk back toward the apartment building. "It's so strange to realize that we're parents and responsible for a child's upbringing," he said.

Polly huffed a chuckle. "It makes me nervous. I still think of myself as barely an adult and now I'm supposed to teach her how to grow up."

"You have me," he said.

She looked at him to see if he was serious. The grin on his lips made her smile.

"Yes I do. You can be the adult when I forget how," she said.

The girls turned a corner and Polly and Henry continued toward Sycamore House. "It's practically on our way," she said.

"I'm sorry, what?"

"The convenience store. Can we stop?"

He laughed. "You're a nut. We don't have enough ice cream at home for you?"

"But this is out-for-a-walk-after-I-found-a-body ice cream. Please?" Polly leaned in against him and tilted her head to look into his eyes.

"How can a man resist that?" They turned down the street and he moved so she was walking on the inside. "Do you think Mr. Greyson killed the girl?"

She shook her head. "I can't come with any good reason. It makes no sense. Why do you do that?"

"Do what?"

"You always move to the outside when we're walking. If a car were to come crashing over the curb, we'd both be dead."

Henry chuckled and shrugged, then brought her hand up to his chest and hugged it close. "It's just something Dad taught me. I watched him do it with both Mom and Lonnie. As I grew up, Mom always moved to the inside so I'd learn. It's not about cars careening into us, though."

"Then what?"

"From what Dad said, it goes way back to before cities had running water. People in upper stories would toss their water and garbage out into the street and if they didn't get it out far enough, the gentleman took the brunt of it."

She laughed. "That doesn't seem fair."

"It was chivalrous. Think about the ladies in their beautiful dresses. Men wore dull suits and a top coat on. They also wore hats. More protection. So they walked on the outside, offering pretty girls all the protection they needed."

"But why do men still do it?"

"Are you telling me your dad didn't move you to the inside when you walked together?"

Polly nodded. "All the time. I never thought anything of it."

"But it's odd for you when I do it."

"No, it's sweet. I guess I finally just asked why."

"We still do it to give our girls some protection. If we were walking along a street and a car went through a puddle and splashed us, I'd take the worst of it. I'd always sacrifice myself for you that way." He stopped and tugged on her hand to turn her toward him, then kissed her.

"You're so good to me," she said. "All of that chivalry and you still let me be independent."

"And I buy you ice cream." Henry opened the door to the store and let her enter first.

Polly nodded a hello to the young man behind the counter, walked to the freezer and peered in. "I don't know what I want," she said. Then she slid the top panel open and took out a toffee and chocolate covered ice cream bar. "This. Something different."

"Good for you," Henry said with a smile. "You're branching out." He took out another item and they went to the cash register.

"That's new," the young man said to Henry.

"He knows my buying habits," Henry said to Polly with a

laugh. "We're trying new flavors tonight. It's always good to be adventurous."

They paid for the ice cream, left the store, and stood in front of a trash can to unwrap their treats.

"I almost don't want to go home," Polly said. "When I get there, I'll have to think about all of the things that are going on in my life right now."

"We can keep walking," he replied.

"Not long enough," she said. "I want to sleep under the stars and dream about worlds where there is no murder and where children stay sweet and kind and never grow up."

They crossed the highway to Sycamore House and Henry led her to the garden. Street lamps glowed and bugs fluttered in their light. "Maybe just a few more minutes out here, then," he said.

Polly swatted a mosquito away. "Nah. We can go in. But thanks for letting me dream a moment." She stopped suddenly and put her arms around him. "How did I get so lucky?" she asked.

He held his ice cream treat away from her face and kissed her, chocolate and ice cream mingling on their lips. "I'm the one who married the greatest girl in three states." He backed up and swept his arm toward the building. "Look at what you've done here. And I get to be a part of all of it."

"You have to be a part of all of it," she said with a chuckle. "Sometimes I feel badly for dragging you into my crazy life. But you're so good for me."

"I *get* to be a part of it." He kissed her lips again. "Don't ever think that I didn't know what I was getting into when I asked you to marry me. I chose to be part of all of this because it is exciting and part of you. You're exciting. You're crazy and wonderful and generous and loving and a little weird and you will never let me be bored. I'm the lucky one."

Aaron's SUV pulled up to the front door of the building.

"Our little love-fest is over," Polly said.

"It's just postponed," he replied and gave her bottom a squeeze. "They can't stay here all night and we don't have a kid in the house."

She chuckled and felt her face flush red. "Don't you dare say anything like that in front of Aaron. You embarrass me!"

He took her hand and they walked toward the front door. "You always surprise me with your innocence. Lydia says much worse things to Aaron when they're with us."

"And that embarrasses me too," Polly said. "So be good."

As they got close to the front door, another car drove up and she turned to see who it was.

Jeff jumped out and said, "I'm right on time. I was afraid you'd be finished with everything and I'd have made the trip for nothing."

"It's twenty minutes from your place to Sycamore House. Not much of a trip," Polly said.

"Well..." He scowled at her. "Whatever. I knew I could put my hands on information faster than you and if Aaron had questions about other employees I should be available."

"I appreciate it," Aaron said.

"The date wasn't worth sticking around for?" Polly asked.

Jeff shook his head back and rolled his eyes. "It was the worst. What a damned diva. I was so glad when you called and interrupted me. It gave me a good reason to say good night and run for my life." He took her arm as they walked to the front door. "The best part? I didn't even give him a chance to ask if we could reschedule. I just threw money on the table and left. It was dramatic and fabulous!"

"You're a nut," Polly said as they walked through the doors that Henry and Aaron held open.

"Polly, I'd like you to go up to Miss Specht's room with me and then I'd like to use your conference room if that's okay," Aaron said.

"Of course," she replied. "You think that being alone with a young woman in her bedroom is a bad idea?"

He let loose a laugh. "The worst. I've stayed out of trouble for all these years, I'm smart enough to continue that trend." Aaron gestured for her to lead the way and they went into the addition and up the elevator to the second floor.

Polly knocked on Camille Specht's door. "Camille? It's me, Polly."

The young woman opened the door. Dressed in shorts and a t-shirt, she held an open book in her hands. The light was on over a wing chair and there was a glass of ice water on the table beside it.

"Yes?" she asked and then she saw the sheriff. "Is there a problem?"

"I'm sorry to interrupt your evening," Aaron said. "But I need to speak with you about one of your employees. Would you please come downstairs?"

"Right now? What's happened?" She shook her head. "Just a moment. I need to put shoes on and..." She glanced down at what she was wearing. "I'm not dressed for this."

"It's okay," Polly assured her. "You're just going down to the conference room. You're fine."

"Shoes. I need shoes. Let me put this down." She tossed the book into the chair where she'd been sitting and then pulled out a suitcase and dug around, coming up with a pair of flip flops. Camille unconsciously brushed her hand across her hair, patting it down and into place. "I'm so sorry. I wasn't expecting to see anyone tonight. I'm a mess. We spent all day working and..."

"It's really okay," Polly said. "You look fine."

The young woman finally nodded and followed them back downstairs. When she saw Jeff in his office, she gave a big sigh of relief. He jumped out of his chair and came out into the main office to greet her, handing Aaron a file folder.

"That's what we have on her," he said.

"On who?" Camille asked.

Aaron pushed the door open to the conference room and gestured for her to go in. "Julie Smith was killed this evening."

Camille looked at Jeff. She hugged herself and took a deep breath. "Our Julie Smith? She just started this week. We all just started. I barely knew her."

Jeff nodded. "Our Julie Smith."

Before he could say anything more, Aaron said, "Please. In here. I have several questions to ask about her and the others."

"The others?" Camille asked. "Do you think one of them did it?"

"We don't have any idea yet," Aaron replied. "We're just beginning to ask questions."

"And you're starting with me?" Her eyes flashed with fear. "Do you think I killed her? I barely knew the poor girl."

"Please, let's go in and sit down. Would you like a glass of water?"

"No," Camille replied. She rocked back and forth. "But could Jeff be in here with me? I don't know what to think."

Aaron said, "Sure. Whatever makes you comfortable."

Jeff and Camille went into the conference room and Aaron turned to Polly and Henry. "You two might as well go on upstairs. We'll be here for a while, but I think Jeff can get everything I need."

"Okay," Polly said. "Let me know if you need anything else."

"I'll be fine. Talk to you tomorrow, though, okay?"

He went into the conference room, pushing the door shut behind him.

"Phew," Henry said, puffing air out through pursed lips. "She was nervous."

"Poor thing. Her first week in town, she has a new job, she's lived in two separate places and tonight the sheriff shows up to talk to her about a murder." Polly took his hand. "I'm just glad it isn't me."

He chuckled. "I'm glad it's not you, too. You've had enough to deal with this last year. I don't think my heart could take another one right now."

"Wimp." She tugged his hand. "Wanna come upstairs and play with your wife?"

"Race you." He let go and ran for the stairway. Polly caught up to him and they ran up the steps side by side.

CHAPTER NINE

"Really. If you will wait one moment, I'll check to see if Ms. Giller is available."

Polly looked up to see Stephanie standing in her doorway.

"What's up?" Polly asked.

"There's a Leslie Sutworth here. She wonders if you have time."

Polly nodded. If someone was this desperate to see her, she'd make time.

The haggard woman who came into Polly's office looked as if she hadn't slept in days with hair pulled back into a ponytail, no makeup and bloodshot eyes. Her fingers rubbed back and forth - the skin on the side of her index fingers red and raw.

"Have a seat, Mrs. Sutworth," Polly said. She gestured to the chair in front of her desk and asked, "Would you like something to drink? Coffee? Water?"

"No thank you," the woman said, taking a seat.

Polly sat across from her. "I'm sorry about what happened with your son, Mrs. Sutworth. Is there anything I can do?"

"Call me Leslie, please," the woman said. She gave a hint of a smile and then looked down at her hands again.

Polly waited.

"I'm not sure what to ask," Mrs. Sutworth started. "This is all so difficult. Denis was in a good place. When he's on his meds, he's tolerable, but then things get out of balance and he gets so..." she stopped. "I don't even know what's wrong with him. He's always been a little different, but it doesn't take anything for him to snap these days. You know?"

Polly nodded. She had no idea what to say.

"They're going to send him home and I'm at a loss." Tears formed in her eyes and she reached up to brush them away.

"How can I help you?" Polly asked.

"On top of everything else, he broke the ankle and femur on his right leg. They're talking about putting him in a rehab facility, but Ms. Giller, if they do that, it will just send him into a spiral."

"That makes sense. Many facilities around here aren't set up for someone his age. But if he needs physical rehabilitation, they'll be able to help him."

"I know. But I don't want him in a place like that and I can't take care of him at home." Now that the woman had started, she pressed forward. "A friend recommended that I talk to Evelyn Morrow and when I did, she mentioned Sycamore House. She said she had been on-site here with someone else and if you had room, it would be a good place. She talked about the horses and other animals and you have kids here and people who are nice. I'd come over when I wasn't working to spend time with him, but..." She looked back at Polly, desperation on her face.

It had never occurred to Polly that her addition could be turned into a convalescent home, but it made an odd kind of sense. "You're hiring Evelyn Morrow to care for him?"

"If I can find him a good place to stay. And I like Sycamore House. There aren't any steps for him to deal with. Since insurance will pay for his rehabilitation, I just need to talk to his doctor and the insurance company about putting him here instead of a cold facility."

This was coming at Polly really fast. She'd never considered this possibility, though she'd wanted Sycamore House to be a haven for people who needed to get away from the rush of the real world. Her mind reeled, trying to think about all of the possibilities and the problems this might bring.

"I have some concerns," Polly said. "I can't put my staff or guests in harm's way."

Leslie Sutworth took a deep breath. "I understand, but he'll be under Mrs. Morrow's care and she'll make sure he takes his medications on time. He's fine when he's regular. She and I will take care of all of his medical appointments and she will also help take him to his therapist's appointments."

"I'd like to help you," Polly said. "Let me talk to my assistant. He schedules the rooms and would know all of the legal ins and outs of taking this on."

Before she could continue, Mrs. Sutworth interrupted. "I'm not asking you to take anything on. I just need a safe place for him to regain his strength."

Polly nodded. "I understand that, but Sycamore House isn't your normal, everyday hotel. We're a family and if Denis moves in, we'll be part of his life and he'll be part of our family."

"I don't know where else to turn," the woman said, leaning forward to put her arms on Polly's desk. "I thought I'd lost him and I just can't face the idea of losing him now just because I had to drop him off in an institution. I can't take care of him at home. You're my last hope."

That nearly did Polly in, but she knew it wasn't fair to accept this responsibility without talking to Jeff first.

"When are they releasing Denis?"

"This weekend as long as we can find a place for him."

Polly took a breath and blew it out through pursed lips. "That's really fast."

"I've called everybody. And I've been at the hospital with him and trying to take care of my other two kids and my work has been patient with me, but I have to go back in a few days, and..." She stopped and looked at Polly again.

"Let me talk to Jeff and we'll make a decision. I'll call you before five o'clock today. That's all I can promise," Polly said.

"My ex-husband sent money," Leslie said, pulling out her checkbook. "I'll write a check so you don't have to wait for the insurance to kick in."

Polly put her hand up. "No, it's not about the money. That's the least of my worries. Let me talk to Jeff and I promise to call you. We won't make you wait for a decision."

The woman sat back, defeated. "I'll wait. I'm sorry to be so insistent. I never beg for things, but I'm at the end of my rope and when Mrs. Morrow mentioned Sycamore House, for the first time I saw hope."

"I understand," Polly said and stood up, hoping Mrs. Sutworth would follow suit.

She took the hint, gathered her things, and stood up. "Please call as soon as you know anything."

"I will." Polly opened the office door and stood in it while the woman walked out. Mrs. Sutworth gave her one more desperate look before turning the corner.

Polly put her hand over her forehead and took in a slow breath, then stuck her head in Jeff's office. "Got a minute?"

He grinned at her. "For you doll-face, I have all the time in the world."

"You're a nut." She went in, shut the door, and sat down. "That was an interesting visit," she said.

"Stephanie said it was a Leslie Sutworth. Any relation to the kid who caused the accident out front?"

"His mother. She wants to bring him here instead of a rehab facility. They'll need two rooms since Evelyn Morrow will be in charge of his care."

He sat forward. "She what? We aren't set up for that."

"I know. But it's not about all of the physical rehab. She says she doesn't have a good place for him at her home. And I guess that makes sense. We don't have any stairs, Evelyn knows the building. The bathroom is handicap accessible, there's plenty of space in the room for him to move, even in a wheel chair."

"I never expected anything like this," Jeff said, putting his head in his hands. "It's a lot of responsibility."

"Exactly. That's what I told her, but she sounds desperate."

He scratched the top of his head. "When do we have to make the decision?"

"That's the deal. They're sending Denis home this weekend. I need to tell her today so they can set the room up. He'll be in a wheel chair and need a hospital bed. I don't even know what else."

Jeff thought for a minute. "Let me call our insurance guy. You check with Evelyn Morrow and make sure she is on board with this. Without her, I don't want to deal with it. Make sense?"

"It does."

"What about you? What's your gut saying?"

"I want to help her, of course, but when that kid was suicidal, he tried to take someone with him. I don't want him messing with our people."

"Yeah. That."

"On the other hand," Polly said. "This is what Sycamore House is all about. It's why I have this building and we certainly aren't using that addition for what I'd planned. It sits empty too often. Maybe this is what we're supposed to be doing with it."

Jeff glanced at his computer and jumped up. "I have to go," he said. "I'm meeting Sheriff Merritt at the coffee shop."

"Oh," Polly said. "How did that go last night?"

"Camille is pretty upset. We Aaron the information he needed. I met him at the inn this morning to see Grey. He said he didn't know anything about it, but that he'd left his walking stick at the coffee shop earlier in the day."

Polly furrowed her brow. "Yeah. That's right. I was there with him. He put it in the umbrella stand."

"And you didn't see him take it out?"

"I don't think so. We went our separate ways after coffee."

"Okay. I'll tell Aaron what you remember." He opened the door and she followed him into the main office.

"When will you be back so we can finish this?" she asked.

"I don't know. But call me if I'm not here after lunch. I'll check on the insurance, though."

"Thanks, Jeff."

She went back into her office and dropped into her seat. She needed to call Evelyn, but thought she'd make one other call first.

"Hey sweet girl, what's up?" Henry asked.

"Am I bothering you?"

"Never."

"No really. I need a few minutes and some advice. Do you have time?"

He chuckled. "I sure do."

"Why are you laughing?"

"Because I'm at the office having coffee with Dad."

"I see."

"Is this important? Should I leave the room?"

"Well..."

"Hold on."

Polly waited a few moments.

"Okay. I'm outside," he said. "What's going on?"

She described the situation to him. He didn't interrupt, just listened.

"Well?" she finally asked after telling him everything. "What should I do?"

Background noise and the sound of his breathing told her he was still on the phone, but he was silent.

"Are you still there?"

"Yeah. Sorry. This is a tough one."

"If it were easy, I wouldn't have called for advice."

"Great. Thanks," he said. "My first reaction is to say no, but that's not who you are. I'm always trying to protect you from things that are difficult."

"Okay. Do you have another reaction?"

"I keep thinking about Rebecca. If you'd listened to me, she wouldn't be in our lives, so I don't know if I'm the best barometer. And you're right about Sycamore House being empty. It's a shame not to use those rooms. Maybe this is your next step. Especially if it's Mrs. Morrow. No one else had to get involved with Sarah Heater's care once she was on-site. She's a take-charge woman."

"Do you think we should do it?"

He huffed out a breath. "I don't know. I don't want to be the one to say no to you. If Mrs. Morrow says she can do it and Jeff says your insurance will cover whatever it needs to cover, there's no reason not to say yes."

"I have your support, then."

"Honey, you always have my support."

Polly smiled and then realized he couldn't see her face. "Thank you," she said. "I love you, too. I'll make more calls and let you know what we come up with."

Before she could call Evelyn Morrow, Stephanie tapped at her door again. "Polly?"

"Yeah?"

"Mrs. Morrow is here to see you."

"Seriously?"

Stephanie smiled. "Can I send her in?"

Polly stood up and walked to the door. "Evelyn, I can't believe you're here. I was just going to call you."

The woman stepped in to give Polly a hug. "I've missed seeing you this summer."

"Me too," Polly said, nodding and backing into her office. "Come on in."

They sat down and Evelyn started. "If you were going to call me, I guess you know why I'm here."

"Denis Sutworth."

"Yes. But before you say anything, I want you to know that I'm not here to press you into accepting him into your home." Evelyn gave her a warm smile. "Because I know that's what it is."

"I have some trepidation," Polly said. "There are so many things that could go wrong."

Evelyn Morrow nodded. "I understand that. I really do. I'd hoped to get here before his mother, but I'm guessing she's already been to see you."

"She was barely willing to leave and let me think about it. I know she's desperate, but this is a lot of responsibility. If she hadn't mentioned your name, I don't know that I'd be considering it at all."

"I'm not here to talk you into this, believe me," Evelyn said. "But I will answer any questions you have."

"Okay then. How can you care for someone with such traumatic injuries? He can't walk. I looked it up. Ankle recovery is six to eight weeks. A femur could take eight to ten months. He's going to need a great deal of physical therapy."

"There is a physical therapist who lives here in Bellingwood. She will come to Sycamore House on a regular basis."

"And you're going to do all of his physical care?" Polly asked.

"For a while. Just like I did with Sarah, I have a team of others that will help. I'll move in next door, though."

"And his emotional and mental stability. With all of the painkillers and other drugs, I don't even want to think about how that is messing with his brain chemistry. And why is he so suicidal? Is it a chemical imbalance or are there other issues?"

Evelyn smiled a sad smile. "Even with chemical imbalances, there are often other issues. Denis has always been frail emotionally. His father was a hard man. Most wouldn't call him abusive, but he was demanding and intolerant of less than perfect behavior. When the man left them, Denis believed it was his fault - that he'd failed his mother. She had to go to work full-time and no longer had time to care for his emotional needs. She blamed herself for his trouble, he blamed himself. The spiral started and neither managed to overcome it. She would rather he live at home so she can keep an eye on him twenty-four hours a day, but thank goodness that isn't practical. He needs to learn to live on his own."

"Are you qualified for all of that?"

"No of course not, but he has a therapist. He needs to be away from his family. I don't think I'm stepping too far out of bounds in telling you that it wouldn't be healthy for him to continue living with his mother. Not for any of them. And especially not for his younger siblings."

Polly knew it wasn't fair, but she had to ask. "Are they as broken as he is?"

Evelyn smiled. "No. They were much younger when their father left and I believe Denis took most of the responsibility on himself. But he's old enough to be out on his own and those two kids need to grow up in a safe and healthy environment. Well, as much as it can be."

"How much will Leslie Sutworth be here?" Polly asked. She knew that she was seeing the woman at her worst. A mother shouldn't have to deal with any of this and it hit her hard all at once. But still, if she showed up on a regular basis, she'd wear Polly out.

"That's one of the things we will have to discuss," Evelyn said. "Once she goes back to work and the kids start back to school, their lives will return to normal. She loves her son very much, but is at a complete loss as to what to do with him. She's been living with so much guilt these last few years it's been nearly impossible for her. And this accident hasn't helped. That poor woman needs a break and I think we're in a position to give it to her."

Polly smiled at the woman sitting across from her. "When do you think you're just going to get rid of your apartment and move in here?"

"Don't tempt me," Evelyn said with a grin. "You take very good care of me here. All of my needs are met and I feel as if I'm spoiled on a daily basis. This is nothing like some of the in-home experiences I've had. I usually end up in a small back room tucked away in a household that isn't prepared for an extra family member. The only thing I can do is focus on the patient. Even if I have a few hours of down-time, I really don't. But here, it's almost a joy care for someone. The grounds are a lovely place for a short walk, I have a great big room with all of the amenities of a hotel. You have a wonderful staff and I love being able to see your animals enjoy their days. If I could convince all of my patients to move into Sycamore House, I'd give up my apartment in a heartbeat. But that's a discussion for another time."

"I certainly wouldn't mind having a qualified nurse around," Polly said. "We could have used you a couple of times this summer."

Evelyn looked at her in surprise. "Was everything okay? You can always call me, you know."

"No, it was fine. Just bumps, bruises and skinned knees." Polly shook her head. "But since I have a real problem with blood, the kids have learned to find someone else if they're bleeding profusely."

Evelyn grinned. "Then it's a good thing you became a librarian instead of a nurse."

"Ha," Polly said. "It was never even a consideration. Dad laughed at me once when I was in high school. He came inside to clean up after cutting himself in the barn. I actually fainted when I saw his arm. He and Mary had to deal with me before she could clean and bandage his wound. I was so embarrassed. He told me that I might want to stay away from anything in the medical field." She put her head down. "I'm not very good at taking care of people either. I want to tell them to buck up and get over themselves."

"You're better at it than you think," Evelyn said, gesturing to take in the building. "Look what you've done here. It's not for you, it's all about taking care of other people."

"This was easy," Polly said. "What you do isn't so easy."

"It's what I love," Evelyn replied quietly. "That makes it easy for me."

Polly took a deep breath, held it and then released it. "I will speak to Jeff again. If he thinks that we can do this, I'll call Leslie this afternoon."

Evelyn stood up and put out her hand. "Thank you for your time, Polly. I think we can make a difference for this boy."

CHAPTER TEN

"Enter," Polly said with a grin after Rebecca had startled her with a rap on the office door. "How was your night with Jessie and Molly?" she asked.

"It was a blast. I think Jessie trusts me more. She wasn't nervous at all when I held and fed Molly."

Polly smiled. "You are pretty trustworthy. Jessie knows you would do everything you could to keep her daughter safe."

Rebecca dropped into the chair across from Polly. "I want to have a big party here for all the girls we know. No boys allowed."

"Okay," Polly said, slowly nodding. "What are you thinking?"

"I'm not sure." Rebecca stood up and shut the door. She sat back down and lowering her voice, said, "I don't think Jessie or Stephanie have very many friends. They both work all the time and then go home. And I know for a fact that Rachel only ever works and hangs out with Billy up at his apartment. I know they're engaged and all that, but she should have girlfriends, too. I want to hook them all up."

"I see. Is there anybody else that should be part of this?"

"Well, what about those girls who are going to work at the

coffee shop? Do they have friends?" Rebecca was sitting forward on her chair, bouncing as she spoke.

"I'm sure they have college friends."

Rebecca sat back, slumping in her chair. "That's the problem. Jessie and Stephanie didn't go to college and since they're not from here, they don't have any way to meet people."

"And you think you should fix this?" Polly wanted to laugh out loud. In a very short time, she'd managed to train Rebecca well.

"Nobody else will."

"Have you and Kayla been plotting?"

Rebecca shrugged. "Maybe. But it's a good idea. I bet if we asked your friends, they'd know more people who are that age. All these girls think they have to have boyfriends, but they should have girlfriends and let boys in only if they're good enough to handle them."

"You're such a smart girl," Polly said with a laugh. "I'd like to record this right now and play it back for you in a few years..."

"I'll always feel this way. Boys are just fine, but it's important to have great girlfriends. Look at you. You have a ton of them."

"Yes I do. And I wouldn't trade any of them away, but I can't imagine living without Henry in my life."

Rebecca shook her head. "I lost track of what I'm saying. Jessie thinks she needs a husband to help her. It's like she thinks she is only half a person because she's not married and then she said that Molly needs a dad. That's crazy!"

Polly nodded, "She's had a rough life and the one person who made sense was her dad, even though he wasn't around very often."

"But I didn't have a dad. Mom and I did just fine without a man."

"Yes you did," Polly said. She smiled. "You two were great together. But Jessie isn't the same person that your mom was."

"That's why she needs more girlfriends." Rebecca stopped, as if she were re-thinking her statement. "I guess Mom didn't have any girlfriends either. We were always moving around too much. She used to say that someday we'd settle down and she'd have time for a best friend again. I wish she'd been able to do that. She was a great friend."

"You know she had friends here, don't you? She told Evelyn she was a friend. And I considered your mom a friend."

"But a best friend is different. You know what I mean."

"I do know what you mean. You do silly, crazy things with a best friend and never worry that they're going to laugh at you."

"Yeah. That. So are we going to hook these girls up with friends or what?" Rebecca sat forward again and thumped her fist on Polly's desk.

"Why don't we do a cookout in the back yard with them instead of a big party?"

"But I want it to be just girls."

Polly chuckled. "You'd be mad if the boys wanted to have a game night and didn't invite you because it was 'just boys.'"

"Not if they wanted to bond and be brothers."

"Bros?" Polly asked.

Rebecca gave her a look. "That doesn't work for you."

"Okay, ummm, wow. I'm not that old." Polly pursed her lips into a scowl. "You stuck a knife right into my heart."

"You're tough. You can take it," Rebecca said, trying not to giggle.

"Let's think about how we can do this. I'd guess that you don't want to be obvious about trying to set these girls up to like each other, right?"

"Yeah, but I think they need help. I mean, Rachel and Stephanie are here in the same building all day, but they do their own thing and then split. They need some encouragement." Her eyes lit up. "What if we went shopping for a day? We could do that! Maybe we could rent a van and go over to the Amanas. Wouldn't it be fun if everybody went with us? All of your friends and these girls. We could spend the night and get up early and eat breakfast and shop all day long."

Polly watched her daughter spin up with excitement. It was strange to think of Rebecca that way, but Polly was trying to get used to it. She had a daughter. "The Amanas would be a great trip, but I think we should save that for later this year when they decorate it for Christmas. It's really pretty then."

"We don't have to do it just once," Rebecca said, pushing her lips out in a pout.

"Maybe you and I should do it by ourselves sometime before we invite the whole world. Where did you come up with this?"

"I heard Rachel and Sylvie talking about it. Sylvie said the restaurants are great. They have the best pancakes. And Rachel said she liked the stores." It was as if Rebecca finally heard what Polly said. She looked up. "Just you and me? All day by ourselves without Henry?"

"Sure. Why not?"

"You never go anywhere without him."

"I go lots of places without Henry. I like traveling with him, but I think it would be fun to go with you and show you around. I haven't been there in years."

"When can we go? Can we go this weekend before school starts?"

"No, not right away. I want to get the coffee shop open before I leave on a weekend. And besides, aren't you shopping with Stephanie and Kayla on Saturday?"

"That's right," Rebecca said. "I forgot about that." She smiled. "There are so many things to do. When can we go, then?"

"Maybe for my birthday."

"Really?" Rebecca's eyes lit up with excitement. "That would be fun. Just you and me? Will we go overnight?"

"We'll see. Maybe. We could go over to Iowa City. I think you'd like to see the campus there."

"That would be fun!" Rebecca picked up her overnight bag. "I should go upstairs and unpack. Are Andrew and Kayla up there? What are we doing for lunch? Can I cook?"

The girl could turn on a dime. "Yes, they're either upstairs or down at the barn," Polly said. "You go on and I'll be up after a while. We can figure lunch out then."

"Thanks!" Rebecca opened the door and ran out, her mind occupied with new ideas.

Polly saw Jeff come in the main door of the office and called out, "Hey you. Funny man. Get in here!"

He laughed. "What do you want, old lady?"

"Can we get back into the coffee shop yet?"

"Not until tomorrow. What's up?"

She nodded toward the chair and he dropped into it.

"Evelyn was in this morning after you left," Polly said.

"What did she have to say?"

"She thinks it would work."

"Do you think we should do this?"

"I'm frustrated." Polly said, sitting forward. "Like things are spinning out of control. I'm nervous about letting a completely broken young man live here. Evelyn isn't worried, so I'm inclined to approve it, but things feel out of sorts. There's too much that's undone right now and of course I had to go and find a dead body last night. We have all of these new employees and just when we're that close," she held her thumb and forefinger up with just a little space between them, "to opening the coffee shop, we're blocked again."

He chuckled. "When have things ever been normal? Three months ago a serial killer kidnapped you and three months before that we were all hiding out because some guy was chasing the Sheriff and his sister."

Polly scrunched up her face and growled. "You're right. Maybe I was hoping that things were starting to settle down. I have a daughter now and I have to think about more than just me."

"I know," he said, nodding. "But change is usually difficult and weird. One of these days Grey and Camille being here will be normal. And whatever happens with Denis Sutworth is going to happen. We can't control everything."

She thought back to all of the crazy things that had happened over the last three years and realized that this was no stranger than anything else. She glanced at the window to the hallway as three young women and a young man walked past.

"Who's that?" she asked, nodding to the glass.

"Must be here for Sylvie. She's ready to start hiring. I think she plowed through a huge list yesterday and honed it to four or five second interviews. She's bringing me in for final conversations, but I told her that I trusted her to approve their credentials and skills in the kitchen. The only thing I care about is whether they'll get along with our family and that they aren't criminals."

Stephanie knocked on Polly's door. "I have the information back. It's in the interview files on the shared drive," she said.

Jeff looked over his shoulder at her. "Thanks."

She went back to her desk and he smiled at Polly. "She's amazing, you know. Bright as can be. It takes nothing for me to train her to do something new."

"That's good. Especially if we're bringing more people on staff."

He leaned forward on her desk. "Are you ready to make more changes?"

"What do you mean?"

"If we keep this up, by next year, Stephanie will need an assistant. Rachel and Sylvie will need an office."

"Where will we put everyone?" Polly asked.

"You should talk to your husband. I think that we move some of this across the hall. Leave the lounge, but turn the classroom into a large conference room, the computer room into a couple of small offices, move Stephanie into this conference room and put her assistant / receptionist out front here."

"Ummm, wow?"

He grinned at her. "You hired me to make this place grow. When you told me last year that you were expanding to the coffee shop and bakery, I realized you weren't kidding. I'm ready to rock and roll."

Polly took a deep breath. "I'm still stuck on wow," she said.

"I'm just waiting for you and Henry to decide what's next. Surely you aren't satisfied with stopping now?"

Polly scowled at him. "So much has been going on, we haven't talked about it. What else does Bellingwood need? I was thinking the other day about an art gallery. And maybe open a craft store. Move those knitting classes downtown and put up quilting frames where people can work on big projects."

He laughed. "Those are interesting ideas. Do you really think we're ready to get into that kind of business?"

"I don't know," she said. "It was what I originally thought of for this place, but then you showed up and the world got bigger than I ever imagined."

"Yeah. I'm good at that. You'll come up with something. And don't forget, there are still plenty of empty buildings downtown and dilapidated homes all over the place."

"I'm not flipping houses," Polly said.

Jeff gave a slight shudder. "That sounds awful - a lot of work in a short time. Henry doesn't work like that. But he's building those new apartments on the east side of town and last week at the Chamber meeting, Bel-Co is announced it's expanding."

"People are moving to Bellingwood. I guess that's pretty cool."

"It's great," he said, nodding. "We're getting great press with the winery. People are talking about Sycamore House..."

Polly interrupted him with a laugh. "You mean, the crazy lady who finds dead bodies?"

"If it's going to happen, we might as well capitalize on it," he said.

She was shocked. "You're kidding. You wouldn't!"

"Of course I wouldn't," he said. "That would be wrong. It would be very, very wrong."

"I don't want to walk around town and have strangers staring at me," Polly said. "It's bad enough that the people who live here act a little afraid of me."

"Last I heard, they took down the pool at the Elevator. You kept branching out and they couldn't keep up."

Polly flung a pencil at him. It missed by a mile and caromed off the wall behind him.

Jeff bent over, picked it up and put it back on her desk. "You're bad at that, you know."

"Shaddup and go back to work. I'm going upstairs to check on the kids."

He stood up and hung back while she exited her office. "What are you going to do about the Sutworth's?" he asked.

"Any reason I shouldn't say yes?"

Jeff shook his head.

"Then I'll call Evelyn Morrow. I'd rather she be the one to work with the mother. I don't want to be responsible for that woman," Polly said.

She looked at Stephanie, who was diligently typing away at her computer.

"What do you think of all the insanity, Stephanie?" Polly asked.

The girl looked back and forth between Polly and Jeff, smiled and said, "I have a great job. It's better than anything I could have ever hoped for." She placed her hands back on the keyboard and started typing again.

"She's good," Polly said with a laugh. "I think we should keep her."

~~~

Polly made sure the kids were set for lunch and changed into a fresh blouse. She was only going to the diner, but since she didn't know Camille well, thought she could dress up. She rubbed Leia's head and ran her hand along Luke's back and up his tail. Both cats were sprawled on her bed, ignoring the daily chaos that happened in the place.

"See ya later," she called out. Rebecca had decided they were having sandwiches and fruit for lunch. The girl knew her mind and it was entertaining to watch Andrew and Kayla acquiesce to nearly everything she asked of them. Polly tried to pay attention to make sure she wasn't unreasonable, but for the most part, it she was the only one willing to make a decision and follow through.

Obiwan followed Polly to the front door and wagged when she rubbed his head. It was never easy to leave him, even if the kids were there. How had she lived all those years without a pet?

She waved to Stephanie through the window to the office and walked outside. It was warm and the humidity was high. She should have driven, but the walk wouldn't hurt her. Polly wandered through the corner garden and waited for traffic to pass before she crossed the street. She started to walk down Elm Street, but remembered encountering the three boys and decided to take another route. That was going to have to be fixed. She wasn't going to be frightened to walk in her own community. Now all she needed to do was figure out how to deal with them.

By the time she arrived at the diner, sweat was dripping from her forehead and she was glad to get inside the air conditioned restaurant.

"How are you, honey?" Lucy asked.

"I'm hot," Polly replied with a laugh. "It's enough to make me whine and complain."

Lucy smiled. "Your friend is in that booth over there." She pointed at the wall where Camille was waiting. "You go ahead and I'll bring you an ice cold Dew and extra napkins. How about something cool to wipe your face?"

"I'll be fine," Polly said. "Thanks though."

She made her way through the crowd to Camille. "I'm sorry if I'm late. I walked."

"I was early," Camille said with a wry smile. "I'm still trying to impress you."

Lucy was right there with Polly's drink. She put a small stack of napkins in front of Polly and handed her a cold, wet cloth. "That's fresh."

"Do I look so bad?" Polly asked. "I'm not that out of shape."

"You're fine, dear. Do you two know what you want to eat yet or do you need a few more minutes?"

Polly looked over at Camille, who nodded. After giving Lucy their lunch orders, she wove her way back to the main counter.

"Do I look that hot?" Polly asked.

Camille leaned across the table. "She's been handing those out since I got here. She offered me one, too."

"Joe's going to love the laundry bill this week," Polly said. "How are you doing?"

"I'm still shaken, but Jeff tells me that it will be okay." Camille looked at Polly and grinned. "He also told me that if I'm going to work for you, I should get used to this."

Polly shook her head. "Don't listen to him. He makes too much out of things. Tell me why you wanted to move back. Jeff said you'd been working at a college?"

"In southern Indiana," Camille said with a nod. "My family is actually from Omaha and I wanted to move closer. I was also ready to leave the university setting. It was a great job, but there's always red tape and regulations. And no matter how far up the food chain you go, there's one more person who has input into what needs to happen. I wanted more control and easier access to decision makers."

"Where else did you look?" Polly asked.

"I applied for a few things in the Omaha area. My mama would have loved that. It broke her heart when I moved to Indiana." Camille smiled across the table at Polly. "I quickly figured out that Omaha wasn't big enough for all of us. I was there for three weeks and felt like running away. Do you think Bellingwood is far enough?"

"I guess we'll see," Polly said, smiling. "You have a big family?"

Camille rolled her eyes. "My daddy has three brothers and two sisters and Mama has five brothers and three sisters. Everyone lives in the Omaha area with all of their kids and a slew of grandbabies. Both of my grandmothers are still alive and they rule the families."

Polly chuckled. "I can't even imagine. It was just my dad and me. Well, his brother was near, but we didn't see much of them."

"Oh girl," Camille said. "You should see it when we get together. We have to rent out the church basement for holiday meals. My family doesn't know the meaning of an intimate gathering. No matter what happens, it's a party."

They waited while Lucy put plates in front of them. "You're looking much better now," Lucy said to Polly. She gestured to the two salads in front of the women. "Are you sure you don't want anything else?"

Polly grinned. "It's too hot for a tenderloin and fries. Maybe next time."

"Wave if you need anything," Lucy said and turned away.

"So is cooking for big family gatherings..." Polly stopped as she looked up and saw Camille's head bowed and her lips moving. "I'm sorry," she whispered.

Camille looked back up. "No, that's fine. Don't apologize. I know I startle people sometimes. Now what were you asking about cooking?"

"Was that why you went into food service?"

"Both Mama and Daddy were the oldest in their families, so it fell on her to organize things when everybody got together. I'm her oldest daughter and since the day I was able to walk and hold onto her apron, I was part of that planning. It was just a natural thing for me. As I grew up, it was my job to assign tasks to my brothers and sisters and the cousins so they'd stay out of trouble until we ate. I learned how to delegate before I was in junior high. Even the toddlers had jobs to do. And when we get together now, it's still my job to keep everyone busy until the meal is served. Mama and I have a good rhythm. We know what the other one needs without anyone saying anything."

"That's so cool," Polly said. "Sometimes I wish I had a big family. And then other times, I'm glad that I don't."

"From what Jeff says, it sounds like you have a pretty big family here in town."

Polly shrugged her shoulders. "I guess I do. I hope you like it here. They're good people"

"So far, so good," Camille replied. "I'm still trying to deal with what happened to Julie. That's more than I know what to do with. But I like Sylvie, and Jeff will be wonderful to work with. Can you tell me what's up with you and your friend Sal? Jeff tried to explain that Sal owned the building and the coffee shop and you own the bakery, but Jeff works for you and he's in charge ..." She left the thought hanging.

"That's essentially it. Sal's from Boston and thought Bellingwood needed a coffee shop. She also wanted to get involved in the community. Once she brought up the idea, it all kind of exploded and we invested in it with her and so, ummm, yeah. Maybe there isn't a great explanation," Polly said.

"That makes more sense," Camille said, shaking her head back and forth. "Or not. Oh well. Sal told me that Jeff is the one who will be working with me, so I guess that's enough information."

The two talked until Polly looked up and saw that the reason the restaurant had grown quiet was because it had emptied out. Their table had been cleared and she'd already paid the bill. She checked the time on her phone and saw that it was two fifteen. "I can't believe we talked so long," she said.

Camille did the same thing. "I guess I'm glad the sheriff has closed the coffee shop. I'd be late. Do you want a ride back to Sycamore House?"

"That's okay," Polly said. "I'm going to the library to say hello to my friend, Joss. She's the head librarian and you'll get to know her. She's as addicted to caffeine as anyone I know and can hardly wait for you to open."

They walked out the front door and Polly reached over to hug Camille. "I'm glad you're here."

Camille's hug was strong. With a large family, she was probably used to affection.

"Me too," Camille said. "You're in for a treat this weekend. Mama is coming to visit me for a day." Then she stopped. "I hope you don't mind that she stays with me at Sycamore House."

Polly grinned and took Camille's hand. "I'll speak to Jeff. While she's here, she might as well stay in the room next to yours. There's no reason you two have to share. I can't wait to meet your mother."

They separated and Polly headed for the library with a lilt in her step. There was nothing more fun than getting to know someone new.

CHAPTER ELEVEN

The next morning, Polly stood at the kitchen sink. Henry had already gone to work and Rebecca was just starting to rouse. Kayla would be there soon and Polly had promised the three kids a ride in her new truck. She looked out the window to see her four Percherons walk past, each with a rider. She recognized Jason and Eliseo and waved they didn't see her. They turned the corner and headed east, toward Sycamore Inn and the winery.

"Polly?" Rebecca said quietly.

Polly jumped and squealed, startling both cats.

"I'm sorry!" Rebecca said.

"No, I was focused on the horses," Polly said, pointing out the window. "I didn't hear you come in."

Rebecca had all of her sheets in a bundle.

"What's up?" Polly asked.

"It started last night," Rebecca said, her head bent down. "Now I'm in hell."

Polly started laughing as soon as she realized what Rebecca was talking about. "Hell? That's one way of putting it. Are you okay?"

"I'm fine. It just surprised me. I didn't think it was ever going to come and now I don't know if I want it to be here. I can't go swimming or do anything anymore, can I."

"You know better than that," Polly said. They'd already talked about this and Rebecca's bathroom was stocked with what she needed. "But you have what you need?"

Rebecca rolled her eyes. "Yes, but promise you won't tell Henry?"

"I don't keep secrets from him, but we certainly won't talk about it in front of you. Shall we treat and wash your sheets?"

Dragging the sheets behind her, Rebecca slumped her way to the bathroom near the media room where they'd installed a washer and dryer. "I don't feel very good. Do I have to go anywhere today?" she asked.

That one threw Polly. She wanted to be as sympathetic as possible, but on the other hand, she didn't want Rebecca turning into a lump every month. "I tell you what. We'll start the sheets, then I want you to take a long shower and put on your favorite shorts and shirt. Make sure you're comfortable. You don't get to sit around and feel sorry for yourself today. You never know, tomorrow might get worse or the day after that might be a bad day and if you give up now, you'll never make it through this."

Polly handed Rebecca the stain remover and let her deal with her sheets, walking out into Henry's office. She'd give her space to cope, but since this was part of every girl's life, Rebecca had to learn to manage it just like everyone else.

She heard the washer start its cycle and waited for Rebecca to come out. When she didn't, Polly went to the doorway and pushed it open. "Are you okay in here?"

At the sound of quiet sobbing, she pushed the door open and found Rebecca on the floor, her head in her hands and her knees pulled up to her chest.

"Honey, what's wrong?"

"I miss Mom," Rebecca said.

Polly slid down to sit beside her and stroked Rebecca's hair. "I'll bet you do. I'm so sorry. And I get it. Mary had to help me through my first time and we weren't prepared at all. She'd completely forgotten that it was going to happen to me. And I was in school when it did. I had to go see the nurse and I was crying so hard they called Mary to come get me."

"Was it embarrassing being at school when it happened?" Rebecca asked.

"It wasn't too bad. I was in the bathroom when I discovered it, then I ran to the nurse's office. I was scared because nobody had ever talked to me."

Rebecca giggled. "It would have been bad if your Dad had to have that conversation."

"No kidding," Polly said. "Luckily, you have a million women around you and none of us are embarrassed about it."

"Kayla started before school was out."

"She did! Have you two talked about this?"

"A little. Am I going to get bigger boobs now?"

Polly started to laugh. "I think your boobs have already started developing. And I'm sorry to say, but your mom didn't have much, so you might not get much more than what you have."

Rebecca looked down at herself. "I thought that maybe my period would give me more. I'm pretty flat."

"You're fine. Whatever you have is perfect for you," Polly said.

"Kayla's boobs are bigger than mine."

"Yes they are, but she's a different girl than you. None of us are identical."

"That's for sure," Rebecca said. "I'm sorry I cried."

"This is one of those times you miss your mom. You're allowed to cry about that whenever you want."

"Mom and I talked about this, too. She kinda scared me, Polly."

Polly scrunched up her eyebrows. "What do you mean?"

"She told me about a time when she was wearing white jeans and she..." Rebecca's voice dropped to a whisper. "Leaked. She was really embarrassed."

"I think all of us have one embarrassing time in our lives. At least one. But look at me and think about your mom. We lived through it. Right?"

"I don't want to do that."

"You need to not worry. We'll do our best to pay attention. Is that why you want to stay home? You're worried?"

Rebecca nodded and dropped her head down again.

"Oh sweetie, I get that. Now, we can stay home today and then what are you going to do about tomorrow?"

Rebecca lifted her shoulders and dropped them.

"And the day after that?"

"I dunno," Rebecca said quietly.

"And what about next month? Are you planning to stay home from school for an entire week?"

Rebecca looked up at her, the question in her eyes.

Polly chuckled. "No. You don't get to stay home because of this. Did Kayla stay home?"

"No," Rebecca said.

"You can't be afraid of this. You can handle it. When we go out today, I'll be sure that we stop at places with bathrooms. This will all be okay. I promise."

"Can I take extra clothes, too?"

"Of course," Polly said with a laugh. "We'll put the bag in the bed of the truck. No one else needs to know it's there."

"Okay." Rebecca stood up and offered a hand to Polly. "I'd better take a shower. Kayla will be here any minute. I'm sorry about being whiny."

Polly walked into the other room with her. "There will always be scary stuff. Just promise me that you won't let them stop you from doing the things you love. Talk to me and we'll find our way through it, okay?"

"Okay." Rebecca turned around. "It's not hell?"

"I didn't say that," Polly said, laughing. "But you'll get used to it."

~~~

"Where's Andrew today?" Polly asked when she walked into the kitchen. "I was going to take the kids out in my new truck."

Sylvie looked up from her laptop. She tapped the screen and turned it so Rachel could read it. "That's what we're looking for. Would you check to make sure we have everything we need?"

Rachel nodded and then grinned at Polly. "She found recipes from the Amanas. We're actually going to make a Boston Cream Pie."

Polly looked sideways at Sylvie.

"It's a cream cake with a ganache," Sylvie said. "This shouldn't be too difficult and if it's as wonderful as I think, it will be a huge hit in town."

"That's my favorite cake in the world," Polly said. "The kids and I will come back and be taste testers."

"Andrew won't be here," Sylvie said. "He's home with Padme."

"Is he sick?" Polly asked.

Sylvie stood up and reached under the counter and came back up with two large bowls. "Nope. Not sick. Just being an adolescent. We're nipping this in the bud today."

Polly chuckled. "Whoops. What did he do?"

"Little boy of mine decided that he was smarter than his mother last night and thought he could get away with telling me what's what. When Jason tried to warn him off, Andrew actually pushed him." Sylvie looked up, laughter in her eyes. "Can you believe it? He pushed Jason. What was that kid thinking?"

"This doesn't sound like Andrew."

Sylvie shrugged. "It's been building. I swear. Sometimes the week or two before school starts is the worst. My boys see it coming and they don't know how to handle themselves."

"What did Jason do?" Rachel asked.

"He was confused," Sylvie said. "They've always wrestled, but Jason usually initiates it. When he started getting stronger, sat talked about being careful. He works at it. I was proud when he backed up and looked at me, as if to ask what he could get away with."

"I'd have let Jason pound on him," Polly remarked.

"That's what Andrew wanted. He was spoiling for a fight. I told Andrew that he needed to apologize to me for being disrespectful and to Jason for getting physical. He informed us that he had no intention of doing either thing. He was right and Jason shouldn't have gotten between us."

"What in the world?" Polly asked. "That doesn't sound like Andrew. At all. He's so easy going. This just isn't normal."

"Trust me," Sylvie said. "I gave up on normal a long time ago. He stormed off to his room last and refused to talk to us. This morning when Jason and I were getting ready to leave, he informed me that he was staying home. I informed *him* that was just fine."

Polly shook her head. "Sylvie, something must have happened."

"You're right. But until he's ready to talk, I can't do anything and I won't put up with bad behavior. He needs to learn that right now. The rest of it will come out when it does and then he can swim back out of the muck he's creating." She looked at the prep table and the ingredients Rachel had assembled. "Do we have everything?"

"It's all there," Rachel said.

"I need to get busy, Polly. I'm sorry if Andrew screwed up your day."

"No, it was no big deal. I'll take the girls. We'll do the day without him. Have fun with whatever you're doing here." Polly went out the back door and up the steps to her apartment. She couldn't imagine what would have set Andrew off enough to bring out this behavior. She hadn't seen much of him the last couple of days, so didn't know if he'd been acting out while he was here. She wasn't bringing it up with Kayla and Rebecca. They didn't need to be part of this. He'd figure it out and the world would move forward anyway.

When Polly got upstairs, she was surprised not to see any of the animals come running. No one was in the media room, so she called out, "Rebecca? Kayla?"

"In here," Rebecca called back from her bedroom. The bedroom door opened as Polly walked into the living room, releasing Obiwan and the two cats.

"What are you girls doing in there?" Polly asked. "Giving the animals a makeover?"

Kayla laughed. "Well, kinda. We shut the door because we didn't want Andrew barging in. Then the cats pawed at the door and whined and when we let them in, Obiwan came with them."

"I see. Well, Andrew isn't feeling well today. He's not coming over, so you're safe."

Polly caught a quick glimpse of shame cross Rebecca's face before she jumped down from her bed.

"Where are we going, Polly?" Rebecca asked, smoothing the comforter where she'd been sitting.

"I thought we might go down to the bookstore in Boone, but since Andrew isn't here, I hate to leave him out of a trip like that. Since you two girls are shopping with Stephanie on Saturday, it doesn't make sense to do that. What do you think?"

"Maybe we should just get lunch and go to the coffee shop. Kayla and I could put the books back on the shelves and help clean up," Rebecca said. "We can do fun things another day."

"Is that what you want to do, Kayla?" Polly asked.

The girl looked at Rebecca and then Polly and then back to Rebecca. "Did you and Andrew have a fight?" she asked Rebecca.

"I don't know," Rebecca said under her breath.

"Why would he be mad at you?" Polly asked her.

"It's nothing. Just nothing." Rebecca pushed past Kayla and out into the living room. "Shouldn't we walk Obiwan before we go anywhere? Let's take him outside, Kayla." She patted her leg. "Come on, Obiwan. Let's go for a walk."

Kayla ran to catch up and Polly followed them to the top of the steps. Rebecca looked back at her with more guilt as she went down the steps. Polly followed the girls outside.

"What are you doing?" Rebecca asked as she opened the door to the back yard. "We can take him out by ourselves."

"I know you can, but I want more information about what happened with Andrew that he might be mad at you."

"I didn't do anything," Rebecca muttered as she followed the dog.

Kayla ran on ahead, trying to get Obiwan to chase her. He gladly obeyed and Polly caught up to Rebecca and put her hand out to catch the girl's shoulder.

"What's up, Rebecca? Andrew turned into a bear last night and is sulking at home today. Did he do or say something to you?"

Rebecca shrugged her off. "It wasn't any big deal."

Polly reached out again and stopped Rebecca, then stepped in front of her. "It might not be a big deal, but you're not telling me what's going on and Andrew isn't happy. Tell me. Now."

"He asked me to be his girlfriend this year," Rebecca said, her eyes dropping.

"And you said?"

"I said no. I didn't want a boyfriend."

"Did you two talk about why you didn't want a boyfriend?"

"No, he just left. Kayla was there and I think he was embarrassed. We were just talking and he blurted it out. It wasn't romantic or sweet or anything. He didn't even ask. He just told me we should be boyfriend and girlfriend because we're always together and everybody thinks we are anyway."

"What brought all of this on?"

The dances at school. You know we're in junior high, don't you?" Rebecca asked, as if Polly was a complete dolt.

"Yes, Rebecca. Yes I do." Polly said. She sat down on the arm of one of the Adirondacks. "Were you three talking about the dances?"

"There's one that first Friday."

"I know. The schedule was sent out a couple of weeks ago."

"Andrew thinks we should be dating so we have someone to dance with."

"What did he think Kayla would do?"

"That's what I said," Rebecca responded. "And he got all hot and bothered. And then he quit talking to us."

"Do you think you hurt his feelings?"

"What about mine? The only reason he wants a girlfriend was so he'd have someone to take to the dance. He could have just asked me to the dance."

"He doesn't have any experience with this stuff. How do you expect him to learn if you won't tell him what you want?"

"I don't know what I want," Rebecca said, throwing her arms in the air. "What if there is somebody new at school and I want to go out with him? Or what if some of the other boys are interested in me and want to ask me to dance? Am I supposed to be tied down to Andrew just because we've always been friends?"

"Uh, wow," Polly said. "I think you're getting a little ahead of yourself." She looked for Kayla and found her with Obiwan down by the pasture. Daisy and Nat were at the fence looking for attention. They had a few more minutes.

Rebecca sat down on an Adirondack. "I probably am. But he just assumed I was going to be his girlfriend. He could have asked."

"And you just said no and didn't explain any of this to him?"

"He should just know."

Polly slid down into the seat of the chair and smiled at Rebecca. "That's not fair and you know it. Don't get me wrong. I understand. I blow things out of proportion with Henry all the time. I explode and say stupid things and get mad at him because he doesn't know what's going on up in my head. But even still, it's not fair. I have to apologize and then we talk about it. Henry usually has a good reason for doing things. But if I just get mad and don't talk to him, we never fix anything. Do you want to be friends with Andrew?"

"He's my best friend," Rebecca said.

"And you want it to stay that way?"

"Of course I do. He's been there through everything." Rebecca looked up. "I wouldn't mind being his girlfriend. I just wish he would have asked me when we were alone. Maybe give me a flower or do something nice."

"Here's the deal," Polly said. "You're too young to be girlfriend and boyfriend. I thought that going steady was the thing to do when I was in junior high, but seriously, you're too young. Neither Sylvie nor I want you to make that kind of commitment to each other right now. You need to talk to Andrew. If you want to tell him that I won't let you, that's perfectly fine. But you need to tell him what you expect. If he's going to ask you to the dance, he needs to ask you. Don't be mad at him because he doesn't understand your rules, okay?"

Rebecca drew in a deep breath and then slowly let it out. "How am I supposed to talk to him if he's not here?"

"Let me work on that. I'll talk to Sylvie..."

"No! You can't tell her. That's embarrassing. He doesn't want her to know about this."

"Whether he wants her to know or not isn't the deal right now. He was rotten to her last night and she needs to know why. I'll see if we can't break him out of his house today. He can help you and Kayla at the coffee shop and we'll make a quick run to Boone this afternoon. How does that sound?"

"It sounds good."

"You go get Kayla and I'll talk to Sylvie. And Rebecca?" Polly asked.

"Yeah?"

"I need to tell you something that my Dad and Mary told me when I was about your age."

"What's that?"

"I'm totally serious now," Polly said. "You can always use me and Henry as an excuse. If you think you're being pressured into doing something or going somewhere that you don't want, tell whomever you're with that we won't let you. We'll always back you up. We just want you to be safe and stay out of trouble. Does that make sense?"

"I guess so," Rebecca said.

"It might not seem like a big deal right now," Polly said. But someday you will remember this and be glad that you can use us. Okay?"

"Yeah."

"Go get Kayla and Obiwan. I'll meet you in the truck."

CHAPTER TWELVE

Henry and Polly walked into the Alehouse and saw Joss and Nate already there. Rebecca was spending the night with Kayla since they were heading out early the next morning to go shopping with Stephanie.

The two young girls were very excited to babysit the twins and Stephanie agreed to supervise the entire affair at the Mikkels' house. Joss bribed her with pizza for the girls and the dinner of her choice from Davey's - as well as an iPad with headphones so she could watch a movie and shut out the insanity.

Kayla and Rebecca were responsible, but even they didn't feel comfortable taking on full responsibility of the two very active one year olds.

"Does it feel good to get out and about?" Polly asked with a smile.

"You have no idea," Joss replied. She pulled the chair out beside her and patted the seat. "I have plenty of adult interaction, but it's never enough. It's good to see you guys."

Nate stood up until Polly was seated and she smiled at him. "You and Henry are real throw-backs, you know," she said.

He creased his brow. "What do you mean?"

"You stand up for a woman, you open doors. The other day I had a conversation with Henry about why he always walks on the outside of the sidewalk. All of this chivalry. I don't know what to do with it." She winked at Joss. "Kind of conflicts with the whole strong, independent woman thing."

"Chivalry was never about removing a woman's independence," Nate said. "It was always about treating her with respect. And chivalry is more than just how a man treats a woman. It's a life of honor and courage, being courteous to everyone, helping those in need or who are weak, and standing on the side of justice."

Joss flipped her head toward him. "Wow. Where did you get that? It's deep!"

He chuckled. "Let's just say that I'm more than just a gear head. I might have been a paladin once or twice in the past."

"Oh," she said. "Those nights."

"What nights?" Polly asked, leaning in.

Joss patted her husband's hand. "Those Dungeons and Dragons role-playing game nights and weekends."

"You did that?" Henry asked. "My buddies weren't into it."

"I started playing in junior high. We were *those* kids who spent time in the basement with classical Russian music in the background while we ate ding dongs, drank Mountain Dew and painted pewter figures. We played through high school and then I found friends in college who played, too. By then, though, we changed out the Dew for beer and the ding dongs for cheap pizza and Doritos." He patted his tummy. "I worked hard for this."

"I wonder if Grey played Dungeons and Dragons," Polly mused out loud.

"Who?" Nate asked.

"The man who was in the accident last Monday," she responded. "He's working out at the inn right now. I keep thinking of him like Don Quixote. He speaks differently than we do and he's all about chivalry. But your description of the word fits him to a tee. I could see him as a paladin or knight. And I don't think he's as feckless as Cervantes's character was. He can handle himself."

The waiter interrupted them and Polly jumped to open her menu.

"Anything to drink first?" he asked.

"Ummm. I don't know." She turned to Henry. "What are you having?"

"A Guinness," he said.

"Do I want that?"

He laughed. "I don't think so. You aren't much of a beer drinker."

"I'm not much of an anything drinker," she said and turned to the waiter. "What do I want?"

"What do you like?"

She shook her head. "I have no idea."

"Tomato juice?" he asked.

"Sure."

"Have you ever had a Bloody Mary?"

Polly looked at Henry, who shrugged.

"Try our Bloody Mary," the waiter said. "If you hate it, we'll talk. But I think you'll like it."

"Cool. Thanks."

Joss and Nate already had drinks. Polly grinned across the table. "Look at me, I'm growing up! It's a real adult drink."

Nate laughed. "For someone who has done so many things, there is still a lot of you that hasn't seen the world."

"No kidding," Polly responded. "Now what's good?"

They ordered a platter of appetizers and burgers. Polly ordered the Bourbon burger.

"You're my little alky," Henry said. "I'm so proud. All of this branching out you're doing."

"It was just easier ordering a glass of wine," Polly said. "And people always served that at weddings and in their homes. I didn't have to think about it."

Joss shook her head. "That's so odd. I was so intimidated by the wine selections that I avoided them. It wasn't until Nate and I were married that I started understanding how to choose one to drink. We went on a winery tour in Napa Valley and I did my best to absorb the information."

"You absorbed more than that," Nate said, poking her in the side. "You started really drinking that afternoon."

"I found what I liked," she said with a laugh. "It got fun."

"I poured her into bed that night and didn't see her eyes until the next afternoon." He turned to Henry. "What does your weekend look like?"

"Why?" Henry asked.

"Joss is spending a week with her mother and taking the kids."

"What?" Polly demanded. "You didn't tell me you were leaving town."

"I didn't know until today. Mom called this morning. Dad has a meeting in Chicago all week. She's riding with him. I'll meet them and she'll ride back with me and the kids. We'll do the same thing next Friday going the other way."

"Have you taken the kids on a long trip yet?" Polly asked.

"Not by myself," Joss said with a groan. "But I've loaded the tablet with their favorite movies and it's only a five hour drive. After that, Mom gets to entertain the little buggers."

Polly couldn't stand it. "Shouldn't you be home packing? What are you doing out this evening with us? I'd be going crazy trying to prepare for a week-long trip with no notice."

"I spent today packing," Joss said with a laugh. "It's no big deal."

"Oh yeah," Polly said. "You're that person. You worry about your house being a mess when one thing is out of place."

"I'm not that bad."

"Yes you are." Polly reached out and gave her a hug. "And I love you in spite of yourself. What about the library?"

"Andy's managing everything. It's the week before school, so we're usually slow. I'll be back before the kids start coming in every day after school again."

"So," Henry said, punching Nate's arm. "You're gonna be a bachelor. Does this mean time in the shop?"

"That's exactly what it means. Do you wanna come build cars with me?"

Henry looked at Polly and she shrugged. "I don't care what you do. Have fun. Rebecca and I will keep ourselves busy."

"I was thinking," Henry said to Nate. He bent in close and started drawing on a napkin.

Polly tuned him out and smiled at Joss. "I don't even want to know."

"Nate insists that his kids will have an appreciation for cars. He says that no child of his will grow up not knowing the joy of grease under their fingers. I believe he wants to prepare Soph to take Danica Patrick's place."

Polly wrinkled her forehead and then chuckled. "The race driver?"

"Yep. He thinks it would be great fun if the kids ended up racing each other in the Nascar Sprint Cup in about twenty-five years." Joss looked at her husband. He glanced up at them and nodded approvingly.

"I wish I knew more about cars," Polly said in a whisper. "But I can't say that too loud or Henry will make me help him change the oil. I don't want to get greasy, I just wish I'd paid more attention so I understood things."

"That's why I married pretty boy over there," Joss said with a laugh. "He knows that if he didn't take care of our vehicles, I'd drop them off at a garage. When he makes me mad, I've been known to threaten to make a call and schedule an appointment."

"You're so tough," Polly said. "Like you'd ever do that."

Joss pushed Polly's arm. "Hush. Don't let on."

Polly watched Joss's eyes try to focus on the other end of the room. "What are you looking at?" Polly asked.

"Who is that?" Joss turned Polly to see and pointed over her shoulder. "He looks messed up."

"Crap," Polly said. "Henry? Look."

He looked up from his conversation with Nate. "What?"

"Down there," she tilted her head in the direction she wanted him to look.

"Okay. What do you want me to do about it?"

"Who is it?" Joss asked again.

"It's Grey Greyson. The guy in the accident last week. Jeff hired him to manage the hotel. I can't believe he's in here drunk as a skunk," Polly said.

Henry put his hand on her arm. "Leave it alone, Polly. Who knows what he's got going on."

"How's he supposed to manage the hotel if he's in here drunk?" she asked, shrugging his hand off. "I'm going to talk to him."

"Polly, no," Henry said, putting his hand back. "He's not hurting anybody."

"Look. I'm all for giving a person a hand, but the first week on a job and you're drinking to get drunk? That's not right."

She stood up and started across the room. Polly wasn't surprised to feel Henry at her side, his hand on her back.

"Ask questions before you blow up," he said.

"I'll be good. I promise." She slid onto a stool beside Alistair and said, "Hi there. I didn't expect to see you up here tonight."

He looked at her, recognition slowly coming to him. "Ms. Giller." He put his hand out to shake hers. She ignored it. "And your good husband, Mr. Sturtz. I didn't expect to see you here either." He wobbled on the stool and slurred his words. "The hotel is buttoned up tight. I promise I didn't leave anything undone."

Polly pointed up at the clock on the wall. "It's only seven o'clock. You're confident there won't be any more customers tonight?"

He dropped his head. "I left my phone number on the front door."

"You're really drunk, Grey," Polly said.

"No I'm not. It isn't as bad as it sounds."

"How many have you had? And what are you drinking."

"Just a couple of scotches."

Polly glanced at the bartender. "How many has he had?"

"Five or six, but he doesn't have a car, so I'm not worried."

"Have you had anything to eat, Grey?" she asked.

He shook his head. "I'll eat at home. It's a lonely little home

117

there. Nobody to talk to. Nights are the hardest." He rubbed his temple. "It's when my demons come up out of their graves to torture me."

"Henry, take him to our table and feed him a burger, would you?" She put her hand on Grey's shoulder. "We'll take you home tonight."

"I'm sorry, Ms. Giller. This isn't what I would like you to know about me."

"Go ahead," she said.

Polly waited until the two men had gone several feet and turned to the bartender. "Has he been in often?"

"Every night this week. Last night, Bud took him home. He was pretty wasted."

She pulled a business card out of her telephone case and put it on the bar. "Call me if he needs a ride again, okay?"

"Really?"

"Yes, really." Polly slid off the stool and slowly walked toward the table. Grey had taken her place and both Joss and Henry were forcing food on him. She took out her phone and swiped a call.

"Hello there," Jeff said. "It's Friday night. I'm still at Sycamore House. What's up?"

"We need to talk."

"About what?"

"About Grey. I'm at the Alehouse and he's here, drunk. The bartender says he's been in every night."

"Damn it. Do you want me to fire him?"

"Not yet. I did when I first saw him, but I have to think this isn't who he really is. Can he fix this?"

She heard Jeff take a deep breath. "I don't know, Polly. If he's an alcoholic..." He paused. "I just don't know."

"We're feeding him and we'll take him back to the hotel tonight. I don't know what to do." Polly sat down at an empty table. She waved at Henry and leaned on the hand with the phone in it.

"He and I agreed that this could end within the month. If it's over the first week, I guess that's it," Jeff said.

Polly sighed. "Grey's a good guy. I don't want to throw him away, but I don't have any experience with alcoholism."

"You won't be able to talk to him tonight," Jeff said. "He'll say anything when he's drunk. The conversation needs to happen tomorrow, when he's sober."

"Will he even remember that I was here tonight? Will he admit that there's a problem?"

"I don't know that either," he said. "You need to tell me how far you want to go to be part of his life."

"He's worth it," Polly said.

"You've known him less than a week."

"He's worth it," she said, this time more firmly. "I'm confident. I have the same feeling about him that I did with Eliseo and with Sylvie. Whatever has brought him to this point needs to be put behind him. From here on out, he needs to know that we're part of his life."

"Are you sure?"

"No," she said weakly. "But I'm almost sure."

"Then I'll wake him up bright and early tomorrow morning and we'll see what he says. Do you want to be there?"

"Unless you want me there, I'll let you take care of it," Polly said. "He said that nights were his worst time. If he can't deal with being alone at night, we'll have to work something else out, though."

"I'll talk to him. And you and Henry can get him home tonight?"

"Yeah. We can do that," she said with a laugh. "My hero helps me take care of everybody."

"Now, there's a good guy."

"Thanks Jeff. I'll see you tomorrow."

"Don't worry. We'll deal with this," he said.

"Thanks." Polly ended the call and sat at the table, watching her husband and friends with Grey. Joss and Nate were working to keep up the conversation and Henry kept looking her way, worry in his eyes. She gave him a weak smile. He trusted her no matter what. Even in the midst of things like this, he stood beside her.

Polly's eyes burned with tears. She was so lucky. He'd argue with her later tonight about keeping Grey on at Sycamore Inn, but he'd also listen and in the end, trust her with whatever decision she and Jeff made.

The moment she stood up, Henry stood and took a chair from the empty table next to theirs.

"We ordered another hamburger for you," he said. "Here, have a bite of mine."

"I apologize profusely for my behavior," Alistair said, attempting to stand up.

Polly put her hand on his shoulder, telling him to stay seated. "We'll deal with that tomorrow," she said. "Tonight let's finish dinner and get you safely home."

She sat down between Grey and Henry just as the waiter slid another plate in front of her. Polly looked up at him and smiled a thank you, then handed him the Bloody Mary and asked for a glass of water. Henry had made sure that Grey had water and that it was kept full.

"You've met our friends, Joss and Nate?" she said.

"A purveyor of healing balms," he replied. "Do you know that the inventor of Pepsi-Cola was a pharmacist? And so was the man who first made Dr Pepper. They originally were thought to help with digestion or even to give people pep." He looked at the water in front of him. "Soda pop might have been a better choice for me this evening. I apologize," he said to Polly.

Nate spoke up. "There have been many famous people who were apothecaries in their time. Even Dante was educated as a pharmacist so that he could become a politician."

Polly chuckled and took another bite of her hamburger.

"What are you laughing at?" Nate asked.

"You never cease to amaze me," she said.

"Why?"

"Tonight I've learned about paladins and chivalry and now I've learned about Pepsi, Dr Pepper and Dante. It's never boring with you, is it?" She looked at Joss.

"Never boring," Joss said. "I have no idea where he gets all of this information, but I do know that whatever he learns, he never loses."

"A wonderful trait, to be sure," Grey commented. He pushed his plate back an inch. "I can find my own way home."

Polly stopped him. "No, please. Let us take you home this evening. Sit with us for just a little longer. Joss? Nate? Is that okay?"

"It's fine," Joss said, smiling across the table at Polly. "You're fine."

"Thanks," Polly mouthed back.

CHAPTER THIRTEEN

Early the next morning, Polly rolled over and snuggled into Obiwan. Rebecca was with Kayla and Henry was already gone. He and Nate planned to forage through Ames and Des Moines for parts they needed for the Woodies they were rebuilding.

After dinner, she and Henry had taken Alistair back to the hotel and driven over to the Mikkels' house. Nate and Henry wanted to look online for the parts they needed. Polly knew she probably wouldn't see much of him for a few days. He didn't take time for his personal projects and he had so much fun with Nate that she was glad he was doing this.

He'd let the dogs out before he left this morning, kissed her goodbye, and told her to sleep in. She wondered how long she'd managed to stay in bed.

Checking her phone for the time, she sighed. "Eight fifteen," she said. "I might as well give up. Sleeping in isn't for me."

Obiwan licked her arm, but when Han heard her voice, he placed his front paws on her side and tried to lick her face.

"Back off, you slobbery thing," she said. His entire body wagged. "I know, I know. You're happy to have your human alive and alert." Polly sat up and he scrabbled into her lap. She hugged his neck and kissed the top of his head before moving everyone to the side so she could get out of bed.

Polly wandered through the living room and into the kitchen, being careful of the two cats who insisted on either stretching out directly in her path or weaving around her feet as she walked. "Death of me," she said. "You're going to be the death of me."

Henry had left a full pot of coffee and she sighed as she poured a cup out and breathed in the scent. She stood in front of the kitchen window and looked out at her little town. Two people were pulling weeds in the corner garden. The man looked up and she realized it was Sam Gardner. She and Henry needed to invite them over for dinner one of these evenings. Jean had taken a liking to Rebecca, inviting her to their home a couple of times. The first time Polly had gone with her. But within minutes, Jean made the girl feel at home in her kitchen and soon the two were chattering as they made a strawberry pie. Rebecca helped Jean with canning, putting up everything from beans and tomatoes to dill pickles and raspberry jam.

At the thought of jam, Polly's stomach rumbled and she sliced some bread and dropped it in the toaster. She wasn't sure how she'd gotten so fortunate in meeting the wonderful people that she knew. Her life as a child was so different than Rebecca's was going to be. It had been wonderful, she loved her Dad, Mary and Sylvester, but she hadn't had been exposed to other adults. There weren't any aunts and uncles in her life and her friends' parents were just nameless entities that gave permission to do things.

But Rebecca was learning about life from so many different people. She spent time with Beryl every Saturday morning and Bill Sturtz had enjoyed teaching the three kids how to carve wood this summer. Jean Gardner was giving Rebecca invaluable experience in the kitchen and the girl was enjoying it all.

There had been some rough nights the first month after Sarah's death. Polly and Obiwan usually crept into her bedroom after she'd spent time crying to make sure that she would relax enough to fall asleep. The dog was gentle with Rebecca, climbing up beside her and settling in. Polly generally sat in the chair beside her bed and held her hand. She wanted Rebecca to grieve and cry, but didn't want her to have to do any of it alone.

After a few weeks, the nights weren't quite as long and the days began to brighten again. In the beginning of the grief process, Rebecca was desperate to see Evelyn. They'd spent so much time together that their connection was strong. Evelyn would pick Rebecca up and take her away, sometimes out for lunch, other times out for a drive and every once in a while, they would sit outside behind Sycamore House by themselves and just talk. This was another adult who was a big part of Rebecca's life.

The toast popped up and Polly reached up for a plate. She buttered it and spread some of Rebecca's jam on top, then sat at the peninsula. She was spending too much time reflecting this morning. But in truth, she didn't know what to do with herself today. It was all hers. She didn't have to be anywhere or do anything. Polly leaned back and stretched. What a great day.

Then she remembered Grey and the conversation Jeff was planning to have with him this morning. It bothered Polly that she hadn't realized. He never seemed hung over and when she'd been with him, there was no hint that he had a drinking problem.

She wanted to text Jeff and ask more questions. When was he going to talk to Grey? Had he already? What was he going to say? How was he going to handle it?

Leia sniffed the plate on the counter and Polly instinctively moved it away. But it broke her concentration.

"No," she said, pushing the cat back. "You don't get my breakfast. I get my breakfast." She picked the cat up, snuggled her and then reached down to release her onto the floor.

"Okay kids, it's time to get moving. First a shower, then I have no idea what. But it's going to be fun!"

~~~

"Hey Andrew, it's just you and me again today. Wanna hang out?" Polly asked, stopping at his nook under the stairs. He'd moved most of his books to his room at home, leaving nothing on the shelves and only pens, pencils and paper in the desk.

"Nah, it's okay," he said.

"Come on. We haven't been alone forever. I want an adventure. Come with me," she pleaded.

"Didn't you already find your dead body?" He scratched a pencil on a sheet of paper, circling round and round until he'd created a tornado.

Polly gently popped him on the back of the head. "Nope. You don't get to mope. You have to come with me. I feel too good to let one of my favorite people feel sorry for himself."

"What's Henry got to do with it?" Andrew asked, looking up at her with a hint of a grin.

"That's right. He's feeling sorry for himself because he gets to spend the entire weekend playing with car stuff. Come on. First stop, the coffee shop and we'll tell your mom that we're leaving town together."

He finally laughed and stood up. Andrew was practically as tall as Polly and he was still just as adorable as ever. She wanted to squeeze him tight, but knew that would make him miserable.

"Let me go upstairs and get my book," he said. "Just in case you find yourself in a girly store somewhere."

"Run. I'll meet you in the truck."

Andrew attempted to move past her to get to the door leading upstairs and Polly stepped into his path. When he moved to the left, she mimicked him.

"What are you doing?" he asked.

She wrapped her arms around him and squeezed. "Hugging you. Thanks for coming out with me today. I wanted a partner in crime and didn't know who I might find."

He went limp in her grasp until she let go, then looked at her, waiting until she moved.

"Fine," she said. "Go upstairs. I'll be the lonely old lady in the truck." She let him pass and smiled to herself. Now the day had potential. Andrew was usually up for anything, no matter how crazy it got.

She sat in her truck and fiddled with the digital readouts. They hadn't taken the time to read the manual, but so far she'd managed to make everything work. She loved the backup camera. One of these days she planned to scare the daylights out of Henry with it.

"I'm ready," Andrew said, climbing in and buckling up. "Do you know where we're going?"

"First to the coffee shop. They're still giving away free coffee and I want to see who shows up."

Andrew put his book on the seat beside him. "You know, don't you?"

"Know what?" Polly asked, backing out of the garage.

"Rebecca told you. I know she did."

"Why don't you tell me your side?"

"Because she hates me. I don't know why I thought..."

"Thought what?"

"It sounds stupid. And really mean."

Polly stopped at the highway, waiting for traffic to pass. She looked at him. "What do mean - mean?"

"I thought she was mine and that just sounds bad. She's not anybody's. But I guess I thought we were together already."

"I suppose that assuming something without having a conversation isn't too bright," Polly said. "Did you think about *asking* her to the dance?"

"I did ask!"

"Are you sure that's how the conversation went?" Polly glanced at him, not surprised to see confusion on his face.

"I asked her to go to the dance with me," he repeated. "What else would I have done?"

Polly pulled into a parking space next to the coffee shop and turned the truck off. "Think back over your conversation. Did you truly ask her or did you make an assumption and set forth an expectation." She opened her car door and smiled over at him.

"A what?" he asked.

"You think about it while we're inside. We'll talk about it when we get back in the car. If you can't figure it out on your own, I'll be glad to help you through it." She held the front door open and breathed in the scent of coffee. It was heavenly. There were several people at tables around the room, all smiling, with drinks in front of them.

Camille waved at her from behind the counter, where she was working with Helena at the cash register. The older woman nodded, taking it all in. Everybody was on site today. Sky and Rena were hovering behind the counter, talking animatedly to each other and Benny was wiping tables.

"What do you think?"

Polly jumped and spun around. Jeff had come up behind her.

"I don't know," she said. "What do *you* think?"

"It's going to be okay. We need to replace Julie, but not right away. It seems kind of crass."

Andrew leaned in. "That was the dead girl Polly found?"

"Yes," she replied, scowling at him. "Go get something to drink and find your mom."

Andrew walked away from them and Polly asked, "How did it go?"

"With Grey?"

"Yes. What happened this morning? I've been dying to know, but didn't want to bother you."

"I talked to him. He's an alcoholic."

Polly's shoulders slumped. "Damn it."

"He admitted it right away," Jeff said. "He's gone through rehab and has been clean for twelve years. He thought he could handle it but after the accident, he just didn't have it in him."

"What are we going to do?"

Jeff shrugged. "That's up to you. He says it is completely up to you. He promised to find an AA meeting and get a sponsor - someone to talk to. But if you want him gone, he'll go."

"I don't want him to go," Polly replied. "But what if he can't get this dealt with?"

"He told me that he was willing to be accountable. He promised to call me this evening and tell me that he'd been to a meeting and had a sponsor."

"And tomorrow? What about tomorrow and the next day?" Polly asked.

Jeff smiled at her. "You do know that one of the major tenets of AA is that they take it one day at a time. If you want to trust him to make these steps, then that's what we have to do. If you don't want to, he'll understand and move on."

"I know it sounds crazy," Polly said. "But I want to trust him. We've only known him a week, but like I told Henry, he's worth it. I just know it."

"That's my girl," Jeff said. He hooked his arm in hers and led her to the counter. "Do you know what you'd like to order today?"

Polly looked up at the wall and then at Sky who had come over to greet her. "Hey there, Miss Giller," he said. "What would you like to drink?"

"I'd like an iced mocha," she said.

"Anything special?" he asked.

"Nope," she laughed. "Just bring on the caffeine."

He smiled and turned back to Rena.

"Is Sal here?" Polly asked Jeff. "She should be enjoying this after all that she's been through to get here."

"She and Sylvie are in the bakery - plotting."

"Polly!" Camille exclaimed. "I'm so glad you're here. Do you have time to meet my mother?"

Polly glanced around the shop. "I'd love to."

Sky handed her a cup, Polly took a tentative drink and scowled.

"What?" he asked in desperation. "Is something wrong?"

She grinned and winked at him. "I'm kidding. It's great. Thank you."

Rena stood behind him, quietly laughing.

"That was mean," he said. "I was going to tell you that Rena made it."

Animated chatter reached Polly's ears before she saw Andrew leading three women from the bakery. Sylvie and Sal were listening to a tall, regal black woman describe a dish she made in her own kitchen.

Camille stepped out from behind the counter and took the woman's arm, stopping the conversation. "Mama, I want you to meet Polly Giller." She turned and said, "Polly, this is my mother, Abigail Specht."

The woman stepped away from her daughter and took both of Polly's hands in hers. "I've been hearing much about you. It's nice to meet you."

"It's nice to meet you too," Polly said. "We're fortunate to have your daughter here in Bellingwood."

"Yes you are," Abigail said. "She's one of a kind." She turned to include Sylvie and Sal in the conversation and said, "Your friends have been showing me your facility. This is quite some adventure you all are on. And Milty here tells me that there's already been a death. That's too bad. I hope it doesn't affect your business."

Polly glanced at Camille. "Milty?"

The young woman shook her head. "My brother anointed me with that name and it stuck. Please forget you ever heard it."

"Does Jeff know?"

"Know what?" Jeff asked. He'd been wandering the room, greeting guests.

"My girl is known as Milty when she's with friends and family," Abigail said. She brushed her daughter's hair back from her face. "It doesn't seem right that the only time she'll hear that name is when she is with us in Omaha."

"Mama," Camille protested.

"If they're going to be your family, they need to know everything about you." Abigail Specht took Polly's arm and pulled her aside. "I'm a tad worried about this dead girl that was found in the alley. Are there any suspects yet? Is my little girl safe here?"

Polly rubbed her chin. This was never easy to explain. "I'm certain that she's perfectly safe. We have a wonderful police department and the county sheriff and his deputies are quite professional. Even though they might not know much right away, they're working on it."

"She's looking forward to this position," Abigail said. "I'd hate for her to regret her decision to move to Bellingwood."

Polly looked into the woman's stern eyes. Nope, she didn't want to ever cross her. "She's safe and we're looking forward to her time with us, too. She'll be working most closely with Sylvie and I think they've connected already."

The woman smiled warmly and said, "Thank you. I just wanted everything to be out in the open between us. She's a special girl and since I can't be here to watch over her, I want to know the people who will."

"Mama, quit scaring Polly," Camille said, pulling at her mother's arm. "You aren't that intimidating. Stop it."

Polly gave her head a quick shake. Abigail Specht was definitely intimidating.

"How are things coming in the kitchen?" Polly asked Sylvie.

"I'll be in here on Monday," Sylvie replied. "I just want to play and make messes and bake before I bring staff in." She looked around the room. "There's no clock in here," she said.

"It's ten thirty," Jeff said. "You're okay."

"No I'm not. I told Rachel I'd be back by now. She's probably worrying." Sylvie nodded at everyone and said, "It's nice to meet you, Mrs. Specht. I hope to see you again."

Before anyone could respond, she ran for the front door and was gone.

"She said it was okay that I go with you," Andrew said quietly. "Are we still doing an adventure?"

"Let's see what we can find," Polly responded.

They said their goodbyes and went back to the truck.

"People are going to like that place," Andrew said.

Polly pointed at his cup. "What did you get to drink?"

"A strawberry smoothie," he responded. "It's too warm for hot chocolate."

"How are their smoothies?"

"Great. You want to try it?"

Polly smiled at his offer. "No thanks. I'll order one another time. Where shall we begin?"

CHAPTER FOURTEEN

Browsing through the bookstore and then wandering through the museum and gift shop at the Boone & Scenic Valley Railroad had taken the entire morning. As they walked back to the car, Andrew asked Polly about lunch. He was starving.

"Where shall we go?" she asked.

"I don't care. Not McDonalds. I'm not a kid anymore."

Polly laughed. "No. You're not. Do you want to drive over to Ames?"

He looked at her, his face alight with expectation. "Really? That would be awesome."

"Maybe when we're done with lunch, we'll go to Goodwill to see what they have for used books. There are always interesting finds at the thrift stores."

"That's where Rebecca and Kayla were going," he said, his shoulders slumping as he thought about his friends.

Polly pressed her fob to unlock the doors on the truck and watched him walk to the passenger side. Once they were in and buckled up, she said, "I suspect they're done at Goodwill. Stephanie was planning to get an early start."

"I don't want to see them anyway," he grumped.

"I know you don't. Where shall we eat?" She could almost see his mind spinning as he considered the possibilities.

Andrew knitted his brows together. "I don't know," he said.

"You have a few minutes to think about it. Be creative. We can go anywhere."

"Is there somewhere you've never gotten to eat?" Andrew asked.

Polly laughed. "There is. Every time I've tried to eat there in the past, something comes up. Do you want to try it?"

"Okay, where?"

"The big barbecue restaurant. Hickory Park. They have ice cream for dessert."

"Yes!" he said with great enthusiasm. "Everybody talks about how awesome it is and I've never gone. That would be so cool." He opened the bag of books he'd purchased at the bookstore and held up a book for Polly to see.

She glanced at it and smiled. "Xanth?" she asked.

"Yeah. Is it good?"

Polly nodded. "It was a classic in its time. Have you figured out what Xanth is?"

Andrew gave her a strange look. "The place?"

"Yes, but say the author's name," Polly replied.

"Piers Anthony?" Andrew asked.

"Say it all together as one word."

"Piersanthony." He heard it. "Xanth! I get it. That's pretty cool."

"It took me a while," she said with a laugh. "If you keep reading his stories, you'll find more and more puns like that. He had fun with it. You will too."

Andrew opened the book, glanced up at her and then started to read.

"You don't want to talk about Rebecca?" Polly asked.

"No," he muttered.

"Did you think about what you might have said to offend her?"

"No. Whatever." He slouched toward the truck door, trying to put more space between them.

"So you want to just keep this all bottled up and be uncomfortable around Rebecca?"

Andrew slammed the book shut - pretty ineffectually since it was a paperback and didn't make much noise. "Sorry," he said, sheepishly. "I don't want to talk about it."

"Andrew, this isn't like you," Polly said. "Your mother said you were rotten the other night. You aren't talking to Rebecca and Kayla and now you're exploding at me. You can't do this. You're sucking all the fun out of your life."

"She hurt me," he said. "I thought she liked me and then she just said no. I get it that I'm a boy, but we have feelings too."

It was all Polly could do not to laugh out loud, but she heard the pain in his voice and remembered that even at this age, love just hurt sometimes.

"Oh Andrew, this is not the last time you are going to be hurt by a girl. It might not even be the last time you get hurt by Rebecca. But you can't let this destroy your whole life."

"It's only bad when I have to talk about it. Maybe we shouldn't talk about it."

"But you aren't speaking to your best friend. That's no fun. You'll need each other this year."

"Can I tell you something and you won't ever tell anybody else, not even Henry?" Andrew asked. "Because this is really, really private."

"Okay?"

"I think I love Rebecca," he said. "Not just as a friend. But someday when we're out of college and grown up, I want to ask her to marry me. You can't tell anybody I said that. Promise?"

"I promise," Polly responded, doing her best to keep her eyes on the road.

"That's why it hurt. She doesn't love me back."

Polly reached out and put her hand on his knee and gave it a squeeze. "Thanks for telling me. Now will you listen while I say a few things?"

"Yeah. You're going to tell me I'm too young and that I don't know what the future will be and yada, yada, yada."

"Well, that's true, too," Polly said with a chuckle. "And that whole too young thing is a big deal."

"I knew it."

"Andrew, you're too young to take this all so seriously. Let it be what it's going to be. Enjoy your time with your friends and with Rebecca. If you want to dance with her at the dance, do it. But I can promise you that if you try to make her all yours right now, she will run away from you."

"Why? We've been friends for ever and I was there for all of her stuff."

"I know. But Rebecca has just been through a horrible loss. She spent the last couple of years not knowing what was happening next. Every morning when she woke up, she knew without a doubt that it was one day closer to her losing her mother. That was on her mind all the time, even if she didn't say anything. As much as she misses Sarah, now she's looking forward without fear. She wants to do everything. She doesn't have to worry about rushing home because she might miss precious moments with her mother. You have to let her live."

"But I could die at any minute, too," he protested weakly.

"Andrew," Polly scolded.

"Well, I could," he said under his breath.

"Is that the tack you want to take with me right now?"

"No," he said sheepishly. "Sorry."

"Give her some rope. Be her friend, but don't strangle her with your friendship. Be the person she trusts. Be there when she needs you. You can do that, right?"

"I have been," he said, still grumpy.

"Yes you have. You've been a great friend. Don't stop now just because of one stupid dance."

"You're not very fun," he said.

"Why's that?"

"Jason complains about it too."

"Jason complains about me?" Polly was stymied.

"He says you always make sense, even when it makes him mad."

"Oh," she said with a laugh. "I can live with that."

Polly pulled into the parking lot at Hickory Park. "Are you ready for barbecue?"

"I guess."

"Are you planning to sulk all the way through the meal?"

"Maybe just until they bring us our drinks?" He looked up at her and grinned.

"Okay. I'll let you have that." She got out of the truck and saw her phone on the console. She was tempted to leave it in the truck, but knew that would just be asking for trouble. She reached back in, snagged it, and jammed it down in her back pocket.

Andrew looked at everything as they walked up to the front door. "This place is huge," he said. "There's a lot of cars here."

"Yes there are," Polly said, wanting desperately to correct his grammar. She chose to let it go. "Let's hope there's room inside for us to sit down."

The host at the front of the restaurant told them there would be a short wait.

"Rats," Polly said as they moved away to make room for others. "That was stupid of me."

"What?" Andrew asked.

"College kids are coming back to school this weekend. Every kid and their family is in town."

"Cool," he replied.

As she leaned against the wall, she thought she heard a familiar laugh. "He did not," she said quietly. She looked at the host and asked, "I think I hear someone I know. Can I just go in and look?"

He smiled and waved her ahead. Polly walked around a corner and saw Henry and Nate sitting at a table. "What are you two doing here?" she demanded.

Henry stood up and guilt flooded his face. "Well, uh, I figured that if I was ever going to eat here, it would have to be with someone else and we're just coming back from a run to Ankeny for parts and there it was just off the highway and we were hungry and thought it was a good idea and..."

She put her hand up. "You need to stop while you're ahead. If you want to redeem yourself, you'll ask us join you."

"We've already placed our order," he said.

"It's okay. We'll read the menus fast and place our order as soon as the waiter arrives. Right, Andrew?"

Andrew looked back and forth between them and then nodded. "I'll read fast."

Henry pulled the chair out beside him for Polly and Andrew slid in beside Nate. The waiter walked past, stopped and looked at them, perplexed.

"We're adding two more," Henry said.

The young man smiled, took their drink orders and walked away.

"Just about the time he thought his day wouldn't toss any curveballs at him," Nate said.

"Did you find what you were looking for?" Polly asked them.

Nate shook his head. "The guy thought he might have some brake parts in his warehouse, but nothing. It was fun to dig through his junk, but frustrating all the same."

"Have you heard from Joss?" she asked.

"They got on the road earlier than she expected." He looked at his watch. "They should almost be there."

The waiter stopped back with drinks and took Polly and Andrew's order. Andrew, true to his word, had scanned through the menu quickly and made a decision.

"This is fun," Polly said. "I can't believe we found you here. The host said it was just a short wait, but there were a lot of people ahead of us."

"Move-in weekend," Henry said.

"That's what Polly said," Andrew exclaimed. "If I go to college here, will I have to live with Mom in Bellingwood, or do you think she'll let me live in a dormitory?"

"You want to live in a dorm," Nate said. "That's where all the fun is. You meet great girls and there are parties and you make friends."

"And you still have to study," Polly interjected.

"Exactly," Nate said, nodding furiously. "You study all the time, in fact."

Henry leaned forward. "Especially if you are going to keep that full-ride scholarship you'll have for being so danged smart. Right?"

"Right," Andrew said. "Girls?" He turned to Nate.

"Lots of great girls. They're everywhere. I met Joss in college."

"How about you, Henry?" Andrew started. Then he looked at Polly. "Oh, I guess not."

The waiter came back and put plates down in front of Nate and Henry, then glanced at Polly. "Yours are coming right out. It should only be a minute."

She nodded. "Thanks."

Henry handed her a French fry. "Want one?"

"You're my hero," she said. Her phone buzzed in her back pocket and she groaned.

"What?" he asked.

Polly reached into her pocket and pulled out the phone. Jeff was calling her. "It's like he knows," she said. She glanced at the diners and scooted her chair back. "I'm going to take this. He knows I'm out adventuring with Andrew." She swiped the call open as she walked back to the foyer of the restaurant.

"Hey Jeff, what's up?" she asked.

"Where are you?"

"I'm not telling. It's better if you don't know," she responded. "Is something wrong?"

"Well, not necessarily wrong, but I need you."

She chuckled. "Of course you do. What's going on?"

Yelling in the background grew closer and Jeff whispered loudly. "Just come back. And hurry."

"Jeff, what?" Polly asked.

"It's not that big of a deal, I guess. But I can't talk right now. Hurry back, will you?"

"Okay. It will take about twenty minutes. I'll leave right away."

"Thanks Polly," he said. "Sorry."

She stared at the phone after pulling it away from her ear. She was never coming to Hickory Park again. It was always something. Every single time.

Polly went back to their table and salivated at the plate in front of her. "I have to go," she said.

Henry looked up. "You're kidding."

"Nope. Now you can be sure of two things about me. First, if there's a dead body, I'm the one who will find it and second, if I try to eat at Hickory Park, some crisis will occur."

"What's going on?" Andrew asked. He put his fork down on the plate and scooted out of the bench.

"No, you stay here," Polly replied and turned to Henry. "Can you two bring him back to Bellingwood? And either enjoy my meal or bring it home with you?"

Nate put his hand on Andrew's shoulder before the boy could stand up. "You'll have as much fun with us as you will with Polly. I promise."

"But my books," Andrew said.

"I'll put your backpack in Henry's truck," Polly said.

He relaxed and slid back in front of his food.

Polly leaned over to Henry. "I promised him ice cream."

"Of course you did. We'll take good care of him. Let me know what's going on."

She nodded and ran out of the restaurant to her truck. One quick stop to drop Andrew's backpack in the back seat of Henry's truck and she was on the highway heading for Bellingwood.

One of the first things she'd learned to do in the truck was how to pair her phone to the main system. She pulled up Sylvie's phone number and placed the call.

"Hello, Polly," Sylvie said. "Is everything okay with Andrew? Is he being respectful?"

"He's fine. Where are you?" Polly asked.

"In the kitchen. Why?"

"Jeff just called and told me to hurry back to Sycamore House. What's going on?"

"Oh that," Sylvie said. "Yeah. He needs you. We're in the middle of a perfect storm here right now."

"What do you mean?"

"He's got a furious bride and her mom and there's a mess going on with that boy who is moving into the addition with Mrs. Morrow. Aaron's here, the boy's mother is here. There was yelling and screaming. The bride is screaming and crying and Jeff's alone. Well, I'm here. But it's not much better in the kitchen. The oven quit working and I'm waiting for a repairman. They didn't deliver the right meat this morning and Rachel's on her way to Ames to pick up what we need. I'm sure I could tell you more if you'd like."

"What about Eliseo and Jason?" Polly asked.

"One of the donkeys is sick. Mark is here."

Polly shook her head. How could so many things have fallen apart in just a few short hours?

"I have to go," Sylvie said. "I think my repairman is here."

The call ended and Polly shuddered. She pressed down on the gas pedal, pushing it as fast as she dared. Thank goodness they were as close as Ames. She turned on the radio, hoping that music would help her tune out all of the questions swirling in her mind. But that didn't help. The last thing she wanted to do was listen to DJs hawking a new product.

Once in Bellingwood, she sped past the winery and the Inn, giving a fleeting thought to how Grey was doing today. She really liked him. He made her smile even though she was worried about him. She pulled into her driveway and parked in the garage, jumped out and ran inside to the kitchen.

Sylvie looked up. "That was fast," she said.

"I was already on my way. How are things in here?"

"There isn't much more I can do unless I move everything up to the bakery and I'm not ready to do that yet."

"You can always use my stove if you need it," Polly said.

"That's okay," Sylvie said with a laugh. "It wouldn't fit. But Emmett will have me up and running pretty soon."

The man with his head in the oven waved a free hand.

Polly patted Sylvie's shoulder. "I'm going to see how I can help Jeff. Where do you think I'll find him?"

"The screaming and flailing about moved into the office. I think he tried to hide them in the conference room. Aaron is back in the addition and today's wedding party is in the auditorium decorating."

"So. Chaos?" Polly asked as she crossed the threshold of the kitchen into the main foyer.

"Pretty standard," Sylvie called behind her.

Jeff and Sylvie were good at keeping things moving without falling apart, so even though Sylvie tried to make a joke of it, chaos was not the usual order of the day at Sycamore House. She walked into the office and didn't see Jeff anywhere, so knocked on the conference room door and opened it. Two women - a young bride and her mother were seated at the table, the bride sobbing with her head down in her arms. The older woman's face was furious, her arms crossed in front of her.

She looked up at Polly and snapped, "Who the hell are you? Do you want to make this situation even worse?"

Polly shook her head, backed up and shut the door. That situation wasn't going to be fixed in a jiffy.

"Yeah, she's pissed," Jeff said, coming into the main office.

"What happened?"

"I'm still trying to figure that out, but the girl is getting married in two weeks and while they say that they scheduled things with us, I can't find any information to verify that."

"Did we miss something?"

"I can't tell. There aren't any emails and I don't have a signed contract. There's a beginning of a contract in Stephanie's pending file, but nothing was ever completed. I haven't met either of these people and when I asked Sylvie if she'd talked to them about catering, she drew a blank."

"What are you going to do with the crazy people?" Polly asked. "I assume they don't care whether or not you get to the bottom of whose fault it is they aren't on the schedule, they just need a location for the reception."

Jeff took a deep breath and let his shoulders fall back into place. "You know what? You're right. They just need me to fix this for them. I'll call J. J. over at Secret Woods. They're still trying to expand their wedding receptions."

"How big is the reception?" Polly asked.

"It isn't even that big," Jeff said, rolling his eyes. "You'd think it was six hundred people the way they're carrying on. But the numbers on the contract show fifty."

"The coffee shop is another possibility. Think about how fun that could be. A coffee bar and jazz on the stage."

More of his body relaxed. "Thanks. I've got this. I'll help them fix it and none of us have to search for blame."

"That might be most of the mother's anger," Polly said. "If she knows her daughter hasn't been dealing with the details, she is probably out-of-control furious."

"Thanks."

"Have you talked to Eliseo?" Polly asked.

"The donkey? Jason came up when Sylvie freaked out in the kitchen. He didn't want to tell her that Eliseo couldn't run up and take care of her stove, but Mark had just gotten to the barn."

"She freaked out?"

Jeff nodded. "It was ugly. Seriously Polly, when I called you, I felt like I was on a firing range. Everything fell apart at the same time and I didn't know where to start, so I stepped into your office, shut the door and made the call."

"I'm glad you did. Okay, the Sutworth's?"

"There's something bad happening over there." Jeff visibly sagged. "I didn't want to get involved in it, but Leslie was crying, Evelyn tried to keep them all calm, the Sheriff wanted to speak with the boy. It's something to do with Julie Smith's death."

"What?" Polly asked. "How are they connected?"

"I have no idea. I had my own crises to manage."

She glanced toward the side door.

"You're going to get involved, aren't you?" he said with a sly grin.

"Would I be the Polly Giller you know and love if I didn't?"

"That's my girl. Thanks for coming back."

"I haven't done anything yet."

"But you came. That was all I needed to know."

"I'll always come," she said.

"By the way, what were you doing?"

As soon as she thought about it, her stomach growled. "Believe it or not, ordering lunch at Hickory Park. It's the last time I ever even try. I'll do takeout, but I can't risk our sanity."

He laughed. "I can always count on you."

CHAPTER FIFTEEN

"Run away," Polly muttered to herself when she opened the door to the addition. Loud wailing coming from the room Evelyn Morrow would use announced the fact that Denis Sutworth had moved in. His mother was letting everyone know that she was present. Polly quietly tapped on the door, hoping no one would hear her.

But the door opened immediately and Aaron Merritt looked at Polly, frustration evident on his face.

"Polly," he said, taking her arm. "Please come in."

"Miss Giller," Leslie Sutworth wailed. "Will it never end? How much more should Denis have to suffer?"

Polly held her finger up to the woman and silence fell. She turned to Aaron. "Where's Evelyn?"

He tilted his head to the other room. "She's in with the EMTs getting Denis settled."

"And why are you here?" Polly asked.

"He has questions about that girl's death," Leslie cried. Her voice went up and down the pitch register. In just a few moments, Polly's nerves were on edge. She couldn't imagine what Aaron was feeling. Leslie went on. "Denis was in the hospital fighting for his life when she was killed. How could he think that my poor boy would be involved in something so awful? Denis wouldn't kill someone."

Polly put her hand back up, silencing the woman once again. "How is Denis connected to Julie Smith?" she asked Aaron.

"That's why I want to speak with him. This morning Stu discovered the two had been dating..."

"But that was over," Leslie wailed. "They broke up. It nearly destroyed him. That was probably why he went off his medication. He has been so distraught. But you can't think that he had anything to do with her death. You just can't. I've spent all my free time with him. He can't walk, much less drive. This is the worst thing that could happen today, when everything is supposed to be so joyful. My boy is out of the hospital..."

"Please stop talking, Mrs. Sutworth," Polly said, interrupting what promised to be an unending flow of words from the woman's mouth.

"But..." Leslie whined.

"No. You aren't helping." Polly stopped before she said anything more. Words like 'incessant whining' and 'helicopter parenting' were swirling around, but she didn't think that she needed to escalate the situation any more than it had been.

Leslie Sutworth sat down in a wing chair and dropped her head into her hands, snuffling and snorting. Polly walked over to the desk, picked up the box of tissues and put them in the woman's lap.

"You've been here for the last half hour?" she asked Aaron.

He took her arm and led her outside the room and pulled the door closed. Once they were alone, he drew her into a bear hug and chuckled when he released her.

"What was that for?" she asked.

"I wanted to put cuffs on that woman and duct tape her mouth shut. But since that's totally inappropriate, I just let her wail. I assumed she probably had a good reason for it, since so much has happened to her this last week."

"It happened to her son. She's just living vicariously through his pain," Polly retorted. Then she felt guilty. "No, that's not nice either. This is going to be a long recovery for all of us if she decides that she needs to spend all of her waking moments here. I wonder how long Evelyn will put up with it."

Aaron leaned on the door frame. "Probably longer than you. I should think about hiring you, though. You don't put up with much crap from people like her."

"I can't bear whining.'

He looked at her and smiled.

"Yeah, yeah, yeah. I know. I whined when Joey and his serial killer friend were in town. I tried to contain it to just Henry, but sometimes it crept out in front of other people."

"The man's a saint," Aaron said quietly, a wicked grin on his lips.

"Henry?" she asked. And then she laughed with him. "He really is. I don't know anyone else who would put up with my particular brand of insanity."

"I guess we each have our own crosses to bear."

"Lydia is a cross you have to bear?" Polly asked.

"Good lord, no," Aaron said, putting his hands up defensively. "I'm her cross."

"What are you thinking about this connection between Denis and Julie?"

He shook his head. "Whenever I discover coincidences like this, I find that it's important to ask more questions. Having two strange occurrences happen in the same week and then finding that the two subjects not only knew each other, but were intimately involved..." His voice trailed off.

"I get it," Polly said. "I was beginning to wonder if anything was happening. I hadn't heard from you and things have been quiet around town. Do you have any idea who might have broken into the coffee shop? Any idea of the timeline from that evening at all? And what about Grey's walking stick. Were there any fingerprints on it other than his?"

"You watch too much television," Aaron said. "I wish we were given fingerprints and other evidence on a silver platter. The only fingerprints on the stick belonged to Alistair Greyson."

"Do you suspect he was involved?"

"No." Aaron shook his head again. "But the absence of anyone else's prints tells me that someone took care to cover their tracks."

"And inside the building?" Polly pressed.

"Nothing to tell us who it was. Unless it was one of the other employees. But we've talked to all of them and they either have very solid alibis or, in the case of Sylvie, I'm pretty sure she didn't beat a young girl to death."

Polly chuckled. "I don't know. You might want to stay out of the kitchen if you don't want to have to revise that consideration."

"Things were a little chaotic when I arrived today," Aaron said.

The door opened and Leslie stood there. "Why won't they let me see my boy?" she whined. Her voice was much quieter, but it still made Polly want to grit her teeth.

"You must be patient," Polly said. "They will come get you when he is completely settled. You don't want to make this any more difficult on him than it already is, do you?"

"No." Now she sounded like a beaten puppy.

Polly put her hand on the woman's arm. "Go on back in and relax. Evelyn will be out soon."

The door closed again and Polly took a deep breath, doing her best not to roll her eyes. "Have you talked to Ken Wallers?" she asked.

Aaron looked at her quizzically. "About what? I usually see him a couple of times during the week."

"About this case."

"Does he know something?"

"Well, he knows about Denis. That accident is his case."

"Of course," Aaron said. "I haven't yet. We just got the information about an hour ago. Stu was in Boone and stopped at the hospital to see if he could talk to the kid and discovered he'd been released to come up here."

Polly lowered her voice. "I can't believe they let him out of the hospital so early."

"Insurance," Aaron said with disgust. "Rehab is less expensive than hospitalization. They patched him up as well as they could and there's no reason to keep him any longer. Insurance forces everyone to make interesting decisions."

"Then I guess I'm glad she got in touch with Evelyn."

"I didn't know you were opening a nursing home," he said with a smile.

"Neither did I," Polly responded. "But it fits right in with what I'd originally hoped for Sycamore House."

The door to the other room opened and two EMTs came out.

"Is everything okay?" Aaron asked.

"He'll be fine," the young woman said. "They sedated him for the ride up here. He's starting to come around again. Mrs. Morrow has it well in hand."

Aaron shook her hand and clapped the young man who was with her on the back. "Thanks for your work. It's good to see you both."

"Nice to see you, too, Sheriff," the young man said on his way out the door.

"I haven't seen much of the girl, Sarah," Polly said to Aaron. "What happened to her?"

"She's moved on. She went to the University of Iowa for a nursing degree. She wants to go to med school, too."

"So young," Polly said. "Big dreams and the energy to make them happen."

Evelyn Morrow came out of the room and smiled at Polly. She didn't carry the smile on to Aaron. "He's exhausted, Sheriff. Surely this could wait until tomorrow."

"Tomorrow's Sunday, Mrs. Morrow," Aaron said. "If I can avoid working, it keeps Lydia happy."

Polly grinned. "And if Lydia is happy, everyone is happy."

"Please keep your visit short, then," Evelyn said. "He's going to have enough to deal with..." She stopped herself. "That was out of line. But don't spend too much time with him. I'll keep his mother busy with paperwork until you're finished."

She slipped into the next room and more wailing erupted from

Leslie Sutworth. Evelyn gently closed the door behind her and the sound was muffled.

"Do you think you're coming in here with me?" Aaron asked with a smile.

Polly looked up at him, giving him as innocent a face as possible. "Do you mind? I really want to know what I've got going on here. I haven't even met this kid and now you're here to talk to him."

"One of these days..." Aaron shook his head. "No. I'm being foolish. I didn't say anything."

"What? What one of these days? What were you going to say?"

"I was going to tell you that you should apply for a private investigator's license, but then I realized what was about to come out of my mouth and stopped myself."

"But you failed," Polly said. "Don't worry. That's a terrible idea. Then I'd have to be involved in things I don't want to know about. Can you just see me sitting outside a hotel with my camera waiting for illicit lovers to leave? Talk about a bad idea."

Aaron chuckled. "It is a bad idea." He put his hand on the door handle. "You can come in with me, but stay quiet. I'm not accusing this kid of anything. I just need to find out if there is a connection between his accident and Julie's death."

"Okay," she said. "I'll do my very best to be good." Polly waved him in. "I promise."

Aaron strode into the room and stepped in front of the bed. It had been angled so Denis could look out toward the horse pasture. Polly had been worried that seeing him here in a hospital bed would bring back memories of Sarah Heater, Rebecca's mother, but the room was nothing like it had been when Sarah and Rebecca were living here. Their lives had filled every available space and this was sterile. Maybe over the next few months it would become more his room, but for now, it was simply an accommodation for a young man who needed help.

"Denis Sutworth, I'm Sheriff Aaron Merritt." Aaron put his hand out, reaching across the bed so Denis could shake it. "And this is Polly Giller. She owns Sycamore House."

Polly nodded and smiled. "I hope you are comfortable here. Evelyn knows that we will do everything we can to make your stay a good one."

"Thank you," Denis said weakly. "Am I in trouble for the accident with you, too?" He turned to Aaron. "I've already talked to the police and they said the man I hit wasn't pressing charges."

Aaron shook his head. "That's not why I'm here. You'll work that all out with Chief Wallers. No, I'm here about Julie Smith."

"Julie?" the boy asked. "What about her? Did she do something wrong? She's a nice person." He craned his neck toward the door. "Is she here to see me?"

Polly and Aaron glanced at each other. A look of surprise crossed his face and Polly felt helpless. There was nothing she could say.

Aaron sat down in the chair beside Denis's bed. "Son, I'm sorry to tell you that she is dead."

"Dead? What do you mean, dead?" Denis gave his head a quick shake. "I know what you mean, dead. But how could this happen. Was she sick? I just talked to her the other day."

"You did?" Aaron asked. "She came to see you in the hospital?"

Denis slumped back in the bed. "No. I've lost track of time. It was before the accident. But a couple of days after we broke up. I saw her down in Boone. She worked at Kentucky Fried. I went in to get lunch."

"Why did you break up?" Polly asked, then pursed her lips when Aaron scowled at her.

He dropped his head down and shut his eyes. "No reason. It was just time. We were moving on."

Aaron leaned forward. "Denis, can you think of any reason why someone would kill Julie?"

"She was killed?" Denis's head shot up and he winced. "How? When? Where?"

"I need you to focus on my questions," Aaron replied. "Do you know of any reason why someone might kill her?"

"She was a sweet girl. No one would want to kill her. The only bad thing that she ever did was decide to be with me," Denis said.

He grew quiet. "When was she killed? Won't you at least tell me that?"

"It was Wednesday," Polly said. "At the new coffee shop. Did you know that she was going to be working there?"

Denis nodded while Aaron scowled at her again. "She was excited about the job. She always wanted to be a barista." He rolled the 'r' in the word. "That's how she always said it. She's taking language studies at Iowa State. She wants to be an engineer and work around the world." He heaved a sigh, then winced again. "She wanted to. I'm sorry."

"Denis," Aaron said, demanding the young man's attention. "I need to ask if there might be any connection between your accident and Julie's death. Can you think of any reason that they are associated?"

"No," Denis said immediately. "There's nothing."

"Are you certain?" Aaron asked.

Denis looked out the window. "There is nothing. I'm sure. I was out of control and that had nothing to do with Julie."

Aaron moved his body to get Denis's attention again. "And you don't know of anyone who would want to hurt Julie?"

"I don't," Denis said, shaking his head. "I'm very tired and my pain is increasing. Could you please ask Mrs. Morrow to come in?"

Aaron stood up, drew a business card from his breast pocket and set it on the table beside Denis's bed. "If you can think of anything that will help us find out who killed Julie, please contact me. We would appreciate your help."

He waited for a response, but there was none. Polly took his arm and they left the room. She knocked on Evelyn's door and waited for the woman to respond.

"Are you finished?" Evelyn asked upon opening the door.

"We are," Polly said. "He's asking for you. Says that his pain is increasing."

"He said those words?" Evelyn asked. At Polly's nod, she smiled. "He's lying. That's the exact phrase the doctor used with him. He was just trying to get you to leave."

Evelyn turned back to Leslie Sutworth. "If you will give me just a minute, I'll make sure Denis is comfortable."

"He's my son," Leslie cried. "I want to see him now. I can comfort him." She rushed toward the door.

Evelyn calmly stepped between her and the hallway and said, "We've discussed this, Leslie. I am in charge of your son's care. If you want me to continue, you have to listen to me. I can't argue with you about how I do my job and take care of him at the same time. Do you understand?"

"Why won't anyone let me see Denis?" she wailed and turned back into the room. "Why am I being denied my boy?"

Evelyn pulled the door shut.

"This is going to be a trial," Polly said patting Evelyn's arm.

"No it's not," Evelyn replied. "She and I have come to an agreement and it's in her best interest to follow my instructions. And besides, she goes back to work on Monday. That woman needs interaction with other people. She is much too focused on her oldest son."

"Let me know if you need backup," Polly said.

Evelyn chuckled. "I might take you up on that." She looked at Aaron. "Did you get everything you needed from him?"

"I got all I was going to get today. No one had told him yet that his ex-girlfriend had been killed."

"Oh my," Evelyn said. "I didn't realize."

"He's still processing that information."

"I'd best get in there and check on him, then," she responded. "Thanks for making it quick."

Evelyn slipped quietly into the next room while Aaron and Polly walked out of the addition and into the main part of Sycamore House.

"Do you think there's a connection between the accident and her death?" Polly asked.

"I don't know for sure," Aaron said. "He hasn't had time to sort all of the information out yet."

Polly followed him to the front door. "If I call you to come rescue Leslie Sutworth from my insanity, will you come running?"

"She's a pip," he said with a laugh. "I'm pretty certain she would drive Lydia to drink. Doesn't she have two more kids at home that she should be taking care of?"

"Yes," Polly said flatly. "If it weren't for Evelyn Morrow, I would never have done this for that family. But she believes that this is the right thing to do."

"She's a good woman." Aaron gave Polly a quick hug. "You both are."

Henry's truck pulled up in front of them and Andrew clambered out of the back seat. "Polly. I have your lunch. And Henry stopped at the convenient store and bought ice cream sandwiches." He rushed over to them and handed her two bags.

She waved at Henry and Nate and watched as they took off.

"Are you going upstairs?" she asked Andrew.

"The dogs need to go outside," he responded.

"Could you put the ice cream in the freezer and the food in the fridge? If you don't, the animals will get it."

"Sure!" he exclaimed, grabbed the bags, and went inside.

"You haven't eaten yet?" Aaron asked.

"Andrew and I were out for the day and stopped at Hickory Park in Ames. Nate and Henry were already there, so we joined them. That's when Jeff called me in a panic. Everything was falling apart here and he needed one more person to manage the crazy people."

"That's a great place."

"It might be," Polly rolled her eyes. "But I'm giving up on eating there. Every time I go, a crisis occurs that drags me home. I don't know which one affects the other, but in order to avoid any more terrible events here, I'm just going to stay away. We can do take out, but I can't eat in there."

"Okay," he said tentatively. "That sounds right for you."

She swatted his arm. "Don't you give me any trouble. I am who I am and there's nothing I can do about it."

"And we like you that way."

CHAPTER SIXTEEN

As Polly walked back into Sycamore House, her phone buzzed.

Henry texted her. *"What was the big crisis and why was the Sheriff there? I didn't want to make a big deal out of it in front of Andrew and Nate. Is everything okay?"*

She smiled. *"Everything is fine. Aaron wanted to talk to Denis Sutworth. He dated Julie Smith. The crisis was everything fell apart all at once and Jeff had more than he could handle. S'all okay. I love you."*

"So you really don't care how long I'm out today?"

"Stay out as long as you want. When Rebecca gets here, she'll want to show me her purchases. We'll have fun."

"You're amazing and I love you."

"I know." Before Polly pressed send, she smiled and thought about adding another 'I love you,' but then laughed and sent it anyway.

She walked back to the kitchen to see if Rachel and Sylvie were finding their way out of their crises, but when she heard Sylvie speaking in short, terse sentences, she turned back and headed for the office. Maybe Jeff had had better luck with the mother and daughter.

The conference room door was still closed and she hesitated in front of it, wondering if Jeff needed help, but jumped backwards when she saw the door handle turn. Polly scooted over to Stephanie's desk and tried to look nonchalant as the two women walked out, followed by a red-faced Jeff Lyndsay.

He waved her into her office and shut the door when they were both there.

"How'd that go?" Polly asked.

Jeff leaned over and banged his forehead three times on her desk. When he sat back up, he whimpered and then put his hand on his forehead, rubbing it where he'd smacked it.

"You can't speak yet?" she asked.

"Dumb. Dense. Thick. Feeble. Dim." He brought his hands to his neck and made a show of choking himself. "I've never dealt with anyone so simple-minded. No, that's too generous for them. It was a flat-out refusal to listen to a single word I said. They had it in their heads that the wedding would be here and they could have a fairy-tale reception. No matter that they had given no thought to what it should look like, who would do the food or the decorations, or even who was performing the ceremony!"

Polly didn't know whether to laugh or be shocked. "What?"

"I'm not kidding you. They honestly thought that all they had to do was put the date out there and the world would give them the perfect wedding."

"Have they bought a dress?"

He nodded. Yes, they have a dress. They bought that two years ago when the daughter announced she was going to find a man and get married. Polly," he said. "They bought the dress and then went out to find a husband to accessorize it!"

"He's the dumb one, then. If he's stupid enough to make a choice to be part of that family, I guess you can hardly feel sorry for him. What are we doing about this?"

"They'll have to go to the courthouse in Boone to get married on Friday. I made it clear that needed to happen without our intervention. Monday morning they're meeting here with a wedding planner friend of mine that owes me a huge favor." He shook his head. "I'll probably owe her a couple after this. But she knows what's going on and apparently, they're willing to pay."

Polly muttered, "The mother probably thinks this is the only way to get that stupid girl out of the house and into someone else's hands."

"She's not much better," Jeff replied. "They haven't even sent out invitations. Which is a good thing, I guess. I talked to Ryan at the winery and there's a room available." He threw his hands up in the air. "I think I did all I could do. How are things in the rest of the world?"

"Aaron is gone and Denis is settling in," Polly said. "I started to walk back to the kitchen, but Sylvie sounded, ummm, snippy with someone, so I didn't go far enough to see what was happening."

"I should go back and help. Just to make sure she doesn't chew up and spit out the repairman." He stretched and leaned back in the chair. "Am I walking out the door yet?"

"Sure you are. I'm watching it happen," Polly said with a laugh.

Alistair Greyson walked in the front door and Polly glanced at Jeff, wondering if he'd seen the man. Jeff's eyes were closed and he was breathing slowly through his nose.

"Grey is here," she said quietly. "Do you want me to talk to him?"

"He is?" Jeff jumped up. "I'll talk to him, unless you want to. I don't want to tell you that you can't talk to him."

"Were you falling asleep?" she asked.

"Maybe a little. I was relaxing as best I could. It was just for a second, right?"

"Go on. Talk to Grey."

He gave his head a quick shake and opened the door.

"Grey," he said. "How are you? Come on into my office and we'll talk."

Polly leaned back in her chair. What a strange day this had been so far and with Henry gone for the foreseeable future, it was going to stay strange.

"Polly?"

She looked up to see Andrew standing in her doorway.

"Hey, what's up? I kind of lost track of you."

"I took the dogs out and I'm bored."

"What do you mean you're bored? You got all of those books."

"I know. But I got used to reading with people around and it's too quiet upstairs. When are Rebecca and Kayla coming back?"

She smiled and gestured for him to sit down. "I don't know. I hope they're having a great time with Stephanie. What do you think we should do to keep you from being so bored?"

"We could go out back and set up the croquet set," he mentioned, his voice laced with hope.

There wasn't anything keeping her inside. "That sounds great. Let me change my clothes while you set up the wickets."

"You'll really do it?"

"Why not?" she asked.

"I don't know. You're an adult."

"I'm not too old to play outside. Now go. I'll be there soon."

Andrew tore out of the office.

Before Polly could get up, Alistair Greyson was standing in her doorway.

He made a sweeping gesture into a bow and said, "I apologize profusely for my behavior last night and for the fact that I caused you to doubt my commitment to the honor you bestowed on me as manager of your fine inn. I hope you accept my sincere apology and will offer me yet another opportunity to prove my worth to you."

She thought through all of the words that he had just spilled out and finally said, "Of course. I assume that you have worked everything out with Jeff."

"I have," Grey said. "He is a man with a generous heart and on my honor I will not disappoint him."

"Mistakes and failures are part of life," Polly said. "Honesty and honor go a long way to covering them, though, don't they?"

He took a deep breath and released it. "I may fail again," he said.

"We all do," she replied. "It isn't the end of the world."

"If I might ask one more boon?" he asked.

"What can I do for you?"

"It's what I might be able to do for you. But I would have to ask that you trust me, and that is something I have yet to earn."

"What is it, Grey?" Polly asked.

He glanced toward the addition. "I'd like the opportunity to speak with the young man who set in motion all of the things that brought us to this point."

Polly hesitated.

"I know that you know nothing of my background, but Mr. Lindsay does. I've spent the last seven years working as a clinical therapist with young people. I would like the opportunity to see if there is anything I can do for him."

"You have?" She didn't know what to make of that. "Why are you working as a hotel manager in a small town?"

"It's the right thing to do in this season of my life," he replied. "But I am qualified."

"I don't have any authority to tell you whether or not you can spend time with him. That would need to be a discussion you have with Evelyn Morrow, his mother, and anyone else who is involved with Denis's care." Polly thought about it. "And probably Denis himself."

Grey nodded gravely. "I understand."

"He has just gotten here," Polly continued. "Let me mention your request to Mrs. Morrow."

He swept his arm in front of him and took another bow, "Thank you kindly. And now I will return to my work. I have been away long enough for this day."

Grey strode out and as she watched him walk past the windows in the hallway and out the front door, all Polly could think was that he needed a cape and a tricorn hat.

Polly's phone rang and she was surprised to see that the caller was Evelyn Morrow. "Evelyn?" she asked. "How can I help you?"

"Would you mind bringing your no-nonsense self over for a few minutes? I'm sorry to bother you, but I'm getting nowhere and I need just a bit of assistance."

"The mother?" Polly asked.

"You are a smart girl. I can't seem to get through to her."

"I'll be right there."

She walked out and stuck her head in Jeff's office. "I'm going to give Evelyn Morrow some backup. If you hear screaming, come get me."

"What's going on?"

"I think she's having trouble with Leslie Sutworth. What happened today? Did we get a crazy-person bomb dropped on us?"

"Can I help?"

"Let me see what I can do. You're close enough that if we need you, we'll let you know."

He grinned and waved her away.

"I don't want to, I don't want to, I don't want to," Polly muttered under her breath as she walked toward the addition. She opened the door and walked down the short hall to Evelyn. "What do you want me to do?"

Evelyn opened the door to Denis's room, where Leslie was kneeling at his bedside, crying and sobbing. "She won't leave." She pulled the door shut again. "I have been firm with her, I have cajoled, I have begged, I have wheedled. I've done everything I can think to do outside of grabbing her legs out from under her and dragging her by the ankles into the hallway. I thought I'd save that for the last resort."

"Physically removing her is off the table?" Polly asked.

Evelyn shrugged. "If it comes down to it, I suppose not. I understand that she's his mother and is worried about him, but good heavens, Polly. He's had issues throughout his life and she's had a full week to get used to his physical disability."

"Having him here is new," Polly said. "She's always known where he was at night. He lived with her, right?"

"I suppose that's true."

"And when he was in the hospital, she knew that he was safe with nurses and doctors. So, this is new."

"You're right. Maybe I just needed you to calm *me* down," Evelyn said. "I've about had it up to here with the woman." She waved her hand in front of her forehead. "She's been hovering in my space since early this morning."

"And here I thought you were one of the most patient and kind women I'd ever met," Polly said.

"I'm good with the dying," Evelyn replied. "Not so good with wailing family members. But I can usually kick them out when they get too far out of control. This woman simply won't listen."

"Let's see what we can do." Polly opened the door, took a deep breath and said, "Mrs. Sutworth?"

When the kneeling woman didn't respond, Polly walked across the room and put her hand on Leslie Sutworth's shoulder. "Mrs. Sutworth, I'm speaking to you."

"You can't make me leave him," Leslie said.

Polly put all of the steel she could muster into her voice. "Stand up." She accompanied her command with a firm grip on the woman's upper arm.

Leslie followed Polly's lead and stood. "You can't make me go away. I won't go. He needs his mother."

"Come with me," Polly said and took Leslie's hand, drawing her across the room to the door.

"Noooooo," Leslie cried and grabbed the door frame.

"Do *not* be a fool," Polly said flatly. "You're acting like an imbecile. Come out into the hallway and discuss this calmly with me." She glared at the woman. "Right. Now."

With a look of defeat, Leslie released the door frame and followed Polly into the hallway. Evelyn quickly stepped inside the room, gave Polly a grateful glance and shut the door.

"You people are horrible," Leslie wailed. "You are trying to keep me from my son."

"No one is trying to keep you from him, but you are making it difficult for the woman you've hired to care for him to do her job."

"But he needs his mother," she cried out.

"Don't we all," Polly replied. "How old is Denis?"

"He's twenty-two," Leslie said. "But that doesn't make any difference. He's still my boy. And he's fragile and can't live on his own."

Polly slipped her arm around Leslie's back and walked her toward the front door of the addition. "He isn't on his own, but he does need you to give him space. How is he supposed to get better when you are in there crying all the time?"

"How does that make it any worse?" Leslie asked. "At least he knows that I'm there and that I love him."

"Don't you think maybe he needs positive emotions right now?" Polly responded. "Fewer tears and more joy? Have you told him yet that you are glad he's here or have you spent every moment that you have with him wailing over his injuries?"

"But he's my son," Leslie protested.

There wasn't going to be any good way to get through to this woman, but Evelyn had asked for help, Polly had agreed, and something had to be done. If Denis's psychiatrists were blaming the boy's father for his issues and not looking at this poor woman, Polly wanted to send them all back to school.

"Yes he is and it is time for you to let him grow up and start living for himself. You can't hold onto him forever."

"But I can't let him go when he's in the middle of a crisis."

"Tell me, Leslie," Polly said quietly. "When were the times in your life that you felt you grew up the most? Were they when your parents did everything for you? Were they when life was easy? Or did your biggest periods of growth occur when you had to struggle?"

That stopped the woman. She stood, staring at Polly with her mouth open, about to deliver another protest. But she had no response.

"Are you trying to tell me that all of this is going to help Denis grow up?" she asked.

"I can't tell you that for certain, but I'm positive that if you hover over him, wailing and crying and throwing tantrums when you have to leave, that isn't helping him. He's the one who has to heal, in body, mind and spirit. You can't do it for him. The only thing you can do is encourage him, pray for him and love him."

"I pray for him every minute of every day," Leslie said.

Polly smiled. "I'm sure you do. Now I also know that you have two other children who probably need to see their mother be strong. You shouldn't force them to be the strong adults in the family. You know that, right?"

"This whole thing has thrown a wrench into my life, Polly. I don't know how I'm going to get through it."

"One of the things I've learned is that every crisis has an end. It might be five years down the road, five days in front of you or it might happen in five minutes. But we can get through it. You can handle this. You've raised three children on your own for several years. You've done that. You can do this."

Leslie's shoulders sagged and she let out a small whimpering sigh. "He'll be safe here tonight?"

"He'll be safe here every night. Evelyn is a wonderful caregiver. You hired her to do this job and she wants to do it well. You just have to let her."

"I haven't cooked or done any laundry for a week," Leslie said. "The kids have tried to keep up, but they have their own lives."

"Go kiss your son goodbye and head home. Try to sleep tonight. I'll ask Evelyn to text you when she has Denis settled for the night and when they wake up in the morning. If there are any problems, you'll be the first to know. And tomorrow, why don't you spend the day with your family at home..."

"We should probably go to church."

"Then, do that and bring lunch over with the other two kids. Make Denis's life here as normal as possible. Then go home and spend Sunday evening preparing for your week back at work. Can you do this for everyone involved?"

All of the exhaustion of the week settled on the woman. Her eyes glazed over, her body sagged with relief and she nodded. "I can be strong. I'll do it for my boy. I'll do it for my family."

Polly walked back to Denis's door with Leslie and lightly tapped on it before opening it.

"Evelyn?" she said. "Leslie is going to say goodbye to her son. She won't be back until tomorrow after church to have lunch with him. I've promised that you will text her when he's settled for the night and when you are both up in the morning. And I've also promised that she'll be the first to know if something goes wrong."

"Of course," Evelyn said and stood up from the chair she'd been sitting in.

Leslie approached her son, bent over to kiss his forehead and then whispered in his ear. She stroked his hair and then walked away from him, tears filling her eyes. She pushed Polly away, when Polly tried to approach her. "I'm leaving now. I don't want to talk to anyone."

Polly stepped out into the hallway and watched the woman walk out the main door to the outside sidewalk and then turned back to look at Evelyn.

"Thank you," Evelyn said quietly. "I don't even know if Denis was fully aware of what was happening here. He's had a long day and has been in and out of sleep."

"I doubt if this is over, but at least you two can rest tonight," Polly said. "Feel free to let me know if you need more help."

"Thank you again," Evelyn said.

"Speaking of help." Polly stopped moving and turned back. "Have you met the other man from the accident?"

Evelyn nodded. "Just once. He came down to see Denis in the hospital. He seems like a nice man."

"He'd like to stop in and spend time with Denis every once in a while. Apparently, he has some kind of therapy background. Can he contact you?"

"We'll see," Evelyn said, her brow furrowed in concern. "I'd like to know more about him and I'd also like to know why he wants to be involved."

Polly chuckled. "He's kind of a knight errant. We all are looking at him as a Don Quixote."

"He does talk funny," Evelyn agreed.

"I doubt that he has any ulterior motive. He's a genuinely nice man. He probably just wants to help."

Evelyn nodded. "Let's see how it plays out."

CHAPTER SEVENTEEN

Vaguely remembering that she had something else to do, Polly flopped down on the sofa. When she realized her dogs were gone, she remembered the game of croquet. Maybe Andrew would get distracted by something else so she could shut her eyes for a few minutes.

The situation in the kitchen had gotten worse while Polly dealt with the Sutworth's. Sylvie had stopped speaking in coherent sentences and the repairman was red-faced as he scrambled to find the problem. When Polly looked in, Rachel gave her a slight head shake and before Sylvie could see her, ducked back down as she created plates of salad. Polly had run for the front steps.

She heaved herself back up off the sofa and headed for the back door. Before she was in Henry's office, the front door opened and close and Rebecca called out.

"Polly, are you up here?"

"Back here, honey. Did you have fun?"

"You have to see what I got," Rachel yelled across the apartment.

Polly glanced at the back steps. Andrew was going to be

frustrated with her. This was bad. She had no idea which way to go. She started for the living room, turned to go to the stairway, moved her body to face the living room and then stopped and laughed at herself. She couldn't move. Either way, one of her favorite people was going to be disappointed.

"Polly?" Rebecca called again, closer as she came toward Henry's office. Rebecca stopped in the doorway. "Were you going somewhere?"

"Andrew is waiting for me to come play croquet. It's been absolutely nuts here today."

Rebecca nodded. "Okay. I guess this can wait. It's no big deal." She headed back toward the living room.

"Wait, honey. I want to see what you bought. I'm so glad you had a great day," Polly ran after her and put her hand on Rebecca's shoulder. "Andrew can wait a few more minutes and tonight when it's just you and me, I want you to model everything. Now, pour it all out here on the sofa and show me."

The girl lit up and ran back into the living room and returned with two large shopping bags and three plastic bags.

"Holy cow," Polly exclaimed. "What did you do?"

"We went to the Goodwill in Boone and then the one in Ames and then we went to Target. Stephanie took us to McDonald's for breakfast and then we went out for lunch and on the way home, even though I was stuffed to the brim, she stopped at Dairy Queen and I had a twist cone. I'm not going to eat for a week!"

Polly stuck her lower lip out in a pout. "And I was going to get pizza for dinner. It's just you and me. Henry is hanging out with Nate all day."

"I'll try to eat a piece," Rebecca said. "Is that okay?"

"I'm teasing you," Polly said with a laugh. "Show me what you bought. Just dump it all out right here."

Rebecca upended the two shopping bags and then shook the items out of the three plastic bags. There were blue jeans and blouses, skirts and t-shirts. They'd bought shoes at Target and Polly smiled to see new underthings. She was glad Rebecca had an opportunity to go shopping with girls.

"I got this for you," Rebecca said and reached into the pile. She came up with a pretty silver pin of a horse.

Polly pulled her in for a hug. "Thank you. It's beautiful."

"I saw things at Goodwill that I wanted to buy for presents, but Stephanie said we were buying school clothes. She said we could go shopping before Christmas if I still wanted to buy them."

"Good for her," Polly said. "There is plenty of time. But this is wonderful. I love it. Thank you."

Rebecca picked up two of the t-shirts, one that someone had tie-dyed and another with wild stripes. "Stephanie called me a hippie. Look at these jeans." She dug in the pile and came up with a pair of jeans that had flowers appliquéd on them.

"You might be," Polly said with a smile. "This looks like an amazing shopping day."

"It was the best." Rebecca hugged Polly again. "Thank you for letting me go with them."

"I tell you what. Let's wash these things while we go outside with Andrew and then tonight, you can do a fashion show for me."

Rebecca looked down at her new clothes and dug into the pile again. "I bought a hat," she said.

"Cool. What does it look like?"

"It's a blue jean hat. Look."

She put on a blue denim beret and Polly chuckled. "You are a hippie girl. We can wash that too. Let's take it all downstairs."

Rebecca stuffed most of the clothes back into a bag and reached for the other one. They took the bags downstairs and sorted clothes into a first load.

"Andrew is going to kill me," Polly whispered to her as they headed for the back door.

"Why?"

"It's been an hour since I told him to set up the wickets."

They found him with Doug and Billy sitting in Adirondacks with glasses of lemonade. Andrew jumped when Obiwan leapt off his lap to greet Polly. Han followed suit and stopped when Andrew held on to the leash.

He turned around in his chair and said, "About time."

Polly saw a book tucked under his leg. "I'm guessing you found plenty to keep you busy. Hi guys," she said to Doug and Billy.

"He was down here looking pathetic and hot, so we brought lemonade." Billy nodded toward a bucket sitting along the back wall of Sycamore House. "We took care of the dogs, too."

"Thanks for taking care of all my boys," she said. "Who's up for croquet?"

"I didn't set it up," Andrew said.

"Why not? I'm ready to play."

"When you didn't show up, I knew you were busy, so I got a book. Then the guys came out and we were talking and now it's this time."

"So, nothing?" she asked. "We have plenty of mallets and balls. We can all play."

"Did you have fun being a girl today?" Andrew asked Rebecca, sarcasm lacing his voice.

Polly waited to see how Rebecca would react. When the girl's face dropped, Polly took a loud, deep breath.

"Come on, Doug," Billy said. "Let's take the dogs upstairs and clean the kitchen before Rachel gets there. She's had a bad day and we have a dirty kitchen."

Doug looked back and forth between his friend and Polly and nodded. He took the empty lemonade glass out of Andrew's hand, bent over and said quietly, yet loud enough for Polly to hear. "You walked into it. Figure out how to walk out before they kick your butt." He and Billy and their dogs went into the garage, leaving a sullen Andrew on his chair.

"They're chickens," Andrew said.

Polly grinned. "I don't blame them. Here's the deal. You have a couple of options. First of all, the two of you can sit here and talk this out. You are both making assumptions about the other person that aren't true." She paused.

Rebecca looked at her. "What's the second option?"

"Yeah. I don't like that one," Andrew said.

Polly laughed out loud. "The second is even worse."

He rolled his eyes. "What does that mean?"

"I sit here and embarrass both of you by asking pointed questions and *making* you talk. Now choose, because this ends today."

Rebecca dropped into an Adirondack across from Andrew. She shrugged. "Whatever."

"Yeah. Whatever," Andrew echoed.

"You two seriously want me to get involved?" Polly asked.

"Well, she won't talk to me. She just shuts me out," Andrew said.

"That's because you just talk and talk and talk and never listen," Rebecca replied. "You say stuff and then it's like it's over."

"I do not."

"Yes you do. It drives me crazy. Who made you the boss of our friendship?"

"Me!" he cried out. "You're the one who's always in charge. You're the one who gets to say yes or no to whatever we do. And most of the time you want to do stuff with Kayla. You never want to do things with me anymore."

Polly patted her thigh to beckon the dogs and backed quietly away from the circle. Even if they were yelling at each other, at least they were talking. The most difficult thing they would have to face was forgiving each other and then letting it go.

~~~

Henry came out of the bathroom, fresh and clean from a shower. When he'd gotten home from Nate's, he was a mess. He'd tried to hug Polly, but she relegated him to the shower with no extra love. Rebecca was already in bed, exhausted from her day.

"How far did you two get today?" Polly asked, putting her book on the bedside table.

He smirked. "I won't even bother to explain it. Your eyes will just glaze over and I'll end up talking to myself."

"Okay," she said. "What percentage of the cars did you finish?"

He sat down on the edge of the bed and pushed Han closer to Polly so he had space to lie down. "I don't know how to measure it," he said. "We spent time working on the frame, blasting rust off and repainting it. It won't be too long until Nate and I are shaping wood panels at my shop."

"See, I understood that," she said. "What was so hard about saying those words?" Polly shifted to her side, doing her best to avoid pushing Leia off the edge of the bed.

"You're right. I'm sorry." He turned inward to face her and pulled Han close so the dog tucked in to him. Han leaned back and gave Henry a sloppy lick on his chin, trying for the mouth, but missing it as Henry dodged. Henry laughed, put his hand on the dog's head and pushed it down.

"Are you going back tomorrow?" Polly asked.

"If that's okay with you. Nate never has time without the twins around. I'd like to take advantage of this."

She nodded. "That makes sense. And you certainly don't have to ask permission."

"I've never done anything like this," he said with a laugh. "It's always been work or you since we got married."

"Then this is a good idea. You should do it more often."

"When the twins are older and don't require so much parental intervention. Maybe," he said. "Nate doesn't want Joss to feel like she's the only caregiver."

"She doesn't," Polly responded. "That's the last thing she'd ever feel. Especially with him. He's a good dad. Can you imagine how insane it will be when they have a bunch of kids?"

Henry stretched and rolled his shoulders. "It's so strange to think about that. What about us? Do you think Rebecca will be the last kid we adopt?"

"I don't think so," Polly said. "But what if she is? I don't want to do what Nate and Joss are doing. I'm not ready to actively seek out babies."

He started laughing and Polly glared at him. "What?" she asked.

"Two things occurred to me in a split second," he replied.

"What?"

"First. You need to quit talking about not wanting to have babies around, because something weird will happen and you'll end up rescuing a family of kids that have babies. So be quiet. Don't say those words ever again."

Polly hung her head in mock shame. "You're right. I'll shut up. What was the second thing?"

"I will always be happy with whatever our family looks like. If Rebecca is the only child we have, that's okay. If we end up with fifteen more, that's okay too." He reached over and rubbed her arm. "The only thing I ever wanted was you. After that, it's all icing on the cake."

Polly leaned across the dog and kissed him, long and slow. When she lay back on her pillow, she smiled. "That was the right thing to say."

"I have my moments." He propped himself up on his elbow. "Did Rebecca have a good day today?"

"She really did," Polly said. "Shopping and eating out with someone other than me. And she came home with a pile of clothes. She's got great taste. We had a fashion show tonight in her bedroom and she showed me all of the possibilities for combinations based on the wardrobe she'd built. After we went through her clothes, she has a few bags to take back to Goodwill. That girl has grown since she got here."

"I didn't even think about it," Henry said.

"Didn't think about what?"

His eyes grew misty and he said. "We should have a place here to mark her height. What if she's already as tall as she is going to be? We never did that for her. Don't you remember your wall?"

"Mine was the bathroom door sill upstairs," Polly said. "I remember doing that with Dad. We always measured me on Saturday mornings before we went downstairs for breakfast." She looked at Henry. "Where was yours?"

"It still is," he said. "If you go upstairs, there's a small corner between my bedroom and the bathroom. Lonnie's was on one side of the corner and mine was on the other. Mom painted the hallway several times, but that corner has never changed color. Can we figure out someplace to do this for Rebecca and keep it up for any other kids that come into our lives?"

Polly smiled at him. "What about the little hallway leading to our bathroom? We don't ever have to paint that wall again. No one will see it. There's plenty of wall for as many kids as we want to have."

"What was the deal with all the craziness here today?" Henry asked. "Did you ever get lunch?"

"Nope," Polly said. "It was one thing after another. I hope Evelyn can manage Leslie Sutworth. She had to ask for my help today. The woman was just plain crazy. She wouldn't leave and with all that wailing and crying..." Polly pursed her lips. "I don't want to be rude, but no wonder that kid has emotional and mental problems. She's a nut. And if his dad was tough to live with, he didn't have a chance. Especially if there was even a hint of a chemical imbalance. He's never had a moment of freedom or peace. If nothing else, I hope we can help him find that here. And maybe give him enough courage to find a way to move out and live on his own."

"How did things work out with Grey?"

"I don't know," she said with a shrug. "He apologized for his behavior last night, but I'm not going to check up on him. I can't imagine that if he's an alcoholic, he can just make a decision to quit drinking and really do it. We'll see, though. I'm not giving up on him."

"Of course you aren't," Henry replied. "You haven't had a good rescue in a long time."

"Hey!" she said, loud enough to cause Han and Obiwan to both look up at her. "Sorry."

"You know Aunt Betty is an alcoholic," he said quietly.

"What? I had no idea."

"She hasn't had a drink in years, but when I was young, something happened and she started drinking. She'll talk to you about the alcoholism, but she still won't talk about what happened."

"Do you think she lost a baby?"

"No, that's not it," he said. "They did have a couple of miscarriages and she was open about those. Dad and Mom probably know, but no one talks about it. She was a mess up until I went to high school. One night Uncle Dick called Dad in a panic. She'd passed out and he couldn't get her up. They took her to the hospital and Dick finally told Dad what had been going on. Dad cried. When Aunt Betty saw that, I think she realized she was at the bottom and got help. But she'll still tell you it isn't easy."

"I didn't know any alcoholics when I was growing up," Polly said. "There wasn't much alcohol in the house. Is that weird?"

He gave a slight nod. "There were probably more than you realized. I worried about some of my college friends. They wouldn't stop drinking. As soon as they got back from class in the afternoon, they had to have a beer, then another and another. Weekends were ridiculous. It was all the time with some of them."

"Well, I hope it doesn't take Grey too long to figure it out," she said.

"What will you do if he doesn't?"

"That's the question, isn't it?" Polly put her head on the pillow. "They say it's a disease. I wouldn't fire someone for being sick."

"But you don't want him to screw things up at the inn," Henry said. "You don't owe him anything."

"I suppose. Except for the fact that he's a good guy and deserves as many chances as I can give him. He didn't hurt anything last night."

"But he was incommunicado. What if a guest had needed something? If it's his job, shouldn't we expect him to be there?"

"Not twenty-four seven," Polly said. "I don't know. I just have a good feeling about him. Even if it takes a while to get there."

"It might." Henry took her hand. "But it's why I love you. You see things in people that I miss. I trust you in that, even if I protest."

Polly leaned over and whispered. "Andrew and Rebecca had their first fight. He thinks they should be boyfriend and girlfriend and go to the dance together. She wants to be more casual."

Henry's eyes grew big and he looked at her in shock. "They should be casual! What's this about being boyfriend and girlfriend? They haven't even started seventh grade yet. She isn't dating until she's at least sixteen. No way, Jose! That's not happening. Not in my house."

Polly started laughing and couldn't stop.

"What?" he demanded.

"You, you big old papa bear, you. This is Andrew and Rebecca. They've been best friends since we've known her."

"Well, they aren't going to be dating," he sputtered.

"That's right. That was what they had the fight about. I think they're both afraid of all the new kids that come into school this year and all of the new experiences. They're growing up. This was Andrew's way of making sure that things would stay the same. But Rebecca is looking forward to changes. She feels the freedom of not worrying about her mom and wants to try new things."

"They aren't dating," Henry said under his breath. "I'll take that kid out behind the woodshed and show him why."

Polly burst into laughter again. "I love you, Henry Sturtz."

"I love you too, but you can't upset me like this. I'll never sleep now."

"I didn't mean to upset you. Rebecca handled it okay. I had to talk to Andrew this morning about giving her some freedom..."

"Freedom? He's not dating her. Not until they're eighteen."

"I thought you said sixteen."

"It's going to be twenty-one pretty soon," he said.

"Got it." Polly wiggled closer to him and pushed Han down and away from Henry.

"What are you doing?" Henry asked.

"I'm going to help you go to sleep. Do you have a problem with that?"

He turned and shut off the light on his table, allowing the moon to bathe the room in its glow. "I'm still upset, but if you kiss me on the lips again, I'm sure I'll relax."

CHAPTER EIGHTEEN

Every muscle in Polly's body twitched when the phone on her desk rang. It never did that. Her friends called her cell and if something came into the main number, Stephanie let her know the call was for her before sending it through. She looked at it and then at Stephanie who was in the doorway.

"It's not from me," Stephanie said.

It rang one more time and Polly snatched it up. "Sycamore House, may I help you?"

"Is this Abby?" The young girl's voice on the other end of the phone wasn't familiar, but she sounded upset.

"No, I'm sorry you must have a wrong number. This is Sycamore House," Polly said. "Can I help you?"

"This has to be Abby. I need Abby. Where is she?"

"You need to try to call Abby again. You punched in a wrong number."

"This is Abby's number. She put it into the phone so I could call if I needed her. I need her." The girl was growing more upset.

"Tell me what your name is," Polly said. "Mine is Polly. Is your mom there? Can I talk to her?"

"I'm Gina and Mom is at work. Abby is supposed to come over if I need her. Bean fell down and hurt his head. He's bleeding all over and I need Abby!"

Polly took a piece of paper out of her desk and wrote on it. *Get Kayla and Rebecca from upstairs? I need them.* She handed it to Stephanie, who ran out of the office.

"Gina, what's your last name," Polly asked. "Can you tell me where you live?"

"Bean is dying. Where's Abby?" The call ended and Polly looked at the phone in her hand. She replaced it in its cradle and realized her hand was shaking.

Rebecca and Kayla ran into the office and Rebecca said, "What do you need? Stephanie said it was urgent."

"I don't know who else to ask," Polly said. "Do you know anybody in the elementary school named Gina? She has a brother that she calls Bean."

The two girls looked at each other.

"There's a Gina Landry," Rebecca said. "She's a second grader and I think she has a brother named Brennan. He's in fourth grade."

"Do they live here in town?"

Kayla looked up at her sister. "They live out by us in a trailer."

"Come with me. We're taking a ride," Polly said.

The girls followed her through the auditorium to the back door and her truck.

"Is something wrong with Gina?" Rebecca asked, once they were settled into the back seat.

Polly backed out of the garage and turned to head for the street. "I don't know. But she just called my office number looking for Abby. She said her brother was hurt."

"He's always hurting himself, if it's the same boy I'm thinking of," Kayla said. "He comes to school all the time with bandages on."

They drove past the inn and Polly waved at Grey, who was standing in front of the rooms, talking to one of the cleaning ladies.

"That man is kinda different," Kayla said. "He talks weird."

"He's a nice man," Polly responded. "He talks the way people used to talk. Very courteous and polite."

Kayla leaned forward as they entered the trailer park. "She lives down a few spaces from us. Turn here."

Polly followed Kayla's directions to a blue trailer with an attractive deck in front and flowers in flower boxes on the front windows. She pulled in beside it and said, "You two stay here unless I beckon for you, okay?"

She didn't wait for them to respond, but jumped out and headed for the front door.

The inside door was open when Polly knocked on the sill. "Is anyone here?" she called out.

A young girl ran to the door and said, "Who are you?"

"I'm Polly. Are you Gina? Were we just talking on the telephone?"

The girl looked at Polly, then back in toward the back of the trailer and then at Polly again. "He hurt himself really bad this time. There's blood everywhere."

"Did you try to call your Mom?"

"She can't take calls at work. They get mad at her."

"I know you aren't supposed to let strangers come into your house, but do you know Rebecca and Kayla?" Polly waved at the girls in the truck, then turned her hand and gestured for them to join her.

"I've seen them before. They're older than me, though."

Rebecca came up to stand beside Polly. "Hi, Gina," she said. "Is your brother hurt?"

"He's bleeding," the little girl said.

"This is Polly," Rebecca said. "She's my mom now. Can she come in and try to help?"

Gina looked to the back of the trailer again and finally she said, "Bean can't talk anymore. Maybe you better." She tripped the lock on the storm door and pushed it open.

"Can you show me where he is?" Polly asked.

The girl took Polly down a hallway and when she turned into

the bathroom, it looked as if there had been a murder. Blood was everywhere. A boy was lying on the tile floor with a towel wrapped around his head.

Polly stepped back out and took a deep breath. She went in, knelt down beside him, and said, "Bean, can you hear me?"

His eyes fluttered open and she breathed a sigh of relief, then drew out her phone. "I'm calling the EMTs. He needs a doctor. Gina, why don't you go out and talk to Rebecca and Kayla while Bean and I wait. Okay?"

Gina shook her head. "I'm not leaving him. We're supposed to take care of each other." She sat down beside her brother and took his hand into her lap, clutching it with both of her little hands.

Polly dialed 9-1-1 and gave them her location and the situation in front of her. When she hung up, she said, "Gina, I need you to find a blanket for your brother. He's lost a lot of blood and his body is going to be cold. He needs to warm up."

"But it's summertime," Gina protested.

"I know, but this is different. Go get a blanket. Hurry." Polly tried to put as much urgency into her voice as possible. The girl jumped up and ran out of the bathroom.

"Someone is coming to help you, Bean. You're going to be okay," Polly said. "Just hold on. Can you tell me what happened?"

He mumbled something and she bent in closer to hear what he said, but that was when Gina came running back in with a comforter. "I took this off my bed," she said. "Well, the end of my bed because it's too hot to have on in the summer. Mom's going to be mad if it gets blood on it, though."

"That will wash out. And I doubt that she'll be mad at you for taking care of your brother."

"He hurts himself all the time. Mom says he's always pulling stupid stunts. She says that sometime he's going to do something so stupid he can't come back from it."

"What did he do this time?" Polly asked.

Gina took her brother's hand again. "He fell off the roof."

"How did he cut his head?"

"When he broke one of Mom's flowerpots out back with his

head. He made it to the bathroom and passed out on the floor and fell down again and hit his head on the pot."

The poor kid probably had a concussion.

"We need to call your Mom," Polly said. "I think he's going to have to go to the hospital. He's hurt pretty badly. Do you have her phone number?"

"She'll get in trouble," Gina repeated.

"I'll make the call and deal with whatever trouble comes from it. Can you get me her number?"

The sounds of sirens interrupted whatever Gina was going to do and Polly stepped out of the room to meet them. The first person in the door was the same young man who had brought Denis to Sycamore House. Polly led him to the bathroom and told him what she knew, then turned to ask Gina for her mother's number again.

It took a few moments to get through the switchboard, but Polly finally made them understand that it was an emergency and they put her on hold.

"Hello, this is Darla Landry. Who is this? What's wrong?"

"Mrs. Landry, my name is Polly Giller. I own Sycamore House here in Bellingwood."

"I know who you are. Why are you calling me?"

"I'm at your home with your children. Your son fell off the roof and cut his head open quite badly and I'm afraid he might have a concussion. We've called the EMTs and they believe he should go to the hospital."

"What? How did you get there?" Before Polly could respond, the woman said, "I'm clocking out and I'll be home in a minute."

"I can tell you everything, but would you talk to the EMT. They may direct you to the hospital in Boone instead."

Polly handed her phone over and after a short discussion with the boy's mother, he handed the phone back and they wheeled him out of the trailer.

"Are you still there, Mrs. Landry?" Polly asked.

"Yes. Do you have Gina? Where's her babysitter?"

"Is that a girl named Abby?"

"Yes. I knew she was going to be late this morning, but she should be there by now. I don't know what to do about Gina."

"I can take her back to Sycamore House with me if you don't mind. My daughter, Rebecca, and her friend, Kayla are with me. They know Gina and Brennan from school."

The woman took a short breath. "Rebecca is the girl you adopted after her mother died, right?"

"That's right. I promise you that Sycamore House is a safe place for kids."

"I know that," Mrs. Landry said. "My kids did the after school program there on Mondays. Gina knows the building. You're okay with this? You don't mind?"

"I don't at all."

"How did you get there, though?"

"I'm not sure how it happened, but the number that the girl, Abby, programmed into your phone came into my office," Polly said. "Gina sounded worried and I asked my girls if they knew who she was and we came down here. Kayla lives not far from you. Can you give me any more information on Abby? What's her last name? I feel like we should check on her."

"It's Abby Belran. I'll try to reach her, but she lives up on Monroe. One-o-nine. It's on the north side. A little blue house. If I hear that she's okay and just skipped out, I'll call you back. This is your cell phone, right?"

"It sure is."

"Does Gina still have the other phone?"

"Yes she does."

"May I speak with her?"

Polly handed her phone to Gina. "Your mom wants to talk to you."

"Mommy?" Gina asked. She listened and looked up at Polly and then glanced at Kayla and Rebecca, nodding the entire time. "Okay. I will." Finally she handed the phone back to Polly.

"Mrs. Landry?"

"Gina knows she's going with you. Thank you so much for taking care of us today."

"No problem. I'm glad I was here. I'll talk to you later when you know more about your son."

They hung up and Polly glanced back toward the bathroom. She thought about the amount of blood that had been in that room and all of a sudden, she saw spots and felt dizzy. She groped for the wall and Rebecca reached out to grab her arm.

"Are you okay?"

"Chair. Sit me down," Polly said.

Rebecca and Kayla led her to the couch, Polly sat down hard, and then dropped her head between her knees. She took a few deep breaths and waited for the dizziness to pass.

"What's wrong?" Kayla asked.

Rebecca chuckled. "Blood." She rubbed Polly's shoulders and said, "I couldn't believe you were in that room taking care of that boy. I thought you would pass out."

Polly looked up at her. "I guess he needed me more than I needed to faint. I hate to ask this of you, but are either of you in good enough shape to be able to gather up those towels and the blanket? I want to take them back to Sycamore House and wash the blood out before it sets in too much."

"I got it," Kayla said. "Do you have a laundry basket, Gina?"

Once they were in the truck, Polly took several deep breaths before driving away. She turned to the girls in the back seat. "Gina, have you ever been to Abby's house?"

Gina nodded. "I know right where it is."

"Okay. I want to check on her next. Does she live with her parents?"

"Her mom is dead," Gina said. "It's just her and her dad. She has a sister in college, but Abby's still in high school. Her dad isn't home much. I think he drives a truck."

Polly drove back onto the highway, turning north on Elm Street. She drove past the downtown and turned left on Monroe Street. Gina pointed to a small blue house and Polly pulled into the driveway. She checked her phone to make sure that Darla Landry hadn't called back, but there had been no calls.

"You kids stay here," Polly said. "I'll just knock on the door and see if she answers. Maybe she overslept and had her phone turned to silent."

She walked up the steps to the front porch. When there was no response to the doorbell, she opened the storm door and rapped sharply on the door. "Abby Belran, are you in there? I'm Polly Giller. Are you here?" She knocked twice more and when there was no answer, she got frustrated and tried the door knob.

The door opened and Polly stepped partway in. "Abby? Abby Belran? Are you here?"

Still no response. Polly didn't know whether to be nosy and check further or just to leave it. It felt wrong to walk away, so she stepped back on the porch and held up a finger to the girls, telling them she'd be just another minute.

"Abby? I'm Polly Giller and I'm here to check on you. Are you here?" Polly had entered into the kitchen at the front of the house. She turned left into a small living room. The door to what looked like a high school girl's room was ajar, so she crossed the room and pushed it open, then dropped to her knees.

"No," she said quietly. "Not again.

The young girl lay half on and half off her bed, blood congealed in a pool below her. A large gash was opened at the back of her head and beside her was a broken marble clock that was obviously the murder weapon.

Polly stepped back out into the living room and then in her need to get as far away from it as possible, walked into the kitchen and made a call.

"Oh Polly," Aaron Merritt said. "What have you found?"

"She's just a high school girl," Polly said. "And she lives with her dad. I know this will destroy him. I can't imagine what Dad would have done if I'd died, too. Her mother is gone..."

"Polly, where are you," he asked gently.

"I'm at 109 Monroe. Abby Belran. I've seen too much blood this morning, Aaron. I have three kids in my truck and I don't know what to do next."

"Can you call someone to get the girls? I'm on my way. Just hold on, I'll be there as fast as I can."

"I'll call Sylvie. Maybe she and Rachel can come up. This has been a rough morning, Aaron."

"Make the call. Go sit outside. We'll be there."

Polly went out the door to the porch and gave a quick wave to the truck and started to call Sylvie, but remembered that she was trying desperately to get the bakery up and running. She'd come, but that wasn't fair. Joss would do this for her, but she was out of town. She made another call.

"Hello, dear," Lydia said. "How are you this bright August morning? Are you ready for the kids to be back in school?"

"Hello Lydia and no, I love having them around. It will be nice to have a schedule again, though. I have a favor to ask. Are you busy this morning?"

"I'm making a chicken casserole for Sandy and Benji Davis. They just brought home a new baby. Why do you ask?"

"Is the casserole in the oven yet?"

"No, I just finished mixing it. Do you need me?"

"I really do. I would have called Sylvie, but she's got too much on her mind this week."

"No, honey," Lydia said. "You were right to call me. How can I help you?"

"I have three girls sitting in the back of my truck and I just had to call your husband."

"Oh, honey. I hoped that poor Julie Smith would be enough."

"Me too, but I walked into it this morning. I swear, Lydia, sometimes the universe goes out of its way to get me involved. Would you be able to pick the girls up and take them back to Sycamore House for me?"

"Kayla and Rebecca?" Lydia asked

"And Gina Landry. We were at her house because her brother had fallen and hurt himself really badly and their babysitter hadn't shown up. Then I came over to check on the babysitter and she's the girl I found."

"This sounds awfully convoluted," Lydia said. "But I've put the casserole in the refrigerator and after I wash my hands and find my keys, I'll be right there."

"Thank you so much. You're a life saver."

Polly gave Lydia the address and ended the call. Now she had to decide what to tell the girls in her back seat. She preferred being up front and honest with the kids in her life. It made answering questions so much easier. She took a deep breath and walked over to the truck.

Rebecca opened the back door and said, "What's up?"

Polly looked at the ground and then back up and said, "I need to tell you what's happened."

"Oh no," Rebecca said and reached out to touch Polly's arm. "Are you okay?"

"What?" Kayla asked and glanced at Rebecca before looking at Polly. "Really? Really?"

"Girls, Abby has died. I don't know how to say it any easier than that. The Sheriff is going to be here in a few minutes and I need to stay and talk to him. Mrs. Merritt is going to take you back to Sycamore House."

"She's dead?" Gina asked. "How?" She burst into tears.

Rebecca and Kayla both put their arms around her shoulders.

"I don't know," Polly replied. "That's what the Sheriff will figure out. But you will be fine at Sycamore House with Rebecca and Kayla. Do you like dogs?"

Kayla leaned in to divert Gina's attention. "Polly has the best dogs. Obiwan is big, but all he wants to do is love you. Han is crazy, but he's a big goofball. And they're named after the movie Star Wars. Have you ever seen that movie?"

Gina looked up at her, tears streaming down her face. "No."

"We'll watch Star Wars." Kayla looked at Polly. "Is that okay?"

"Of course it is."

"I just saw it the first time this year," Kayla said. "And now I've seen it like a million times. They love it at Polly's house."

Kayla continued to talk to the little girl and Rebecca turned back to Polly. "Are you sure you're okay? Do you want me to stay with you? Kayla can take care of Gina."

Polly reached in and hugged her, then whispered in her ear. "You're amazing. I'm fine. It's been a lot of blood this morning, but once you three are back home and the Sheriff takes care of things here, I'll settle down."

Rebecca pointed at Polly's pocket. "You should call Henry. You know how much he hates it when he finds out about this stuff from somebody else."

"I think I'll keep you. Is that okay?" Polly asked with a smile. "I love you."

"I love you, too."

For the second time that morning, Polly knew that the sirens coming through town were for her. She backed away from the truck as Lydia pulled in behind her.

"Are you okay?" Lydia asked before she was all the way out of her Jeep.

Polly smiled. "I'm fine, but I'm glad you're here. It would be good if the girls could get out of here before it turns into a big scene.

Rebecca unbuckled her seatbelt and reached to unbuckle Gina's. "This is Mrs. Merritt," she said. "She's the Sheriff's wife. We're going with her now."

Gina and Kayla climbed across the seat and stepped down beside Polly.

"You will be fine," Polly said to Gina. She bent over to give her a quick hug. "I promise it will all be fine."

"Not for Abby," Gina said.

Polly knelt down beside her. "You do know that Abby doesn't feel anything right now. Do you believe in heaven?"

Gina nodded.

"Then you have to believe that's where she is. She isn't thinking about dying or pain or anything. Isn't that right?"

"I guess so," Gina said.

"Come on girls," Lydia said, putting her hand on Kayla's shoulder. "I know where everything is in Polly's kitchen and I think today would be a good day for chocolate chip cookies."

Polly watched them drive away as the first sheriff's vehicle pulled in. She took a deep breath.

CHAPTER NINETEEN

"Darn it, Polly," Aaron said. "I wish you could identify the murderer as easily as you find the bodies." He nodded at his team as they headed for the front door.

"Where's the fun in that?" Polly asked. "I shouldn't have to do everything for you, should I?"

"Most of the time, you do anyway. Now tell me again how you came upon this scene?"

Polly explained the odd phone call and her discovery of Gina and Brennan Landry and then, the mother's concern over their babysitter not showing up.

"And Mrs. Landry is in Boone now at the hospital?"

"I suppose," Polly replied. "I think the boy hit his head hard a couple of times, so there is at least one concussion." She shuddered. "I should try to find someone to clean that bathroom up. Between him passing out and his sister trying to help him, there was a lot of blood."

"You've had more than your share of blood today," he said. "And I've seen its effects on you. How ya doin'?"

"Okay, I guess. There wasn't anyone else around to take care of things, so I just kept moving without thinking." Polly glanced at the back of her truck. "I have the bloody towels in there. I should start soaking those pretty soon."

He patted her shoulder. "If Lydia is at your place with the kids, ask for her help. She's gotten pretty good at cleaning up bloody messes."

"You? Were you hurt often?" Polly frowned at him.

"No, not me," he said with a laugh. "But five kids create plenty of blood. And poor Jill had bloody noses all through her adolescence. Plenty of blood in Lydia's lifetime. Ask her. Please. I don't want to have to send a unit to rush you to the hospital because you passed out and hit your head on the washing machine."

"Do you think Abby's death is connected to Julie Smith's?" Polly asked. Before Aaron could answer, she continued. "And do you know yet to who trashed the coffee shop and killed Julie?"

He shook his head. "We've talked to most everyone who knows her. I can't make a connection between her death and Denis Sutworth. There's nothing there. We talked to a few friends that she planned to meet that evening at the General Store. They assumed she was worn out from starting work and stayed home."

"I'm surprised she didn't text them," Polly said. "Kids know everything about each other's movements these days. Not much is left to the imagination." She sighed. "I know Rebecca is going to need a cell phone pretty soon, but I'm not ready to lose sight of her face and only see the top of her head."

He nodded. "Our kids were pretty much done growing up by the time everybody had cell phones. I can't imagine what Lydia would have done if she'd caught them with their faces buried in electronic devices. Video games and computers were bad enough. They thought she was a mean, mean mama."

"They all turned out pretty well," Polly said, smiling up at him. "I think both of you did just fine."

A deputy called Aaron's name and he turned and acknowledged it with a wave. "I'm needed. You've had enough of a day that maybe you should go home and put your feet up."

Polly checked the time on her phone and saw she had missed a text from Henry. "Maybe I'll avoid everything and take the kids and Lydia out to lunch at the diner. I could use comfort food."

He gave her a quick hug and went inside the house. Polly backed out of the driveway, carefully avoiding the emergency vehicles. She breathed a sigh of relief once she crossed the highway and pulled into her own drive. After turning the truck off, she shut her eyes and thought back over the absolute insanity of the morning. Was there anyone else in the world who had things like this occur as part of their daily lives? How in the world did an unpublished number get into Gina Landry's phone? She hadn't thought to ask anyone yet what Abby's actual number was.

Then she remembered Henry's text and swiped the phone to look at it.

"I'm going to be late tonight. There's a problem at the Harris house in Ogden. How's your day?"

Polly texted back, *"That's cool. Do you have a minute to talk?"*

Her phone rang and she swiped the call open. "Hi there, hot stuff. No time for me or for Nate tonight, huh?"

"It was you ... all you," he said. "My time is always for you. So what's up?"

"I did it again."

"Oh no." His voice fell. "I can get someone else to handle the Ogden job. Maybe Dad would go down."

"No, no, no," Polly said. "That's not why I told you. I just didn't want you to hear it from someone else." She chuckled. "Well, okay. Rebecca reminded me to call and tell you so that didn't happen."

He laughed. "I think we should keep her."

"That's what I told her this morning. She was terrific. Henry, I love her so much. How did we get so lucky?"

"Sarah did a wonderful job raising her," he replied. "If we don't screw it up these next few years, she can do anything with her life that she wants to do. Now tell me what happened?"

Polly described her morning to him and he made enough noise as she retold the tale to assure her that he was listening.

"Do you think the two murders are connected?" he asked.

"I asked Aaron that same question and didn't get a good answer. He wasn't avoiding me, there was just too much other stuff going on. But think about it, Henry. When have I ever found two dead people and not had the deaths be connected?"

He sighed loudly. "Why am I not more upset at the fact that you just said that last sentence out loud?"

"Because you're getting used to me?" she said with a weak laugh.

"I guess that's it. Are you sure you're okay?"

Polly nodded. "I'm fine. Just sitting in the truck in the garage. Lydia has the kids upstairs. I need to get the towels inside and have her help me de-blood them and then I am taking everyone out to lunch."

"I love you, sweetcakes. Take care of yourself until I get home tonight, will you?"

"Thanks, Henry. I love you too. And to tell you the truth, I feel better now than I did before you called. You always do that to me."

"That's me," he said. "Your human Valium."

"You're just as addicting."

"Go do your thing. I'll be home as soon as I can."

Polly sat back in the truck seat when the call was ended. She didn't want to go upstairs and deal with people. If she just sat here and took a quick nap, she wondered if anyone would notice. But there were too many things to deal with. She got out of the truck and walked to the bed where the basket of bloody towels had been hidden. Taking a deep breath, she took the basket out and went inside. She was at the top step when Obiwan skidded to a stop in front of her. Laughter and noise filled her apartment. There were more people here than just Lydia and the three girls.

"Too many people here to let you keep an ear out for me?" she asked the dog.

She put the basket up on Henry's desk so the dogs couldn't get into it. The last thing she needed was bloody towels strewn around the house. Rebecca had put a dirty towel atop the others so she didn't have to look at the blood, but Polly needed to get away from the coppery scent.

A large party greeted her in the dining room. Beryl was at one end of the table with Rebecca and Kayla, while Gina was in the kitchen with Lydia and Jean Gardner. Jeff and Andrew were setting the table while Eliseo, Sam Gardner, Jason and Ralph Bedford were peering at a computer tablet in front of Jason.

Jeff looked up and saw her and crossed the room. "There you are," he said. "We decided you needed a party. Lydia and Jean have been cooking up a storm. All we needed was you."

"I..." Polly looked around. "It hasn't been that long," she said. "How have you been cooking up a storm?"

"Lydia called me," Jean said. "We haven't cooked much, just bacon for BLTs. The tomatoes and lettuce are from the garden out back and the bread is Sylvie's. I whipped up cole slaw and beans and Lydia just took cupcakes out of the oven. We'll frost those after everyone has eaten."

"You whipped up cole slaw and beans," Polly said, shaking her head. "How does that even happen? I was going to take us out for lunch. I didn't expect this."

Beryl looked up. "Sometimes we just need to be reminded that life is easy. You can't accuse me of making cooking easy, but I can certainly enjoy the easy life."

"Why are you here?" Polly whispered to Beryl when she got close enough.

"Lydia called and told me what you'd been through this morning. It was either have lunch with you or sit in front of a blank canvas, frustrated because it hasn't yet told me what I'm supposed to paint." She winked at Rebecca as if the two of them had a private joke. "I'm hoping that all of you will inspire me so that the afternoon is better than the morning."

Polly glanced at Eliseo. "I can't believe you're up here, too. That's awesome."

He shrugged. "We had to eat and when Lydia called and asked if we had any tomatoes and lettuce in the garden, she invited us to come up and have lunch."

"What about Sylvie and Rachel?" Polly asked. "And Evelyn?"

Lydia smiled. "Don't worry. I checked on them all. Well, I had my helpers check on them. Sylvie is up at the bakery and Rachel is catering a luncheon at Memorial Hall. Kayla and Rebecca delivered lunch to Evelyn and Denis and I think that pretty much takes care of it, don't you?"

"Seriously," Polly said. "When everything falls apart, you're the only person in the world I want to organize my life. Thank you."

"I spent years taking care of and organizing the lives of five kids. I miss it. This is my favorite thing to do in the world. All it takes is a few phone calls and a little time." Lydia put a bowl of baked beans at either end of the table and then came around to give Polly a hug. "You needed some love today."

"Thank you," Polly said. "I have one more favor I need to ask of you, though. How do you take blood out of things? I have a basket of towels from the Landers house. They're covered in the red stuff and I can't think about them any longer."

Lydia grabbed Polly's hand and then released it. "Where's the basket? We can't let that set."

"It's on Henry's desk in there," Polly said, nodding to the office.

"Jean," Lydia called. "I'll be back in a few minutes. Are you good?"

"You go on," Jean Gardner said, waving Lydia away. "I have plenty of good help." She took two bowls of slaw from the counter and handed them to Andrew, talking quietly to him and pushing him toward the dining room.

Lydia left the room and then put her head back in. "Don't use your bathroom in here for a while, Polly. I'm going to soak them in the tub. Is the salt still in the same place downstairs?"

Polly's brows furrowed as she looked at Lydia. "Yes? Why?"

"Don't think about it. I've got this." Lydia smiled and soon Polly heard the water turn on in the small bathroom.

Where in the world would she be without this woman? And why didn't Lydia's daughters rely on her more? Polly often felt like she absorbed an awful lot of Lydia's time, but the woman never complained and was always available when needed.

Beckoning Jeff over, she said quietly, "Gina and her brother made a horrible bloody mess in their bathroom. I can't clean it up. Do you think that if I paid Barb and Cindy an ungodly amount of money, they'd meet me there and scrub it down?" Barb and Cindy Evering were the mother and daughter team who cleaned rooms at Sycamore Inn.

He shrugged. "I can't imagine why not. But why don't you wait until after lunch and check with Gina's mother. She might not want people in her house, especially if she comes home this afternoon."

"You're right," Polly said. "I was just trying to help."

"We'll eat. You'll call her and find out what's happening and then, if you still want to, I'll call Barb. I'm sure they'd be glad to help. Especially for an ungodly amount of money," he said with a grin.

"I'd pay anything to not deal with that," Polly said. "Anything."

~~~

Polly was surprised that she hadn't heard from Darla Landry. The house had finally quieted down enough to think about something other than interacting with people. Eliseo and his crew had gone back outside, Jean Gardner was helping Kayla and Gina cook in the kitchen, Beryl and Rebecca were still at the table working in a sketchbook, and Andrew had taken the dogs out. Lydia was nowhere to be found. Polly couldn't imagine where she might have gone, but wasn't too worried.

She looked at her phone and back at Gina. The girl would probably want to talk with her mother, but first Polly wanted to find out what was happening with Bean. She went into her bedroom and closed the door, then called the number in her phone.

"Darla Landry," the woman said.

"Hi, Darla, this is Polly Giller. I'm calling to check up on your son."

"He'll live, that little brat," Mrs. Landry said. "They're going to keep him overnight for observation. He's pretty banged up and there's evidence of a concussion. At least he didn't break anything this time."

"This time?" Polly asked.

Darla sighed. "He is always into something. I keep thinking that someday I will be able to afford a large enough place that he can play outside without jumping off roofs or doing crazy things, but if I stop and think about it, that would just give him more room to find potential danger spots. He's broken his arm twice and a leg once. The number of split lips and gashes on his knees and elbows has gone beyond what I can count. Other than putting him in a padded room, I don't know what else to do."

"He's a boy, I guess," Polly said. "Have you thought about what you're doing tonight?"

"I suspect I will come home. The Sheriff has already been here to tell me about Abby. The hospital will watch Bean and Gina has no place else to go."

Polly looked toward her kitchen. "If you want to stay with your son, Gina could spend tonight here at Sycamore House with Rebecca. Maybe I'll invite Kayla to stay and they can have one last sleepover before school starts."

"I wouldn't want to do that to you. You've done enough already. No, if Bean is going to hurt himself, maybe it's time that he learn that I can't be there for him."

"Are you sure? He's just a kid," Polly protested. "If you want to come home tonight, I understand that, but if you're doing it because you don't want to put me out, you won't. I have plenty of room. I have a built in babysitter with Rebecca, and Gina is having fun with the dogs and cats. There is plenty to do and she'll be perfectly safe."

"I'm not worried about her with you. Everybody in town knows who you are," the woman said with a chuckle. "Are you certain?"

"Absolutely. I'd love to have her."

"I probably need to speak with her about Abby. It will crush her."

"Mrs. Landers," Polly said. "I hate to tell you this, but Gina was in the truck when I found Abby. She knows all about it."

"She didn't see anything, did she?"

"Oh, no, no, no. Not at all. She stayed in the truck with Rebecca and Kayla. Mrs. Merritt came to get them before the Sheriff and his team arrived. But she knew what happened. She cried a lot with Rebecca. I think the girls were probably good for her. Right now she's in the kitchen making up some concoction with another friend, Jean Gardner from down the street."

"I know Jean. She's a good woman. What's she doing there?"

"You would be surprised at the number of people who are in and out of my house on a daily basis," Polly said. Then she remembered, "Speaking of being in and out of the house, there was a lot of blood in your bathroom. We've brought the towels here and they're soaking in salt water, but it looks like there was a murder in that room."

"Ugh," Darla said. "If he wasn't going to be such a mess for a few days, I'd make the brat clean it himself, but I guess I'll have to deal with that."

"Well, no," Polly interrupted. "Not if you'll allow me to take my cleaning team over from Sycamore Inn. Please don't say no. They will have it cleaned up in a jiffy and then when you get home you can focus on your kids and going back to work."

"Work. I hadn't even gotten there yet. What am I going to do with those kids until school starts?" She coughed and said, "No, that's not your problem. I'll find someone. When I think of what happened to poor Abby, this is minor."

Polly spoke quietly. "I can help you, you know. There are only a few more days. Gina is having a good time here and she can come play with Kayla and Rebecca. If Bean needs to be quiet, we have video games and movies. Andrew Donovan is here every day and he can help entertain your son."

"You do have quite a large group of people around, don't you?"

"Yes I do," Polly said. "And it is very simple to add two more into the mix. Please think about it before you say no."

"I don't know how I could possibly say no to that. I don't have any other options right now. I'm taking tomorrow off and maybe Wednesday, but then I need to get back to work."

"Let me help, then."

"I don't know how to thank you," Darla Landry said. "I haven't even met you yet and I'm in your debt."

"No you aren't. It's why I'm here."

"I've heard that about you, too," Darla said. "The reason you're here is because you find dead bodies. I can't believe you found someone who was close to me, but I guess I'm glad it was you."

"Did Aaron ask you about Abby's father?"

"Yes, I have his information and gave it to the Sheriff. He was going to contact him this afternoon. The whole thing is so sad."

"It really is. She was too young."

"Thinking about it makes me want to hug my kids. Even if I want to beat the tar out of my stupid son."

Polly smiled. "Would you like to talk to Gina?"

"Yes, thank you. And thank you for taking care of her."

"I'll let you tell her that she's staying here. We'll go over and pick up clothes for tonight and tomorrow and make sure everything is turned off and locked up."

"Thank you so much."

Polly went out and beckoned to Gina, then parked her on the sofa with the telephone. Darla had not said no to the bathroom cleanup and had obviously forgotten about it. That just made it easier to make sure it was taken care of. Jeff had reached out to their cleaning team and they would meet Polly at the trailer whenever she could get there. This was why she loved knowing so many people. There was always someone to help.

CHAPTER TWENTY

After everyone but the kids had left that afternoon, Polly was ready to drop. She took Gina home to pick up whatever she needed in order to spend the night and to meet Barb and Cindy Evering. After introducing them to Gina, they brought in their buckets, brushes and cleaning materials and went to work.

"You're going into third grade this year?" she asked Gina.

The little girl rushed to her dresser and took out a pair of lime shorts and a brightly colored shirt. "These are my first day of school clothes. Mom bought them last week. Aren't they cool?"

Polly smiled. "They're great. That color looks terrific on you."

"That's what Mom said." Gina pulled open her drawers and pointed. "Mom organizes all of my clothes into sets for me. She says I have to learn how to match things up but she..." Gina stood up taller and spoke in a higher pitched voice, mimicking her mother. "Despairs of ever having a daughter with a sense of style."

"It will come," Polly said. "It will come. I promise. And maybe you will develop your own sense of style along the way. Who knows, maybe you'll become a fashion designer when you get older."

Gina rolled her eyes. "I'd rather be a cowboy. I want to learn how to rope cows and ride horses."

"Rope cows? Whatever gave you that idea?"

"That's what my daddy does," Gina said. "He lives out in Wyoming. He doesn't live with us anymore." She slumped. "I heard him tell Mom that he loved us kids, but he couldn't live with us anymore. Mom's sad because of that."

"I'm sorry," Polly said.

"We never see him. Sometimes he'll send a letter or call us, but he doesn't remember birthdays or Christmas. Mom says that's okay. She loves us enough for a hundred daddies."

"I'll bet that's right," Polly said. Her heart broke for this little family. No wonder Bean was all over the place. He was just trying to grab as much attention as he could and had no good way to focus his energy.

Gina plopped herself down in front of the closet and was pulling things out.

"What are you looking for?" Polly asked.

"There should be a pair of cowboy boots in here. Daddy bought them for me a long time ago. Do you think they'll still fit?"

"I doubt it," Polly said with a chuckle. "You've probably grown since then. Does your mom know you want to ride horses?"

"She says they're too expensive right now, but when I get older and get a job, I can save money for a horse. I read stories about them and I have pictures." She dropped her head and said shyly, "We drove by your house and took pictures of your horses. They're big."

"Do you know what they're called?"

"Everybody knows that," Gina said. "They're Percherons. The whole town knows about your horses. It's cool when you take them out for Halloween. They're spooky all dressed up. We always go to the parades when you ride them. And I saw you last winter with the sleigh one time."

"Maybe when you get up tomorrow morning, Kayla and Rebecca will take you down to the barn to meet them. Would you like that?"

Gina sat back and stared at Polly with her mouth open. Finally she spoke. "Do you mean it?"

"Of course," Polly replied. "They love visitors. Do you know which one you like the best?"

The little girl nodded. "I like the one that you always ride. His name is Demi? Is that right?"

"That's absolutely right. You do know a lot about my horses. Demi is pretty laid back. He lets the barn cats sleep on him at night and the donkeys try to get into his stall all the time."

"That's funny," Gina said. She leaned against the closet door frame. "I can't believe I get to see them face to face."

"How about I talk to Eliseo. He's in charge down there and maybe he'll let you sit on Demi's back. What do you think about that?"

Polly thought the child would swoon. Having these horses was better than the Beatles coming to town for a child this age. She had to figure a way for the horses to spend more time with kids.

"Polly?" Barb Evering was standing in the bedroom door.

"Are you finished?"

Barb nodded. "It wasn't as bad as you thought. We just needed to scrub a few things clean and it's back to normal."

"You can't believe how a little blood could be very bad for me," Polly said, laughing. She stood up and walked over to the door. "Thank you so much for doing this. Mrs. Landers doesn't need to bring her son home and then have to clean up a mess like that."

"We're glad to help."

"How are things at the Inn with Grey?" Polly asked. She heard a slight chuckle from the bathroom as Cindy was packing up the supplies.

"He's different," Barb said. "But he's a very nice man. He's always asking us if we'd like him to help, but we've got a schedule. If something breaks or needs fixing, though, he's right on it and he's got a new plan for keeping inventory of supplies." She dropped her voice to speak in a whisper. "He said he wants to get us one of those electronic tablet things so we can do inventory on that and order supplies faster. And so we can keep in touch with him during the day. But he's right down the way. It's only a few steps more to go and talk to him. I don't understand why filling out the sheet is any different than clicking a box on some electronic gizmo."

Polly nodded. "Do the guests like him?"

"I guess," Barb said with a shrug. "I don't see them very much. They're always out of the rooms by the time we get started. He likes chatting it up with them when they come and go. If he isn't talking to them in the lobby, he's outside working and talking to them. He's awfully busy. And he talks funny. You know, like in olden times. All proper and polite."

"He is polite," Polly said. "I like that about him."

"I guess. Well, we'll be out of your hair. Thanks for the extra work. Any time you need us, we're available."

"Thank you, Barb. I appreciate your help." Polly walked them to the front door and then called out, "Do you have everything you need, Gina?"

Gina came into the living room with a backpack stuffed to the brim. "I think so," she said breathlessly. "I don't want to forget anything. How long am I staying at your house?"

"Hopefully your brother will come home tomorrow." Polly flipped the living room light off and took the key that Gina handed to her. "You want me to lock the door?"

"Bean always does because I get scared that I'll forget."

"Okay. I can do that." Polly pulled the door shut and locked the deadbolt, then tugged on the door. "Here, you tug on it, too. That way both of us will be sure that it's locked."

When they were finished, Gina ran for the truck and stopped beside the passenger door. "Do you have a husband?"

"Yes I do," Polly said. "His name is Henry." She opened the door and waited for Gina to climb in. "Why do you ask?"

"Will he be mad that you invited me over?"

"Nope. Not at all. He's a pretty good guy."

Gina let out a sigh of relief. "My daddy didn't like guests. He was always tired when he came home and said that his house was his castle and nobody was going to bother him. We had to be quiet when he was sleeping and he always took a nap right after he walked in the door. Usually in front of the TV so we had to play quietly in Bean's room."

"You'll soon find out that nobody is very quiet at my house," Polly said. "If Henry needs privacy, he just goes into the bedroom and shuts the door."

As they drove up to Sycamore House, Gina caught a glimpse of the horses and sighed a huge sigh. "I can't wait to see them in the morning. They're so pretty."

"Do you want to drive down and meet them right now?"

Polly watched Gina's face in the rear view mirror. The girl lit up, then grew serious and said, "No, I can wait. You'd better take me back to the house."

"Why do you say that?" Polly asked.

"Mom says that I expect too much and she's always talking about how people are just nice because they have to, not because they want to. Tomorrow is okay."

"Honey," Polly said. "I offered to take you to the barn because I enjoy seeing my horses, too. I'll be busy in the morning and I'd like to introduce you to Eliseo and Jason. Jason is Andrew's older brother."

"Are you sure it's not too much trouble?"

Polly turned the corner and drove into the parking lot so they could walk to the barn. "It's no trouble at all. Come on. You can play with the other kids later." She opened the back door and waited while Gina unbuckled her belt and hopped down to the ground. "Come on. It will be fine."

She opened the gates for Gina and then walked into the barn. "Anyone here?" she called out. When there was no answer from humans or equines, she said, "Well, everybody must be outside. How many horses did you see out there?"

"Two," Gina said quietly.

"And donkeys?"

The girl nodded and Polly took her through Demi's stall to the pasture. He was standing at the back fence with Daisy and she called his name. "Demi!"

The horse looked up at her voice, threw his head in the air and nickered, then trotted across to see her. Daisy looked up to see what the commotion was and raced to catch up to him.

"Demi and Daisy, this is Gina," Polly said. "She wants to be a cowgirl someday. What do you think?"

Gina backed up at the approach of the immense horses. Polly turned and put her hand out. "It's okay. They are big, but Demi is as friendly as they come. Remember, I told you that he lets the cats sleep on him at night."

"He's bigger than I thought," Gina said, looking up at the horses with immense eyes.

Polly put her hand on Demi and he dipped his head closer to Gina. "Go ahead and rub there just above his nose. He loves that and it is very soft." There was no other spot on the horse that Gina could reach from the ground unless it were his legs or his belly.

Demi pushed at Polly's hand with his head. "I don't have anything for you, ya beggar," she said.

Not to be outdone, Daisy crowded in, looking for attention. Polly pushed her back. "You're going to scare the girl. Be polite."

Before she knew it, Tom and Huck were on the other side of Gina, pushing at her hand. The girl giggled. "What do they want?"

"They probably think you have treats. That's how we usually introduce strangers to them."

"They're not as big," Gina said.

"No they're not. And they're fun. When you come down tomorrow, maybe Eliseo or Jason will put a saddle on one and you can ride. If you fall off one of them, it isn't as far to the ground."

Daisy snorted and turned to run for the far side of the pasture. She got halfway there, stopped and turned as if to ask Demi why he wasn't following her.

"Go on," Polly said. "Keep her company. We'll be back tomorrow." She patted his shoulder and ran her hand down it, caressing him. She still couldn't get over the fact that these beautiful horses lived with her. He took off and soon the donkeys followed.

"I didn't upset them, did I?" Gina asked.

"Oh no," Polly said. "I suspect the other two are working in the pasture on the other side of the creek and these guys are wondering why they're stuck in the same old place."

They walked back to the truck and Polly drove to the garage. She took Gina's backpack and carried it upstairs. "Anybody here?" she called out. The two dogs came crashing into Henry's office to greet them and Polly stopped and knelt down to accept their affection so they didn't barrel Gina over onto the floor.

Andrew strode into the office and said, "I'm bored. They're being girls again."

"But they *are* girls," Gina said, knitting her brows in confusion.

He nodded toward the other room. "They're in Rebecca's room and talking about clothes for school. It's all stupid."

Polly handed Gina her backpack and said, "Go ahead. You'll have fun."

"Why did you have to bring another girl into the house," Andrew asked with a whine. "It's not fair."

Polly grinned at him. "How long have they been in Rebecca's room?"

"They just went in there."

"And what were you doing before that?"

"I beat them in a game."

"A racing game?"

"Yep."

She laughed. "You're so put upon. How about we give them a few minutes to do their thing. After that we'll walk to the coffee shop and to the General Store for ice cream."

"You like ice cream," he teased her.

"Yes I do," she said. "Got a problem with that?"

He threw his arms up in defense. "No problem at all."

"That's good, because I wouldn't want to tell your mother that you were a brat."

Andrew hung his head in shame. "She already knows I am."

"Oh Andrew," Polly said. "I was just kidding."

"Didn't she tell you how bad I was?"

That caught Polly off guard, because of course Sylvie *had* told her. She didn't want to lie to him, but she also didn't want him to worry that he couldn't mess up in the safety of his own home. There were some things that needed to be protected.

"She said you were having a rough time, but I thought you and I talked about stuff on Saturday. Did you do something else?"

"No," he said, shaking his head. "But that was bad enough." He looked up at Polly, worry on his face. "Am I always going to be stupid because of girls?"

She laughed out loud and pulled him into a hug "I love you so much."

He struggled and pulled away, a wan grin on his lips. "You *hug* me too much."

"I don't hug you enough and yes, you are probably always going to be stupid because of girls. You should ask Henry if he still gets stupid because of me. We can't help it when our hearts and our heads get confused because of love."

"It's not love," he said. "Mom called it puppy love. That sounds dumb."

"No matter what you call it, love messes with your heart and your head and sometimes your stomach. I promise that you will live through it as long as you don't piss your Mom off so much that she wants to kill you."

He glanced up at her and grinned.

"What?" she asked.

"You said 'pissed.'"

"I guess I did," she responded. "Are you telling on me?"

Rebecca came into the media room, dressed in a long denim skirt and bright, flowery blouse. "Can I wear this the first day of school?" Her hair had been pulled back into a pony tail, with casual, loose tendrils brushing her cheeks. She looked older than her twelve years.

"Sure," Polly said, shaken that the girl was growing up in front of her eyes. "You look fabulous." She looked over at Andrew who was staring with his mouth open. "We're thinking about walking up town for ice cream. Do you want to put your shorts back on so you're comfortable in the heat?"

Rebecca turned and ran out of the room.

Polly reached over and with her index finger, pushed up on Andrew's lower jaw. "Shut your mouth," she said. "You could catch flies with that trap."

"She's so..." He pursed his lips and scowled at Polly. "Whatever."

"She's so grownup? So pretty?"

"Whatever."

The three girls came running back into the media room, Rebecca and Kayla pulling Gina with them.

"Gina says she can't go with us because she doesn't have any money, but I told her it was no big deal," Rebecca said.

"It's no big deal," Polly repeated. "I've got this. I can afford ice cream for one little girl."

"But Mom said..." Gina started to protest.

"It's okay," Rebecca said, kneeling down to get closer to Gina's size. Polly wanted to laugh. It hadn't been that long ago, she'd done the same thing to Rebecca. "Unless you're allergic to ice cream, Polly's got it." She looked up at Polly. "Right?"

"Right," Polly said, nodding. "Now you aren't allergic to ice cream, are you?"

"No!" Gina exclaimed. "It's just that you're doing so much."

Polly sat on the arm of the sofa. "Sometimes the only thing you can do is say thank you. That was one of those things that my mother insisted I learn how to do."

"You didn't know how to say thank you?"

"Not at your age. But I learned," Polly said. "It's right up there with the most important words you'll ever learn how to say."

"What are those?" Gina asked, confused by this point.

Polly held her hand up and with the other, flipped down a finger as she recited the list. "I love you, I'm sorry, please, and thank you. As long as you use those words and phrases, you'll do well. That's what my mother said. When you're with me, unless you think something is going to be bad for you or hurt you, don't worry it being too difficult or expensive. If I offer and you want to do it, just smile and say thank you. Deal?"

Gina looked at each of the other kids in turn. They nodded in agreement.

"That's how Polly rolls," Andrew said.

"Okay." She processed for a moment and then said, "Thank you."

"Let's head out. I want to check on the coffee shop and then we'll get ice cream."

They left by the back door. Polly and Andrew found themselves at the back of the pack as Kayla and Rebecca taught Gina how to skip.

"We've been down this road before," Andrew said, sarcasm thick in his tone.

"We'll be down it again," Polly replied. "Stop being such a stick in the mud."

They waited to cross the street and as Polly turned the corner on Elm Street, she saw the same pack of boys that had come after her the day she was out with Alistair Greyson. She didn't want to run into trouble today. Not with the kids. The boys were loitering beside a building and weren't yet paying attention to Polly and her pack.

"Girls," she said "Stop and come back here."

"What's up?" Rebecca asked.

"I know them," Andrew whispered.

Polly pushed the girls behind her and turned back around. "We're taking a different route today. Let's walk down the highway and go up Maple Street. It's a couple of extra blocks, but that's okay."

Kayla whispered. "Is it because of those boys? They've been making trouble this summer. The tall one is mean. I heard he wrecked his dad's new truck and his dad wanted to kick him out of the house."

"Let's just go get ice cream," Polly said. "They can do their thing. We'll do ours."

CHAPTER TWENTY-ONE

Rebecca, Kayla, and Gina ran to the coffee shop after eating ice cream. The older girls promised to show Gina all of the books they had for kids. Andrew walked in the front, door, eyed a chair in front of a set of shelves and made a dash for it. He sat down, shut his eyes, reached onto the shelf and took out the first book he touched. He opened his eyes and nodded nonchalantly before turning to the first page. The boy could read anything.

"Hello, Ms. Giller," Helena Black said, coming around a table. "How are you today?"

"I'm fine, thank you," Polly replied. "Is Sylvie in back?"

The woman nodded and walked with Polly down the hallway. "There's a lot of excitement around here, you know."

"There is? What's going on?"

"Well, you know," Helena's voice dropped to a loud whisper. "The murder and everything."

"That was last week. Surely things have settled down."

"Do you ever think they settle down after something like that? But people keep coming in and ordering coffee. Maybe it was a good thing for us."

"I don't believe it was a good thing."

"No, no, no. That isn't what I meant. I just meant that all of the additional attention would bring more business in and that's what you always want as an owner, more business, right? I haven't had a chance to talk to Miss Kahane much about it. She always has her nose in that computer of hers or is too busy to chat. Do you think she'll be a good owner? Your employees talk about how good it is to work for you. But you two were friends before you came back to Iowa, isn't that right? You know her better than anyone."

"Helena?" A voice from behind them called out.

Polly and Helena both turned to see Camille Specht standing there.

"Yes?" Helena responded.

"You were working on re-stocking. Let Ms. Giller find her own way to the bakery."

"We were just chatting. I enjoy talking with the owners," Helena said. "They're so interesting, don't you think?"

"It was nice talking to you," Polly said. "Go ahead. I need to see Sylvie."

Helena moved in toward Polly and spoke softly as Camille went back into the main part of the coffee shop. "I don't know how she's going to do as manager. People probably wanted to have someone manage the shop that was from here."

"I think she'll be fine. She's a wonderful person," Polly said.

"But you don't understand. She's not like everyone else in Bellingwood. That's going to keep customers away. And like I said, owners want more business."

Polly pursed her lips and drew in a deep breath. Now was not the time or place to be having this conversation, but if this woman insisted, she'd let it happen. "I hope you aren't saying what I think you're saying," Polly said.

"All I'm saying is that there are people in Bellingwood who aren't as open minded as you and me."

"Then maybe they'd better get their coffee elsewhere," Polly said. "And as for open minded, that has nothing to do with anything. You don't need to be open minded, you just need to be a human being. Am I making myself clear? Because if you have a problem with Camille Specht as your manager, you and I will have a different conversation."

Helena Black shrugged. "It's up to you. It's your business. I was just trying to be helpful. I can't help it if people in town gossip and say things."

"Yes you can. You can stop it and insist that they have a little respect. But then," Polly said. "It's up to you." She spun on her heels and strode back down the hallway to the kitchen. By the time she walked in the doorway, she was seething.

"Hi there," Sylvie said.

"Hi," Polly spat.

"Uhh, what's up?"

"I just had a pointed conversation with Helena Black. Apparently, she's been hearing gossip about Camille."

Sylvie chuckled. "Do you remember when I warned you about people's reactions to Eliseo?"

Polly rolled her eyes. "Yeah. And I got mad then. But I think I'm madder now."

"Well, I learned my lesson that day," Sylvie said. "And you were right. Whatever the bigots were going to say about him just wasn't important. Camille is a wonderful person and Bellingwood can't remain isolated in its white little world forever. We're too close to the cities for that to remain a reality. They'll just have to suck it up and deal."

"Why is it that people even have to *deal* with this any longer," Polly said. "It's ridiculous." She shook her head. "I'm sorry. I wasn't expected to be blindsided by that today. I just wanted to come say hello and see how you're doing."

"I'm okay. It's going to be slow for a while until I can get my feet under me, but I'll get there. I pulled loaves of bread out of the ovens this morning and they're already sold. All of the pastries I made this morning were gone before eleven o'clock. I'm testing the ovens for cakes this afternoon. I'm building a wedding cake for Saturday. If I have to go back to Sycamore House to finish it, I want to know before Wednesday." She looked around and whispered. "Don't tell anyone, but I'm doing better than okay. This is fun."

"Have you talked to Rachel?"

Sylvie smiled. "Quite a bit. She's lonely all by herself. But she's busy, so at least that keeps her out of trouble."

"Do you or she need anything?"

"Five more people, but we can't afford that many right now," Sylvie said.

"You've talked to Jeff?"

Sylvie nodded. "We have a plan. Two girls are coming on next week, they'll move back and forth between the two kitchens. Hannah's little one is nearly four and starting pre-school this fall, so she wants to come over a couple of mornings during the week."

"Time has passed too quickly," Polly said. "I can't believe she's that old."

"Andrew is going into junior high and Jason will be a sophomore. What am I going to do when they're out of the house and going to college?" Sylvie asked. "I'm not ready for that."

Polly put both her hands up and said, "Whoa. Stop. You have years before that happens." Then she gave Sylvie an evil grin. "And who knows, maybe you'll have another baby and then you'll have decades ahead of you."

"How about we make a pact," Sylvie said, curling her upper lip in a snarl. "You have a baby first. Then I'll think about it."

"Got it," Polly said, laughing. "I'll be good."

Both of them turned when they heard a commotion.

"Polly!" Andrew yelled. She was already heading his way and nearly ran into him coming down the hallway.

"What's up?"

He grabbed her hand and pulled her back into the main room, where two of the boys who had been on the street earlier were standing over a table with a couple of high school age girls. The girls had pushed their chairs back against the outside window - fear evident on their faces.

Camille was striding across the room toward them and Skylar had the phone in his hand.

"I've got 9-1-1," he said.

"Stop it," Camille said sharply to the boys.

The two boys turned to her and laughed. A tall, blond boy said, "What 'cha gonna do to us? You can't put a hand on me or I'll sue your ass."

She stood firm and Polly stepped in beside her. Camille continued. "We're calling the police. You are threatening my customers and that gives me permission to put a hand on you. Now, back off."

"We aren't threatening anyone," he taunted. "We're just being friendly." He turned to the girl closest to him and reached out to touch her. She flinched. "Right, Janelle?"

When she didn't say anything, he repeated the words. "Right, Janelle? Tell the nice ladies that we're friends."

Polly moved to step between him and Janelle. "My manager asked you to stop. Now I'm asking you to leave. You are no longer welcome here. If you attempt to come in again, we will call the police and have them escort you out every single time. Now, go." She put as much strength and venom into the last two words as she could, but to no avail.

The boy stepped closer to her. "You don't have your protector with that big stick here today. I'm pretty sure I can take you."

"You don't scare me, little boy," Polly said. "I've seen your kind before. Do you wanna know where?"

He sneered at her. "Where?"

"Eldora. I don't know who you think you are, but you don't scare me and you can't intimidate me. If you hurt me, it just makes life more difficult when the police actually get here. Look around, you stupid little boy. This room is filled with people who can identify you. You can't hide, you can't run. One or two questions and I know who your parents are, where they work, and why they let you run loose. Figure it out soon, because your life isn't going to be worth anything if you continue like this."

Polly's heart was racing so fast, she was sure her face was beet red. The only thing she could see was the boy in front of her, everything else had dropped out of her vision. Her mouth was cotton-dry and she waited for him to punch her in the nose or slap her face. A small part of her wanted him to do just that. She could take the punch, but at the same time, she knew exactly what it felt like and wasn't in any hurry to repeat the pain. Explaining another black eye to Henry wouldn't be easy.

"Whatever, bitch," he said, backing up. "Come on." He grabbed his friend by the shirt and pulled him to the front door, only to be met by Bert Bradford, who backed him into the coffee shop again.

"You two again?" Bert asked. "We've been over this before. I'm tired of hearing about you intimidating people downtown. I told you the last time that if we heard another complaint, I was taking you in."

"I want a lawyer," the kid said. He turned to his friend. "Record this on your phone. It's police harassment. Make sure you put it up on YouTube. They can't treat us like this. When my lawyer hears about this, he'll have your badge. And we're going to own this stupid coffee shop too. I'm suing you all."

Bert sighed and grasped the kid's upper arm. He spun him to the door and with his other hand, grabbed the second kid's arm. "It's just a short walk to the police station," Bert said. "You can videotape anything you want. Notice me being quite polite to you. I haven't pushed you into a door frame or anything yet. Now keep moving."

He turned back to Polly and Camille. "As soon as I handle these two, I'll be back to take statements."

Polly knees went weak and she reached out to stabilize herself on the table in front of her. "Entitled much?" she said quietly.

"Are you okay?" Rebecca asked. She pulled a chair out and put it behind Polly.

"I think so. Why do I open my mouth like that? If he'd punched me, Henry would have killed me."

The two girls, Janelle and her friend, were still plastered against the window, but now they were staring at Polly.

"Do you go to school with those two?" Polly asked them.

Janelle nodded. "Ladd's going to be a senior."

"Have they always been like this?"

The other girl looked at Janelle and shrugged her shoulders. "Yeah. They call themselves a gang. But the ones who kinda kept them in control graduated. They think they're going to run the school next year. But they're stupid because they're just from Bellingwood. Nobody in Boone cares. They think they're all tough, but they aren't. They got beat up a lot last year."

"So they take it out on people that can't protect themselves," Polly said. "Are you two okay?"

The girls nodded.

Camille bent over the table. "You need to stay to talk to the police. Would you like another smoothie or something to eat? It's on the house. Go on up and tell Sky what you want. We've got this." She nodded at Sky and then said, "Maybe you should call your parents and tell them what's going on. Just in case."

The girls headed for the counter and Janelle turned back to Polly. "You were pretty cool. I wish I would have stood up to him like that. But I didn't want him to hurt me."

"He wasn't going to hurt anyone. Not in front of people." Polly grinned. "And besides, what if he did? A bloody nose or a black eye would only hurt you for a while, but the assault charge would stay with him for a long time. Sometimes you have to balance the odds."

"I never thought about it like that," Janelle responded.

Polly finally felt her mind come out of the fog and she looked for the rest of her entourage. Kayla and Andrew had taken Gina to the other side of the shop. Andrew was sitting with the little girl on an oversized chair, reading a book out loud, while Kayla sat next to them, effectively blocking Gina's view of the action.

"Who decided they should do that?" Polly asked Rebecca.

"I told Andrew to get her out of the way," Rebecca said. "She's just a little girl and didn't need to be involved if things got ugly."

"You are amazing." Polly reached out and pulled Rebecca close, then wrapped her arms around the girl. "I can't believe your mother chose me to live life with you. Every single day you make me proud."

"Even when I screw up?"

Polly chuckled. "Especially then, because it reminds me that you're human and not some crazy little angel sent into my house."

"Yeah. I'm so not that," Rebecca said. She gently pulled away. "You scared me."

"I scared me a little too," Polly replied. "But bullies will always be bullies until someone stands up to them. Today it was my turn."

All of a sudden, Helena Black rushed up to Polly and said, "Are you okay? Did he hurt you? What will we do if they come back and you aren't here? There isn't anyone here who can pull off what you just did. It's because you're the owner, isn't it. What if he had a gun? He might have killed someone. I know he's just an angry young boy, but what are we going to do?" She spun on Camille. "What are you doing to keep us safe? Do you have a plan for this? You're the hot young manager. How could you let this happen?"

"Helena," Sylvie said quietly. "Stop it. Your mouth is running away without engaging your brain. You and I both know this was a fluke. Now why in the world are you behaving this way?"

"Because she isn't cut out to do this job and none of you will see it. Things like this are going to keep happening and it won't be my fault." Helena stalked away and whipped out a cloth to wipe down tables.

Polly looked at Camille and Sylvie and mouthed, "What in the hell?"

Both women shrugged and Camille said, "We might need to talk about this."

"Yes, I think we might," Polly said. "Do you think you can fix this or should we cut our losses?"

"We have ninety days," Camille replied. "But I'm not ready to make a big decision yet. We've only just gotten started."

Sylvie stepped in closer to them. "But you don't need a terrorist on your staff. Everyone else is excited about working here and making this place fun. I don't know for sure what her agenda is."

"I'd fire her right now," Polly said.

"Yes," Sylvie said with a laugh. "But you're on a roll. You need to calm down before you engage in any more hot encounters." She gave a rapid shake of her head. "Hot encounters? Where in the world did that come from? Sometimes I open my mouth and weird phrases come out."

Camille winked at her. "Could it be the knight without a steed who was flirting with you when he was in earlier?"

"Grey was in?" Polly asked.

"And looking for Sylvie. I don't know what they talked about, but he was definitely flirting."

Polly stood up and pushed the chair back in under the table. "When were you going to tell me about this?"

"I wasn't," Sylvie said. She gestured to Rebecca. "And hello. Young ears."

"Did he ask you out on a date?" Polly asked.

Sylvie flicked the towel in her hand and tucked it into her waistband. "You're nuts. I don't have time for this. Someone come get me if Bert needs to talk to me. I'll be in my kitchen." She tried to stomp, but her tennis shoes absorbed most of the sound, so she turned back around and stuck her tongue out at Polly and walked toward the hallway and back to the kitchen.

"She sure told me," Polly said. "With emphasis."

Chief Wallers walked in the front door and took in the room before walking over to Polly, Camille and Rebecca. "I hear you had some excitement," he said.

"I was glad to see Bert show up," Polly replied. "Did they get a good video of him roughing up the suspects?"

Ken chuckled. "Yeah, that's my Bert. I've had a few boys on the force who might have been tempted to do that, but never Bert. He's a quiet sort. Are you going to file a complaint against the boys?"

Polly and Camille looked at each other and Polly nodded, then said. "Yes, I think we will. I don't want my customers to be uncomfortable here." She gritted her teeth and said. "Bellingwood should be safe. This is ridiculous. Just the other day those boys tried to intimidate me and Grey Greyson on the street."

"They always come up just short of doing something that will get them in real trouble," he said. "I need them to hit someone or do something stupid."

"They almost hit Polly," Rebecca said.

Ken looked at Polly. "They did?"

"I might have gotten up in the blond kid's face. Maybe I was daring him to follow through on his threats." Polly looked down at the floor. "You don't have to tell Henry about that, do you?"

"I should," Ken said, laughing. "But I suspect he'll hear about it before the day is over. I need to take statements from y'all. Where should I start?"

Janelle and her friend had taken another table and were glancing at Ken before darting their eyes away.

Polly gestured toward them. "Those two girls had to put up with the boys' initial attention. Start with them so they can get on with their day. The rest of us will be available."

Ken stopped at the counter to order a drink and then sat down in front of the two girls. Polly headed for Andrew, Gina, and Kayla with Rebecca in tow. She arrived to hear Andrew growl.

"What are you reading?" she asked.

"Beauty and the Beast," he said. "I'm letting Gina read the Beauty parts."

CHAPTER TWENTY-TWO

Engaged in a book, Andrew chose to stay at the coffee shop until Sylvie was finished so they could go home together. Since Kayla planned to spend the night with Gina and Rebecca, Polly was just as relieved not to have to deal with him sulking about the girls doing their girly things.

What she wanted to do was go home and flop on the sofa for an hour or two, but there was supper and an evening of entertainment ahead and that was before Henry got home, exhausted from his day. Yep. She'd be glad when school started again. Summer break was wonderful, but a schedule was just as wonderful when it came around.

They walked home and when they got inside, Polly sent the girls upstairs and called the dogs to come down. She snapped a leash on each of them and walked across the lot to the highway, crossed it, and wandered into the woods behind the swimming pool. The quiet of the trail was a welcome relief from the day. Had all of that excitement happened only this morning?

Obiwan and Han were glad to be out and she kept pace with them, stopping when one or the other found something interesting to sniff. If she continued long enough, the trail went between the vineyard and the hotel and then on out of town. She smiled at a young couple jogging toward her. Han came to attention, but Henry had taught her several of the click techniques he used. The young dog came to heel beside her, on his best behavior.

"You are such a good boy," she said, kneeling down beside him after they passed to give him a hug. "I'm proud of you."

Obiwan nuzzled her face and she hugged him. "I'm always proud of you. You're a natural at this. But your friend here had to learn his good behavior." She rubbed their heads and stood back up. Polly glanced back along the trail, considering whether or not she should return, then decided that the girls could take care of themselves for just a little longer. If she couldn't crash on the couch, the least she was going to do was take a long quiet walk with her boys.

As she walked, Polly thought about the two murders. They had to be connected because otherwise, there were two murderers in town and that just hurt her head too much to think about. She gave a quick shudder, thinking back a few months when her old boyfriend had shown up in Bellingwood with a serial killer. She felt terrible for Joey because she still had soft spot in her heart for him. He'd deteriorated since she first met him. Maybe he'd always been that way, but she worried that she'd been the catalyst for his rapid descent into madness.

The only comfort Polly had was that his mother was as mad as he was. She just hid it better. Polly shook her head. How in the world did people like that manage to live within society, doing all that woman did, and never be caught in their insanity? Did her acquaintances ignore that part of her personality or just refuse to see it?

A tug from Obiwan made Polly realize that she'd stopped in the middle of the trail. She paused to get her bearings. No wonder she'd stopped.

"Hey," she said to the dogs. "At least some part of my brain was paying attention."

They'd come out on the street leading south from the vineyard to Sycamore Inn. She could retrace her steps on the trail, but was much more curious about how Alistair Greyson was getting along. Jeff thought he was doing very well. He'd rearranged furniture to make the front room nicer for guests and was talking to Eliseo about bushes and trees they could plant to bring color to the front of the building.

Polly walked between two buildings to enter the courtyard in the center of the complex and heard someone whistling. Grey looked up from a picnic table when Han gave a yap.

"Ms. Giller," he said and stood up, moving across the lawn to greet her. "How are you this fine evening? I see that you are accompanied by two very handsome young beasts. Out for a stroll?"

She shifted both leashes to her left hand so she could accept his outstretched hand to shake. "We are. We took the trail. The boys needed exercise and I needed peace."

Grey reached for the leashes and she allowed him to take them. He gestured to the picnic table. "Ahhh, peace. One thing we don't often find, though our souls desperately crave it. I find that life in a small town can offer more or less depending on how we choose to live."

"I suppose so," Polly said. "How do you like it here?"

"In my own search for inner peace, I find this space to be quite comforting," he replied. Then he pointed to the center area. "This has not always been a lawn. Might I ask what used to be here?"

She nodded. "It was a swimming pool, but it had been pretty much filled in by the time we purchased it. Things were a horrid mess."

"I see," he said. "Might you consider ever opening that back up again?"

Polly looked out over the beautiful lawn and scowled. "No, I can't imagine why I'd want to do that. I don't want the liability or the maintenance of a pool. Why do you ask?"

"Curiosity," he said. "You left the pool intact, but filled it in?"

"Yes. Now I'm curious. Tell me what you are thinking?"

"Nothing much. And certainly nothing that I'd want you to consider until you knew me better. We'll discuss it later."

Polly chuckled. 'You have no idea how much I hate surprises and I am not terribly fond of cryptic questions and statements either."

"Please allow me time to line up all of my mallards before pursuing this," he said.

"Get your ducks in a row?"

"That's one way of putting it." He reached across the table and placed his hand on top of hers. "Am I to understand that you encountered another vicious murder this morning? I am sorry you are constantly exposed to such darkness in the world. You are a shining light. It doesn't seem fitting for this to be your calling."

"It certainly is something," she said. "But if someone has to do it, I'm glad it's me." Polly looked into his deep blue eyes. There was caring and understanding there, as if he'd experienced the greatest depths of pain and the highest heights of joy. Every time she was with him, she felt comfortable and safe. The dogs must have felt the same way. Obiwan was lying under the table, almost exactly between them, and Han had taken a place beside Grey, his head lolling over on the man's foot.

"Why do you say that?" he asked.

As he spoke, Polly watched the lines on his face shift with the formation of words. She was so focused on him, she missed the question and had to slow her mind down to think back on what he had said.

"Say what?"

"Why are you glad that it's you?"

"I guess I know that I can handle it. Death doesn't frighten me. Sometimes I'm startled by it, but it isn't scary or dark or awful. Whatever that person felt before they died, it was over in a split second and they've left all the pain behind. Their last moments, whether horrifying or peaceful, no longer mean anything to them. They've moved on to the next step and have no physical ties left to their lives." She shrugged. "It would have been awful if Abby's father or sister had found her this morning. Neither of them need to have that memory chiseled into their minds. I was the one who was there. As awful as losing her is going to be for them, at least they will be remember her as a happy, sweet girl."

"What about your memory of her?"

"I didn't know her before today, so she's just become part of me now. I was the one who protected her father and sister from that. I don't take it in."

He didn't look as if he wanted to accept that. "You have to take it in. It's a powerful moment. You shouldn't just toss it aside."

"You're right," Polly said. "I don't toss it aside, but I don't let it eat away at me. I'll hold on to my dogs a little tighter tonight and I'll snuggle in with my husband, maybe hug Rebecca one or two times more than usual."

"So you let your friends and family help you through this."

"They aren't helping me through anything. They're just part of my life."

Grey smiled at her. "You've figured this out by surrounding yourself with good people. You don't let many toxic folks into your life, do you?"

"I ignore them as much as possible. I don't have time for their bitter anger."

"I don't suppose you would," he said. "Especially not if you are the body finder. That takes emotional energy. Energy that the rest of us expend on those toxic, bitter people. You're a smart woman, Polly Giller. You've figured this out without all of those pesky psychology degrees."

She nodded and he allowed silence to surround them.

"I should get home to the girls," Polly said, swinging a leg out from under the picnic table.

"This isn't all that easy for you, is it," he asked quietly.

"Death?" Polly shrugged. "It is what it is."

"And everyone lets you get away with saying those words. You pass it off as if it is easy for you and you try not to think about it after it's over."

"You're right there," she said. "I don't need to think about it again. It's not my job."

"You don't spend time with their families. I'll bet there are some you've never met. You leave that all to others. Am I right?"

Polly thought back to the girls who had been killed by her ex-boyfriend a few months ago. She'd never met any of those families. She didn't want to. She knew that it made no sense for her to feel guilty about their deaths. Joey was the one who obsessed over her and committed the murders to get her attention. She had no interest in meeting Julie Smith's family or Abby's father and sister. She thought back further. It wasn't completely true. She'd gotten to know Thomas Zeller's old girlfriend and her family and she'd found Henry's Uncle Loren.

"Those don't count," she muttered, then looked at Grey. "You're right. I avoid those situations as often as possible. I don't want to see the shock in their eyes and have to deal with the grieving of someone that I don't know. That's such a personal time and having a stranger gawk at you while you try to process a loss like that isn't fair. They need privacy and family, not me." She gave him a wry grin. "It's bad enough that people see me as a grim reaper."

"You make jokes, but it isn't easy, is it?"

"We all make jokes," she said. "It's about the only way to handle it. I mean, look at me." She gestured at herself. "I'm a normal, Midwestern girl and my super power is finding dead bodies. I have a super power. Who else can say that? Everybody around me lives normal lives and do normal things. But when the Sheriff sees my phone number show up, he knows I've found a dead body." She hit the table with her fist. "Three months ago they had to send me out looking for a girl who had been killed. I was the only one who could find her. The police had looked for days, but in just a few short hours, I tracked her down. I didn't want to be strange and odd. I didn't want to be infamous. I just want to be Polly Giller and live a quiet life in the middle of Iowa."

"This frustrates you. And you won't talk about it."

"No one wants to hear me whine about something as silly as this. I can't make it stop, so why complain?" She grinned. "And I have plenty of other things to whine about."

"I doubt that. You know, a person once said something about cursing someone by wishing them an interesting life."

"Confucius," she said. "May you live in interesting times. But I don't think he said it."

"Anyway. You have an interesting life. Whether it's a curse or a blessing is your decision."

"Tonight it feels like a curse," Polly said. "It was a long day with no sign of growing shorter." She looked out over the lawn and said, "You won't tell me what you're thinking of back here?"

He laughed. "You don't forget a thing, do you?"

"Not really."

"Do you know why I limp?" he asked.

"Something about hockey?"

"I was pretty good in my day - being recruited by the pros. Then came a rather horrendous car accident and my pro career was over before it had even begun. I had to re-start my life while I lay there in that hospital. Before I left, I decided that I hadn't always been defined by hockey and I could choose to be anybody I wanted to be. So, I made some interesting choices and years passed and here I am."

Polly looked at him and said, "There must be more of a story in those years that passed, yes?"

"Aye, my friend, but those stories will be told another time. For the purpose of this conversation, the fact that I still love hockey is enough."

"Wait," Polly said. "That day you swept the kid's legs out from under him. Did you learn that playing hockey?"

He chuckled. "Well, not that exact move, but I can still face down an aggressor."

"Now, tell me what you are thinking." She gestured to the grassy area.

Grey stood up and walked away from the table, stirring the two dogs into life. Han sat up and Grey stopped to pick up his leash. He handed Obiwan's leash to Polly. She walked with him.

"I'd like to put ice in here this winter. Maybe teach some of the boys and girls how to skate and find out if any of them show any skill for the game. You have a league in Des Moines and several young teams in the state. Maybe someday we could do something in Bellingwood, but we need to start. This isn't much, but even a little bit of ice for a short period of time could be interesting." He turned and grinned at her. "There's that word again."

"That's a pretty big dream," Polly said. "I can't even imagine how to make it happen."

"I'm sure your husband can. And don't forget your groundskeeper. Both of them are quite creative and practical. They both understand how to create something from nothing."

"Henry is amazing. It still astounds me that he can take my ideas and turn them into something like Sycamore House and then, this place. I start dreaming and he makes it happen."

Grey was walking close to her and nudged her arm. "The two of you are very fortunate to have found each other. It's a joy to see you together. You fit."

She nodded. He was right. That was a perfect description. They fit together. Sometimes it was so natural she couldn't believe they hadn't always been together. Polly looped her arm through his as they walked. "Who are you thinking will come skate with you?"

"That young man in your sickroom. He needs me. He sees nothing out there in front of him for his life. All he ever focuses on is the pain that he's in. And those young men who assaulted us. They are so wrapped up in their anger that they have lost their true north. They don't know who they're supposed to be and right now, no one is helping them discover that. The world is afraid of them. Their parents are afraid of them, their teachers and friends are afraid of them, so they live in a bubble, knowing that at any moment it could break and they'd be lost."

"Wow," Polly said. "I'm just mad at them. Who in the hell do they think they are, treating people like that? Do you know that two of them were in the coffee shop today and were taken out by the police?"

He stopped and turned to her, pain in his eyes. "I'm too late."

Polly put her hand on his. "Grey, you've been here less than two weeks. You can't save the world in that amount of time."

"You said there were two boys today. We were attacked by more than that."

"One of the boys who lives with his aunt and uncle on their farm wasn't there. I don't know what happened to him."

"I want to meet him. He'll remember me. Maybe he and I can start moving earth here in preparation for the ice this winter."

She tightened her grip on his hand. "You are a character. I will find out who he is. Henry told me the other night and I've forgotten. His parents were killed, so I'm sure that he is as lost as you can get."

"You give me permission to begin this project?"

"Talk to Henry," Polly said. "If he thinks it is possible and the two of you can come up with a budget we can manage, my answer is yes."

"The budget is not something I will saddle you with," he said. "The boys and I will raise the funds and I have money of my own."

"No big decisions today," Polly said. "I'll tell Henry you want to make an appointment to discuss this and we'll move forward from there. You are a character, you know."

"It's my best trait," he responded with a smile.

CHAPTER TWENTY-THREE

Nobody moved the next afternoon when Polly asked if they wanted to go to the library and then get ice cream. Kayla and Rebecca sat on either end of the sofa in the media room with Andrew in the middle playing a game. The girls whimpered and Rebecca gave a weary shake of her head.

Gina was a very active girl and had kept the three older kids moving all day long. She'd kept Rebecca and Kayla up late the night before, begging them to talk about boys, teachers at school, the horses and donkeys at the barn - anything she could come up with. Polly had checked on them a couple of times, but finally gave up and went to sleep.

The little girl had gotten up when she heard Polly and Henry moving and in her excitement, stirred Rebecca and Kayla awake. She begged to go to the barn, so by eight o'clock they were out of the house. Andrew showed up soon after and Polly sent him down to join them. They had ridden horses, much to Gina's delight, taken a wagon ride, and helped Eliseo in the garden. As soon as the swimming pool was open, Gina pulled out her swimsuit and announced that she couldn't wait, so off they went.

When Darla Landry showed up with her son, Polly was certain that she'd sent the young girl home completely exhausted. Darla wouldn't have to do much this evening to entertain her daughter.

Polly was in the kitchen mixing a marinade for the chicken they would grill this evening when Rebecca came over.

"What's up?" Polly asked.

"Can Kayla and Andrew spend the rest of the evening with me? We won't be able to relax like this when school starts. I'm not ready to have them go home yet."

Polly shrugged. "They have to ask permission, but I certainly don't care. What are you planning to do?"

"Not much. Just sit around and talk. We won't get in your hair or anything and Henry usually watches TV in your room if he isn't working in the office. We'll stay out here."

"That's fine," Polly said. "Don't worry about getting in our hair. We're both kinda used to you all. As long as Stephanie and Sylvie don't care, I'm fine with it. In fact, tell Kayla to ask Stephanie if she wants to eat dinner outside with us. I have plenty."

Rebecca gave her an odd look, but said, "Is there anything we can do to help?"

"You can start on the corn," Polly said, pointing to a bag filled with corn on the cob. She opened the refrigerator and took out a container. "I've already mixed up the butter and herbs."

"Do it in the garage?" Rebecca asked. She'd been through this routine several times already.

Polly handed her a box of aluminum foil and utensils. "Thank you."

"Kayla, I need help," Rebecca called across the room after dropping the aluminum foil on the floor the second time. She handed the bag of corn and the butter to her friend and gathered the rest into her hands. Kayla shared another of those odd looks with her friend, but Rebecca pushed her forward.

Polly smiled as she watched them walk across the room. Rebecca was always going to be in charge. All she would be able to do was watch and guide her as best as she could.

"Henry's here," Rebecca yelled back from the stairway.

Han and Obiwan went tearing through the house to greet him. He walked in from his office and put his hand out toward Andrew, who gave it a high five slap and went back to his game.

"What are you doing?" Henry asked. "I came home early."

"I'm getting supper ready. Are you good to grill tonight?"

"They did it again?" He shook his head.

"Who did what? The girls are taking care of the corn. I have the chicken and there are salads in the fridge downstairs."

"Not them they, but they they." He gave her a look of disgust. "She calls and asks if I will be able to make it home in time to deal with dinner so that you're free, but does she call you?"

"Who?"

"Where's your phone. Have you had it on today?"

Polly thought back through her day. She'd been busy enough to not pay much attention to whether or not her phone was working. She'd made some calls in her office, but maybe not on her phone. That didn't make sense, though. She used that phone for everything. She patted her back pocket and realized it wasn't there.

"I don't know where it is. Did you try to call me?"

"No, I was too busy trying to get things wrapped up so I could get home on time."

"Dial it, would you?"

He used his phone to call hers and when she didn't hear his ring tone, Polly panicked. "I can't believe I've lost my phone. You know how I depend on that thing."

"It has to be here. Where did you go today?"

She thought back over her day. "I haven't left the property. I was down in the barn for a while, I walked the dogs a couple of times, and I was in my office."

Henry walked over to their bedroom. Polly followed and so did the dogs. The cats jumped down from their ledges on the cat tree when Polly and Henry entered the room.

He strode over to her side of the bed and picked up her phone. "Things were a little chaotic this morning. But I still can't believe you walked out of this place without it."

"I can't either." Polly took it out of his hands and sat down on the end of the bed. When she swiped it, nothing happened. "I think it's dead."

"Of course it is."

"This has never happened to me before. Am I losing my mind?"

He chuckled. "Three girls, two dogs, two cats and a husband are too much for your early morning workout, eh?"

"I guess that's over my limit." She plugged her phone in. "So who called me and what did I miss?"

"That's what I don't fully understand. I can't believe she wasn't here worrying about you when you didn't answer your phone. She never called me back all worried either."

"Who?"

"Lydia. Something about an important girls' night tonight."

Polly jumped at the knock at their front door. "You don't suppose that's her, do you?"

"I'll go see," he said.

Her phone had just crested the one percent mark for power. "I can. You change. We need to talk about tonight."

He looked at her, his brows knit together.

"No big deal. Get comfortable. I'll see who it is." Polly walked across the living room to the front door and found Jeff there with his hand raised to knock again.

"I'm so sorry, I'm so sorry," he said. "I totally forgot to tell you."

"Tell me what?"

"Lydia stopped by while you were across the street at the pool getting the kids and I was supposed to have you call her right away. I got busy with those crazy church ladies and totally forgot. She's going to kill me."

Polly laughed. "It's my fault. I forgot my phone this morning and it's dead. I'll call her now. Henry just told me."

He ran the back of his hand across his forehead with great drama. "Thank goodness. I thought my life had ended. She's no one that I want to have angry at me."

Polly patted his shoulder. "You'll live. I'll take the hit on this one. But you owe me."

"Uh huh. I could have made you talk to those little old ladies."

"Jeff?" Stephanie's voice came up from the bottom of the stairs.

"Be right there, my sweet," he called back. "See. It never ends."

"You're a nut." Polly grinned as he ran back down the steps. It should have felt weird to have her home and business in the same building, but it couldn't be any more normal. She loved having these people around.

"Is it charged enough yet?" she asked loudly after shutting the door and starting back to the bedroom.

"I dunno," Henry said.

Polly shut the door to the bedroom once she got in there. "I don't want to go out tonight. This has been a crazy day and I just let Rebecca invite Kayla and Andrew to spend the evening. I hate leaving you with that."

"Because they're so hard to get along with?" he asked. "It's fine. I have work to do in the office anyway."

"But I'm making you cook dinner and everything."

"If I were you, I wouldn't worry about it. Call Lydia. Tell her you're alive and that you'll be there. It's been a while since you've all spent time together. Go. Get silly."

~~~

Polly walked into the coffee shop and looked for her friends. After Lydia had bawled her out for being unavailable all day and terrifying her to within an inch of a heart attack, she finally told Polly that they were meeting at six o'clock. She sat down at a table, arranging herself so she could see the front door.

Most of the shops were open in the evenings this week before school started. A couple of stores had started it the summer Polly moved into town and in the last two years, it had taken on a festival-type atmosphere. Kids had one last hurrah with their friends before homework and activities absorbed their evenings. Stores offered great deals on back-to-school items before they put everything out for clearance and the whole community enjoyed beautiful summer evenings in town.

Polly had promised Rebecca that they could come up Friday night for the street dance.

"Do you want something to drink?" Polly looked up to see Jeff standing over her.

"What are you doing?" she asked.

"Camille and I are taking care of the evenings this week. The young'uns are back in school and you know how evenings are on campus. None of them had planned on working these hours. I'd forgotten about this week. So, we've got it."

Polly smirked at him. "No Helena?"

"She might have gotten fired today," he said with a smile.

"Sylvie says she's always quit before she got fired. But I'm glad. She had some interesting ideas about who she would work for."

"We don't need that," he replied. "This place should be relaxing and fun for everyone, including my manager. She doesn't need an employee terrorizing her. None of us do."

"That's good." Polly said. "Have you seen Lydia? I'm supposed to meet her."

"No," he said. "And I didn't forget to give you any other messages from her. I promise."

"Don't worry. It was my fault."

"So... coffee?"

Polly glanced up at the menu on the wall. She was hungry, but since Lydia hadn't told her what was happening tonight, she didn't feel safe in ordering. "No, I'd better wait."

"Let me know," Jeff walked away to a table filled with high school girls. He stopped and talked to them, then moved on to another table with two women.

Polly watched him work the room and grinned as she realized she was feeling proud. He was natural and comfortable with people.

After a few more minutes of waiting, she couldn't stand it and sent a text to Lydia. *"You said the coffee shop at six, right?"*

"We're here, where are you?" came back the reply.

Polly recognized a few people, but none were her friends.

"What in the hell?" she sent. *"You're freaking me out."*

"Serves you right."

The front door opened and Lydia came bustling in with Beryl. They made a beeline for Polly's table and the two women each grabbed an arm and lifted Polly out of the seat.

"Mess with my heart, will you?" Lydia said. "That is unacceptable."

"I said I was sorry. I had no idea that I'd gotten that far out of contact with you," Polly protested. Then she locked her legs in place to stop their forward movement. "And besides, isn't this whole thing a little last minute?"

Lydia grinned at her. "You're so easy. Come outside. Sylvie's on the patio with Andy. We figured you would see us out there."

"What are we doing tonight? I'm starving," Polly said. She waved to Sylvie and Andy when they turned the corner.

"We're working for our dinner tonight," Beryl said, dropping into a chair beside Sylvie. "Sit and I'll explain."

"Do you know what's going on?" Polly asked Andy, who shook her head no.

Beryl pulled up two manila envelopes. "We're breaking into two teams and each is responsible for parts of our dinner. Inside the envelope is your first clue. Go to the shop or house that the clue refers you to and they'll give you the dinner item and your next clue. Since it's my game, I'm playing along the route. You'll see me at random times. Polly, you and Andy are one team while Lydia and Sylvie are the other. Are you ready?"

"Is the food going to go bad before we get to wherever we're going?" Lydia asked.

Beryl gestured with her head to two red coolers behind them. "Lydia, you take one for your Jeep and Polly, you take the other in your truck. There's ice in each of them to keep things cool enough. Any hot dishes will be insulated." She wriggled her nose at Lydia. "I may not be much of a cook, but I know how to avoid poisoning my friends."

Andy raised her hand and waited for Beryl to acknowledge that she had a question. "Where are we supposed to go when we're finished?"

"Don't worry," Beryl said. "That's the last clue." She waved the two envelopes in front of them. "Just so you know, there are prizes. You might want to think fast. Are you ready?"

Polly nodded at Andy, who took the envelope that Beryl was waving in front of her face. Lydia snatched the other one and scooted close to Sylvie so they could read it together.

"I've got the cooler, Andy," Polly said. "Let's go." Polly picked up the top cooler and carried it with her to the truck. She put it in the back behind her seat and climbed in, waiting for Andy to shut the door. "Okay, what does it say?"

"She dances rings round you and me, her waifs fly to the bumblebee." Andy said.

"Lisa Foster's dance studio?" Polly asked. "I can't believe they're open tonight. It's just up here around the corner."

Andy nodded. "My granddaughter was in her show last spring. They did *Flight of the Bumblebee.*"

Polly drove around the block and pulled into a space in front of the studio. Lights were on so she and Andy jumped out and approached the door. When she tugged on it, it opened and they went inside.

"May I help you?" a young girl in tights asked from behind a counter.

"This is going to sound crazy," Polly responded, "but do you have something for Polly Giller and Andy Specek?"

The girl laughed and bent down. She came back up with a small basket. "You guys must have fun."

Andy laughed. "We do. We always do. Is there a card in there?"

Polly opened the basket and the smell of garlic wafted up from within. Bundles wrapped in foil were nestled in red and white checked fabric, a tablecloth from Dylan Foster's pizza shop, Pizzazz. His wife, Lisa not only owned the dance studio, but was Mark Ogden's sister. She handed Andy the card.

"Thank you," Polly said as they left.

"Have fun!"

"Where to next?"

They climbed back into the truck and Andy said, *"From the*

highest heights to the lowest lows, you need his help if you don't have the goes."

"What?" Polly asked, laughing. "The goes?"

Andy dropped her head and Polly watched her mutter the rhyme again. "She wouldn't mean the pharmacy, would she?"

Polly thought about it. "Ahhh, of course she would." She laughed and laughed as she backed out of the parking space and headed back downtown. They parked in front of the pharmacy and went inside, heading for the back.

Nate was waiting for them with a bag in hand. "I think this is for you," he said.

"Do you help people who don't have the goes?" Polly asked.

"What?"

"Never mind. Beryl dropped this off, didn't she?"

"Yeah. Earlier this morning. She said you'd be in. I haven't opened it. I hope I'm not helping pass contraband."

Polly opened the tote bag and saw red checked napkins and plastic wine glasses. "Nope. Just helping us put dinner together. Have you heard from your wife? Is she having a good week?"

He nodded. "She actually sounds more relaxed than she has in a long time. Her mother is doing everything and forcing her to rest and just play with the kids. I'm glad she went."

"Awesome. When are you and Henry getting back to the cars?"

"That's up to you," Nate said. "You give him the night off and I'll have someone here to work for me."

Polly scowled at him. "He can have any night he wants. I don't make his schedule."

Nate chuckled. "I know. Just messing with you. He said something about maybe tomorrow night. I'm flying out to drive back with Joss this weekend. She thought her dad was staying in Chicago longer than he really is. She shouldn't have to make the whole trip alone."

"You're a good man," Andy said. She tugged on Polly's sleeve. "We'd better hurry. What's the next clue?"

Polly used both hands to open the bag in front of Andy, who reached in and took out a third white card.

"She walks in beauty like the night. You'll find her tools a great dee-light."

Both of them said, "The beauty shop."

"Thanks, Nate," Polly said as they left the store. She put the bag in the back seat and followed Andy to the beauty shop. The owner's name was Dee Ryder. Polly didn't know her well. There were two shops in town and she'd ended up at the other one.

When they walked in the front door, Beryl spun on a stool and said, "You'd better hurry, Lydia is ahead of you and you don't want the loser's prizes tonight."

Andy crossed to the counter and said, "How are you, Dee? Do you know Polly Giller?"

The woman put her hand out. "It's nice to meet you. You're friends with these two?"

"I claim Andy all the time," Polly said. "But Beryl is a risk. I only claim her when I have to." She jumped as Beryl slid her arms around Polly's waist.

"What are you doing?" Polly asked.

"Just testing a theory."

"What theory is that?"

"You like me better than you say. You didn't even hit me."

Polly chuckled. "Do people often hit you when you sneak up on them?"

"You'd be surprised," Beryl said as she hustled them toward the front door. "Now you two better hurry and get out of here. You don't want them to beat you."

Andy headed for the front door and then turned back. "Hey," she said. "Stop that."

Beryl cackled. "Got 'cha." She took the tote bag from Dee and handed it to Polly. "Put that in the cooler. Dee kept it in the fridge for me today."

"Nice to meet you," Polly said as they left. She opened the cooler and put the tote bag in, then remembered that she needed the card from inside it.

When they were back in the truck, she handed it to Andy. "Okay, now where."

"Verdant growth, be it blue or green. The boys are cute, though no Charlie Sheen. Drive away, sweet girls, to the end of the lane and find our libation, though it be this group's bane."

"Secret Woods Winery," Polly said, laughing. "I wonder how much she had them set aside for us."

"Please not that much. I still haven't heard the end of that from Len. He can't believe I got drunk at my age."

"At your age?" Polly said. "What does that mean?"

Andy swatted at her. "I know! That's what I asked. Then I told him that he didn't marry an old lady and he couldn't treat me like one."

"Good for you." Polly drove down the highway and turned just past Sycamore Inn.

"How's your new guy working out?" Andy asked. "I've heard he's kind of a character."

"He is such a nice man. There's just something about him that makes you feel instantly safe and comfortable. I hope he stays for a long time." Polly pulled to a stop between two cars. "Well, let's go in and see what we've got."

They walked up to the front door and went inside. Sounds of a party came from one of the back rooms and a young man in a black vest and tie came forward. "May I help you?" he asked.

"I'm Polly Giller and this is Andy Specek. Do you have something for us?"

He nodded. "Just a moment."

Andy took a deep breath. "I wonder what Beryl's prizes are. She scares me. That woman likes to play games."

"How bad can it get?" Polly asked.

"You have to ask?"

Polly chuckled. "I suppose I shouldn't. Do you think we're nearly at the end of our trek?"

"I hope so," Andy said. "I'm starving. That garlic bread is killing me. Why did she make us pick it up first? To torture us?"

J. J. Roberts came out with an insulated bag and handed it to Polly. "Sounds like you girls are having quite the party tonight. Are you sure you wouldn't like company?"

"How much wine is in there?" Andy asked with a gasp.

"Just six bottles," he said.

"Six bottles! What does that woman think she's doing to us? I'm not getting drunk again."

He laughed. "I'm just kidding. There are only three in here. She told me about your last escapade. I'm just glad we were a small part of it." He handed a white card to Andy. "And I'm supposed to give you this, too. Have a good time tonight."

"Thanks, J. J.," Polly said. "Everything going well out here?"

"It's been a good summer," he replied. "Patrick is back in California for a few months. They needed him to work with Sword Lords, but he'll be back right at harvest." J. J. shrugged. "You know, the first couple of years are tough. But we're sticking with it. You guys have been great. Rachel is a great chef and Jeff Lyndsay is good to work with. We appreciate the extra business he throws our way."

It made Polly feel good to know that he trusted these guys with his guests. "I'm glad we can work together," she said.

"We need to hurry," Andy said, then looked at the two of them. "I'm sorry."

"No, you're right. We'll talk later, J. J.," Polly said.

He held the door for them as they left.

"Well, where do we go now?"

"What we call the beginning is often the end. And to make an end is to make a beginning. The end is where we start from - T.S. Eliot." Andy replied.

"Are you kidding me?"

"What do you mean?"

"We're going back to the coffee shop," Polly said, shaking her head.

CHAPTER TWENTY-FOUR

Once they got back downtown, Polly drove to the side of the coffee shop and parked in front of the patio. Lydia and Sylvie weren't back yet, but Beryl was at their table, spinning a bright yellow parasol over her head. She snapped her fingers as Polly got out and Rebecca, Kayla and Andrew came out of the coffee shop, dressed in black pants and white shirts. They did their best to keep straight faces as they crossed to Polly's truck.

"What are you three doing?" Polly asked.

"We're here to serve, ma'am," Andrew replied. "I will escort you two beautiful young women to your seats, while my associates retrieve your packages."

When Rebecca walked past her, Polly put her hand out to stop the girl, but Rebecca neatly avoided her touch and moved on.

Andrew stepped between Andy and Polly, bent both of his elbows and tilted his head, indicating they should take his arms. Once they obeyed, he led them to the table, pulled a chair out for Andy first and then for Polly. Rebecca presented him with the bag Polly had picked up at the pharmacy. The two of them shook out the red-checked tablecloth and with only a little help from the adults, soon had it situated. Kayla bowed formally and presented him with the napkins. He snapped out one and placed it in Andy's lap, then snapped the other and reached to place it into Polly's lap.

She tried to help and he scowled. "I have it, ma'am," he said.

Giggling from the two girls had him turning to both of them with that scowl on his face. Kayla smirked. "He's been practicing for hours," she said.

Rebecca handed the bag from Secret Woods Winery to Beryl.

"They're too young to serve wine," she said, opening the bag. She took a bottle out and placed it in a wine bucket beside her. "I felt it best not to corrupt them at such an early age, but aren't they spectacular?"

"How long have you been planning this?" Polly asked.

"I talked to Jeff this afternoon and he set it up with Rebecca."

Lydia pulled her Jeep in next to Polly's truck and parked, causing Andrew, Rebecca and Kayla to scurry away. They repeated their earlier performance for Sylvie and Lydia, who smiled through the surprise and allowed Andrew to escort them to the table. He snapped two napkins open and placed them in their laps and then stepped back and stood at attention.

Sylvie whispered at him, "What are you doing here?"

He ignored her and smiled.

"They're under strict orders not to fraternize," Beryl said. "There's a tip in it for them if they keep it professional tonight. But you girls have to be nice, okay?"

Andrew joined Rebecca and Kayla at the next table, helping them to lay out the food items. Kayla brought plates and silverware over and set it out in front of each woman, followed by Rebecca with their wine glasses.

Polly turned and snuck a glance, catching Andrew scooping soup into bowls. When Kayla and Rebecca returned, he pointed at the bread and they unwrapped it and dropped it into a couple of baskets. Kayla returned with the baskets while Rebecca and Andrew carefully delivered bowls of soup to each person.

"No one spilled anything," Polly said. Rebecca turned away from Beryl and caught Polly's eye, then rolled her eyes in relief.

"Wine?" Beryl asked, uncorking the bottle. She filled the glasses and took another bottle out to chill in the ice.

"Where's the soup from?" Andy asked.

"She sent us to Davey's," Sylvie responded. "What was that clue? Something about a slutty bartender? I'm glad Lydia remembered that evening. It seems so long ago."

Polly swallowed the bite of bread she had in her mouth. "How long have you been planning this evening?" she asked Beryl.

"A few days. It's no big thing."

"For someone who likes to think of herself as a hermit hiding in a small town, you certainly know plenty of people," Polly replied. "They did all this for you with no question?"

Beryl laughed. "There were questions, but once I explained, they thought it was great fun. I didn't know when I was going to be able to pull it off, but then I remembered that this week was when everything was open and decided to see what I could do."

The kids had their backs to them at the other table and were fussing about.

"Do you need help?" Beryl asked.

"No, I think we've got it," Rebecca replied. She started whispering to Andrew and Kayla. Andrew turned around. "Whenever you're ready."

"Where's the main course from?" Polly asked.

"That has to be what we picked up at the barn," Lydia said.

Andy's head shot up. "The barn?"

Lydia laughed. "The clue said they were the biggest beasts on four legs we'd ever seen, so we drove to the barn. Eliseo put a box in the Jeep and told us we couldn't look." She swatted at Beryl. "Just tell me it isn't some strange exotic meat."

"Alligator, coming right up," Andrew announced and with a flourish, presented a plate to Polly, upending it into her lap. "I'm so sorry," he cried. "I'm so sorry!"

Polly laughed and picked the plate up and then worked to retrieve her meal. Two pieces of fried chicken were still sitting on her legs, she'd caught the plate before too many baked beans had fallen, but lost most of the potato salad and corn bread.

Andrew was in shock and his face crumpled as he realized what he'd done. She was afraid he might cry, but instead, he rushed inside the coffee shop.

"I've got this," Beryl said, starting to stand up.

"No, he's my son," Sylvie replied. "I'll talk to him."

Rebecca and Kayla couldn't move in their shock until Beryl said, "Go ahead girls. It's okay. Nobody is upset over a little spilled food. Serve the rest. We have plenty to refill Polly's plate."

"My dad would have been really mad if we ever did anything like that," Kayla said. "I can't believe nobody's upset."

"Andrew is," Rebecca reminded her.

"Yeah, but he did it," Kayla whispered back. "None of the adults are mad."

"It's just a little food and everything will clean right up," Polly said. "In fact," she handed her plate back to Rebecca. "I should go inside and wipe off my leg. Fill me up again, would you? The chicken is fine. It didn't make it any further than my lap and that's good for longer than the ten second rule." She stood up and patted Beryl's shoulder. "We're not ruining the party. We'll all be right back, I promise."

"You'd better," Beryl said. "I haven't handed out prizes yet."

"I can't even imagine," Polly said with a laugh, opening the door into the coffee shop.

Andrew was tucked into his mother's shoulder in a corner by the back bookshelves, his shoulders shaking. It killed her to see him react so hard to something that was such a non-issue, but she walked past to the bathroom, nodding at Camille who was cleaning up behind the coffee counter.

Sylvie came into the bathroom while Polly dried her legs. Her skin caught most of the food, leaving her shorts relatively clean.

"Andrew feels horrible," Sylvie said. "But I think he was more embarrassed than anything."

Polly smiled. "I hope he's okay. Poor kid. It was no big deal."

"I think it was to him. I loved that he was having fun, but he was getting a little cocky out there."

"Well, of course he was. The only boy with all of those women and girls. He was hot stuff. And you know he's mortified that Rebecca saw him make a mistake.

"It's all about her, isn't it," Sylvie said with a sigh.

"I'm afraid she's going to torture him for a while. He's comfortable with her and she's just starting to find her freedom again. I've talked to both of them," Polly said, "But neither of them will figure it all out until they go through it." She laughed. "We know what that's like, right? I mean, really. If I would have listened to Mary and Dad when they tried to hint at the boys I should avoid, I wouldn't have had some of those awful dates."

"My mother liked Anthony," Sylvie said, with a touch of disgust in her voice. "She thought he'd take good care of me. That woman was not a good judge of male character." She put a bright look back on her face. "But I keep telling myself that he gave me Jason and Andrew and they are wonderful. Now if we can just get Andrew to perk back up and finish the evening."

"Was he crying?" Polly asked.

"Yes, the poor thing. I told him to go wash his face and order fruity drinks for him and the girls. He can hide until his face quits being splotchy, but he *is* coming back. He can't run away from every embarrassing moment."

"Good. We'll be kind." Polly thought about it. "Well, most of us will be kind. I have no idea what Beryl will do. Whatever it is, I hope he can laugh."

Sylvie chuckled. "Me too. He'll be fine. Everybody has to face things like this in their lives. I'm afraid this will be the least of his embarrassing moments." She held the door open and followed Polly back through the coffee shop to the patio, deliberately avoiding Andrew, who was sitting at the coffee bar.

Kayla and Rebecca had taken seats at the other table and were eating. Polly found her plate refilled and sitting in front of her seat. "Everything okay out here?" she asked.

"Is our boy gonna make it?" Lydia asked quietly.

Sylvie nodded "He'll be fine."

They all glanced up as he came out the door carrying drinks for Kayla and Rebecca. No one said anything to him, just watched in silence. He placed the drinks in front of the girls, then sat down with his back to the women's table.

"Nothing like spilled milk to kick an evening off to a rollicking start," Beryl said. She lifted her wine glass. "I suggest we toast to good friends, our worst embarrassing moments and life that continues no matter what."

"Here here," the ladies said, tipping their wine glasses at each other.

"Garçon," Beryl said. When no one responded, she spoke a little louder. "Ahem. Garçon."

Rebecca poked Andrew and he looked up.

"That's you, young man," Beryl said. "You're the garçon. Remember?"

He shook his head and stood up, then came over to stand beside her. "How may I help you?" he asked politely.

"You may ask the ladies if they would like anything more." Beryl pulled his sleeve, so he would bend toward her. "The world didn't fall apart," she whispered, loudly enough so that people could hear. "You're still adorable and well-mannered. None of that has changed. Do you understand me?"

His face flushed bright red and he nodded.

"Now, after your girlfriends and you have made sure that everyone here has had enough to eat, I want the three of you to take your plates and go inside. The rest of the conversation between us old ladies might be too much for small ears to hear. I'd hate to embarrass any of you any more than we already have."

Beryl turned to the rest of the ladies at the table. "We haven't talked about sex or anything, have we?"

Andy dropped her fork back to her plate and started to laugh while Lydia's mouth dropped open. "Beryl!" she said.

"I was just asking. I didn't think we had, but I couldn't remember. It's been so long since I've given it much thought that I was worried the conversation might have happened without my knowing."

Sylvie dropped her head into her hand and Polly sat back and grinned. Rebecca and Kayla took their cue from her and giggled.

They picked up the salad bowls and brought them to the table, placing them in the center.

"We could serve you," Rebecca said, "but I think it might be good for us to go inside as soon as possible. Isn't that right?" She looked at Kayla who couldn't take her eyes off Beryl.

"We'll take care of it from here," Andy said. "Please go inside before the woman embarrasses us any further."

"They all know that you got drunk at the last big party, don't they?" Beryl asked, doing her best to portray innocence.

Sylvie stood up and opened the door. "Go in. Now. I can't stand this. Please hurry before we have to kill her to protect you."

Andrew shook his head and went inside, followed closely by Rebecca and Kayla.

"Beryl Watson, you are absolutely insane," Sylvie said.

Beryl shrugged. "I took the pressure off the boy, didn't I? The story he and those girls will remember from tonight is going to be about how crazy I am, not that he dumped a plate of food in Polly's lap. I'm an old lady and no one ever knows what is going to come out of my mouth. I can take the heat."

Sylvie's eyes filled and she bent over to hug Beryl's shoulders. "You are an amazing woman. It's too bad that more people don't understand how terrific you are. Thank you."

"Ain't no big thing," Beryl said.

Lydia looked across at her friend. "I take you for granted far too often."

Andy nodded. "We always have. I've been her friend for as long as I can remember and every time we're together, she surprises me." She smiled at Beryl. "I'm awfully thankful for you."

Beryl picked up her parasol and tapped Andy on the head. "Stop it now. You're embarrassing me and you know I don't like it if I'm not in control. Finish your meals." She looked at Polly. "I want to hear more about that nice young man out at the hotel. I understand he's taken a liking to our Sylvie."

"How do you hear these things?" Sylvie asked, putting her fork down firmly on her plate. "You live by yourself, you never get out and yet you always know things you shouldn't know."

"I have spies everywhere." Beryl crouched forward, her eyes darting back and forth. "You never know where they're hiding."

At that moment, the sound of a child's scream rang out. Polly jumped from her seat and ran toward the sound. On the other side of the street, a young woman was fighting with a high school aged boy for her purse. Her daughter was screaming in fear.

Polly didn't even think about it, but ran across the street to help the woman. "You there. Stop what you're doing," she demanded.

She realized that she was about to confront Heath Harvey again. He was with one of the boys who'd tried to bully her and Grey the other day. By the time she put her feet on the sidewalk, the boys had taken off, running south.

"Are you okay?" she asked.

The woman nodded and wrapped her arms around her daughter.

"Call the police," Polly yelled and took off after the boys. She wasn't going to let them get away. She'd already told herself that they couldn't do much to her other than punch her a couple of times and she was betting that they wouldn't even do that. She saw them duck into the alley and stopped at the end, wondering if she wanted another black eye.

Footsteps behind her caused her to glance up, only to see Rebecca, Andrew and Kayla coming.

"What are you three doing?" she asked.

"We saw you chase someone and thought you might need help," Rebecca said.

That clinched it for Polly. It was one thing to put herself in danger, but the last people she wanted to see get hurt was these three kids. She looked down the alley and then back at Rebecca.

"I know who it was," she said. "I'm not walking into a fight with them. Not tonight. Let's go back and see if the woman is okay. She had a scare."

They walked back up the block and found a small crowd surrounding the woman and her daughter. Bert Bradford was walking down the street toward them and Polly waved at him.

She stopped and put her hands on Rebecca's shoulder. "Go on

back to the coffee shop. Tell them that I'm fine. I'll be there in a few minutes."

The kids hesitated and she said, "Go. I need to talk to Officer Bradford."

Rebecca scowled and harrumphed, but finally walked back across the street with Andrew and Kayla.

"What happened?" Bert asked after they left.

"Heath Harvey and one of the boys you took in yesterday tried to steal this woman's purse. I chased them into the alley, but decided not to follow any further."

He nodded. "I'm glad. We'll keep an eye out for them."

"What did you do with the other boy?" Polly asked.

"Ladd Berant," he said. "We couldn't keep him. The chief did his best to frighten him, but there are just some kids who are too cocky for their own good. He thinks he is smarter than all of us put together. It's too bad, though. One of these days he's going to go too far."

"How long do they get to get away with harassment like this?"

"You're certain it was Heath Harvey?" he asked.

"Absolutely."

"Attempted theft is more serious than intimidation. We'll find him and maybe this will put the fear of God into him." Bert gritted his teeth. "He usually doesn't do things like this on his own. Berant is the leader of this little gang and the rest of the boys do what he says. More than likely he's close by, giving directions."

"This is going to be a rough week for you guys if they're here with everyone on the streets."

Bert nodded, then looked over his shoulder at the group still gathered on the sidewalk. "I need to take care of her. Thanks for your help, but please don't get yourself in trouble chasing down our local gang members. There are people above me who wouldn't be pleased if you got hurt."

"Got it. I'll try to be good," Polly said. She smiled at him and walked back across the street. Yeah. This was going to take some explaining.

CHAPTER TWENTY-FIVE

Too much had happened and no one felt like continuing the party, so Polly took Kayla home. Lydia had asked Beryl to save the prizes for another evening, but the wild woman was not to be dissuaded. She took out four gift bags and passed them to each of her friends. Lydia and Sylvie were hesitant, knowing they'd lost the competition. Sylvie laughed out loud when she pulled out a bright red feather boa.

"What is this?" she asked.

Beryl nodded to the rest of them. "Open yours."

Each woman found the same thing in their gift bag.

"These aren't winner or loser prizes," Lydia protested. "They are crazy."

Beryl took another boa out and wrapped it around her neck. "I get tired of being the only wild person in this group. You all need to join me. From now on, whenever we get together, I demand that we wear these. Especially if we go out to dinner. Are you with me?"

Polly looked at her friends, who all had huge smiles on their faces. "I'm in for the boa. Who needs to be boring?"

Andy tossed hers around her neck, then pulled some of it up under her eyes. "Am I mysterious?"

"You'll do it?" Beryl asked, quite flabbergasted.

Lydia sat up straight and wrapped her boa from the top of her head to under her chin a few times. "Of course we will. But you don't care how we wear it, do you?"

"You're the best," Beryl said. "Sometimes I worry whether or not my whimsy gets under your skin."

"We're with you, crazy woman," Andy said. "You're the only reason I don't wear dark blue suits every day, even when I'm playing with my grandchildren."

They'd helped clean up and pack everything back into Lydia's Jeep. Sylvie left with Andrew, and Polly put the girls in her truck.

After she dropped Kayla off, Rebecca climbed into the front seat. "You have fun with your friends, don't you?" Rebecca asked.

"They're nuts, but I love them."

"Do you think Kayla and I will always be friends?"

"I think you have a good chance. But you'll make new friends as you grow up. You'll meet people in high school and more when you get to college and then when you start working. You'll never stop making friends."

"Kinda like you and Joss?"

"Exactly like that. I don't see my high school friends very often, but when I do, I still love them. Our lives just changed and we weren't together all the time. Sal's the only friend I see from college, but if she hadn't moved to Bellingwood, we wouldn't see each other that often."

"And that's okay? I'd miss Kayla if I couldn't see her."

"It's always okay to miss friends you aren't with," Polly said. "But you can't focus on that or you'll miss out on getting to know other wonderful people."

"Like you," Rebecca said. "I have so much fun with you."

"And I do with you, too," Polly replied. "I would have been a different person if you weren't in my life."

"I miss Mom, but it isn't as terrible as I was afraid it would be." The light from the street lamp illuminated tears on Rebecca's face.

"Do you feel guilty about that?" Polly asked quietly.

"Sometimes. For a long time I thought that it was bad that I was having fun again. Everybody kept asking me if I was okay or if I was sad. And I was okay. I think they wanted me to be sadder than I was. Mom was so sick and she hurt all the time. I didn't want her to stay alive when she felt like that."

Polly pulled into the driveway and pressed the button to raise the garage door. She drove in and turned off the truck. "Your feelings are yours. They're okay no matter what. Other people don't want to lose that feeling of sadness because it reminds them of the person they lost. That's okay too. When it comes to death and living without someone we love, feelings are going to be very different and very personal. Whatever you feel is okay."

"I'm glad Mom made me live with you before she died. That made it easier," Rebecca said. "It would have been bad to just move in that first night."

"Your mom was an amazing woman," Polly said. "She loved you with everything she had."

"I love her too."

"I know you do."

"But it's okay that I love you. Mom told me that I had enough love for as many people as I wanted to love."

Polly smiled. "She was right. That's a great way to look at it."

Rebecca opened the car door. "Look at us," she said. "Talking about this stuff and not crying on the side of the road. I'm proud of us. We're growing up."

Polly laughed out loud. "You're a nut, girl. And I love you."

"Do you want me to walk the dogs tonight?"

"Nah," Polly said. "Send them down. I ate so much, I should at least get a little exercise. Tell Henry I'll be back in a few minutes."

The dogs ran down. Han waited patiently for the leash. Polly didn't feel like being on top of his behavior tonight, so leash it was. She walked back into the garage and jumped when Obiwan barked. He rushed toward the back of the garage.

They'd emptied most everything from her father's home, except for a few stacks of boxes. Slowly but surely, she was making her way through them, but it felt like a never ending process.

"What are you doing?" she asked.

Han growled as Obiwan's barking grew louder and more insistent.

"Obiwan. Come," Polly commanded. She wanted to get him out of there and back inside. Someone or something was hiding behind her boxes and she didn't want her dog in trouble.

"It's just me," a husky voice said and Heath Harvey stood up.

Polly pulled Han back and said again, "Obiwan. Come here."

"I won't hurt him. I won't hurt you either."

"What are you doing in my garage?" she asked. "Aren't the police looking for you?"

He rolled his eyes. "That's why I'm in your garage."

"Obiwan. Come." This time, Polly snapped the words out and her dog obeyed. He trotted to her side, trying to keep an eye on the young man at the same time. "I don't know why you've chosen my garage to hide in, but I'm the wrong person to mess with."

"Yeah. Whatever. I'll get out of your hair."

Polly opened the door to the storage room and pushed the dogs inside, then pulled the door shut again. "Why did you choose my garage tonight?"

He snarled at her. "The door was open. Nobody would think to look in the great Polly Giller's garage for a loser like me. You'd never have anything to do with me."

"I don't have much to do with losers," she said. "But that seems to be your choice, not a general assumption by society."

"Well, I'm a loser and I'd better go."

"Wait a minute. Where will you go from here?"

He shrugged. "I dunno. I may as well leave town. My uncle will beat the hell out of me and probably kick me out anyway."

"He beats you?"

The kid shook his head. "No, but after tonight he won't hold back. He hates me. I'm surprised he hasn't kicked me out."

"I doubt he hates you," Polly said. "From what I understand, he took you in even though he never had kids around before."

Heath looked up at her. "He said it. He told me that if I'd been in the car with my parents, I would have died too and then he wouldn't have to be responsible for me. He calls me a hoodlum and says I'm an embarrassment."

Polly pursed her lips. "I don't think he's wrong about the last part. You've been acting like a hoodlum this summer and I'm sure it's been quite embarrassing for your aunt and uncle. You know that you are responsible to people other than yourself, right?"

"Well, he should be responsible to me, don't you think?"

"That's crap. He takes care of you, gives you a roof over your head and puts food on the table for you. He doesn't embarrass you or talk bad about you to other people. He is responsible to you."

"Take his side. Everybody always does. You're just like them."

"Probably," Polly said. "Why would you think I'm any different."

He looked away and started to walk toward the open garage door. "No reason."

"Stop," she said. "Tell me why you think I'm different." Polly moved to intercept him before he could leave.

"Just people talking," he muttered.

Polly finally got close enough to touch his arm. He flinched and stepped back.

"What do people talk about?" she asked quietly.

"That you listen and don't judge. Everybody thinks I'm a bad kid."

"I think you're a bad kid," she said. "You pissed me off when you tried to intimidate me. You had no right. Who in the hell do you think you are?"

"It was just a thing."

"It was just a what thing?" she demanded. "Were you trying to impress those boys you were with? What else? Did you think that if you hurt me you would prove how strong you were? I'm a girl. You're bigger than me. What does that prove?"

"Nothing," he said, keeping his head down. "It was stupid."

"Damn right it was stupid. Why did you do it?"

"Because."

"Because why? That's not a good answer." She spat the word. "Because. That's no answer at all."

"Because Ladd said."

"If Ladd told you to jump off..." Polly stopped herself with a chuckle. Such a well-worn phrase. She just couldn't bring herself to repeat it. "What else has Ladd told you to do?"

Heath looked up at her, panic in his eyes. "I didn't do it," he said. "I swear I didn't do it." He ran out of the garage before she could catch him.

Polly followed, putting on speed, trying to keep up with this kid who was so much bigger. But he didn't have the advantage of months of running with her dogs. As he crossed the parking lot, she caught up and grabbed his sleeve.

"Why are you chasing me?" he asked, coming to a stop.

"Because you're running away. Now tell me what has you so shaken up."

"I can't."

Polly took a long, deep breath, keeping her hand on his sleeve. "Come inside with me. Whatever it is that has you so upset, you need to tell someone and apparently tonight, that someone is me. You came to my place because you want to tell me. Am I right?"

"No," he said, his eyes alight with fear. "I don't want to tell you any of this."

"Come on. You're going inside. I'm not standing out here on the road while you hem and haw about whether or not you're going to finally spill whatever is eating you up."

He looked up at the lights on in her apartment. "Are there people up there?"

"My husband and our daughter."

"Then I'm not going. This was a bad idea." He tried to pull away.

Polly held tight and tugged him toward Sycamore House.

"Lady, I'm stronger than you."

"Uh huh. Come on."

She practically dragged him to the front door of the building, waited as it unlocked and then took him inside. When they got to the stairway, he stopped. "I'm not going up there."

"Look," Polly said, still holding on to his shirt. "I've had a long few days. I'm tired of arguing with you. We can continue this as long as you like, but here's how it's going to go down. You'll say no and I'll push a little harder. You'll keep saying no and I'll keep pushing. And at some point, I'm going to win. It's what I do. You came to my place for help. I'm going to give it to you and at this point you can't stop me. Let's skip past all of the saying no and pushing and move ahead to your acquiescence. Okay?"

"You're crazy."

"That I am. No one will disagree with you. Now, head up those steps. I don't want to go through this up and down stuff with you any longer tonight. Move."

He trudged up the first few steps while Polly watched.

"I'm just going to make sure you don't back out. Keep going," she said. "I'll be right behind you."

When he got to the top of the steps, she took his arm, opened the front door and led him inside.

"Polly?" Henry asked coming out from the kitchen. "Who's... oh. Okay. Where are the dogs?"

"They're downstairs by the back door. Would you mind?" she asked.

"You're going to explain all of this to me later?"

Polly chuckled. "Sooner rather than later, I'm guessing. Where's Rebecca?"

"She's in her room. Something about friends and crying. I didn't understand it all."

"We'll be in the kitchen when you come back. You're welcome to join us. I think Heath has a story to tell."

"Okay," Henry said with hesitation. "Are you sure you're okay?"

"Yeah. I'm okay," she said. "Thanks."

Heath stood waiting at the front door. Polly took his arm and led him into the kitchen, then pointed at a stool in front of the peninsula. He sat down and she went over to the refrigerator.

"Something to drink?"

Luke jumped up and wandered over to sniff at the stranger. Heath reached out and let the cat sniff the back of his hand, then slowly moved it so he could scratch Luke's head. He ran his hand down the cat's back and up his tail, then repeated the motion. Soon, Luke was purring and flopped down in front of the boy.

Polly filled a glass with ice and lemonade and took a container of cookies out of the freezer. "I love frozen chocolate chip cookies," she said. "Have you eaten anything tonight?"

He shook his head, all the while focused on the cat in front of him.

"I have cold chicken in here. Would you eat a couple of pieces?"

"I'm fine."

She took the container of chicken out and dug around to find leftover fried potatoes. Henry had sliced the corn off the cob, so she put some of each on a plate and put it in the microwave. When it came out, she put two pieces of grilled chicken on the plate and set it down beside the cat.

"He'll go away if you put him on the floor," she said. "He's actually quite polite about the whole thing, but if you want him to stay close, he's always glad for the attention."

"What's his name?" Heath asked.

"That's Luke and the other cat is Leia. The two dogs are Obiwan and Han. Obiwan was the one who found you in the garage."

"Weird names."

"Star Wars. You've never seen that movie?"

"I don't watch movies."

"I see." Polly scooted the cat down and pushed the plate in front of Heath, then handed him a fork and a napkin. "Eat and I don't want to go through the whole arguing thing. Remember. I'm going to win. You might as well just start caving in now."

"You're pushy."

"That's not new information," she said with a laugh. "Now eat. Because I think you're going to need a full stomach to tell me whatever it is you have to tell me."

He was only about halfway through the plate of food in front of him when the two dogs came barreling in from Henry's office. Obiwan sniffed at Heath's legs and looked up at Polly.

"He's fine. We invited him in," she said to the dog. She took two treats from the cupboard and handed them to Heath. "Give one to each of the dogs. It will help them get to know you."

He looked at her in wonder, took the treats and then got down from his stool and handed the first to Obiwan and the second to Han, rubbing each of their heads before standing back up. "They're good dogs."

"Yes they are." She nodded to the plate. "Finish your food. You're about to have to spill your guts."

He looked at her.

"No, there won't be any arguing. You're beginning to learn, aren't you?"

"Yes ma'am."

She smiled. She so badly wanted to pat him on the head, but they weren't there yet. This poor boy desperately needed someone to talk to. If it was going to be her, then she was just going to have to suck it up and do her thing.

Henry came in. "I shut the garage up. Right?"

"Yes. We're in for now," she said. "Thank you for doing that."

He came over and stood beside her, wrapping his arm around her waist. "What do we have here?" he asked.

"I'm not sure yet." Polly watched Heath take a final bite. "Drink your lemonade. I'll refill it before we get started. Then you can work on the cookies."

Heath glanced at Henry, then back to Polly and took a drink from the glass. Polly poured more into it, then looked at Henry, asking the question.

"I'm fine," he said. "I've had plenty. So conversation in here or on the couch."

She picked up the container of cookies and said. "Let's get comfortable. This is going to take a while. Take your glass, Heath."

He picked up his glass and followed them into the media room. Henry gestured to the sofa and Heath sat down, putting his glass on the table in front of him. Polly put the cookies down beside the glass.

"Now," she said. "You came here for a reason. I've fed you, I've tormented you, and I've made you crazy. It's your turn."

"He'll kill me."

"Who will kill you?" Henry asked.

"Ladd Berant. I'm not supposed to tell anyone anything."

Polly dropped her head, shaking it in mock frustration. "Remember," she said quietly. "I always win. Just start talking."

"He killed those girls."

Both she and Henry sat back. Neither of them expected to hear that.

"Ladd Berant killed Julie Smith and Abby Belran?" Polly asked with a gasp. "Why?"

Heath swallowed hard and put his hand over his mouth. "I'm gonna puke."

Polly jumped up and opened the door into the bathroom. "Right in here."

He rushed in and shut the door. She and Henry listened as he vomited over and over. They waited until the toilet flushed and they heard the water turn on in the sink. When he finally came back out, his face was red and his eyes were swollen.

Heath sat back down and Obiwan jumped up to sit beside him, nuzzling his hand until he started stroking the dog's back.

"I'm sorry I forced so much food down you," Polly said.

"It's okay." He looked up. "It hadn't had much time to process."

She tried to stop the chuckle, but couldn't. "I guess not. Can you go on?"

He nodded, his hand stroking Obiwan's back. The dog moved in and lay his head across Heath's lap. "We were messing around up town. Ladd always tests the doors. The coffee shop was open, so we went in. He told us to mess it up, so we did. Pulled books off the shelves. Just messed it up. Then the girl came in. She got mad and told us to leave. Ladd got all up in her business and started pushing her. She yelled at him and he grabbed that stick out of the pot by the door. He threatened her and backed her up through the building. I thought he was just going to do what he always does. He always gets mouthy, but walks away."

He drew in a breath and stopped, concentrating on the dog.

"The girl got pissed and said she was going to call the police." Heath shuddered. "Do you know what it sounds like when somebody's head gets smashed? It was horrible. He took her outside and then hit her in the head over and over and she fell down beside the dumpster. Ladd wiped his fingerprints off the stick and then we all ran away."

"Who is 'we all'?" Polly asked.

"That's the thing," he said.

"What's the thing?"

"Abby was with us. She was scared. She dated Ladd sometimes. Her dad didn't like him, but he's never around. She thought Ladd was cool, but he always got her in trouble."

Polly nodded. "Abby threatened to tell the police, didn't she?"

"She said she wouldn't at first. Ladd promised all kinds of stuff. They'd go to prom together and he'd buy her things." He shook his head. "He wasn't going to. He just wanted her to calm down. She was okay for a few days, but then she started talking about it. I told her to shut up. Ladd freaked out and I didn't know what he'd do."

"How do you know that it was him who killed her?" Henry asked.

"He told me the next day. Told me that if I even thought about talking about it, he'd do the same thing to me. He said how he went over there and she made him promise to talk to somebody." Heath shuddered. "He said if he hadn't killed her, he should have made her pregnant, so she owed him."

"That's ridiculous," Polly said under her breath.

"Ladd's out of control. Tonight he made us steal that lady's purse. He's trying to get money to get out of town. He told me that if we didn't get him five hundred dollars, he was going to make us regret it."

"We need to call Aaron," Henry said. "Do you know where Ladd is hiding?"

"After he got yanked in by the police he said he wasn't going home again so he broke into the old shoe store. He's hiding there."

Polly looked at the boy on her couch. He'd transformed from being a bully to scared boy. She didn't know if it was real or just in her mind. In the last hour or so, he'd become a real person to her, no longer a kid who was part of the crowd. She desperately wanted to help him.

"I'll call Aaron." She stood up and said to Henry, "Find out who the other kid is. We need to make sure he's safe." She stepped into Henry's office and took out her phone. Was it really just earlier today that it had been lost to her?

"Polly Giller, haven't we had enough for one week?" Aaron asked, when he answered the call.

She walked toward the back of the apartment and stood by the railing. "I need you to come over. Heath Harvey is here and has told us that Ladd Berant was the one who killed Julie Smith and Abby Belran."

"What?" Aaron demanded. "How did he get to you? Do you believe him?"

"He was hiding in my garage. And yes, I believe him. I want to help this kid, Aaron. He's a mess."

"Of course you do. It's been a while since you've rescued someone. Like what? A week?"

"Stop it. Just come over. You've still got access to the building, right?"

"Yes, ma'am. I'll be right there. I don't know why I'm even needed in this county," he muttered. "As long as Polly Giller is around, she'll find the bodies and catch the killers."

"Stop it. I'm not catching any killer. I'm safe in my own apartment. You're going to go catch the killer."

"Yeah, yeah, yeah. You just need me to do the dirty work. Fat lot of good I am."

Polly laughed. "Quit whining. You love me and you know it."

"It's a good thing, too. I'll be right there."

CHAPTER TWENTY-SIX

Gently closing the door after Aaron and Stu Decker took a very willing Heath Harvey downstairs to the conference room, Polly leaned against it and took a deep breath. When she asked Heath if he wanted her to call his aunt and uncle, he broke down.

"He won't care," Heath said. "He'll make them send me to jail just to get me out of his hair. You just wait. You'll see."

"What about your brother?"

"No. Please no. He never comes back here. He's got a whole life. Don't screw it up because of me."

"He'd want to know that you need him."

Heath's eyes begged her to listen. "Please don't call him yet. His classes just started and he doesn't need this right now. He's doing really good. I'm the loser in the family. Leave him alone."

After he was gone, she went into Henry's office and called the phone number he'd given her for his uncle's house. A woman answered and Polly started in. "Mrs. Harvey?"

"Yes. Who's calling please?"

"Mrs. Harvey, this is Polly Giller at Sycamore House in Bellingwood. I need to speak with you about your nephew."

"What's that boy done this time? We aren't responsible for his actions. He won't listen to us."

Polly didn't want to tell Mrs. Harvey that yes, she was responsible for Heath's actions if they were his legal guardians. That might cause more trouble than he needed right now.

"He got himself into trouble this evening, but he needs his family to take care of him more than anything. He was witness to a murder and is taking to the Sheriff."

"I knew it," she said, a sharp edge in her voice. "I told my husband that he was going to grow up to be a no-good piece of trash, just like that woman his father married. You can't trust people like that. He was headed down this path from the day he was born. He looks just like her and is just as bad. It's all in the genes, you know."

Maybe it wasn't the uncle. This woman was a joy.

"He will need legal help. Does your family have a lawyer?"

"We're not getting any lawyer for that boy. He burned his last bridge with us. We tried. We really did, but it was no use. He was never going to amount to anything."

"Ma'am, Heath is a junior in high school. He's just a kid. You can't expect him to handle this on his own."

"Of course we can. We've done more than our share for him. It's over. I wash my hands of him."

"I hate to push this issue, but might I speak with your husband?" Polly asked.

"He'll tell you the same thing," Mrs. Harvey responded. "But just a minute. Will? Will Harvey come here! I know you aren't too deaf to hear me yelling. Come talk to this lady from town. She says Heath is in trouble again and I told her we ain't gonna bail him out. He got himself into it and he can get himself out of it."

Polly waited and finally heard the phone change hands.

"Hello?" The man sounded like he had just come awake.

"Mr. Harvey, this is Polly Giller at Sycamore House in Bellingwood. Your nephew is here this evening talking to Sheriff Merritt. He witnessed a murder last week and has been in trouble. He's going to need his family and a good lawyer."

"I see," he said.

Polly waited for him to say something more and when he didn't, she pressed on. "Does that mean you will help him?"

"No, miss, it doesn't. My wife was right. We've invested money and effort into that boy and he don't appreciate any of it. We put a roof over his head and food on the table. He won't work on the farm and ev'ry time I turn around, he's hopping a ride into town and don't come home until all hours. Sometimes we haven't seen him for a week until he comes back for more clothes. If he made this bed, he's going to have to sleep in it."

"This is your brother's son, Mr. Harvey. You're just going to hang him out to dry?"

"Well, missy, I'm not sure as to how it's any of your business, but it's high time we start protecting ourselves here. He's just going to be like pouring money down a rat hole and some one of these days he's going to do something that will cost so much money to fix he'll bankrupt me. After all these years we've put into the place, it would be a shame to lose it because of a half-assed kid who can't see fit to take responsibility."

"So okay," Polly said. She didn't want to end the conversation because she didn't want this to be real. Heath Harvey knew exactly what his aunt and uncle were like. No kid should have to live like this. She wondered how broken he was by this point and if he could be salvaged. "Can you give me his brother's phone number?"

"I don't have it," Mr. Harvey said. "He'll call on Sunday, looking for the boy. We'll tell him to contact you at where did you say? Never mind, he can look it up for himself. Good-bye now."

Polly stared at her phone, not believing that he had just disconnected. He'd almost sounded relieved at the end. Maybe he and his wife could sleep well tonight, knowing where Heath was, even if it meant they'd left him to the wolves.

She saw Rebecca standing in the doorway. "How long have you been there?"

"A while. Is this about the boy who went downstairs with Sheriff Merritt?"

"I thought you were in your room."

Rebecca smiled at her. "It's not like I can't hear things. I peeked out and saw. Is that the people who were taking care of him?"

"His aunt and uncle. Heath's parents were killed in a car accident."

"Don't they want him?"

Polly pursed her lips and slowly shook her head. "I believe he's too much for them. They don't have any kids of their own and he's been a handful."

"It's because he thinks he's all alone. He needs someone to show him love - like you do with me. If I had to go somewhere strange after Mom died and they didn't love me, I'd be mad all the time, too. It isn't fair that he's punished because his parents died."

"You're right," Polly said. "It isn't fair."

"But he hasn't done anything really bad yet, has he?"

"I don't know," Polly said. "I just don't know. He should have gone to the police after his friend killed Julie and especially after he killed Abby."

"He's just a kid, Polly," Rebecca said. "And that Ladd Berant is mean. He scares everybody. If he tells people to do something, they either do it or he hurts them. He killed two people. Doesn't it make sense that Heath would be scared?"

Polly beckoned for her to come over to the desk and wrapped her arms around the girl, burying her face in Rebecca's hair. "You're right. It does make sense," she whispered. "I don't know what to do about this."

"We should have a family meeting," Rebecca declared, stepping back. "Come with me." She reached down and took Polly's hand.

Polly let Rebecca pull her out of the chair and into the media room.

"Sit there. I'll get Henry," Rebecca said.

In a few moments, the two were back and Rebecca pointed to the space beside Polly on the couch. Henry gave Polly a wry grin and sat down beside her.

"Family meeting?" he asked.

"I dunno. She's in charge," Polly said.

"We won't take notes or anything," Rebecca announced, "But this is our first official family meeting. Do either of you have anything that needs to be brought up before I begin?"

Henry and Polly looked at each other, shook their heads and Polly said, "No, I believe you have the floor."

"Okay then. I just listened to you talk to Heath Harvey's aunt and uncle. They don't want anything to do with him and I believe that he's not a lost cause. Do either of you disagree with me?"

They looked at each other again and Henry asked, "Where is this going?"

"Just answer the question." Rebecca started firmly and then put a hint of pleading in her voice. "Please?"

"Okay, I don't think that very many people are lost causes," he said. "I'd have to get to know Heath better before I answered that with any confidence, though."

"Polly?"

"Well, it says something that he came here. He knew he'd find help. And once he started telling us what had happened, he was pretty upset about the whole thing. He knows his life is in the toilet and has accepted that." Polly looked up. "I guess I don't know for sure."

"I do. No one is a lost cause. I think you should make him part of the Sycamore House family."

Henry started to protest and Rebecca put her hand up to stop him. "Since I got here and since your businesses have grown, you have gotten safer. You don't take as many risks."

'That's not true," Polly said. "Denis Sutworth is downstairs and I hired Grey at the Inn."

"Those aren't risks," Rebecca said. "You aren't involved with Denis Sutworth, you're just giving him a place to recuperate. Evelyn's doing all the work. And Grey isn't that big of a risk. If you don't like him, he's gone. And what have you done lately, Henry? Have you gone out of your way to help someone?"

"Uh, that's not what I do,'" he said. "I support Polly."

"That was a lame answer," Polly said with a laugh. "But he's right. His strength is what allows me to be risky."

"Then I think you need to risk it with Heath and Henry needs to support you. That boy needs to be loved and he needs strong men around him to teach him how to be a man, not a jerk. You have Eliseo and Henry and Jeff here. Look at what they've done for Jason and Andrew."

"But those two have a strong mother. She believes in them and loves them," Henry said. He looked at Polly. "I don't think this is a good idea. We have no idea what kind of trouble this boy would bring with him."

Polly sat back on the sofa. She loved the fact that Rebecca saw herself as part of the family and yet wasn't overly protective of her relationship with them. That was really something. In fact, Rebecca was really something. Could they handle a sixteen year old troubled boy? She glanced at Henry. It was a lot to ask of him. He'd gotten a whole lot more than he bargained for when he fell in love with her. It wasn't that the two of them expected to have a traditional family, but this was over the top.

Rebecca walked over to the bookcase and looked across the titles until she landed on what she was looking for. "Do you remember this book?" She handed it to Polly.

"Crap," Polly said, her eyes filling with tears. "Jo didn't think she could do it either."

"But she did and she changed their lives," Rebecca said.

Henry bent over to see what Polly was holding. "Little Men?"

"You're Daisy, aren't you?" Polly asked with a smile.

"And you're Jo and he's Papa Baehr," Rebecca responded.

Polly tried not to giggle. It was just a day or so ago that she'd called Henry 'papa bear' because he was so protective of Rebecca.

"That's where the horses' names come from," Polly said to Henry. "Demi and Daisy were twins in the story. Jo had inherited land from her Aunt March and started a school where children who needed to learn and to be loved came to live - Plumfield. The first boy to join them was Nat. He was shy and played the violin." Polly smiled. "Let's just say that he's our Andrew, okay? And then came Dan. He introduced all sorts of bad behavior to the school. And that's where Heath comes in, isn't it."

"Dan needed Plumfield, but they needed him, too," Rebecca said. "Heath needs you guys. Really bad."

"How much did you hear tonight?" Polly asked.

Rebecca tilted her head down. "Everything. I sat down on the floor out there and listened."

"Not much privacy around here," Henry said with a laugh. "Polly and I need to talk about this privately, Rebecca. You understand that, right?"

She nodded. "Of course I do. I'm just the catalyst. You guys have to do all the hard work. And if you decide that it's not the right thing to do, I'll understand. I didn't want a chance to do the right thing get away from us, though. He's going to need a place to stay tonight. I'll make the bed in the front room." Rebecca ran out of the media room before they could stop her.

"Did we just get played?" Henry asked.

Polly laughed. "I think so. But dang, Henry, she vocalized everything I've been processing on. I wish you could have heard his aunt and uncle. They're harsh. That woman said terrible things about his mother and that her genetics were the reason he was this way. If his dad was anything like this Mr. Harvey, the only hope Heath had was with his mother."

"His parents weren't anything like them," Henry said. "I only knew them superficially, but they were good people. No one's sure why Heath's aunt and uncle are so bitter and mean, but they are. The court assigned them to be his guardians since his parents hadn't made any plans for him if they died. It was either that or foster care and Heath's older brother begged them to take him in."

"Do you have any idea what he was like before his parents died?"

Henry looked off into space and finally shook his head. "No. He was just a kid. Maybe you should ask some of the teachers at the elementary school. They'd remember him."

"What do you think we should do?"

"What I think is that you and little girl back there have already made up your minds. I can either get on board or beg for a life preserver."

"That's not true," Polly said. "If you think this is a bad idea, I don't want to disrupt the life we've started here. We have to think of Rebecca now. Will he make things rough on her?"

"Our Rebecca?" he asked. "That child will make things more difficult on him than he can ever imagine. The first time he gets out of line, he won't have to worry about answering to anyone but her." He reached over and took Polly's hand. "Did you hear what she said?"

"The whole 'us' thing?" she asked, a grin creasing her face. "Wasn't that great? And a family meeting. I was almost giddy when she said that." Polly glanced over her shoulder to make sure Rebecca wasn't in the room with them. They were going to have to watch themselves. That girl was much too quiet when she wanted to hear what was going on.

"I don't want to make this kind of a decision tonight," Henry said.

"Neither do I. And maybe Heath wouldn't even be interested," Polly observed. "But what about him staying here for a while until things settle out."

He nodded. "I can agree to that. He needs a safe place while all of this comes together." Henry released her hand. "If he chooses to stay here and Aaron approves, don't worry. I'll go get his things from his aunt and uncle. Neither you nor he should have to put up with abuse from them. It won't bother me. I'll take Dad. He can talk to anybody."

"I love you, Henry Sturtz," Polly said, brushing her fingers across his face.

"I'm not going to be a teacher," he said, nodding toward the book.

"You already are. You might not teach history, languages, math and science, but you teach simply by being a good example."

Polly took out her phone and texted Aaron. *"Heath is staying with us tonight unless you have other plans. Have you met his aunt and uncle? They're horrible."*

"In that case, we'll bring him upstairs," Aaron texted back. *"We'll discuss the Harveys another time. Thank you for doing this."*

"Are we taking care of his legal issues, too?" Henry asked.

Polly smiled up at him. "If he stays here for a while, yes. Otherwise, that's someone else's trouble."

"After I talk to Aaron, I'll get hold of Al tomorrow. I had no idea we'd be keeping him this busy."

Al Dempsey was an old friend of Henry's and a lawyer. He'd advised the two of them after Polly's kidnapping several months ago and when it came time later this fall for her to be in court, he agreed to prepare her for whatever might come.

Henry was in the living room by the time Aaron knocked on their front door. He escorted a quiet young man in and Polly invited them to sit down.

"We've talked to Heath and I called Ken. They should be pulling Ladd Berant out of the old shoe store any minute now," Aaron said. "Stu has gone to Andy Otis's house to make sure he's safe. I guess that just leaves Heath's immediate future up in the air. He's made it quite clear that going back to the Harvey's house is a bad idea and I tend to agree."

He looked at Polly, who, in turn, nodded at Henry.

"Heath," Henry said. "We'd like to invite you stay with us."

The boy's eyes shot up. "Here?"

"We have plenty of space. Rebecca is making the bed up in the front room. For tonight at the very least, we hope you'll stay."

"Why would you do that?"

"Son, this is a good offer," Aaron said. "I'd rather not have to take you to Boone and meet up with someone from child services. Especially if you refuse to go home."

"It's not home," Heath said. "It's never been home."

"That's an issue for another day," Polly said, moving closer to Heath on the couch. "Will you stay where you're safe tonight? I don't want to worry about you."

"I can take care of myself," he said gruffly, glancing toward the door of the front bedroom.

Rebecca chose that moment to open the door and come out. "No you can't," she said. "You can't take care of yourself. You've screwed everything up for yourself and now you're here."

"Who's she?" Heath asked, turning to Polly.

Polly had yet to identify Rebecca to anyone. This was her next risk. She didn't want to upset or offend Rebecca and wasn't sure which way she should go. "She's our daughter," was what came out of her mouth before she could think any further.

"You need to say yes and thank you," Rebecca said. "Polly and Henry are great people. They'll take care of you and if you let them, they'll love you. And when you can take care of yourself, they'll even back off. Don't be stupid."

"I'm not stupid," he said. "And you're pushy."

Rebecca smiled at Polly. "I'm learning." She turned back to Heath. "I might be pushy, but I haven't said anything yet that is wrong, have I?'

He turned away. Rebecca put her hand out and took his. "Come on. Let me show you around. I know you don't have any clothes here, but maybe you can sleep in one of Henry's t-shirts tonight and we'll wash your clothes. Tomorrow we'll get you some more. It's going to be okay. I promise." She took him into the front bedroom and Polly could hear the girl chattering away.

"That child is a little scary," Aaron said. "She's just like you."

"I don't think so," Polly responded "She scares *me*. But it looks as if Heath is spending the night."

"I told Polly I'd get his things from his aunt and uncle tomorrow" Henry said. "He'll be safe here for a while. Are there going to be any charges that we need to deal with?"

Aaron stepped forward and looked into the bedroom. Polly followed his eyes. Rebecca was pulling the comforter back and patting the pillows. "I doubt it. He's just a scared kid. But he needs to stay out of trouble for a while. That's a lot to expect of the two of you. Are you sure about this?"

Henry laughed. "We haven't even fully decided if we're jumping in. His staying here is temporary."

"Uh huh," Aaron said. "That sounds about right."

Polly pushed him toward the front door. "Go home to your wife and tell her what insane thing I've done tonight. She and I will talk tomorrow."

"We have some of Jim's old things that would probably fit him," Aaron said. "I'll call Lydia on my way home and come back with a bag of things so he doesn't have to live in his old clothes tonight. Why don't I just put it downstairs and you can pick it up. That way I won't bother you any longer."

"You're never a bother, Sheriff," Henry said, reaching out to shake his hand. "Thanks for everything."

They shut the door and stood there looking at each other. Finally Polly burst out laughing. "What have we done?"

Henry reached forward, kissed her cheek and whispered in her ear. "What you always do. We're rescuing the world."

CHAPTER TWENTY-SEVEN

One last time before going down to her office, Polly checked on Heath. He'd been unable to sleep the night before and she'd finally fallen asleep on the sofa while he watched television. He woke her about three thirty to tell her that he was going to bed and she dragged herself into her own bed, disturbing all of the animals.

Rebecca and Henry had gotten up about the same time and made French toast. Rebecca intended to mother this poor boy until he couldn't take any more. She assured Polly that they'd be fine and when he finally woke up, she'd make sure he ate something.

There wasn't much to do in the office today, but Polly felt like she needed to make sure the world was spinning in the right direction. After last night, she just wanted normal. Rachel was in the kitchen when Polly stopped at the counter to get coffee.

"You look tired," Rachel said.

"I am. It was a long night."

"Word is you had the Sheriff here because you know who killed those girls."

"It was Ladd Berant."

Rachel grimaced. "He was always a brat. Maybe he's Caleb's

age or a little older. I can't believe he killed someone, though. That's crazy."

"It is. Kids just don't realize how they throw their lives away because they can't control their anger," Polly said. "Do you know Hayden Harvey? Was he about your age?"

"I think he plays basketball at Iowa State." She made a quick connection and said, "His brother got caught up with Ladd. I saw them in town with another younger kid. That boy is a mess. After their parents died, I think he went to live with his aunt and uncle. And they're really weird."

"What's Hayden like?" Polly asked.

"He's okay, I guess. He nearly quit at Iowa State to take care of his brother. I think he works construction around the state in the summer. That's why he's never around. It's the only way he can afford to live in Ames. He's a good kid, I think. And a pretty good basketball player. He's got a scholarship for it." Rachel smiled. "He used to date a friend of mine. He wanted to be a doctor. He's pretty smart."

Polly took a drink of coffee and enjoyed the moment. "Did you know their parents?"

"They were okay. Nice enough. I don't think they were real involved. Except basketball games. Mr. Harvey is nothing like his brother. Like I said, those people are weird. Nobody could believe they took Heath in." She shrugged. "Like it did him any good. He'd probably have been better off in a foster home. Hayden couldn't take care of him. He works all the time that he isn't practicing or studying."

"You wouldn't know how to get hold of Hayden, would you?"

"I guess I could call Tam. She might still have his cell number. Why?"

"I just need to talk to him. If you get his number, would you let me know?" Polly refilled her coffee mug and went to the office.

"Good morning," Stephanie said. "Your mail's on your desk and Jeff is at the coffee shop. He said he'd be back before noon."

"Thanks. Anything else?"

Stephanie turned the computer monitor so Polly could see it.

"Grey figured out how to get me all of the registration information at the hotel. It's nearly real-time. He knows how to do this stuff." She turned the monitor back. "He said he was coming over, that nearly everyone is checked out. I like him. He's a good listener."

"Yes he is," Polly said. "And I'm glad you two are working well together." She rubbed her eyes with her thumb and forefinger. This was going to be a long day if she didn't get a nap and right now there was no hope for that.

Polly had barely sat down at her desk when Rachel came in. "Here's the number," she said. "Tam says his Fridays are pretty free, so you should be able to get him."

"Thank you," Polly said, taking the piece of paper. She waited until Rachel left, then punched in the numbers and swiped to make the call. She might as well deal with this while she was thinking about it.

"Hello?" a young man's voice said.

"Hayden Harvey? My name is Polly Giller. I own Sycamore House in Bellingwood. Do you have a few minutes?"

"Uh, yeah?"

She felt herself relax. He really was just a kid. "Hayden, your brother is staying with my husband and me. I don't think your aunt and uncle want to deal with him any longer. They as much told me so last night when I spoke with them."

"Yeah, I know. But they didn't tell me where he was. He's at your place?"

"Yes, he is. I'm glad you talked to them. Your uncle told me he wouldn't speak with you until Sunday."

"Whatever," he said with anger in his voice. "They couldn't wait to tell me that they were kicking him out."

"We need to make some decisions for Heath."

"They said he was in trouble, that he helped murder someone. I've been sick to my stomach and he won't answer his phone."

Polly hadn't seen a phone on Heath. "I don't think he has his phone."

"That old hag probably took it away from him." He took a deep breath. "I guess I can put him on my plan. This is really fast, though. I have to move if he's going to live with me. And then I have to figure out how to get him registered for school. Damn, I can't believe they did this to us."

"Hayden," Polly said, interrupting his flow.

"Wait. Maybe I should be talking about getting him a lawyer. Did he really help murder somebody? Is this one of those girls that was killed in Bellingwood?"

"It is. Julie Smith. But he didn't do it. He came here last night and after some convincing, told me and then the Sheriff what had actually happened. It was Ladd Berant..."

Hayden's guttural growl stopped her. "That jackass. I told Heath that he shouldn't be hanging out with him, but it's my fault. I wasn't there to stop him or give him any guidance. I thought my aunt and uncle would take better care of him."

"Hayden," Polly said. "We need to talk. All of us. You, Heath, my husband and me."

"Why?" he asked. "What do you have to do with this?"

She sighed. "I know this won't make any sense to you, Hayden, but I think Heath showed up here for a reason and I think that I'm supposed to be involved in his life."

"Who are *you*?" He was suspicious and she didn't blame him.

"I'm nobody. But when I see that someone needs help - and Hayden, both you and your brother need help right now - I tend to stick my nose in and do what I can."

"We can take care of each other," he said, but he didn't sound terribly sure of himself.

"You're right. But you need to take a few minutes to think about this practically. Can you take care of a high school kid and still get yourself through college? And can you help him be everything he should be?"

"I'm not giving him up. There are only a few more years until he's eighteen. We can make this work."

Polly knew he was right. They could make it work, but it didn't have to be difficult. "Would you consider coming to Bellingwood and meeting me? I'm not trying to take your brother away from you. I promise you that. If you want guardianship of him, those are the papers we will prepare for you. If you want to take him back to Ames and figure out all of those logistics, you know what? I'll help you do that."

He interrupted again. "But why? Who are we to you?"

"You're a couple of boys who lost their parents and had your lives turned upside down. You're working your tail off so that you can finish this part of your education. You haven't let your parent's death destroy your dream."

"If I make good money, I can take care of Heath."

"Hayden, by the time you are making good money, Heath will be on his own. This is an immediate issue and all I want to do is help."

"I don't understand that," he said.

Polly let out a small breath of air, "I know. I guess I'll never fully understand how the world got so twisted up that we can't help each other out without there being an agenda. People have been helping me since I moved to town and every once in a while I find a person who needs me, so I do what I can."

"You're that lady that finds dead bodies, aren't you. I just realized that."

"That's me. It's my other superpower."

"Did you find the girl that Berant killed?"

"I did."

"Okay. I can be there about three thirty. I have an appointment that should be done by three. Will you be around?"

"I will. And can you stay for the evening? We'll have dinner and there's a street dance up town."

He laughed. "I'd forgotten about those. Yeah. I'll stay. Don't you have a hotel in town? Maybe I could rent a room there tonight and Heath and I will go get his stuff. Gah, I don't want to see those people. They'll just yell at us. I can't believe they let Heath out on his own."

"I've stuck my nose in it again," Polly said. "My husband is going out there today to deal with them. He was so mad I'm surprised he didn't wake them up in the middle of the night. But he'll force them to give him everything that belongs to Heath."

"If he'd gone last night, my uncle would have turned a gun on him. But I can't believe you're doing this for us. You don't even know us."

"Henry does. You know, everybody I've talked to feels terrible that this happened to your family. Nobody knows how to help. But I do, if you'll let me. It will be up to you and Heath, but we'll talk this afternoon. Okay?"

"Lady, you're strange. Can I talk to Heath?"

"He's upstairs, still asleep. Do you want me to wake him up? He's had an awful couple of weeks."

"This is probably the safest he's felt in a year," Hayden said. "Leave him alone. I'll see him later. Thanks."

"Goodbye, Hayden. It's going to be okay. I promise."

She put the phone down and took another drink of coffee. It didn't surprise her that Hayden was wary of this. It made so much sense to Polly, but he didn't know her at all.

"Hello, Miss Giller."

Polly looked up to see Grey standing in her doorway. "Hi there. What are you doing here today?" she asked.

"I'm spending time with your guest."

"Heath?"

He tilted his head and furrowed his brows. "No, Master Sutworth. He and I are building an interesting relationship."

"You are," she said. "We haven't taken the time for you to explain why you're in Bellingwood working at my hotel and not as a therapist somewhere."

Grey sat down across from her. "I closed my practice earlier this summer. Some horrendous things happened and I escaped while my own sanity remained somewhat intact. But if someone is in need of my skills, how can I stand by and not offer to help?"

"That sounds right," Polly said, smiling at him. "I just had the same conversation with another person." She creased her brows. "Do you think you can help Denis?"

"While Mrs. Morrow helps to heal his body, I have agreed to work with his therapy team to bring healing to his mind and heart. There is no reason that young man can't find wholeness."

Polly was skeptical. "Have you met his mother?"

"Ahh, yes I have," Grey said with a smile. "She agrees to be part of the healing process in a positive manner. And while we take care of the son, we will care for the whole family."

"That's quite a goal you've set for yourself," Polly said.

"Without goals, what would life be?" He stood back up. "I don't want to be late. There are many things that need to be accomplished in this day." Grey stepped to the door and then turned back to Polly. "I'm going to speak with your groundskeeper about finding a sturdy branch. I miss my walking stick. Do you know anyone who carves wood?"

"I think I do," Polly said. "Let me ask some questions."

He smiled as he turned to Stephanie. Polly didn't hear what he said, but soon he was on his way, his limp still noticeable. She'd talk to Bill Sturtz this weekend about carving something for him.

~~~

Polly sat back in her lawn chair and smiled across at Henry. He was helping Gina and Bean Landry tie a balloon to Gina's wrist. Darla tried not to hover over her son, even though she couldn't keep her eyes off him. He had two brand new bandages on his knees. Gina couldn't wait to tell Polly that he'd tripped going up the steps that afternoon and skinned his knees. Polly shook her head. Having a klutz in her life might drive her nuts. She was glad he was someone else's son.

Rebecca had run to Jessie and Molly's apartment to help them get ready for the evening. The band was warming up at the west end of the street, while tables and chairs filled in the other end. People brought picnic suppers and came out early to enjoy the last Friday evening of the summer before school started.

"I can't believe I haven't seen you this week," Sal said, coming up behind Polly. "Where have you been? Have you seen the numbers yet? We're doing great for not even really being open."

Polly stood up and gave her friend a hug. "I think you're open. For good. It's going well."

Sal leaned in. "I'm so glad Camille fired that Helena lady. She was strange. Always talking to me about what I should be doing to run the place. I couldn't get any work done." She bent over and picked up her dachshund.

"Where's the other one," Polly asked.

"With Mark somewhere." Sal looked around. "He's decided that it's okay if he walks with a dog that is orders of magnitude shorter than him."

"Because it was either that or...?" Polly asked.

"Or I got creative with torture. He didn't want to find out what I meant by that."

"Do you want to join us? We have plenty of extra chairs. Henry put everything we had into the truck."

"I'm going to the coffee shop. Camille has been putting a lot of hours in this week, so I said I'd help."

"You? Make coffee?"

Sal laughed. "No. I'm not making coffee, but I am good at taking money and chatting it up with the customers. I need to find Mark and hand off a dog. Stop in later. I miss you."

Polly gave her another quick hug and watched her walk away.

Lydia, Andy and Beryl crossed the street, laden with totes. Well, Beryl was carrying a card table.

"Can we join you?" Lydia asked.

"Of course," Polly said. She took one of the totes from Lydia and put it in her chair, then helped Beryl snap the legs out on the table.

"Sweetums boy is coming with chairs," Lydia said. "He made me late. You know how I hate being late."

"How did he make you late?"

Beryl snorted with laughter. "You know them, they were probably necking in the kitchen and she couldn't get her food packed up."

"Stop it, you," Lydia said. She reached out to swat her friend, but Beryl danced backwards, nearly falling into Henry.

"Whoa there," he said. "I've got you."

She fell into his arms and swooned. "Yes you do, hot stuff.

Would your wife mind terribly if I fell for you?"

He whispered, "I won't tell if you don't."

"Oh, he's a good one," Beryl said, standing up and wiping her brow. "Where's the rest of your crew?"

Polly looked up. "My crew?"

"Yeah. Your people. You have a lot of them, you know. Where are the kids and Eliseo? Where's Sylvie and that cute girl who runs your office?"

"I don't know," Polly said with a laugh. "Rebecca went to get Jessie and Molly. Sylvie is probably at the bakery and after that, I've got nothing."

Lydia stepped over to Polly and slid an arm around her waist. "Do you or do you not have another family member? And did Jim's things fit him?" She released Polly and took up the tote bag from Polly's chair.

"Jim's things were perfect. I think he appreciated having extra clothes and for now, I do have another family member. He's with his older brother tonight. They're here somewhere. But I think they need to spend time together. Hayden came this afternoon and after quite a bit of discussion, tears and other emotions, Heath is staying with us for the immediate future. His brother can't manage all that he has going on and try to take care of a high school kid at the same time. We can help, so we will."

"This isn't going to be easy, you know," Lydia said. "That boy's been nothing but trouble since his parents died."

"Do you blame him?" Polly asked. "Everything I know about his aunt and uncle tells me that he didn't have a chance. Henry and I will give him the best chance we can and I have plenty of people around who will help."

"Yes you do," Beryl said. "And I've never known anyone like you when it comes to making people think that the best thing they could do is help you out. It's amazing. You really let people do what they're good at."

"I can't do it all," Polly replied. "Heck, I can't do any of it. I don't know the first thing about raising kids, but I do know when someone needs to feel safe."

"He does need that," Lydia agreed. "Aaron said Rebecca pretty much took charge of him last night."

Polly laughed out loud. "He's putty in her hands. She'll be the one who makes sure he turns into a nice young man. Every single motherly instinct in that little girl found a place to land. It's too bad she won't be able to keep an eye on him during the day, but heaven help him if he gets out of line. This afternoon I heard her going through his things with him. She told him what he could and couldn't wear to school. And then she took off on a diatribe about good grades and how those would get him a scholarship so he could go to college and not be a drain on his brother. Since he had two years left in high school, he'd better make sure that he hunkered down and did the work." Polly looked at her audience. "She used those words, 'hunker down.' I just tried not to laugh."

"What are you doing about all of this legally?" Andy asked. "Don't his aunt and uncle have custody?"

"They're turning it over to us as soon as papers get drawn up," Polly said. "We offered to let Hayden be his guardian, but all of us think it makes more sense for me and Henry to do that. We can afford it financially - health insurance, any legal fees that come up from this trouble with Ladd Berant, school stuff. When he graduates from high school, he'll be eighteen and can decide where to go from there. If I could, I'd take both boys into our family, but Hayden has been independent since his parents died. We don't want to take that from him. However, he knows that we're here for him. He gets it."

"I don't know how you do it," Beryl said.

"What?"

"You just met these boys and you've already become their family. How do you do that?"

"I don't know," Polly said. "It's the right thing to do and nothing is going to change except that Heath has a safe place to live with people who will care about him."

"But you're going to be their family for holidays and birthdays, aren't you," she said.

"I suppose. Why wouldn't I?"

Beryl shook her head. "You don't even understand how odd it is. That's what we love about you. Your heart is right out there and the world just accepts that. How have you not been tainted by the cynicism that the rest of us carry?"

"I'll let you hold onto it for now," Polly said. "Because what you give me is love. Look around," she said, gesturing to the street that was filling with people. "There are very few people who wouldn't help me out if I needed something from them. Right?"

Beryl nodded in agreement.

"Then why wouldn't I do whatever I can to help someone else?"

The woman threw up her hands and turned to her friends. "We've just got to let her be who she is, don't we."

Lydia smiled. "And we'll do our best to back her up." She pointed up the street. "Look who's coming. I haven't seen this baby in weeks. She's growing up so fast."

"Polly!" Rebecca called, pushing the stroller beside Jessie.

"Hi honey," Polly said. "Hi Jessie."

Jessie smiled. "How are you? Rebecca says you've taken in another stray."

"I didn't call him a stray," Rebecca protested. "He's just a kid who needs us."

Jessie winked at the girl. "You know you're learning from the best, don't you?"

Rebecca reached in and picked Molly up, then handed the child to Lydia. "You look like you need a baby fix." She turned to Polly. "I know you don't need one." As soon as she released the baby, she took Polly's hand. "You really are the best. This year is going to be great."

Henry put his hand on Polly's shoulder. "Are they giving you trouble about rescuing people again?"

"They never stop," she said. "But that's okay. They're the reason I have the courage to keep at it." She turned and kissed his cheek. "And you too. I couldn't do any of this by myself."

Bill and Marie Sturtz crossed the street toward them. Marie had a basket in one hand and a chair in the other, while Bill carried another table.

A tap on Polly's shoulder caused her to turn around. Jason was standing there with his two friends. He handed her another basket. "Mom sent that," he said. "Eliseo's on his way up. We're going to go see who's here."

"Where's Andrew?"

"He's taking care of Padme and then is coming over."

"Okay, have fun."

Kayla and Stephanie walked down the sidewalk toward them and Rebecca broke away to greet her friend.

"This family just keeps getting bigger and bigger," Henry whispered in her ear.

"I'm having the time of my life," she replied.

THANK YOU FOR READING!

I'm so glad you enjoy these stories about Polly Giller and her friends. There are many ways to stay in touch with Diane and the Bellingwood community.

You can find more details about Sycamore House and Bellingwood at the website: http://nammynools.com/

Join the Bellingwood Facebook page:
https://www.facebook.com/pollygiller
for news about upcoming books, conversations while I'm writing and you're reading, and a continued look at life in a small town.

Diane Greenwood Muir's Amazon Author Page is a great place to watch for new releases.

Follow Diane on Twitter at twitter.com/nammynools for regular updates and notifications.

Recipes and decorating ideas found in the books can often be found on Pinterest at: http://pinterest.com/nammynools/

And, if you are looking for Sycamore House swag, check out Polly's CafePress store: http://www.cafepress.com/sycamorehouse

Made in the USA
Columbia, SC
11 December 2020